AVID

READER

PRESS

Also by Christina Li

YOUNG ADULT FICTION

True Love and Other Impossible Odds

MIDDLE GRADE FICTION

Clues to the Universe

Ruby Lost and Found

THE
MANOR
OF
DREAMS

a novel

CHRISTINA LI

AVID READER PRESS

New York   Amsterdam/Antwerp   London
Toronto   Sydney/Melbourne   New Delhi

AVID READER PRESS
An Imprint of Simon & Schuster, LLC
1230 Avenue of the Americas
New York, NY 10020

This book is a work of fiction. Any references to historical events, real people, or real places are used fictitiously. Other names, characters, places, and events are products of the author's imagination, and any resemblance to actual events or places or persons, living or dead, is entirely coincidental.

First Avid Reader Press hardcover edition May 2025

AVID READER PRESS and colophon are trademarks of Simon & Schuster, LLC

Simon & Schuster strongly believes in freedom of expression and stands against censorship in all its forms. For more information, visit BooksBelong.com.

For information about special discounts for bulk purchases, please contact Simon & Schuster Special Sales at 1-866-506-1949 or business@simonandschuster.com.

The Simon & Schuster Speakers Bureau can bring authors to your live event. For more information or to book an event contact the Simon & Schuster Speakers Bureau at 1-866-248-3049 or visit our website at www.simonspeakers.com.

Interior design by Ruth Lee-Mui

Manufactured in the United States of America

1   3   5   7   9   10   8   6   4   2

Library of Congress Cataloging-in-Publication Data

Names: Li, Christina, author.
Title: The manor of dreams : a novel / Christina Li.
Description: First Avid Reader Press hardcover edition. | New York : Avid Reader Press, 2025.
Identifiers: LCCN 2024035713 (print) | LCCN 2024035714 (ebook) |
ISBN 9781668051726 (hardcover) | ISBN 9781668051740 (ebook)
Subjects: LCGFT: Gothic fiction. | Domestic fiction. | Novels.
Classification: LCC PS3612.I133 M36 2025 (print) | LCC PS3612.I133 (ebook) |
DDC 813/.6—dc23/eng/20240823
LC record available at https://lccn.loc.gov/2024035713
LC ebook record available at https://lccn.loc.gov/2024035714

ISBN 978-1-6680-5172-6
ISBN 978-1-6680-5174-0 (ebook)

To my found family

"To hold the garden's fragrance in one vase;
And see all autumn in a single spray?"
—**Cao Xueqin, "The Crab-Flower Club"**
(*Dream of the Red Chamber*)

part one: root

根

one

NORA Deng was informed of two rules before the reading of the will.

The first was not to speak to the Yin family without a lawyer present.

The second was to never go into the garden behind the Yin family house.

Nora didn't argue when her mother told her these rules. She didn't say much on the hour-and-a-half drive from their home in San Bernardino out west to Vivian Yin's estate. She'd already exhausted her questions days ago, when Mā shared over dinner that a former actress named Vivian Yin had died, and that their family was included in the will. It was the first time Nora had ever heard Vivian Yin's name. A quick search on her phone at the dinner table revealed that she was a Chinese American actress who was known for her movies in the eighties. She'd even won an Oscar for Best Supporting Actress, in a movie called *Fortune's Eye*.

Nora was surprised. How in her twenty-one years had she never heard of this person? There were a few scattered tributes to Vivian Yin on the internet. A brief *LA Times* section on her. Nothing more.

Nora also had no idea why they were included in the will. When she'd asked, her mother had given her a long, hard look. The kitchen light shone harshly over Mā's head, seeping into the lines around her eyes and reflecting off her silvery strands of hair. In Mandarin, she said, "I don't know."

"Is there some family connection? Are we a long-lost relative?" Nora had seen that in the movies; people plucked from suburban anonymity to discover that they were heirs to royalty. That would be nice.

"No," Mā said sharply. "Why would you think that?"

"So we don't know them and they don't know us?"

Her mother paused. "My parents knew her."

"Then . . . we're family friends?"

Mā's lips flattened into a thin line. "Will you help me clear the dishes?"

That Saturday they took the exit off the I-210 in the direction of the forest. The San Gabriel Mountains loomed in the distance. Nora glanced out at the low, misty morning clouds. Today was unusually overcast for August.

The house was in Altadena and rose up out of the hills. Mā turned onto a lone road that ended at rusted gates. She didn't pull into the elongated driveway. Rather, she idled to a stop beside the curb. "Remember," she said. "Don't wander by yourself. Don't go into that garden behind the house. Okay?"

This house was large; Nora hadn't realized that until they got out of the car. There was a strange, dismal beauty to this place. It looked abandoned, almost sunken in shrubbery. The front yard was overgrown, the grass yellowing. Shriveled, emaciated vines crawled up the pale stone walls. But it still possessed a gentle grandeur that drew Nora's attention, with its symmetrical sloping roofs, the balconies framing tall, arched windows crowned by florid embellishments, and the elegant curve of the front door that stood behind two columns.

As they walked up to the front door, Nora saw a minivan parked to their left in the circular courtyard and driveway in front of the house.

"Nora," her mother said. "Promise."

Nora glanced over. She tucked her short hair behind her ears and tugged up her jeans. Mā's gaze unnerved her just a bit. "Okay."

The cavernous doors opened.

MADELINE Wang sat at her grandmother's dining room table the day after her funeral and looked at the person sitting across from her, who happened to stare right back. This person—Nora Deng, she'd introduced herself as—looked to be around Madeline's age, right out of college or maybe still in it. Cropped hair fell around her sharp jawline. Her fingers toyed with a loose thread on her sleeve. Slightly to Nora's right was a middle-aged woman wearing an ill-fitting red sweater, whom Madeline assumed was her mother, Elaine Deng.

So *she* was the person Mā was talking about on their way here. The one person outside the family who made it into the will.

Madeline felt small in here. The ceiling stretched over them. Spare, listless light filtered through the drawn curtains, revealing the thick layer of dust on the long mahogany table. The house had this persistent and unpleasant sour smell of mildew and damp wood, and the chairs groaned every time someone shifted positions. Madeline silently urged the white man presiding at the head of the table to just read her grandmother's will already and get it over with.

Her chair creaked loudly, and her mother shot her a look. Lucille Wang clasped her hands and looked ahead expectantly. She'd strategically taken a seat closest to the lawyer, her notepad in front of her. Her dark hair was pulled back in a bun. A half-inch or so of silver roots showed. She wore a navy blazer. Madeline knew this was her war suit. Mā was a lawyer too, and in this moment she was making sure everyone knew it. Madeline's yí mā, Aunt Rennie, on the other hand, leaned away from the table and looked like she wanted to disappear. She wore an oversized shawl-like cardigan. Her dark brown hair was starting to slip out of its clip.

The lawyer cleared his throat. Madeline was sitting close enough that she could see the name on his binder. *Reid Lyman.* "Are we all settled?"

Madeline nodded with everyone.

"We are gathered here to hear the last will and testament of Vivian Yin." He had a deep voice. "I have been named the executor of the will. Thank you to all parties for being present for the reading upon her request."

Madeline remembered precisely the day and the moment when her mother came home early from work. Mā had entered the living room with a vacant look in her eyes and dropped her bag to the ground, and that was when Madeline found out her grandmother was dead. They'd sat on the couch together in silence for what could have been minutes or the better part of that day. Mā then called Aunt Rennie; it went to voicemail twice before she'd picked up. When her aunt finally answered the phone, Mā disentangled herself to go upstairs and shut herself in her room.

And then, that next day, her mother abruptly kicked into action. She drafted the obituary and planned the funeral, which had originally consisted of her and Madeline and Aunt Rennie. Madeline's dad eventually came up for the day, a gesture of kindness that softened her mother, if only momentarily. She pestered the *LA Times* to include the obituary, calling the Entertainment desk over and over.

And then, finally, Mā told Madeline about Wài Pó's house. "We'll just stay there for a short time," she'd said. "You and me and your yí mā. Two weeks at most to get everything in order. And then we sell it."

"But that's your childhood home," Madeline had said. "Don't you want to keep it?"

"No. We don't."

They'd driven up two hours from their home in Newport Beach with their bags that Sunday morning. They were all supposed to meet at the house an hour before the reading of the will; Aunt Rennie didn't come until fifteen minutes before, citing car issues and having needed to hail a rideshare. Mā was slightly irked. But now they were all here. Madeline arched her head up, staring at the way the reddish ceiling beams curved toward each other with intricate wood carved corners, observing this house as she would an artifact in a museum. Whatever had been painted up there was long faded, cracks splitting through the paint.

She felt detached from this place. Her mother was the one who grew up in this house, with Aunt Rennie, with Madeline's grandmother—her wài pó—who once was an actress in Hollywood. 外婆 had been married to another actor, too, named Richard Lowell; Aunt Rennie's father and Mā's stepfather. He'd died when Mā was seventeen and Aunt Rennie was fourteen. And then Mā left for college and never really lived here again.

Suddenly Madeline's passing curiosity twinged into a sharp longing to have lived here; to have known her grandmother beyond her fleeting childhood memories. When she was little, Wài Pó would come to their house in Newport Beach. She would make dumplings for lunch. Then 外婆 would take her to the nearby park, her hand clutching Madeline's.

But then she started fading from their lives. Mā wanted Wài Pó to sell her house and move in with them; Wài Pó refused. She turned down holidays. Mā tried calling her, but she would rarely answer. When Madeline was eleven, she watched a pixelated, pirated version of the movie that won her grandmother her Oscar, *Fortune's Eye*, where Wài Pó played a Chinese American woman looking for her brother in the gold rush. The camera work was jarring, the music brassy and melodramatic, but still her grandmother was captivating in every scene. It felt strange, unauthorized almost, to witness the younger, animated version of the person who now shut them out. Madeline never mentioned it to anyone; no one ever brought that movie up.

"The first matters are of her finances," the lawyer said, bringing Madeline back to the present. Her mother leaned forward. "To her daughters: Yin Chen, Lucille Wang, and Yin Zi-Meng, Renata Yin-Lowell—she intends to distribute a sum of forty thousand dollars to be divided as the two beneficiaries see fit."

Madeline watched Mā's glance dart down the table at Aunt Rennie. "That's—" She swallowed her words. "Forty thousand?" she said, in hoarse Mandarin. Aunt Rennie was frozen. And then, almost immediately, Mā's shock folded shut. "There must be a mistake," she said in English.

The girl across from Madeline just watched, her expression flickering with scorn. Madeline felt jarred by Mā's outburst. It still was a substantial figure. Madeline wanted to melt into the floor. How much money had they been expecting, exactly?

But then again, if her grandmother lived in *this* place, shouldn't she have had more?

Mā was still bewildered. "This is the entirety of her inheritance? What about her accounts? Her investments?"

"This was all decided on," the lawyer said. "The monetary inheritance. And for the next—"

"We're not done here. Where's the rest?"

"Let him finish, will you?" Elaine Deng finally spoke up.

Mā's glance cut over to the woman across the table. "I'm sorting out *my* family matters."

Elaine said nothing more but smiled, spitefully polite. Aunt Rennie reached out a hand. "It's okay," she said softly, sounding unsure herself. "There's the house."

"Which leads us to the next clause," the lawyer said. "The estate." He shifted in his chair and looked, not at Mā, not at Madeline's side of the table, but to the two people seated across from them. "Vivian Yin has decided that upon her death, the ownership of this estate and all its matters will hereby be transferred to Elaine Deng."

two

RENATA Yin-Lowell flinched as Lucille stood abruptly, her chair skidding backward. Rennie watched in slow motion as it tipped over. The back of the chair slammed into the ground and everyone jumped. "This house belongs to us."

Elaine retorted, "That's not what the will says."

"It's ours," Lucille insisted. She righted her chair. "Our dad's family lived here for generations. Our mother lived here for the past fifty years. You're not taking it away from us."

"Like you wouldn't immediately put it on the market to make up for that pathetic inheritance your mother gave you?" Elaine's voice was caustic. Next to her, the girl stared at Rennie with the same contemptuous look.

While Rennie racked her mind for anything to say to back Lucille up, she registered something in the corner. A figure materialized. But it was quite hazy when she tried to look at it straight on.

She clutched the edge of her seat and blinked, hard. Nothing. It was nothing! Just dust in the sun.

"It belongs to us!" Lucille's raised voice hauled Rennie's attention back to the table. "None of this should have been allowed to happen."

"What, your mother isn't allowed to decide what to do with her own house?" The girl finally spoke, tipping her chin up. Her short hair framed insolent narrowed eyes.

Lucille's cheeks suffused with color. Elaine said in a low voice,

"Nora. Let me handle this." She spread out her palms. "I don't know why I was added to the will—"

"Don't you?" Rennie's sister spoke quietly, in that cool, lethal tone. She turned to the lawyer, Reid Lyman, who peered at them through his glasses with a slightly bewildered expression. He looked familiar, though Rennie couldn't place him. "Was the will changed recently?"

Reid shifted. "It was, actually."

"When?"

"A few . . . well, two weeks ago. Late July."

Lucille then turned to Elaine. "Well. The will gets conveniently changed shortly before our mother's death so that you get the estate. Isn't that interesting?"

"What are you implying?"

Lucille tilted her head.

Elaine stood too, her petite frame belied by her flashing eyes. "Believe me. I knew nothing about this will before today. I'm here because I was *asked* to come. By your mother."

Lucille's gaze shifted to Rennie. She couldn't play hardball like Lucille, but she could plead their case. She cleared her throat. "Come on. This isn't—fair to us."

It sounded feeble even as she said it. Her older sister pursed her lips slightly, in a way that indicated her disappointment.

"Fair," Elaine said slowly. "The daughters of Hollywood elite want to talk about what's fair."

The shimmering in the corner was back. *It wasn't dust.* Rennie's heart tapped out a wild beat. A prickling sensation came over her. She rocked onto the edge of her seat. Her niece, Madeline, glanced at her, and Rennie tried desperately to stay calm.

"Our mā came to this country as an immigrant," Lucille said. "She, more than anyone, *worked* for this—"

"And you expected to step right into it," Elaine said. "Maybe this was her way of telling you that you didn't deserve this. The *great* Vivian Yin has passed on, and all you say in her memory is that the money she left you is nothing. All you care about is who inherits her home." She pursed her lips in disgust. "Look at the state of this place. Did you even care for her in her last years? Or did you just abandon her in this house and leave her to die?"

Rennie curled into herself, feeling sick.

"Don't you dare speak about our family like that," Lucille spat. "You don't know us. You never did."

In that split second a figure appeared behind Elaine. Rennie was immediately flooded with a childlike burst of relief as she looked upon her mother. *She's back; she's here to explain things—*

And then she remembered that they were all here because Mā was very dead.

Her mother grabbed the back of Elaine's chair and looked straight at Rennie. She was wearing the same blue blouse as she had been the last time Rennie saw her. Her inky eyes bulged. Mā opened her mouth wide, as if to say something, and dirt spilled out.

Rennie lurched up, pointing, just as her mother disappeared. Everyone stared at her in alarm. She bolted from the room, heaving the contents of her stomach into her purse.

She settled on the cold granite floor of the empty foyer against the banister of the stairway and stared high up, where the chandelier glittered. The ridged ceiling plaster was cracking. Strange, discolored stains dripped down the wall now, like spindly, elongated fingers. She didn't want to go back into the library and face the other family. Or hers. Because what Elaine had said was exactly what her mā had told her the last time Rennie visited her.

A visit Rennie wouldn't ever tell anyone about.

She hadn't told Lucille what their mother had looked like then. How paper-thin her skin seemed, how pale she was in the waning light. How it seemed a miracle that Mā was sitting up at the kitchen table, as if she was animated only by her furious gaze.

How pathetic Rennie was, coming to ask her for money.

"看," her mā had said, looking off to the side. *Look.* "She's back."

Rennie didn't know what to say then. *Who's back?* Her mother refused to even look at her. But she simply nodded. If she wasn't desperate, she would never have come in the first place. She had returned in hopes that her mother would do what she had always done: bail

Rennie out. After a nasty, expensive divorce with a manipulative and powerful art collector, and a career dead end with ruinous amounts of credit card debt, she thought that her situation was dire enough that Mā might be sympathetic.

"The thing about you, my daughter"—she spat the last word out—"is that you became soft. You never grew up to be great." Her breath rattled in her chest. She coughed, and spittle dripped from her lips. "You're waiting around, aren't you?" Mā accused. "I know what you're thinking. Who gets the money, who gets the house? I built this up. I endured more than you can imagine. And now you and your sister are just circling me. Like vultures."

"No," Rennie whispered. "No, *no*, that's not—"

"And you didn't—*call me*." Her mother's voice collapsed into a croak. Rennie wanted to fall on her knees right then and there and weep. The sky had darkened in the windows. "All those years. You only ever came when you wanted to take something from me."

"Mā," Rennie pleaded.

"You were the one I wanted to hear from the most. You were the most like me, my 亲女儿." In the dim light Rennie could see that her mā's teeth were darkened and rotted. Mā's eyes narrowed. "You became the cruelest."

Those words had punctured Rennie, and she'd lost all sense of feeling. She'd turned on her heel and stumbled out of the house to her car. She had driven by instinct down the deserted road, away from the house, in the dusk, not realizing that her headlights were busted until she was almost a mile out.

Now, Rennie leaned against the staircase. She couldn't stand to be here. She wasn't capable like Lucille, who could bend things to her iron will. Rennie was simply ready to give in. Twenty thousand was enough for a few more months on her sublet and some crucial payments. She just wanted to leave with the money. But she knew Lucille would never leave without the house. If anyone could negotiate to get it back, it was her.

And if that happened, it would be worth staying.

She collected herself and went back into the dining room, leaving her purse out in the foyer next to the stairs. All eyes latched on to her. "Sorry." She swallowed the remnants of her stomach acid. "I'm back."

Her older sister's eyes narrowed in question. Rennie kept her gaze blank. Lucille looked back toward Reid. "As I was saying. I would like to discuss this with my family in private. Will you excuse us?"

Elaine looked toward the lawyer. He paused. "Of course. I can give you a moment to discuss this in private."

"Yes," Lucille said. "Just a moment."

LUCILLE herded her daughter and sister into what used to be their family's library and shut the doors behind her. She strode across the room to the office table in front of a wall of inlaid bookshelves, and they followed her. Rennie still looked ill. Lucille frowned. "Are you okay? What was that?"

Rennie nodded, not quite meeting her eyes.

Then Madeline said, "Did Wài Pó really . . . cut us out? Of her will?" Her daughter stood uncertainly to the side, her arms wrapped around her willowy frame.

Lucille shook her head. "I don't think that's what happened." She nodded toward the door. "Okay. She was involved in our mā's death. I'm sure of it."

Madeline tilted her head. Rennie looked up.

Lucille mouthed, *Elaine.*

She watched the shock fall over both.

"I was watching her the entire time. She told me to let him finish reading the will. It was like she knew she was getting the house. Her face gave it away when I pressed her on it. She looked guilty. Didn't she?" Lucille had decades of cases under her belt as a personal injury attorney. She'd conducted enough depositions to know how someone's expression could reveal a key truth. She could sense it; the way Elaine's eyes had widened the moment Reid read out the terms of the estate. It hadn't been a look of surprise. It had been one of fear.

"Lucille," Rennie whispered. "You're saying she could have—?"

Lucille nodded.

"Are you sure?" Rennie asked. "That's—that's too far, isn't it? There could have been so many other reasons. Maybe Mā . . . changed her mind! Or had some kind of dementia. Or—"

"You think Mā had such severe dementia she accidentally gave the entire house to *Elaine Deng*?"

Rennie chewed on her bottom lip.

Lucille told herself to focus on the facts. "The will was changed two weeks ago. She was found dead a week ago. Elaine hasn't spoken to us in thirty-four years. She walks back into our lives the morning the will is read. The timing can't be a coincidence."

"Elaine said she had no idea," Rennie said.

"And we believe her?" Lucille paused. "After everything that's happened?"

"What happened?" her daughter asked. "How do you guys know each other?"

Silence.

"She knew our family," Rennie said quietly. "Elaine's parents worked for us."

Madeline nodded. Her expression changed slowly. "*Oh.*"

"There's also an autopsy report with a toxicology component," Lucille cut in before Madeline could ask another question. "We won't get finalized reports for months, but the preliminary results should be in soon."

She had ordered it as an errant precaution. The doctor said it was a heart attack. But Lucille had a feeling. When Mā hadn't been answering her repeated calls in late July, she had reached out to the nursing agency. It was then that Lucille found out that Mā had fired her nurse several weeks ago. Lucille had hired a new nurse, only for the nurse to go to their house and call Lucille, shrieking, that their mother was collapsed on the back terrace. Her body was long cold and stiff. Already in the stages of decomposition.

Lucille had ordered the toxicology report because of a gut feeling. She didn't trust that old nurse. Maybe something—wrong medication, some kind of neglect—had led to her mother's death. But now Lucille thought about Elaine in the dining room, successfully having swept their inheritance out from under them.

Now she had a new gut feeling. No—something more certain than that.

"So," Rennie said slowly, "if Elaine were involved . . ."

"Then it would be a murder case," Lucille said. Madeline's eyes widened. Lucille tried to keep her voice steady. "We take this to court. She no longer is a beneficiary of the will. There's a term for it. The slayer statute, I think."

Rennie shuddered at the phrase. "That's dramatic."

Lucille considered her younger sister. It was strange, seeing her age. Even with the emerging wrinkles around her eyes, she still had this lost dreaminess to her, something Lucille had come to resent over the years. Rennie had always been the softer one. Too willing to believe people at their best. Lucille felt both irritation and pity. Her voice hardened. "So, what? We lose the house and let her get away with this?" She paused. "Just wait until the autopsy report comes in. Okay? Trust me. I know something's wrong here."

Rennie shrank and crossed her arms. "Okay. Okay. I trust you."

There was a knock on the door. They turned.

"What do we do now?" Madeline whispered. "What do we say to them?"

"We should leave," Rennie insisted. "We can figure this out outside the house."

"We can't," Lucille said tightly. "They'll never let us back in. They'll change the locks on us. We need to stay here or we'll be shut out." She stared her sister down. Rennie had to see that there was no other way.

Her sister didn't say anything for a long moment. "Fine," she said faintly. "How do we do that?"

Of course now it would come down to Lucille to scrape things together. She was always the one to be there for Rennie when she crashed and burned, to hire nurses and staff for Mā in her aging years. And now she was the only one who could contest the will. She wasn't an estate lawyer, but she was a lawyer. She could investigate the circumstances of her mother's death. She had to step up. Within seconds she pieced together a plan. She steadied herself against the table for a moment and then faced her family.

"We need to buy time. We're going to go out there and say that we need a few days in the house to sort through our mother's things. The preliminary autopsy should come in the next few days. And during that time, I'll figure out what happened between Elaine and Mā before her death. If Elaine did indeed have something to do with it—" Her voice dropped. "We get justice for ourselves. And for Mā."

NORA watched Vivian's family file into the dining room. They sat back down in their chairs quietly.

"All right," the lawyer said, his dark eyes settling on each person around the table in turn. "Should we proceed? Are there any further questions?"

"Reid, we'd like to make a request," one of the women spoke. The pushy one with the sharp suit jacket. Lucille. "There was no specification as to whom the tangible property in the house belongs to. Which means that by California probate code, it de facto belongs to us. The surviving relatives."

Legal jargon. Nora exchanged a look with her mother.

"Come on," the other woman—Renata?—said. She leaned in and searched their gazes with doe-like, brown eyes. "You don't want my mother's old clothes, do you?"

She was the one who acted weirdly, pointed at Nora's mother, and ran out. She seemed a little . . . scattered. But earnest. Her hands were shaking. Nora actually felt a pang of sympathy for her.

"No," her mother conceded, though Nora could tell she was irritated. "You can have that."

"Thank you," Lucille said. "Can we have a few days to collect her belongings? There are . . ." She looked around the dining room. "Many things of hers. We'd like time to process."

A long moment passed. Reid, the lawyer, looked to her mother. Nora did too.

Her mother took a deep breath and nodded. "Just a few days."

"Okay," Lucille said. "We'll stay here, then."

Mā stiffened at Lucille's statement. "As will we."

Lucille set her jaw. Reid glanced around uncertainly. "Well," he said.

"In that case, if everyone has reached an agreement, I will leave it at that. A copy of the will has been forwarded to your emails. If you have any more questions, here is my business card." He stood and shuffled the files into a manila folder. Nora saw him glance at Lucille one last time before he gathered his things and hurried out.

Nora watched the Yin family leave the room and go upstairs. The daughter looked over her shoulder and met Nora's eyes for a fraction of a second. She looked just like Lucille. Beautiful and brittle, with full lips and rounded cheekbones. She wore pearl earrings, and Nora thought she saw the glimmer of gold rings on her fingers. She'd said virtually nothing. But her calm gaze had needled into everything. Private school pedigree, some Ivy probably, Nora assumed. Not that it mattered. They would never cross paths again after this.

Nora had a weird feeling. Before Vivian's family had gathered in the library, they had been so adamant about the house. Now there was no mention of it. She had known them for all of an hour, but they didn't seem like the type to back out without a fight. Especially not that prickly lawyer, who now marched them up the stairs.

"They're already taking the second floor," Mā muttered to Nora. "Of course they are."

"Why did you let them stay?" Nora asked in Mandarin.

Her mother turned to look at her. Her gray hair was fraying out of its bun. "They're grieving, Jiā-Jiā." She used Nora's Mandarin name. Her voice had softened, and Nora knew she was thinking about her own late mother, who'd passed away when Nora was fourteen. "I am not cruel. This is my last favor to them. And then we will never have to see them again."

"And what about this house?"

"We'll sell it." Mā lowered her voice. "It'll pay for your medical school. And we can donate the rest. I have a few organizations in mind."

three

NORA'S mother clearly knew her way around the house. She led Nora out of the dining room, across the massive ivory-tiled ocean that was the foyer, into another dim hall, and then, finally, to one of the rooms at the end. "You can hang out in here. Keep an eye on them if you hear anything," she said. "But don't talk. I'm going to go back home to get some things for our stay. *Don't* leave the house until I'm back."

"Okay."

"The oldest is a lawyer. You really can't say a word."

"I'm not dying to talk to these people," Nora said wearily. "Don't worry."

Now she was alone on the first floor. She could hear the voices of the Yin women talking upstairs. She started to climb the staircase, thinking she could eavesdrop a little, but the wood creaked under her feet. She gave up and decided to take herself on a tour of the house.

The rooms stretched on, stale and airless. Off to the right was the dining room they had sat in for the reading of the will. The foyer contracted into a hallway as it led to the back of the house, and at the other end Nora could see leather couches and a ticking grandfather clock. The living room, she guessed. But she was more interested in the door on her left, with a set of detailed wrought iron knobs. The room in which Lucille had gathered her family for a private discussion. Nora pulled the doorknob. It stuck for a moment, but with a few tugs and some jiggling, she got it open. Once she stepped in, it swung smoothly shut behind her.

Nora arched her head up to take in with awe the high, vaulted ceilings, the built-in shelves, the inlaid chestnut-colored cabinets. The wall panels were a sun-paled mahogany color, glowing reddish in the afternoon light that flowed in through arched windows constructed of thick, geometric panes of glass. Silk screens painted with elaborate mountains and clouds perched behind the twin armchairs in the corner, with a green glass lamp poised between them.

These people were *rich* rich. Across the room there was a discolored rectangular expanse on the wall, as if a painting had been removed. A mid-century desk stood in front of what looked like a sealed fireplace. Built-in bookshelves rose on either side. Windows lined the left wall, the view outside obstructed by strands of ivy, though Nora could see the circular driveway through the patches the vines didn't cover.

On the desk was an archaic-looking desktop computer straight from the mid-2000s, with that giant, blocky computer case. She eased out the chair and sat on it gingerly. It was made with some saggy upholstery. The desk had drawers underneath it. She tugged on the one in the middle and found magazines, flaked and brittle with age and water damage. A spread of photos. Nora stared at a young woman with black hair that crested around her shoulders and lips dark with lipstick.

There was a bright magnetism to her eyes, even in this discolored, creased photo. A beauty mark under her right eye. *Should I know you?* She stood and surveyed the sprawling bookshelves. Some titles she knew. Faulkner, Fitzgerald, Woolf, Thoreau. There were some Chinese texts, too. Nora only knew some of the words in passing from her years at Chinese school. She recognized one: 红楼梦. *Dream of the Red Chamber.*

She pored over the philosophy section. Rawls. Rosseau. Her mother had been a philosophy major. She'd studied it along with political science at Berkeley. She was two years into her PhD in political philosophy when she'd gotten pregnant with Nora and dropped out. She'd always said that leaving school was independent of having Nora. Academia wasn't for her anyway. Grad school funding wasn't enough to support herself, much less two. And it had always been just the two of them: whichever man had pitched in for her existence didn't stick around. If anything, her maternal grandparents had helped raise her.

Nora sensed that her mother gave up more than she let on. Mā could have been a professor or diplomat instead of working a dull city government admin job that Nora knew she didn't like. These days, what really animated her mother was the organizing work she did on the weekends—driving around, canvassing for housing justice coalitions in San Bernardino and Riverside, phone banking.

Nora eyed a copy of a collection of poems by W. B. Yeats. It jutted out ever so slightly. She'd just touched the spine when the door behind her opened and heels clicked in.

"Oh," Lucille said.

They stood and looked at each other for a moment.

Lucille gestured to the phone in her hand. "I need to take a call in here. Do you mind?" Her voice was clipped.

Nora raised an eyebrow. "What, the fifteen other rooms in this house are all occupied?"

Lucille froze. Nora threw a polite smile over her shoulder as she left the room. She could feel the lawyer's eyes drill into her back. *Good*, Nora thought. *I've rattled her.*

LUCILLE watched the girl go. She shut the library doors with more force than required and the hinges groaned. She winced. She couldn't take her anger out on this place. The house had fallen into disrepair. The faucets were rusted, and the sink handles screeched. Certain balusters on the stairs had come loose. Cracks and stains crept down the walls. Old paint warped and bubbled. And dust seeped and clumped in every ridge in the crown molding and the baseboards, along the windowsills and the mantels. Dirt, too. *How did so much dirt get in here?*

The house was like one filthy, skeletal husk. The last time she had been here was five years ago, but she hadn't made it beyond the foyer then, and now, as she ventured farther into the house, she could see just how much it had decayed.

Lucille sat down at the desk. The cushion sagged underneath her. She pulled out her phone and stared at her ex-husband's number for a few long moments. At her mother's funeral he'd found her in a spare room she'd shut herself in. He'd cradled her, and it had been almost too much, being shown unusual tenderness by someone who'd ruined their marriage years ago with an affair. Still, he had shown up to her estranged mother's funeral, an act of enormous kindness. Now, here in the library study, she called him.

He picked up on the second ring. "Lucy?"

She closed her eyes at the calm, deep sound of his voice and her old nickname. "Hi. I need advice. Assurance, really." They had always loved discussing cases back in the day, late at night, curled into each other on the couch, books pushed among empty beer bottles and take-out on the coffee table. In many ways, he was still the one who knew her best.

"Sure thing. But before that, how are you doing? How's Madeline?"

"Fine." Lucille swallowed. "Mā gave the house to *Elaine*."

There was a pause. "Who?"

"Elaine. Deng. Daughter of Mā's former housekeeper. From ages ago. Of all people." She shook her head. "It makes no sense why *she* would ever be the beneficiary of anything from Mā. But here's the thing. The will was changed two weeks ago."

"Okay. That's odd."

"I was looking at Elaine the whole time. She looked like she knew. I think something's up with her." She paused. "You're following me, right?"

"Ah." His voice hardened. "So you think—"

"I know, Daniel. I can't explain it."

"And is there evidence? An autopsy report?"

"Ordered with a toxicology report. Just waiting for the results. There's a case here, isn't there? From a legal standpoint?"

"Have you consulted a probate lawyer?"

"You're family law. That's adjacent. Come on. I just need your thoughts on the situation."

"That's . . . Okay. There could be. You'd have to prove that it was intentional and without legal justification."

"As in, Elaine didn't kill Mā in self-defense? Yeah. I doubt that." She straightened up. "Thank you for your read."

"Really, Lucy. I'll pass on a contact of mine. Alexis Kahan. From our year at Stanford. It's no problem. He's taken care of things like this before."

"Sure." She cleared her throat. "I don't know. I might keep this to myself for a bit. Family matters are always . . . delicate."

There was a long silence. "You're not thinking of taking this on yourself, are you?"

She fixed her eyes on a book that was sticking out from the others on a shelf. "And what if I did?"

"This is entirely different from your kind of litigation, Lucy."

A part of her knew he was right. But she pushed on. "I'm allowed to. Legally, I can. And I know this family best."

"You have a tendency to take on too much. More than you can handle."

"Now what does that mean?"

He sighed. "I don't want to get into it. You know what I'm talking about."

She knew he was referencing her failed congressional campaign. It always came back to this. It had marked the end of her political aspirations and her marriage. Things were never the same after that. "Well," she said scathingly. "Thanks for the vote of confidence. And the honesty."

"I'm sorry. I—"

"No, I mean it." She ended the call and stared at the screen. *Mistake.*

She let her gaze drift to the desktop computer in front of her. She reached out and pressed the power button. She must have bought this for Mā decades ago. It whirred to life and dust motes billowed out.

It still worked. A miracle. She shut it back off.

Lucille stood up and stretched, facing the bookshelves in front of her. She'd spent weekend afternoons reading across from Dad in the armchairs, the glow of the green lamp between them, books stacked high on the table. They'd talk about the news and international institutions and moral fallacies, until Mā came in and told them it was dinnertime. President Lucy, Dad used to call her, the affectionate moniker he bestowed upon her when she argued at the dinner table. President Lucy. What an embarrassment. In the end, she couldn't even win her own congressional district.

The book that stuck out was a collection of poems by Yeats. What had made the girl choose this book? Lucille pulled it out and cracked open the book.

Something fell from inside the brittle pages. A dried rosebud, and then a line, in faint penciled underline.

When all the wild Summer was in her gaze.

Lucille slammed the book shut and shoved it back on the shelf. She sank into a chair. She held up the rosebud and it crumbled in her hands. A slow, cold awareness washed over her, as if she were inching herself into an ice bath, until she plunged in all at once. Her breath quickened. She was out of her body, watching herself panic. She could do nothing but sink into it and wait.

Eventually—after a few minutes? An hour?—her heartbeat slowed. Lucille pushed herself to stand, feeling dizzy. She took a moment to steady herself on the desk. She had to leave this library for now.

Eventually she ended up at the dining table, watching the dining room chandelier gleam dully above her. The expanse of mahogany stretched out before her. An hour ago she'd faced off against Elaine. In many ways it had been like it used to be. The two of them sitting across from each other over dinner. Locked in ongoing debates. Both sides refusing to let up. But now this wasn't about lofty subjects like socialist collectivism or nuclear disarmament; this was about her mother's death.

I do everything for you. I am setting you up to be great. Remember that. Mā told them this on the nights she came home late from days on set and film premieres, her permed hair loose around her shoulders, her sweet, velvety Guerlain perfume settling around them as she shrugged off her fur coat and slid out of her slingback kitten heels. After filming on location, she would come back to tell them how much she had missed them. How much she loved them; how she couldn't wait to see what they would do to make her proud. What happened? Had her love dried up? Had they disappointed her so deeply that she wanted to bar them from their childhood home?

Did you even care for her in her last years? Elaine's spiteful words tormented her now. *Or did you just abandon her in this house and leave her to die?*

Elaine didn't know that Lucille had tried to help. For years and years. Lucille was the eldest daughter who tried to pull what was left of their family together. Every year she invited Mā to holidays; to recitals; to family vacations. Mā never showed up. Not even for Madeline, her granddaughter, who used to ask about her all the time. Each time Lucille called, Mā would say she was fine out here by herself. Whenever they visited the house, Mā hurried them out. When Lucille hired her a nurse, Mā fired her. Mā exiled herself here, in this house that they had all grown up in, and that they were now severed from.

Reid hadn't even been able to look her in the eye this morning when he read the terms of the will. He knew something was wrong, too. Lucille stood and her chair scraped behind her, rattling across the floor. She picked up the business card that Reid had left behind on the table. His name was printed in spare font. There was an office number and a mobile.

Her fingers trembled slightly as she started a text message.

> This is Lucille. I need some clarification
> on the will. Can we talk?

Her fingers hovered over the send button. It was too easy to reach out to him like this. She remembered when she used to stare at the phone in the library and try to guess the precise moment Reid would call. Was this a good idea? She was still smarting from her conversation with Daniel. But she'd reached out to her ex-husband out of vulnerability. This was a necessity. She needed more details from Reid. He was one of the last people her mother had communicated with.

Lucille sent the text and set her phone face down on the table. She looked around the room. Certain parts had kept well. The table was still smooth. The teal-blue bar cart in the corner was covered by a thick layer of dust but in pristine condition, untouched. She watched the muted light shift across the floor. She remembered her ten-year-old self, with a full set of cutlery and dishes before her, watching the chandelier glimmer while her parents talked to their guests at the other end. She observed the way important people talked, with volume and vigor. At fourteen she had read Woodrow Wilson's biography at this table. At seventeen, in the summer of 1990, she had poured a drink from that bar cart and met eyes with a cute boy. He had been talking to someone, so she headed to the back of the house. Whitney Houston and the Talking Heads streamed through the living room and the windows were flung open, the curtains billowing out like sails. Lucille had stepped out onto the terrace, looking out at the roses and lavender and bougainvillea that draped the terrace and the fountain that poured lightly as a fresh spring. And then the same boy from the dining room had stepped out onto the terrace, too. That was the first time she spoke to Reid Lyman.

He'd wanted to become a writer. He was headed to Princeton to study English and carried a quiet intensity about him; she told him how her dad called her President Lucy and he didn't scoff. They had talked for hours that afternoon. *Tell me when you win that Pulitzer*, she'd said. He grinned. *You can congratulate me from the Oval Office*, he'd responded. When he spoke to her, she got the feeling that they were fastening into orbit around each other, like fusing stars. It hurt, how clearly she remembered that moment. She thought that night would earmark the beginning of the rest of her life.

Her phone buzzed.

Of course

Come to my office

I have availability tomorrow morning

She exhaled and typed.

See you then.

• • •

RENNIE knew how to be quiet.

That night she padded across the second-floor hallway. Her bare footsteps skimmed over the old floorboards. She passed by the rooms where her older sister and niece slept and pried open the door to her mother's bedroom. The air was colder. The large bed stood in the center of the sparse, moonlit room. There was a nightstand, a dresser in the far corner, and a vanity. She knew Lucille would come soon to pack the clothes and possessions away for storage and to argue over. Rennie had to claim things while she still could.

She walked across the room and sat in front of the vanity. She wasn't as nimble as she used to be. She went to look at herself in the vanity mirror, but realized suddenly that it wasn't there anymore. She'd looked into that mirror so many times as a teenager. She used to come in and open the little drawer with a tiny golden key she'd slip from Mā's key ring. She'd try on her mother's jewelry for fun. Later, she'd learned how to pick the loose lock so she didn't even need the key.

Now it was muscle memory. She slipped a bobby pin from her bun, pulled it open, and jammed the metal tip against the rusty pins. The drawer stuck for a bit, but with a bit of wiggling, slid open. Pearl necklaces gleamed in the low light. There were fan-shaped drop earrings and bulky chain bracelets. A herringbone necklace; a solid golden cuff; a dragonfly pin with a smattering of jade—*oh, wasn't it all so beautiful?*

Rennie's eyes were drawn to something new. A ring that glimmered in the corner.

Dad's signet ring.

Rennie picked it up, feeling the solid weight of pure gold curled in her palm. She turned it over, looking at the leaves that crawled up the sides, the initials engraved on the surface worn away over time. Dad had worn it on his pinky. Rennie had a vivid memory of falling asleep between her parents on the couch as a kid, her father's arm tucked around her, the television humming in the background, the ring winking in and out of her vision like a star.

She slipped it onto her index finger and stood. Before she could lose her courage, she swiped the emerald drop earrings, a solitaire bracelet, and the herringbone necklace and slipped them in her pocket. She waited another moment, and then took the jade dragonfly pin and the golden cuff bracelet, too. Who would stop her now? Lucille would never know; she never poked around here. Rennie could sell them all if she had to. Each item would be worth a couple hundred apiece. She felt bad, but she knew that her sister would just lock it all up in airless safes, where it would never see the light of day. And that would be a pure pity. Better it went to Rennie.

She closed the center drawer and opened the one on the left. Hairpins and flakes of paint, an old sewing kit. Nothing of value. Halfheartedly, she opened the deeper drawer on the right.

There was a pile of hairpieces, the pearl scratched and the metal rusted, and silk scarves, which still carried a cloying trace of perfume. Through the folds of fabric Rennie recognized the outline of something and caught a flash of gold. She clapped her hands to her mouth. Slowly, she reached through and uprooted the statue of Mā's Academy Award.

The statue was buried, as if Mā had shoved it in there and never intended to look at it again. It was heavier than she remembered. The metal was so cold it felt like it was burning her. She shoved the award back in the drawer, closing it with finality before she quietly walked out.

Rennie made her way downstairs and headed for the wine pantry. She grabbed a bottle of dusty merlot and a corkscrew. She tiptoed back up the stairs, her ear trained for any extra creaks as she retreated into her room. She sat on her bed and pried the cork off the wine. Everything in here seemed smaller than she remembered. She was fourteen when she left this house for boarding school. Now, the wallpaper was brittle and cracked. Her bedsprings were merciless.

The cork popped quietly. She took a deep gulp from the bottle, her mouth puckering from the acidity. The signet ring glittered on her finger. She hoped she wouldn't have to sell it. Twenty grand should be okay for a while.

She closed her eyes. She wanted to be anywhere but here. Scenes from the cities of her youth—Paris, London, New York—filtered dreamily through her mind. Back then, she drifted from one place to another, charming strangers, crowding into sweaty apartments, and lingering on rooftops with a cigarette in her hand and pills dissolving on her tongue with cheap, carbonated wine. She wanted to be twenty-five and auditioning—for movies in LA, for plays in New York, booking shitty commercials in between, chasing down taxis and elusive phone numbers.

Rennie stared at her distorted reflection in the wine bottle. Her eyes were more deep-set and prominent with age, her nose more angular. She had Mā's cheekbones and Dad's widow's peak. But where Vivian was known for her precise monolids, Rennie had double eyelids, the creases deepened from too many nights of not bothering to remove her makeup. Vivian Yin had enviable, jet-black hair, and Rennie's was a dark shade of brown, the tips lightening to gold in the sun. But besides that, she bore the image of her mother.

Of course, Rennie had always wanted to be just like her. A Chinese actress who'd singlehandedly made a name for herself. Her work ranged all genres, and her presence could summon a room. Rennie had hungered for that kind of success and charisma. Even after that summer when the family ruptured apart. Or maybe especially after that summer. But now Rennie was back, broke, sitting in her childhood bedroom with plans to pawn her late parents' valuables. A bit pathetic. She took a deep breath and drank. Wine was the only thing that aged well in this place.

Something creaked outside her door. Her heart stuttered. Rennie tried to stay calm. Maybe if she stayed still, nothing would happen. And then she heard the voice from behind her.

"Mèi mei."

She dropped the bottle. Wine splashed out on the floor, spreading into a crimson bruise. Rennie shoved her forehead between her knees and squeezed her eyes shut.

This time, it wasn't her mother.

Rennie could feel the presence surround her. She locked her jaw so tightly, her teeth ground into one another. *Please go away.*

At some point she felt the presence ease, and she knew she was alone again. Shakily, she sat up and swiped the tears from her cheeks. She hastily threw a shirt on the spill to soak it up. She got into bed and pulled the covers over her head, staring into the darkness under the blanket as she twisted the ring around her finger. Finally, she felt the wine sink through her and drag her into sleep.

four

AUGUST 2024
DAY 2 IN THE HOUSE

NORA was too tired to study for the MCAT, but she couldn't put off even a day. Not with the test looming in three months. She'd understudied for her first test the summer after her sophomore year and eked by with a mediocre score. She needed to be serious.

She pored over pictures of the venous system. Vasodilation. Vasoconstriction. She followed the path of veins and arteries with her fingertip. If she stared long enough, she could almost see them expand and ripple, like an optical illusion. She curled around her textbook. Could diagrams sink in through osmosis? She hoped so. The lone light in the room flickered weakly by her bedside. She was surprised it still worked, all things considered.

Nora heard her mother's snores from across the hall. Her mother had almost claimed the twin bed across from her. "I can sleep here too if you need," she said. "Just in case."

"I'm twenty-one, Mā. Take the other room."

Her mother shifted from foot to foot. "This isn't a normal house, Jiā-Jiā."

"Well, I do have to study. And focus."

That did it; her mother left. Now it was past midnight and Nora was alone, drifting into sleep in this lumpy bed. Which was *just fine.* This was temporary. This was just a very weird family vacation.

Varying topographies of dust accumulated on every surface. The curtains were soft and made of a splotched, yellowing linen. The wallpaper was a simple patterned taupe. There was nothing on the nightstand aside from an unplugged digital clock and a fountain pen. The nightstand stood between two twin beds that smelled of white flower oil and mothballs. That 白花油 scent reminded Nora of her grandmother. She had never been close to her grandparents. She mostly just remembered spending Sunday mornings with them at the stern, stuffy Chinese church.

Biology terms floated in front of her heavy eyelids. Suddenly her bed jolted, once, twice, and she was jostled awake. The digital clock rattled on the nightstand. The light flickered. The pen clattered to the floor.

Then everything stilled.

Nora picked the pen up off the floor and set it on the nightstand. Was it a small earthquake? What was that?

She glanced at her phone. It was 12:38.

Fully awake now, Nora peered through the slit in the curtains. The stone steps from the terrace arced down into the garden. For a moment, Nora imagined what it would have looked like with flowers in bloom and the fountain full.

Then she realized it *was* full.

How had she not noticed it before? In the center of the garden, Nora could see water spilling over the sides of the fountain. The space around it was flooded with vivid blooms in every color. Someone stood among the flowers, but Nora couldn't make out who it was. Maybe the daughter of the other family?

How bizarre. Inside, the house was falling apart. But someone had been taking care of the grounds? Maintained an immaculate garden? And if so, why did her mother not want her to go near it?

Nora sighed. She crawled back into bed. She didn't know if the bedside light was flickering again or if she was just struggling to keep her eyes open until she slid into sleep.

MADELINE held on to a dim memory from five years ago when Mā had brought her to this house to visit her grandmother during Thanksgiving. They'd only stayed long enough to drop off food and groceries.

Madeline remembered her mother and Wài Pó having a hushed, tense conversation in the foyer. "Get out," Madeline had heard her grandmother say sharply. "I don't want you here."

"I didn't want to come here in the first place," Mā had shot back.

Her mother was silent on the drive home to Newport Beach. On the way, Madeline had asked what happened. "I suggested hiring a nurse to take care of her," her mother had said, her fingers clutched tightly around the steering wheel. "And I invited her to come down to us for Thanksgiving. She said no to both."

"Why?"

"She wants to be alone in that house," Mā snapped. "So be it."

"Why don't we have dinner at Wài Pó's house?" It was big enough, wasn't it?

Her mother didn't answer.

Why had her grandmother kicked them out? When she came to Newport Beach during Madeline's childhood, she'd stay for weeks at a time. Mā would put together elaborate dinners. She'd hire a cleaner. Wài Pó would drift around, taking Madeline to the park and the ocean. And then after a few weeks she would pack her bags. Madeline always begged her to stay. "I can't, 宝贝," her grandmother would say. "I need to be home." Mā would be in a stormy mood the rest of the day. Madeline would always feel like she'd disappointed her own mother in some way by failing to charm her grandmother into staying.

What had led her grandmother to become such a recluse that she avoided her own family? Her passing left Madeline with her own half-sketched questions. What had they done to her? Why would Wài Pó give this house away to another family?

In the early morning, Madeline paused at the top of the wide stone terrace behind the house, one hand on the carved balustrade. Gingerly, she stepped down, surveying the gardens before her. Or, the remains of a garden. Dark roots, long overgrown and rotten, sank into the earth. The mottled grounds stretched out far before her, and the unkempt tangle covered every inch. Madeline could just make out the remnants of walking paths, which cut through the gardens like a cross. In the middle was a cracked stone fountain, moss etched into its rippled grooves. Vines clung to it, knotting into one another as they crawled up from the mess of roots and dirt. It was August, but not a single thing was in bloom.

It must have been beautiful once. But even with the grounds in this state, she felt a keen sense of envy every time she looked at it. Sure, Madeline had grown up without worry about her family's financial situation. She'd gone to a private day school and her parents had paid for college. But she'd never lived anywhere that had this kind of grandeur before, and now she was only here because her grandmother had died. She had felt like a child again at the dining table yesterday, everything argued over and predetermined for her. As the only child of two lawyers, that was often the case. And it only got worse after her parents' divorce. She had to be the tiebreaker and the peacemaker. It was instinctive now to play neutral and absorb other peoples' emotions. Placating her mother was always the first step. She preferred to manage her own emotions—her anxiety, her panic—alone.

Madeline walked across the grounds. The choppy, uneven grass was shriveled and yellow, wilting in the dry heat. There were impending signs of wildfire season. The summer after her sophomore year of college, she'd been a volunteer lookout in Tahoe. She'd rise before the sun, shivering to the bone, and keep an eye on the shape of the clouds, the direction of any smoke. On good days, when the sky was clear, she marveled at the divinity of the landscape before her, at the tree line and the gentle layered slopes of the blue mountains cresting into the lake.

Mā said a degree in environmental studies was useless. How could you change the course of the earth? What jobs could she get? But Madeline had clung to her major. Mā had been right about the job prospects, though. At least here, in this house, with its spotty cellular connection, Madeline could take her mind off the silence in her inbox.

She surveyed the matted blanket of vines and roots and weeds. Everything seemed beyond reviving. But maybe after the dangers of wildfire season had passed, they could remove all this and plant a new garden? She at least knew how to take care of plants and help flowers sprout. That was a start.

Then, as she was scanning the trees that rimmed the perimeter of the garden, her eyes caught on color. At the other end of the garden, she knelt down, teasing the vines apart with her fingers to find a single rose.

A large, half-hidden bud, with soft, fresh pink petals was half-submerged among the parched stalks and shrubbery. Madeline reached for the flower on instinct. Maybe this garden *would* heal. She stood and wiped her hands on her jeans, glancing up at the house as she wondered how to tend a rosebush . . . .

Someone stared at her from one of the first-story windows. After the initial jolt of surprise, Madeline recognized her short hair. Nora. Madeline offered a tentative smile.

The curtains snapped shut.

The girl hadn't spoken to anyone. Madeline had thought that them being around the same age might even evoke some transient affinity between them, but clearly she had been wrong.

Madeline dusted off her carefully maintained white shoes and walked back up the house and into an empty kitchen. The faint scent of rose clung to her, undercut by something sharper and metallic. Rust.

Guilt washed over her. She should have reached out to her grandmother more, tried to know her better. But her estrangement must have been intentional. Madeline's family had been less than a hundred miles away. Something must have happened here, but now all Madeline knew was the fallout.

NORA must have been dreaming about the garden.

She woke up that morning with the corner of her textbook imprinted on her cheek. She yanked open the curtains to find the fountain covered with a fine layer of moss, the roots tangled, and everything else dry and brown. But her dream had been so vivid. Nora was sure she'd seen flowers blooming last night and Madeline pacing among them, just like she was now.

Right then, Madeline looked up and a curious smile lit up her eyes. Maybe it hadn't been her in the dream? Nora snapped the curtains closed, aware she'd been caught staring, and walked down the hall. "Mā?"

Her mother was curled in a fetal position in bed.

"Mā?" Nora moved quickly to her mother's side. "You okay?"

"Mm," her mother groaned, a hand cupping her eyes. "头疼."

Nora looked at the nightstand. An open bottle of ibuprofen. Her mother was having one of her migraines. Calmly, in Mandarin, Nora asked, "Want anything? Something to eat? Water?"

Her mother's voice was muffled. "Go take care of yourself."

Nora made her way into the hallway. The two older women and Madeline stood in the kitchen talking. They stopped right as Nora approached. They stared at her as if she were the one trespassing.

The lawyer—Lucille—said, "Can we help you?"

Nora stood up straight, only to realize she didn't know where anything was. "Are there cups somewhere?"

Lucille pierced her with a hard stare. Renata, the anxious-looking one in a loose dress with hair a shade lighter than the others, pointed at a cabinet. Nora reached for it, feeling all three sets of eyes on her. She went for the tap.

"Drink from that," Madeline spoke up. She gestured to the kettle. "It's boiled water."

Nora nodded, filling a cup for herself and then another for her mother. She observed Madeline watching her curiously. Nora remained stoic. She was usually friendlier when someone as pretty as Madeline smiled at her like that. But Nora was operating under strict, albeit odd instructions.

What a dysfunctional family. Nora had looked them up yesterday afternoon with her spotty cell data. Lucille was a personal injury lawyer, the kind you'd see smiling hawkishly from a highway billboard. Renata had a more elusive and scattered profile: a few small movie credits from the '90s and early 2000s to the name Rennie Lowell, and a 2022 TMZ article about her contentious split from a famous art exhibitor in New York, in which he accused her of stealing one of the pieces in his collection.

It was a little dramatic, but nothing out of line. After she'd looked up Vivian's daughters, she'd searched the actress herself, more thoroughly than before. She scanned the details she knew: a 1986 Academy Award for Best Supporting Actress, a few movie credits, a late husband named Richard Lowell. Nora had searched that name and found a long list of acting credits, an Academy Award Best Actor nomination for the same year Vivian had won, and an obituary attributing his death to an accidental overdose at age forty-four in New York. Nora had also looked up Madeline, only to find private social media profiles. Berkeley Environmental Studies, graduated spring this year. A year ahead of Nora. In pictures she had the same calm gaze and half smile. Nora had recognized her pearl earrings. The cell service dropped, and the page went blank.

Nora finished her tepid cup of water and brought the other mug into her mother's room. "Here," she said. "Water."

"Thank you, Jiā-Jiā."

Nora paused at the doorway. "Did you feel a small earthquake last night?"

Her mother shifted, keeping her eyes closed. "Hm?"

"Never mind," Nora said. It must have been part of the dream, too.

five

LUCILLE pulled into the parking lot of the law firm in Pasadena. It was half-hidden off the side of the road and hard to find even with her navigation. Her phone lit up with a notification, and she snatched it out of her bag. Any email could be the toxicology report. But this one wasn't. It was just a work email. She'd been getting a steady stream of them—briefs to look over, contract language, indemnity clauses, forwarded communications meant to snare her in the CC trap. Her usual urge was to open them and fire off responses, to show how hard of a worker she was even during her time off. But this was too important.

She walked into the office and felt the cool hum of the air-conditioning. She adjusted her blouse. "I'm here to see Reid Lyman."

The receptionist peered toward the offices in the back. "He'll be with you in a second."

Lucille cradled the printed copy of the will in her handbag and picked at a loose string on her pleated pants. She needed to get these tailored again.

"Lucille?"

There was his familiar warm tone. Lucille smiled wanly. "Hi, Reid."

"It's good to see you. Come in."

Lucille followed him to his office. It was a corner room with light wooden walls, bare except for a clock and a Pepperdine Law diploma. She sat in the chair across from his desk, which was strewn with papers. There was an old coffeemaker, the carafe ringed with a gradient of stains. He pushed aside his keyboard and leaned forward. She was a little caught off guard by the intensity of his gaze. She thought of the first time their eyes met thirty-four years ago, those few electrifying weeks after her party. Her cheeks warmed. She slid the copy of her mother's will between them. "Thanks for taking time out of your day for this."

Reid raised a hand. His sleeves were pushed up. "We're past those formalities. I'm sorry about your mother. I want to be here for you."

She paused.

"I mean it, Lucy."

Lucille had come to despise her old nickname because her husband had always sounded exasperated when he used it. But Reid said it softly. With care. She looked up. She wanted to shout across the desk: *How could she do this to us?* Instead, she stayed businesslike. "How did she change the will?"

He exhaled through his nose. "I got a call on my cell during the weekend, which was strange. I asked if it could wait until Monday, but Vivian said it was urgent. That was when she said that she wanted to make a change referring to the inheritance of her estate. To write a codicil. She wanted the estate to go to Elaine Deng."

"*She* said?"

Reid nodded. "Your mother wrote and signed the codicil." He paused and held up a piece of paper with creases in it. "Here is the original document. It *was* her handwriting and signature, wasn't it?"

Lucille stared at the familiar words that had been photocopied into her copy of the will.

I devise and bequeath my estate and all its matters to Elaine Deng.

I revoke the prior devise and bequest of my estate and all its matters to my daughters, Yin Chen, Lucille Wang, and Yin Zi-Meng, Renata Yin-Lowell.

It all would have been theirs. Hers, and her sister's. It should have been.

There was her mother's unmistakable, betraying signature. And the date: July 20.

Lucille ground her teeth. *Keep going.* "And in this call. Did my mother mention any other financial assets? Or funds?"

Reid gave her a strange stare. "There's no other money that she mentioned."

No other money. It didn't make sense. Between her late mother and stepfather, they'd accumulated wealth, generations of it, she thought. Enough to send them all to years of private school and college. Enough that Mā had paid half the down payment for her and Daniel's house. Enough that Mā used to send checks for Madeline's day school tuition. But now it was all gone? "Okay. And what time was this again?"

"Hm." He pulled out his phone. Squinted at it. "Around 5:32 p.m. She'd written up the amendment after and mailed it to me. I received it by Monday. The 22nd."

"And did you ask her why? Why she changed this detail?"

"I did." His eyebrows knit in focus. "And she said this one thing I couldn't make sense of. She said, '*My daughters can't have this house. It will ruin them.*'"

The clock ticked.

"Ruin us," Lucille whispered. *Ruin?* Her mouth was dry. She swallowed. "What does that mean?"

"I asked her. She didn't say."

"That doesn't sound like her at all. Mā wouldn't say that."

"She did." Reid's voice was soft. "I heard her, Lucy."

There had to be more to this. "When she changed the will. Did she seem like she was under the influence of something? Under duress?"

"If you're referring to her mental acuity, she seemed sound of mind. At least to me. But she didn't have witnesses so . . . I don't know."

"Does that even make the will valid?"

"Technically, yes. It's handwritten. Still, contestable."

She gripped the sides of her chair. "It sure is. Because none of this *seems like her.* She doesn't change her will for decades, and then she does this, and a week later she's found dead?"

He gave her a long look. "What did she die of, if you don't mind my asking?"

"Doctor said heart attack. I'm getting an official autopsy report."

He nodded. "That's what I would have done. It may have been . . . planned."

"You think my mother killed herself?"

"I—" Reid swallowed, not quite meeting her eyes. "I didn't mean— It's not appropriate for me to speculate."

He was the last person Mā had spoken to. It hadn't been one of her children. For a moment Lucille felt a cold and total sense of anger possess her. "Ruin us," she echoed. Her voice started to tremble. "She said that giving us the house would—ruin us?"

"I'm so sorry. I didn't know what was going on."

"As if we're not ruined now," she whispered. Every single emotion she had pushed down over the past two weeks flooded her now, the grief rising in the same tide as the anger, all the horrific possible circumstances of her mother's death, along with her own helplessness. And the worst thing was that she was spiraling, publicly, in the middle of Reid's office.

"Lucy," she heard Reid saying. She was only dimly aware of him coming around the desk, putting his hand on her shoulder. "Are you all right?"

She swiped furiously at her face with her sleeves. Lucille looked up and saw Reid leaning over. His hand now cradled her forearm. She held still for a moment, their faces inches apart, his warm brown eyes searching hers, and felt a brief, deranged urge to reach for him. She felt intolerably vulnerable. Why was he looking at her like this? Was it pity or concern?

She rocked back. Reid moved his hand. Lucille stood stiffly from her chair and swept the will into her bag. "Thank you. That was all I needed to know."

Lucille was still in the parking lot of the law firm. Her swollen eyelids ached from being rubbed raw. She needed to drive home, but now she just sat numbly in her car.

Mā said that the house *would ruin them.*

What did she mean? Lucille had always assumed it was obvious that they would sell the house and split the money. They all would have been better off for it. Rennie would have enough money to get back on her feet after her big divorce. Lucille would help recoup some of the money she'd lost in her soul-sucking, fruitless congressional campaign and her divorce. They would deal with their own grief, separately. Life could start again. But now they were stuck. Trapped within the consequences of their mother's erratic final decisions.

It infuriated her.

Whatever it took, she would get her childhood home back. There was no way Mā had given the house willingly to Elaine, that scheming vulture. Had Mā been under the influence of something? Had her mental state deteriorated? Lucille didn't quite trust what Reid said. She needed confirmation. She went back to her phone and searched frantically through her emails until she found the number for the agency.

A nasal voice came from the other end of the line. "Hello. Heartspring Home Health Care."

"I'd like to speak with one of your nurses. Shelly Liao."

"One moment." Tinny music played, and then there was a click.

A Chinese-accented voice said, "This is Shelly."

"Hi," Lucille said. "You were employed by my mother, Vivian Yin, through Heartspring, right?"

"I was. Until late June."

"I see. And why were you let go?"

There was a pause. "I don't know. You should ask her that."

Lucille steeled her voice. "Well, she's dead now, so I figured I could come to you."

"Oh." The nurse faltered. "I'm sorry. When did she . . . ?"

"End of July."

"天啊. I'm so sorry." She clicked her tongue, something that Mā also did when expressing pity. "I think—that your mother didn't want to be taken care of."

"I see."

"I did what I could. Her movement wasn't very good. She needed help getting around, up stairs and into the shower and all. I tried to keep her company in that big house of hers. But she didn't like it. She wanted to be alone."

"Did she seem . . . okay? Mentally?"

"Most times. But she had her own habits. When I would try to eat with her during meals, she'd make me go away. She always wanted me to prepare an extra plate for her. I'd go eat in the kitchen. And then your mother would sit in the dining room, just her and the two plates in front of her. Just talking."

"Talking to . . . ?"

"No one," the nurse said quietly.

Lucille realized she was holding her breath.

"She would use this voice like she was trying to get a child to eat. Of course, I was always the one to clear the plates. It hurt my heart to see the food get thrown out. But she always insisted on that second plate. And I always made it for her." She paused. "She was very insistent about a lot of things. But that's how the elderly are. I assumed she had some kind of dementia."

Lucille's head spun. *Dementia.* So that *was* a possibility. "What were the rules?"

"Not a single object could be moved from its original place. She refused to leave the house when I was there. She had her groceries delivered and she'd watch through the security cameras she'd had installed. There were certain areas of the house I was allowed in. I never went behind the house, for example. She did pay me well. I thought she was satisfied with my work. But clearly she was not."

"Okay." Lucille paused. "Did a woman named Elaine Deng ever visit the house?"

"Elaine . . . ? No. No one came."

"Right. Okay. Were there any other times her mental state seemed . . . particularly questionable?"

Silence.

"Hello?"

There was some muffled shout from the background, and then Lucille heard her say, in Mandarin, "Aiyah, wait a second."

A moment, and then she was back. "Sorry about that. There was one incident I remember," the nurse said. "I was waking her from a nap in that book room and she looked directly at me and said—" She paused. "She said, '*I can feel her. She's coming for me.*'"

Lucille's stomach plummeted. "What? What does that mean?"

"I don't know. I tried asking her. It was strange. But when I brought it up again, she didn't remember it at all. Then *I* started feeling strange. Like I was being watched. I asked her once, 'Doesn't it scare you, living alone in this big house?' I figured that must have offended her in some way, because the next morning she told me I was let go."

"Huh," Lucille said.

"I didn't mean to imply anything," Shelly said. "I just couldn't believe that Ā Yí was living in this house all alone. If I had daughters, I'd sell the house and have one of them take care of me, la."

Lucille bristled. The judgment in the nurse's voice was palpable. *You don't understand*, she wanted to shout into the phone. *I tried everything I could to bring my mother into my life, and she refused.* "Well," she said through gritted teeth. "Thank you for telling me. I appreciate it."

"Of course," the nurse said. "I'm sorry about your mother." There was a click as she hung up.

At the house, Lucille went straight to the bathroom to compose herself. Thankfully, no one had seen her come in. Everyone must be in their rooms. She turned on the faucet to splash water on her face.

Had she been such an awful daughter? Lucille's eyes smarted. Hadn't she spent years begging to be closer to her mother? It was humiliating to continually plead for scraps of her presence, only to be rejected again and again. Mā had chosen that. What Lucille could not accept was that Mā had chosen Elaine.

There were still two possibilities Lucille couldn't rule out. Mā had made this decision out of pure dementia, or she had been coerced. By Elaine.

She gazed down at the sink bowl. There was something collected at the bottom, around the drain. Dirt or some kind of sediment.

How did that get there? She reached out and turned on the sink again, but the water that came out wasn't quite clear. She scrubbed at the bowl furiously with her bare hands. The dirt eddied away, but there was still a rusted tinge to the water and now a coppery smell. She glanced up. On either side of her, sconces shone dimly against the dark green wallpaper. As she peered at her sallow reflection, something shifted in the background. In an instant her reflection warped. A dimple appeared on her cheek.

She looked down again. The water had started to run brown.

Immediately she shut the water off. When she looked upon her reflection again, the image she saw was grotesque.

Her eyes bulged out of her sockets. An open gash festered across her forehead. Blood dripped through her swollen, bloated lips.

A scream rose in her chest. She slapped her hands to her face, raking her fingers down her cheeks, as if she could claw the hideous mask off her. She felt nothing on her fingers, but the image remained in the mirror. She flung the bathroom door open and fled to the library, sagging into the armchair.

She focused on slowing her breathing until she dared a peek at her dark phone screen. Her reflection was back to normal, aside from two long red scratches down her right cheek. Lucille pressed the pads of her fingertips to the raised, irritated flesh.

It was just like the time when she was in the house over winter break, more than thirty years ago.

Get it together. She went to the desk and tugged open the drawers, uprooting all the files until they were sprawled across the surface. Her hands shook and papers slid out of the folders, but she didn't care. She would go through all of them. She turned on the computer and the machine slowly whirred to life, casting an eerie blue glow over the rest of the desk. It was an old Windows. Lucille remembered how she and Daniel had installed it for her mother a few years into their marriage. She clicked on the generic chess pawn icon and it took her straight through. Mā didn't even have a password.

Only the most perfunctory programs were downloaded. Mā had still used Internet Explorer. Lucille pulled up the browser history. The last thing her mother searched was the name of Reid's law firm. Lucille logged onto her mother's email; she was pretty sure she'd set that up for her too. Not that her mother used it. The inbox was empty. She barely even called. If she did, it was always during an errant time when Lucille was getting ready for bed or when she was buried under things at work, and it was never for long. Lucille now perused the computer files. There were the pictures of her and Madeline and Daniel, back when they were a Christmas card family. Madeline had been so young, with a wide, gap-toothed smile and short bangs.

In the Documents folder there were forms, mostly scanned tax returns from recent years. Lucille was about to pore through them when she noticed another folder on the computer; she clicked on it. Video clips. One showed an aerial view of what she recognized as the driveway.

She understood immediately what it was: security camera footage.

She had told Mā to do that, too, living all alone here by herself. Lucille deciphered the file labels; the dates led all the way up until July 20. She hovered the cursor over it.

Her phone rang in with a call from an unknown number.

Lucille paused and then picked up.

"Hello?"

"Hello. Is this Lucille Wang?"

"Speaking. Who is this?"

"This is Scott Felim from the medical examiner's office. We have preliminary results of your mother's autopsy. Do you have a moment?"

six

MADELINE liked wandering the house. As she made her way down the carved, creaky staircase, the wood gave just slightly beneath her feet. At the bottom was the foyer, complete with a chandelier, this magnificent circular structure with layered, tapering rows of delicate glass like sheets of rain. To the right was the closed library study and to the left, the dining room. She walked past them both into the hallway and emerged into a grand living room. She sunk into the cracked leather couch, eyeing the grandfather clock across from her on the marble mantel. It felt strange to be this deep in the house. She had never made it farther than the foyer when Wài Pó had been alive.

Quick footsteps sounded behind her. Mā was at the entrance, back to the hallway. "Go to the library. I need to get your aunt."

Madeline stood. Her mother looked alarmed. There were two scratches down the side of her cheek. "Everything okay? What happened to your face?"

But her mother turned without a word.

Madeline made her way into the library just as Nora was emerging from the branch of the hallway to Madeline's right. They almost ran into each other. Nora averted her gaze and pushed past Madeline as if she didn't exist, toward the kitchen. Madeline stared at her retreating figure. Moments later she heard the hushed voices of Mā and Yí Mā as they descended the stairs. They all gathered in the library. Mā waved them over to the desk.

"The preliminary autopsy came in." Mā pulled something up on her phone and showed them. "Toxicology is inconclusive. Which means that there must have been something in her system."

Madeline sucked in a breath through her teeth and stared at the small words on the glaring screen. An eerie tension hummed through-out the room.

"My God," Aunt Rennie whispered. "What toxic substances?"

"It doesn't say. It will be weeks before we have the full report. Months, maybe." Mā set her phone down. "But now we know it wasn't a heart attack. It wasn't a natural death at all."

Aunt Rennie looked faint. "So you're saying . . ."

"She could have been poisoned," Madeline heard herself say.

"She *was*." Mā started to pace. "Now we *know* Elaine's behind all this. She changed the will and killed our mother."

"Hold on," Aunt Rennie said. "Someone else can change Mā's will? What did the lawyer say?"

"Not exactly," her mother said. "Mā did change the will herself."

Madeline spoke up. "Well, that doesn't add up, then. You're imply-ing Elaine forced Wài Pó to change her will, and then she poisoned her?"

Her mother fixed her with a calculating stare. "That is *exactly* the scenario I'm thinking of."

Madeline shifted uncertainly. "It just . . . seems a little extreme."

"And what's extreme about it?"

"That Wài Pó would just . . . go along with it?" Already Madeline felt herself withering in the face of her mother's resolve. She looked away. Her gaze trailed past the bookshelves and to the windows.

Small cracks branched out from the window casing into the walls, but they seemed to be . . . growing? Moving? Was it a trick on her eyes? And then she realized that they were *vines.* It was as if they had crept indoors somehow through the cracks in the window trim.

Her mother's voice snapped Madeline back to the conversation. "I just talked to her nurse. She said that Mā had been exhibiting strange behavior. That it resembled dementia."

"How so?" Aunt Rennie asked.

Mā hesitated. "She said some weird things. Point is, our mother was already in a fragile mental state."

"You don't think she could have . . ." Aunt Rennie's voice lowered. "Done it to herself? Overdosed?"

"She would *never*," Mā snapped. "Don't you even say that."

Aunt Rennie shrank. Madeline protectively inched closer to her aunt.

Her mother's voice rose. "It's clear. Elaine coerced Mā into changing the will and then she murdered her to get the inheritance. And now we have proof. At the very least we could settle. And at most, well, we can prove murder."

"Okay," Madeline said cautiously. "What now?"

"We just have to buy time. I found some things the other day. I—"

But Madeline never heard the end of the sentence, because Mā fell silent for a long minute. She tilted her head and slowly looked off to the side. Before Madeline could ask what she was doing, Mā was wrenching open the door, revealing Nora Deng in the hallway.

NORA ran. She heard Lucille shouting at her across the foyer as she ducked into the hallway leading to her and her mother's rooms.

She knew the Yins had been plotting something with their whispered conversations and secretive meetings.

She murdered her to get the inheritance. And now we have proof.

Nora knew they were talking about her mother. But what was the proof?

She raced straight to Mā's bedroom. The curtains were drawn. Mā shifted in bed, blinking against the light. Nora tried to keep calm. "They think you had something to do with Vivian Yin's death to get the inheritance. They say they have evidence."

"*What?*" Mā pushed herself off the bed. She staggered past Nora and into the hallway to the foyer. Nora followed her. The other family had emerged from the library. Lucille marched toward Nora. "You had no right—"

"I'm kind enough to let you stay in my home," her mother said with a shaking voice. "And you're investigating me?" Lucille stopped in her tracks.

"*Your* home?" Lucille said incredulously. "Fuck off."

Her mother drew herself up. "She gave it to me."

"You took it." Lucille gave Mā a withering stare, looking her up and down in disgust. Nora realized then that she was self-conscious Mā was wearing mismatched pajamas. "We got the autopsy results. Her toxicology report was positive."

Silence fell. Nora glanced at Madeline. The daughter's eyes flickered uncertainly between her mother and Nora's.

"Mā didn't die of natural causes," Lucille continued in a steely voice. "She was poisoned."

"I see. And you're trying to imply that I had something to do with this?"

"*I* didn't say that." Lucille's eyebrows raised, clearly implying *but you did.*

Nora blurted out, "You can't be accusing her of *murdering* somebody. That's insane."

"Jiā-Jiā!" Mā said sharply, and Nora swallowed, her cheeks burning. Mā turned back to Lucille and took a deep breath. "I had nothing to do with Vivian's death. I didn't even know I was being put in the will."

"That's a lie," Lucille retorted. "You've had it out for us from the start. This is an estate in the San Gabriel Valley. These don't just fall into people's laps."

They stared each other down.

"There could be many explanations for this toxicology report. It could have been anything. An overdose. A suicide." Her mother looked between Renata and Lucille. "Or . . . even someone in the family."

Nora watched Lucille's younger sister tremble in the corner. She hadn't said a word during this entire exchange.

"You're saying that one of us killed our own mother?" Lucille scoffed.

"You *do* seem desperate to inherit the house."

Clever, Nora thought, how Mā now shifted the suspicion onto them. This seemed to touch a nerve in all of them. Lucille started, "You—" But Mā stopped her, raising a hand.

"You know what? You should leave."

"Absolutely not," Lucille declared.

"If you had time to pursue this ridiculous accusation, I assume you've already collected your mother's things. Get out or I'll have you thrown out."

Lucille planted her feet. "Let's play this scenario out. The moment you kick us out of *our* home, I will contact the nearest police department. I will hire a detective. I will have them open an investigation. And no matter what, I will sue the hell out of you."

Nora saw her mother's expression fall slack.

"But," Lucille continued, "there is an alternative. Like you said, there isn't full clarity around what happened to our mother. So, I propose we investigate this ourselves. You let us stay in this house until the end of the week. If I can't find any evidence of wrongdoing in this home—"

"Which there hasn't been."

"If there isn't, then the house is yours. We will put this matter to rest and leave for good."

Mā straightened up. "And you will never contest the will or contact us again."

Lucille paused for a long moment. Then she nodded.

"Fine. You have until the end of the week. That's it."

"Thank you," Lucille said evenly.

"But I want all of these terms in writing. And once the week is up—"

"We will leave promptly," Lucille said. "We promise."

Nora's mother retreated to her room and Nora followed. The blinds were still closed, and the bedroom was dark and stuffy. The moment she sat down, her mother seemed to deflate and sag back into the bed.

"Mā, you have to tell me *something*," Nora insisted. "None of this makes sense."

Her mother closed her eyes. "My parents worked for the Yins," she admitted faintly. "Mā was their housekeeper. Bà was the groundskeeper. We moved into the house when I was a kid."

Nora started pacing. So this was how Mā knew her way around the house. She *had* lived here. And in coming back together, the families had snapped back into a hierarchy that Nora hadn't known existed.

Now she was angry. "Then Vivian did know you. You have a right

to the house. You grew up here, too. Maybe she hated her daughters."
Or maybe it was more theoretical. What was the likelihood an elderly
movie star was interested in wealth redistribution? "They shouldn't stay
here, then." Nora nodded to herself. "They made it out like you were
a stranger, but you're not. And the house is legally ours. You can kick
them out now."

Her mother's eyes flew open. "And what? Give them free rein to
frame me for murder? Or sue us into bankruptcy, regardless? I didn't
have anything to do with Vivian's death, but they will have come to that
conclusion themselves." Her voice rose sharply. "Please, Jiā-Jiā. Leave
me alone. My head is still killing me."

Nora felt another tremor that night. This time it was strong enough
that the bed lurched back and forth. Nora scrunched the blankets to
her chest and curled up in a ball. One of her study books thumped to
the floor. It went on for what felt like minutes. After everything had
gone still, she sat up and looked around her.

Another earthquake? What the hell was going on? Two earthquakes
in a week wasn't necessarily alarming in California, but she still felt an
inching sense of dread. She stared at the study book that now lay on
the ground. She was probably just stressed about this test. Sometimes
anxiety gave her nightmares. Being in someone else's weird house didn't
help, either.

She needed a walk. She threw her blankets off and shuffled out of
her room. The first night here the hallways had been freezing. But now
it felt warm and damp. Humid, almost. Like the walls were sweating.
She paused in the kitchen and turned the light on. It flickered.

Nothing here worked. Moonlight streamed in through the glass
door to the terrace. The door was ajar; Nora moved toward it. Outside,
a figure stood on the terrace steps. Nora sucked in a breath when she
realized that it was her mother.

She stepped outside. Her bare feet touched the cold stone ground.
In her thin T-shirt, she crossed her arms against the damp chill. "Mā?"

Her mother didn't respond. Nora called louder, "Mā?"

She crept down the stairs. Sharp leaves and debris jabbed into her feet and she grimaced. Still she tread carefully over to her mother, who faced the garden. "Mā?"

"She's there." Mā stretched her hand out. Her fingers were streaked with dirt as if she had been tearing at the ground with her bare hands.

"Who is? What happened?"

Nora reached out to put a hand on her mother's shoulder. Her mother jerked around, and Nora scrambled back.

Mā's lips cleaved apart in a silent scream. Tears streamed down her cheeks. She took short, fast breaths and turned her glassy eyes to Nora.

Then her features relaxed. She said softly, "You're *here*."

"Yes," Nora said. "I am, in fact, here. You should go inside. 你会着凉的." *You're going to catch a cold.*

Her mother stared at her, unblinking.

"Come on," Nora urged. A small laugh of disbelief escaped her. This felt wrong.

She was about to head back when she felt fingers clamp down on her wrist. Nora gave a yelp and whipped back around to see her mother's eerily calm face again.

"You've been here all this time," her mother whispered tenderly.

Nora tugged, harder than she should have. "Come *on*, 妈." Her voice rose, as though the problem was Mā's hearing. "Let's go in."

Her mother stood shakily, squeezing Nora's wrist. She followed Nora back to her room without easing her viselike grip, until she was settled into bed. As Nora tucked the blankets around her, her mother finally looked up at Nora's face. "You haven't left," Mā said. "You've always been here waiting for me."

Nora didn't respond. Mā pulled the blankets to her neck like a child while Nora carefully stepped away. When she slipped out the doorway, she felt her mother's eyes on her back.

Nora brought her mother a cup of hot water in the morning. When she walked in, Mā stirred and shifted toward the direction of the steps.

Nora put the cup on the dusty nightstand and sat at the edge of the bed. "How are you?"

"Migraine's worse today," her mother mumbled. She eased herself up. Her wispy hair, which was usually tied back, fell over her shoulders. The curtains were still drawn.

Nora looked toward the side table, where tissues were crumpled with dried blood. "Are you okay?"

"出鼻血. It's too dry out here."

Nora had seen Mā get nosebleeds before, but still, it worried her to see her mother in this state. Especially after last night.

"You shouldn't have been outside," Nora said. "It was cold. I knew it wouldn't be good." She paused. "What happened, anyway?"

Mā stared at her. "I wasn't outside."

"Yes, you were." Did Mā not remember any of it? Nora had seen the pain on her mother's face with perfect clarity every time she closed her eyes last night. "You were out in the garden. You spoke to me. Don't you remember?"

Her mother sat up and narrowed her eyes. "Nora, I was asleep."

Nora reached for her mother's hand and held it to the light. Dirt was still caked under her nails. "Look. Look at this. You were walking in the garden. I came out because there was an earthquake earlier in the night, and—" She faltered. "You really don't remember?"

Mā looked from her hands to Nora, her eyes blank. Then she winced, holding her fingertips to her temples as she sank back down and curled up again.

Was her mother lying? Confused? Or did she truly have no memory? Mā had never sleepwalked before, as far as Nora knew, but it was the only explanation that made sense. Stress could make your body do strange things.

She pulled up the sleeve of her sweatshirt. There was a small bruise. Nora could remember her mother's fingers digging into her wrist, her glassy stare.

She didn't dream any of this up. Not this time.

seven

MADELINE observed the next day unfurl through each tense hour. Aunt Rennie stayed in her room. Mā shut herself in the library and locked the door. Madeline sat on her thin green sheets, poking at mattress springs and feeling invisible. She turned the events of the past few days over in her head. The toxicology report seemed damning. But would Elaine really walk right back into a murder scene of her own making?

Now that all pretenses had fallen away, the house had become a strategic map. Madeline's family occupied the library and the entire second floor. Her mother would leave the house for a while and come back, but no one else went anywhere. Nora continued to avoid her. It made more sense *now*, but still, Madeline wished she knew why she was disliked from the start. She passed time by making conjectures and theories about Nora. What did she think of everything? What was her relationship with her own mother like? Her grandmother? Madeline would likely never find out.

The once sprawling house now felt claustrophobic, and no one spoke without first glancing behind them. The drain groaned and plugged up when Madeline ran the shower. Same with the sink. Whenever she tried to unclog them, she wound up finding clots of dirt. And every once in a while, she would catch the scent of something festering and metallic—like meat? Or blood?—at different places throughout the house, though she could never trace it back to its source.

Late that night Madeline sat on the terrace steps to get some fresh air. She looked up at the intricate, cracked cornices that adorned the sides of the house. The sky was clear and dotted with stars. The property was surrounded by trees and miles away from the nearest grocery store. It seemed as though this place was unmoored from time. Had it only been two days since the reading of the will? Three? Was it Monday or Friday? Instinctively she checked her phone and the bars flickered. The cell service seemed to be getting worse by the day, too.

Madeline heard the door open behind her. "Oh, Yí Mā. Hi."

Aunt Rennie pointed at the step Madeline sat on. "Can I join?"

Madeline nodded.

Her mother's half-sister wrapped the skirt of her gauzy linen dress around her. She settled on the step with a sigh, her delicate features relaxing, and offered Madeline her glass.

Madeline took a sip. "I don't know why adults like red wine."

Her aunt smiled. "You're an adult now, aren't you? 长大了, Madeline."

She spoke Mandarin with a rounded accent. Madeline conceded, "I guess. I don't really feel like it."

"Sure," Aunt Rennie said. "Twenty-two is young. You spend your early adulthood thinking you're still a child, and then one day you wake up and you're almost fifty." She held up her glass. "I used to hate this stuff, too. But you get older and some things you used to hate as a kid don't seem so bad anymore." She drained her glass and squinted out at the garden, frowning slightly.

A nighttime breeze cut across the terrace. Madeline shivered. Aunt Rennie glanced over. "Should we head in?"

Madeline wavered. "I don't like being inside. It's . . ."

Her aunt smiled. Her teeth were stained from the wine. "Unsettling? Hostile?" She drew out her words, punctuating each consonant.

Madeline nodded. "Yeah. With everything that just happened." She paused. "Do you know where Mā went today?"

"She left?"

"Yup. For like an hour."

"No idea."

"Do you really think she's right about what happened to Wài Pó?"

"About whether the Dengs were involved, you mean."

Madeline nodded. ". . . Right."

"I don't know." Her aunt fidgeted with the gold ring on her index finger.

"She's so sure of it. And it's clear that she and Elaine hate each other. I mean—she used to be your housekeeper, right?"

"Daughter of the housekeeper. And the gardener. They were married and Elaine was their kid."

"Oh. So maybe something happened to her that could have led to her doing something to—to Wài Pó."

Aunt Rennie wavered. Madeline could sense that the conversation had started to turn. Her aunt seemed to tense. "That's what your mother thinks."

"What do *you* think?"

"None of it really makes sense to me. It could have been an overdose, but Mā was always careful with medication. It's even harder to believe that Elaine would do something like this to her though. But that's what your mother seems most convinced of at the moment. What I think doesn't really matter much, does it?"

It matters to me, Madeline thought. "She's always been like this to you, hasn't she?"

Aunt Rennie gave her a long look. "She's like this to most people."

"But she's always harder on you."

"Oh, sweetie. It's because I have the specific role of being the family fuckup."

"That's not—"

"I have no job. I'm always moving from one Los Angeles sublet to another. My marriage imploded so badly it ended up tabloid clickbait." She gave a small, resigned laugh. "I know what people say about me."

"I have no job either," Madeline said plainly.

"But you have time. I ran out of that a while ago."

Madeline looked toward the trees. When she was younger, her aunt would sometimes visit. She always swept in with only a few days' notice. Sometimes she'd be in between auditions and regale them with stories for hours. The parties she snuck into, the celebrities she'd met who were kindest. Then she gave up on acting and did a series of odd theater-related jobs. She would promise to come by for Thanksgiving, but something would always come up last minute. Sometimes Mā would text her for days before she would respond.

The last time Yí Mā visited, she announced she was getting married to an art collector in New York and invited them all to the wedding. Months later she called Mā and told her that they'd eloped in Italy on the Amalfi Coast. Her mother had been furious. Madeline understood it stung to be cut out, but she still admired her aunt's erratic romanticism. She loved Yí Mā's free and fleeting joy; how easy it was for Madeline to confide in her; how once, sitting at the dinner table, she noticed that her aunt and her mother shared the same smile, the way their lips dimpled in at the corners.

Now Aunt Rennie simply looked deflated. She drifted through the house, left plates unwashed in the sink, and cupboards hanging open. Madeline asked, "What do people say about you?"

Her aunt shrugged. "*Rennie doesn't know how to handle money.... Rennie runs away from her problems.... Rennie wasted her talent instead of pursuing a stable career.... Rennie sees things like a crazy person.*' Haven't you heard it all?"

Madeline had heard all but the last. A peculiar sensation settled over her. "What do you mean, see things?"

Aunt Rennie frowned. She opened her mouth as if to say something, and then shut it. "Never mind."

"What do you see? Like—ghosts?"

"It's not—" Her aunt faltered. Already she seemed to close off. She gathered up her skirt. "I don't know what I'm saying. It's cold out here. I want to go in." There was a rustle as she stood. Madeline watched her head in, and chewed on the inside of her cheek.

After a while, the door opened again. Mā stood over her, her arms tightly crossed.

"Oh. You're back. Where'd you go?" Madeline asked.

Mā didn't answer. "What were you and Yí Mā talking about?"

"Nothing, really." Madeline craned her neck to look into her mother's face. "Did something happen in this house? Between you and Elaine?"

"No," her mother said brusquely. "Why? Did Yí Mā say that?"

"No, I just—"

Her mother switched to Mandarin. "You shouldn't spend so much time out here. It's late. And cold. And dirty."

A long pause. Madeline bundled her knees to her chest. "I'm okay for now."

Her mother's presence didn't budge. Finally, she said with a sudden sharpness in her voice, "Madeline. Go inside."

In any other circumstance, she would get up. But Mā's tone grated on her. This was the first time she had seen her mother all day and she hadn't even asked how Madeline was doing. She felt like a scolded child.

"I heard you," Madeline said without moving.

Her mother went in without another word.

Madeline didn't know how long she had been outside. At some point the cold set in and her fingertips went numb. But the wine lingered in her head and kept her warm on the inside.

She made her way to the cracked stone fountain in the garden and looked back at the exterior of the house. It really was beautiful. As she stood watching, the lights in the windows went out one by one. Her mother and Yí Mā must be preparing for bed.

The round lights on the terrace didn't work anymore, so as she walked on, she relied on the bright moon to light her way. Slipping her hands in her pockets, she stepped onto what seemed like the remnants of an old path, and, stopping to the left of the fountain, carefully picked her way to that perfect rose. Several pale pink buds, almost luminescent at the tips that surged to a deep red toward the center, formed bursts of color among the roots and overgrown vines. Madeline took in a breath and reached out for the petals. They were light and fluid, as if they were crafted from silk.

She leaned in, expecting the buds to have a faint, sweet scent. But instead the petals emitted that raw, sharp odor of rust.

The air was clear with no mist, but the ground felt damp to the touch. Madeline glanced back at the darkened house again and saw the kitchen light from downstairs sputter on. Who had gotten up?

Suddenly she stumbled, as something laced around her ankles and pulled.

She pitched forward. She scrambled, first in confusion, then in panic, to grab at what had now fastened itself around her feet and seized her ankles.

They were *vines*. Thick and unyielding as rope.

Her panicked breaths rushed in and out. She grasped the vines, dug into them with her fingernails, trying to pry them off, but they didn't budge. Even the ground was unsteady. The dirt was warm and soft, pulsing like a living thing, giving way beneath her.

A whimper escaped her lips. She wrapped both hands around her leg in an effort to tug it free, but it was useless. New vines shot out from the ground and lashed around her knees, dragging her farther into the dirt.

She was going to have to cut herself free. She fumbled around in her pocket. Nothing. A pen. She pulled it out, stabbing at the vines around her, and she almost breathed a sigh of relief when they seemed to retract, like a wounded animal, but it was only for a second. Before Madeline could react, the vines surged forward again with a vengeance and lashed around her arm.

Something punctured into the skin of her arm, and she screamed. She heaved onto her elbows and stomach, her face only inches away from the roses she had just been admiring. The rotten, revolting smell of rust rose from the dirt itself. She tried to find purchase, but her fingers sank into soil that seemed to be rising around her. The vines laced around her back now, and her breath sputtered out in frantic gasps. She could feel the cords creeping up her back, to her shoulders.

Madeline tried to scream louder, but the vines pulled her face forward into the dirt. Wrestling her head to the side, she tried to keep drawing air into her lungs, but she sucked in dirt instead and now she was gagging on it.

Dirt filled her mouth, choking out her screams. Madeline imagined for a fleeting moment what it would be like to be buried alive, to be crushed under the leaden weight of the earth.

And then she felt someone's fingers grab on to her.

· · ·

NORA set the kettle on the stove. It made a clatter and water sloshed out. Impulsively, she cringed and looked around, hoping no one else was there to see. But this instinct to be invisible made her angry. So what if she made a sound? She was tiptoeing around, eating after the Yin family had eaten, like she was the help, even though this was technically her mother's house.

She turned the stove on. The burner glowed to life, and she peered out at the garden, looking for any sign of her mother. If Mā didn't remember gripping Nora hard enough that she'd left a mark, what else could she do in her sleep?

But Mā wasn't out there tonight. Nora was just on edge. The water came to a boil, and she cut the flame and poured it over her tea. She was practicing taking deep breaths when she saw something move in the garden.

Nora nearly dropped her tea. It splashed on the table and over Nora, burning her. She yelped in pain and marched to the glass kitchen door. She wrenched it open. *Was* someone out there?

If this place is messing with me again—

She heard a shrill scream and saw the flash of a white sleeve.

Madeline.

Nora didn't think. She bolted down the stone steps and out onto the grounds, trying to follow the sound. There was another flash of white and she ran toward it.

At first, Nora couldn't see Madeline at all. Breathing hard, she found herself standing in front of what looked like a large tangle of dead vegetation, until it dawned on Nora that it was moving. Madeline must be underneath, covered—no, swarmed—with vines. She heard a stifled cry and saw another flash of Madeline's shirt to the left. She was reaching out as roots wrapped around her feet and her stomach, across her shoulders.

Nora leapt over and grabbed Madeline's arm. She yanked ferociously on a thick handful of the vines. Digging her heels in, she threw her weight backward, but as she pulled, thorns sliced through her palms, causing her to jerk away.

Her blood dripped onto the vines as she stood over the tangle, her mind blanked with panic and in pain. Gathering herself, she reached for the vines again and pulled, gritting her teeth through the sharp pain. This time, the vines slackened.

Nora's knees buckled from the sudden lack of resistance, and she fell back, pulling some vines with her. Madeline ripped one arm free. Nora tugged on Madeline's arm, out of the vines. All at once the vines retracted and they tumbled, hard, against the ground. The back of Nora's head hit the ground, hard. Dazed, Nora heard Madeline's ragged gasps against her ear and registered her weight on top of Nora.

Looking around her, Nora realized she was now eye level with several roses. *Roses?* When had these appeared in the garden? She had thought everything out here was dead. But these were a beautiful light pink, though something like mud seeped from their centers.

No—it was *blood*.

Madeline and Nora sprang apart. Madeline flung the remaining vines off. "Get—away," Madeline choked. They raced back toward the house. They ran up the steps and tumbled onto the terrace. Nora knelt on the ground, panting. Madeline coughed and gagged, heaving over the stones.

Nora looked over and her first thought was: *she's bleeding.* So was she. She could feel the searing pain at the center of her left palm where the thorns had cut the deepest. Blood was welling up inside the other cuts and dripping down her arms.

Madeline looked up, saliva pooling on her lips, her delicate features frozen in terror and her face streaked with dirt. The words lodged in Nora's throat. They'd never spoken. She had to say *something*, but she didn't know how to start. Her voice came out hoarse. "My mom told me never to go into the garden. You shouldn't either."

Madeline just stared.

Nora curled her hand into a fist, pressing her fingertips onto the wound to staunch the blood. A long silence passed between them until Madeline pushed herself to her feet without a word and walked back into the house, leaving Nora alone and shivering.

eight

NORA stumbled toward her room. She needed to clean the wound. She scrounged up her mini first aid kit from her bag and took out the disinfectant and gauze. She paused and stood up shakily.

Madeline was somewhere in the house. Bleeding. After almost having been *swallowed* by the garden. Nora thought of her half-sunken among the writhing vines. A fresh wave of terror flooded her.

If Nora hadn't been there, what would have happened?

The kitchen was empty. The only sign that Madeline had been there was her muddy shoes by the door. Nora's cup of tea lay on the table, untouched. She ran toward the main staircase and up the first few steps before she stopped. There were a few drops of blood on the carpet. Nothing else. Her hand rested on the carved railing. What was she going to do, go search out Madeline's room? She could end up accidentally knocking on Lucille's door.

She returned to the downstairs hallway and went to the bathroom. In the mirror, her chest heaved. Nora turned on the water. It was lukewarm and had a brownish tinge. She shut the tap and went into the kitchen, splashing the remaining water from the kettle over her cut. Fresh blood welled up. She dried her hands and applied pressure.

Returning to her room, she stripped off her dirt-stained clothes and sat on the bed. She didn't realize how tightly wound she still was until her neck started to ache.

That had been nothing like what she'd seen the other night. There had been no blooming flowers. This wasn't a dream. Or maybe it was just some new, fucked-up permutation of it? Would she wake up in the morning and run into Madeline in the kitchen, unscathed? But some part of her did want it to be a terrible dream this time. Because there was no logical explanation for how Madeline ended up half-buried in the ground, nearly devoured by plants.

In fact, nothing that happened today seemed real. Back at dinnertime, when Renata had headed upstairs and Lucille was talking to Madeline on the terrace, Nora had snuck into the library. She'd found a manila folder on the table and rummaged through the contents. She didn't look carefully. She just took pictures of everything.

Now, as she clenched her throbbing left hand, she flicked through the pictures on her phone again. Pages of the will. The toxicology report. All of this information she already knew. She scrolled to the last picture that she'd taken. A printout of a security camera image, taken of the front yard with the date and time clearly marked.

July 20. 1:28 p.m. Two weeks ago.

In the center of the frame was a car that Nora instantly recognized. And though the photo was slightly blurred, she could still make out the numbers of her mother's license plate.

LUCILLE went downstairs in the early gray light and washed her face in the kitchen sink. She had coffee over the granite island. She went to the library and locked the door behind her.

The manila folder was still sitting on the desk, on top of the files she'd upended from the drawers. There were the files she'd printed at the local library yesterday. A paper copy of the updated will. The security camera footage up until July 20, five days before Lucille found out about Mā's death. Why was there no video beyond that date? Even in the last few hours of recording on the afternoon of the twentieth, something was increasingly obstructing the camera lens until nothing could be seen.

Lucille walked outside and peered up at the spot where the security camera would have been. It was too high up for her to reach. All she saw was ivy crawling up the eaves.

At least now she had the evidence that she needed. Because on July 20, there it was—a photo of the same red Honda that now sat next to the curb.

Elaine Deng *had* been here. A righteous fury surged through her. The dates matched. She was still waiting on the rest of the autopsy results, but she had key details. Now she just needed to continue to build the rest of the case: Assemble the evidence. Construct it into an irrefutable narrative.

The morning passed in silence as she pored over all the files from the drawers. Lucille's gaze swam over more than thirty years of taxes, receipts of payment, and carbon copies of checks. There were astronomical property taxes and years of cleaning service invoices, up until around ten years ago when Mā fired them. Receipts of payment for Rennie's acting programs and Lucille's law school tuition. Years of checks to Rennie, all throughout the nineties. Half a down payment on Lucille's house, the starter house she shared with Daniel in Burlingame before they moved to Newport Beach. All this and not a single cent of income in the last thirty-four years.

No wonder they were left with virtually nothing. All the value was in this property. Lucille leaned back in the desk chair, and then stood to stretch. Idly, she stared at the ceiling, which bloomed with brown splotches. Water damage, probably from burst pipes.

Across the library two green velvet armchairs faced each other with a small table between them. When she was younger, books would stack up on that table. "Is that your interpretation?" Dad would ask, settling into the chair across from her and putting his glasses on, crossing his long legs, rolling down his cuffed sleeves. "Do you believe that journalists have an uncontested obligation to the forum of public reason?" Sunlight would expand into the room on afternoons like that; Lucille would feel almost consumed by the intensity of his gaze. Dad had studied the classics and political science at Yale. She would carefully build her arguments before she spoke, trying to preempt every weakness. Sometimes he stoically absorbed her words; sometimes he'd break into a smile. *President*

Lucy, he'd say, and Lucille would feel euphoric. At some point Rennie would barge in and Dad's attention would vanish. But Lucille clung to those small moments of warmth. The fragments of validation. She savored the moments when Mā smiled approvingly at her grades, when Dad turned to focus on her when a guest at the dinner table praised how well-spoken she was.

To some the affinity for being loved came naturally, like with Rennie. Lucille knew it was true, even now, from the way her own daughter gravitated toward her sister. But Lucille was never easily adored, nor did she need to be. She worked for it. She never trusted anything she didn't have to prove.

Lucille returned to the desk and doggedly sifted through the papers. Something was stuck at the bottom of one of the drawers. She reached in and pried up brittle, yellowing papers that were stuck together. The edges were jagged, as though they had been ripped out of a book. Lucille slowly eased them apart.

It was a biography about a railroad magnate turned congressman in the late nineteenth century, with passages on Chinese railroad workers. She strained to read notes in traditional Mandarin scribbled in the margins. She saw *gold rush*—this must have been Mā's character research for *Fortune's Eye*. Traditional Chinese cursive swam in front of her. She couldn't decipher it. The thought of something else of Mā's lost to her forever pierced through her. Lucille pushed the pages to the side. A magazine peeked out from under one of the file folders.

It was her parents' 1986 profile in the *American Film* magazine. Lucille already knew where to flip to. Across the two-page spread her parents lounged on the living room sofa. Mā wore a deep blue chiffon butterfly wing dress and her kitten heels, staring solemnly at the camera. Her stepfather had a playful smile, an arm draped around Mā. His dark hair was carefully slicked back, his eyes peering out from rounded glasses. Lucille did see a lot of him in Rennie these days: the widow's peak, the wavy hair, the strong jaw, the hopeful eyes. The title read, in block letters:

THE POWER OF A DRAMATIC DUO

Mā had won her Oscar in 1986. Lucille had been thirteen. Back then she had practically memorized every word of this profile. Now she read it again.

> An actor classically trained at Yale and an ingenue who'd grown up in the Chinese opera, this unconventional pair found each other at an awards show eleven years ago. Their marriage is a seamless partnership both on and off screen. Their home is furnished with an effortless mélange of East and West, from brush paintings to neoclassical and Italianate architectural influences.
>
> Vivian Yin and Richard Lowell are both dynamic new talents, drawn to ambitious projects. This year Richard starred in Hamlet and Vivian in Fortune's Eye. These roles catapulted them both to the Academy Awards, with Richard receiving a nomination for Best Actor, and Vivian receiving, and winning, Best Supporting Actress. . . .

Lucille shut the magazine. She was losing focus. She was supposed to be gathering documents of legal and defensible use, not looking through mementos. What was the point of reminding herself what their lives used to be like? The portrait of their family that had hung across the room was now long gone. Mā had so carefully chosen someone who would paint them in the style of Renoir; it had taken multiple sessions, and the result was magnificent. Now there was no trace of it, save for the outline of the frame, the paneling that hadn't touched sun for years. But how much of it did Lucille want to remember, anyway? The summers at Lake Tahoe at a spacious rented cabin, the winters up in British Columbia? Her old day school, perched on a hill overlooking the Pacific; the cool blue nights she stayed up listening to Dad's Van Morrison vinyl float up from the living room, with its familiar skips and scratches? The years of observing her parents' lavish dinner parties? How could she endure those recollections, knowing how it all ended?

Something nagged at her. She peeled open the magazine again and then picked up the torn book pages she'd discarded. She looked at the portrait of the railroad magnate, and then at the photo of Dad.

They resembled each other. The more Lucille stared at it, the more she could see it.

part two: bloom

nine

VIVIAN Yin met Richard Lowell at a film festival in Los Angeles.

She had been invited because of her role in *Song of Lovers*, and now she found herself nominated for an award, draped in a red satin jacquard dress she'd borrowed from one of her aunt's friends. It fit well enough. It showed off her delicate collarbones, which she considered one of her best features. She stood unsteadily on the red carpet trying to conjure her old confidence as she tilted her body to face the flashes of the cameras.

Back in Hong Kong, Vivian had loved movie premieres and festivals. In San Francisco, she enjoyed the premieres in Chinatown, which eventually became cozy after-parties that flooded a director's favorite restaurant's back room, with dishes loaded upon the circular tables. Los Angeles was foreign to her and surreal in its beauty. But here she didn't know a soul aside from her co-stars, and even then, the only one she felt comfortable with was Daisy. There were other Chinese actors working in film, too, but most of them were extras and weren't invited to the parties. So she followed her cast and crewmates around, hearing them laugh and joke in English, their vowels drawn out and flattened in the American way.

She hadn't won the award and she was partly relieved, because the thought of speaking in front of the crowd made her want to vomit up the water she had taken small sips of prior to the event. She hadn't eaten anything in the afternoon so she could fit into the dress. Sweat collected at the nape of her neck, and a hidden metal clasp dug into her rib. Her body had changed after the children, and she wasn't quite sure what looked flattering and what didn't, so she contracted in her stomach and hoped for the best.

She had half considered not coming at all. Maybe she should go home and try to see if her hotel room had a phone so that she could call her family before bed. For the past year and a half, she and her daughters had been crammed into a one-bedroom in San Francisco with her aunt and uncle. Her aunt was good at taking care of them, but still, it pained Vivian, being this far away. She felt light-headed from all the lights, the perfumed air, the sequins and satin and bright camera flashes.

But this was a chance to get noticed. And at least she had Daisy. Daisy Rubin had an endearing gap-toothed smile, a heart-shaped face framed by loose, deep red curls, and a loud, warm voice. But now Daisy was across the room talking to someone, her sequined dress winking all around her, so Vivian ordered herself a cocktail that Daisy told her would keep her awake.

The drink the bartender handed her was sweet and creamy. She stood at a table with her co-stars and noticed a lean, dark-haired man with a double-breasted suit across from her, another table over. When he looked up, their eyes met until she looked away, embarrassed. She watched her co-stars drink and laugh. Eventually they drifted off, leaving Vivian standing alone.

All she could think about now were her pinched feet. Maybe this was the moment to make an early exit. She had an entire, luxurious room to herself at the hotel. She could even draw a nice, hot bath.

Out of the corner of her eye, she saw him lean in, his arrival marked by a deep, smoky cologne.

"Is that any good?"

His voice was surprisingly light. Vivian turned slightly and found the handsome man she'd made eye contact with earlier gesturing toward her drink. A quick scan revealed a smart, fitted blue suit filled out by broad shoulders, a checkered tie, a clean-shaven profile, and slicked-back hair that was so dark it was almost black. A silver watch peeked out of his sleeve.

Vivian met his eyes. Through his rounded glasses they were the most remarkable jade green flecked through with brown, framed by long lashes. He was young, Vivian thought. Or he had this tentative, inquisitive smile that made him seem so. Another actor, perhaps.

Maybe she had looked lonely and he felt bad for her. In crowds like these, Vivian was used to being all too conspicuous while feeling invisible at the same time. She looked into her glass and tried to keep her voice steady. "It's strong."

"Seems about right," the man said. "Should I get one?"

"I recommend it," Vivian said.

"Good. I hold your recommendation in high regard."

Vivian chuckled.

He tilted his head. "What?"

"You put lots of trust in strangers."

"I don't usually," he said. "But you seem like you know what you're doing. When everyone else is drinking champagne, a white Russian stands out."

"Oh, I'm just trying not to fall asleep."

He was silent and Vivian looked up.

He smiled. "Bored to death, are you?"

Heat flooded her cheeks as his words drifted in. "Oh!" She blurted out. Had she offended him? "No, I don't mean *that*, I mean—" She searched for words. English could escape her when she was nervous. "I haven't been sleeping good lately. That's all. This is wonderful." She searched his eyes. They glittered mischievously.

"I was just giving you a hard time. Don't worry. I'd be happy to get you another one if it'll keep you out longer?"

She smiled politely. "I'm okay with just one." She hurriedly added, "Thank you, though."

He looked at her thoughtfully. Vivian felt like she was under a spotlight. She wondered if he was going to start asking her questions, the ones the others did when they were drunk, or sober, if they were the more brazen type. Would he ask her where she was from or just start guessing?

Instead, he held out his hand. "I'm Richard Lowell. It's nice to meet you."

Richard Lowell. That name sounded familiar, but she couldn't remember why. He had to be an actor. She shook his hand. "Vivian Yin."

"I figured," he said. "You were great in *Song of Lovers*, by the way. A brilliant performance. You're a natural."

Vivian lowered her eyes. English-speaking movies were new for her, but she had more experience than people imagined. She'd been training since childhood and acting in operas all her life. What surprised her was that he recognized her. And watched her movie. "We had a great director," she demurred.

"Sure, I know Don Corcoran's work. But it takes a certain beautiful talent to bring his vision to life."

The air between them stilled. Vivian looked up. *Ah.* Heat bloomed up her neck and across her cheeks. She hadn't flirted in a long time, but here she was. "Well, I'm glad you saw it," she said, offering what she hoped was a beguiling smile.

"Of course." He took a breath. Vivian fidgeted with her glass, trying to think of what to say next. Her heart raced and she was very, very awake now. She watched him take out a pen from his inner suit pocket. He wrote something on the napkin and slipped it to her, face down.

"What's this?"

"I don't want to keep you up. But I would love a chance to chat with you more about movies. Give me a call if you happen to have some free time tomorrow. If you'd like." Vivian could see that he was starting to get flustered. It thrilled her to see the boyish tinge of pink on his cheeks.

"That would be nice," she said. "Well, it is good to meet you, Richard."

"Likewise." He looked at her, hesitantly, then again, and slipped away into the crowd. Vivian clutched the napkin dizzily as Daisy fluttered back to the table. How she could walk in such high heels, Vivian had no clue. Her co-star was a natural on the red carpet. Her dress's sequins flowed like liquid gold over her curves.

"Oh. My. *God.* What did Richard Lowell say to you?"

Vivian looked up. "What movie is he in?"

"Vivian!" Daisy arched a thick eyebrow. "He was in *The Great Gatsby*. He knows *everyone.*"

"*Oh.*" And it hit her then that *he* was Hollywood's new rising star, barely under thirty, or around it. She'd heard her own notoriously difficult director discussing him like he was a beloved son.

"Tell me *everything,*" Daisy whispered, tucking her hair behind her ears. "What did he want from you?"

Vivian considered what she'd say. She didn't want rumors to swirl, not while she was just about to head home. "Nothing much. Just wanted to tell me he watched our movie and appreciated my performance." Her hand was under the table, his phone number clutched in her sweaty palm. "I was thinking I might take a taxi home."

"Aw." Daisy frowned. "You're okay?"

Vivian gave her a smile and matched Daisy's warm tone. "Fabulous." Daisy liked saying that.

"If you say so." Daisy smiled back and blew a kiss.

"Good night," Vivian said. She wobbled toward the entrance on her lower, but still-terribly-painful heels.

Back in her hotel, it was too late to call home, so she filled the tub with water and soap and stretched out her limbs. She reveled in the space. This one hotel room was the size of her aunt's apartment. She held the napkin up to the light. The faintest bit of his cologne still lingered on it, and something inside Vivian unfurled at the scent.

She went to bed with the napkin on her nightstand. In the morning she woke up early and stared at his phone number.

At the very least, it was smart to get to know someone well-connected in the industry. Especially one who thought she was talented. But that wasn't the only thought pushing her to reach for the phone.

She wondered what exactly compelled her toward him. There was something about him that she wanted to be near, to look level. Maybe it was his smile or his confidence, his playfulness, how he seemed at once uncertain and also completely at ease. She watched the clock hit nine and reached for the phone.

The last time Vivian was with a man, he had abandoned her and the life they'd built together.

She didn't know what to tell Richard Lowell about that, and so she revealed none of it. They sat a table in the poolside hotel cafe that he'd chosen—it was a well-known place, he said, where famous writers from New York liked to frequent, where studio executives met investors, where business magnates stayed on and off over years. He even discreetly pointed out Diane Keaton across the room.

She wore a simple sleeveless pink dress with a knotted collar. Drinking her white wine, she let her head tip back when she laughed. She wanted him to see her as a young and promising actress; and an attractive one, too. That morning she'd dabbed red on her full lips and lined her eyes, applying just a bit of shimmery powder to her eyelids. It couldn't hurt for her to shine a little. Vivian wanted another role. And he knew people. He could help her.

"Tell me about how you got to Hollywood," he said.

She set down her glass delicately and watched the afternoon light cut ribbons on the water's blue surface. Everything was so full of color. It reminded her of Fujian, except here there was no thick, humid blanket of heat. She didn't sweat much. "I was performing in some theaters in San Francisco," she said. "And a casting director was looking for a Chinese actress to put in his movie. So he found me and signed me on."

"You grew up in San Francisco, then? Or abroad in China?"

Vivian paused. She couldn't pretend like she grew up in San Francisco. Surely he heard her accent. But how much did she want to reveal? How her family was from Fujian but had moved to Hong Kong right before she was born? How her bà, who was an English teacher, and her mā, who was a store clerk, had called her the songbird of the family and enrolled her at the opera to train as a performer? She'd gone to movie theaters and seen Shaw Brothers productions after her classes with her friends. She dreamed of acting in Xianxia films and palace dramas. Bà took her to Hollywood movies on the weekends, where she had picked up English. Her mā, a proud, exacting woman, told her: "Be glad I gave you my beauty. It's a gift." According to her parents, Yin Zi-Lian was destined to be an actress.

And so she was. When she was eighteen she was cast in a film production of *Dream of the Red Chamber* as Lin Daiyu. She was performing one of her last nights at the opera when the man who would become her husband walked in. His hair was cropped short, and he had a quiet, solid presence. He sat at a table and watched her, never taking his eyes off her. Then he would leave. Every time she looked back at him and their eyes met, she felt this pull toward this man who would only look upon her but never speak. After one of her shows, he had finally gone up to the manager and asked for her name, and when she came out of the dressing room after taking off her makeup, he was there waiting for her.

Yin Zi-Lian was twenty and in love. He was a twenty-six-year-old business owner who worked in kitchen supplies. He bought things for her: a dress, jewelry. He was discreet about it. Vivian married him quickly. On their wedding night he brought up the idea of moving to America, to San Francisco, to expand his business. He always had grand dreams, and Vivian was drawn to that. The thought of America thrilled her. Chinese movies were made there too, someone had told her. She had family there. One of Bà's cousins had settled in California a long time ago.

After Vivian wrapped up filming on *Dream of the Red Chamber*, they flew to San Francisco. Her mother didn't come to see her off; she didn't approve of Vivian's husband and felt like Vivian was abandoning her. Bà sent them off instead, with the gift of a Chinese-English dictionary.

They moved into a small, one-room apartment in Chinatown. The ocean was close enough to walk to. Sometimes Vivian would go to the pier and just look out at the fog and the sea. San Francisco was a marvel, but still she felt untethered. The English she'd picked up from the movies and from her bà was no match for how fast Americans spoke. She stayed in neighborhoods where she would be surrounded with the familiar sounds of Cantonese or the Mandarin that her parents had spoken to her. At night she made dinner for her husband. He talked about his plans with her, his business. They saw movies at the local theater.

Vivian asked around to see if she could meet any producers. She had just started auditioning when she felt sick one morning and realized she was pregnant. She stopped auditioning. By the following spring of 1973, a year and a half after she had arrived in this country, she had given birth to twin girls.

Acting slipped from her mind as she took care of her daughters. Lucille, whom she named after Lucille Ball, whose show Vivian's neighbor always played, and Ada, a name that sounded beautiful to her. Seasons passed. Her husband worked, often taking trips to and from Hong Kong. Vivian stayed behind with the children. She'd reconnected with Bà's cousin, her aunt, and her aunt's husband, her uncle. They'd immigrated into the country five years before. Now they lived just blocks away and came over to help with the twins.

She loved her daughters and adored being a mother, but she could not face herself in the mirror. She could no longer squeeze herself into her old clothes. Her breasts swelled and her nipples cracked and bled. She wanted desperately to get back into acting, but how? Her life was now consumed with the care of not one, but two infants. And her husband had become absent and irritable. When he was home, he talked about moving them back to Hong Kong. Vivian was lost. It was hard enough to come here; how could they move their young children across the ocean? He said his business was going through hard times. In June 1973 he went on a trip to Hong Kong. He was due to return in two weeks. He never came home.

First, Vivian was angry. Then she grew anxious. She wrote letter after letter. She placed frantic international calls that cost a fortune. She begged her parents to ask around, but no one had seen him or heard from him. And then someone wrote back and said that they'd seen her husband. He'd been gambling. She waited for him for weeks. One month stretched into two. Alone, in a foreign country, with two babies. She thought about going back to Hong Kong. But what was there for her? She would be returning a single mother, with a missing husband. The landlord put up an eviction notice. She was running out of time.

And then her uncle offered to house them.

With rent taken care of, she was ready to build herself anew. She moved into her uncle's apartment by the end of summer. They all lived in the apartment, above an apothecary where she got a temporary job. The twins cried and fussed. Ada didn't sleep well. Lucille wailed during the day, loud, piercing shrieks that seemed to flatten every thought.

Vivian changed diapers. She changed her children's English and

Chinese surnames to hers. Lucille was Yin Chen, named for a silver dawn. Ada was Yin Xue-Hua, named for snow and flowers. If her husband wasn't going to be around in their lives, then her daughters would inherit her own family name. Yin Zi-Lian became Vivian Yin. And all that time she kept watching movies, Chinese ones down the street and American ones in Nob Hill. She pitched down her tone and taught herself to form the words slowly in her mouth, flattening them so she sounded like an American. She auditioned to perform at the opera place down the block and got a small role. She could still sing. She could perform. And it was at the opera house where an American director first saw her. Don Corcoran was directing a noir film set in Chinatown: *Song of Lovers*, a feature film about a lovesick opera singer in Chinatown whose affair ended in tragedy. He wanted to cast her as the supporting character.

Hollywood was where the money was. But as she got more and more into acting, each following role that she fought for, each part that barely had any lines, came with a sour feeling: they had her play a spy, a prostitute, a crime lord's daughter. They had her amplify and distort her Chinese accent instead of trying to speak English like an American. Directors told her how to sound. It didn't feel right. But most of her sets were around San Francisco, which allowed her to be near her family. And she was making enough of a living to help pay for her part of the rent. So she swallowed the bitterness and kept going. One role gradually led to another. *Song of Lovers* released, to praise on her role. Suddenly her name appeared in reviews in newspapers. The film led her to the awards show where she met Richard, and then to this very cafe at the hotel where he was staying.

Now she set down her wineglass and looked directly at him. She would tell him none of this. The sunlight glittered off the swimming pool. "I have family in San Francisco," she said with practiced ease. "What about you? Where are you from?"

ten

VIVIAN and Richard were having dinner later that spring in a red booth at a dimly lit restaurant. She had come to that dinner with a speech prepared. She wore a plain suede jacket over her jeans. She was going to order the cheapest entrée on the menu and offer to split the bill. She was going to walk away. This would be the end.

The last two months had been an enchanting fever dream. What started out as a mid-afternoon wine at the Beverly Hills Hotel lasted into the cool twilight hours, which Vivian finally ended by saying that she had to get home to prepare for an audition the next day, coinciden-tally for one of his friends. Richard told her that he would like to see her again. She went to the audition and got the part. Only later would she wonder if Richard had spoken to the director, or if she got the role herself. Either way, she didn't question it.

She went back to Los Angeles a week later for table reads, leaving the twins in the care of her aunt and uncle. Vivian both adored and feared the city. She felt so small in the face of the billboards, the wide swaths of highway, the landscape itself. Daisy generously offered to let her stay at her place on the corner of Fountain and Sunset, a little one-bedroom apartment up three flights of stairs that teemed with color inside, full of mismatched furniture that had either sentimental value or was pulled off the street. Daisy had painted the walls herself and splotches of lilac and deep-blue paint spilled from one corner to an-other, but it was all charming to Vivian. And it was very characteristic of her friend, who dressed in sequins and bright geometric prints and big earrings and uneven sleeves, who tried to pull her out to dance at night.

The one time Vivian relented, they went out to West Hollywood. Daisy kept pointing out famous musicians and actors who drifted down the street, talking about the parties in their homes that she'd gone to. How as a teenager, she'd snuck into one of their mansions in Beverly Hills and spent the night wandering around on magic mushrooms and getting lost in all the mirrors. Vivian kept her head clear and refused every pill that was offered to her. But still, even standing in the line outside a bar in a loose chiffon collared blouse, wide-leg jeans, and heels, with her blown-out hair fanning around her, with billboards and posters that dripped down from over two stories, she felt an electric, youthful rush. It was like she was being reinvented out here, born anew into this cosmic current of excitement and chatter, music and chaos, where she was only herself, untethered to anyone. At the end of the night, though, with her eyes aching and the music pounding in her head and her heels rubbed raw, she was pulled back into her old life, her real life. She missed her daughters. The next morning, when she looked through Daisy's bare fridge and found nothing but bits of food in take-out boxes and bread rolls, she yearned for braised pork in a thick congee.

During free days when filming, Richard drove her in his convertible over canyons and hills, to Malibu, to the ocean. He told her about how he'd worked with Roger Corman–like directors who would steal onto film sets without permits and let anyone take a shot at cutting and editing. He'd gone everywhere: charmed shipping magnates and princes on a boat in southern Italy, accidentally entered a rodeo and broken up a gunfight in Wyoming. He'd booked one of the top managers in the industry by walking into his office and telling the secretary that he had a meeting scheduled, didn't she remember his call? He told Vivian all of this with a sheepish dip of his head, as if even he couldn't quite believe his own nerve, but Vivian could; who wouldn't be charmed by that easy, hopeful smile? But for every story he told, he asked her even more questions, about her childhood, her hometown, her parents. She found herself telling him everything, down to what she would do after school and the fruits she'd eat on the way home. Everything *except* her marriage and children. She often looked into his eyes and was so enthralled by his sincerity, his abundant and unending curiosity, that she found herself launching into one story, one detail after another.

She told him she wanted to drive someday. He promised to teach her. He'd drop her off afterward at Daisy's place, and on the way up the stairs to Daisy's apartment, clutching her friend's spare key, she'd still be laughing. She and Daisy would perch on Daisy's little balcony, smoking cigarettes, while Vivian recounted Richard's stories second-hand, although never with his charm. She'd catch her grin in the reflection of the window and be entranced by her own joy. Daisy teased her, saying that she was in deep, that soon enough she would be moving down here, that she couldn't wait to meet Vivian's daughters.

Could Vivian see a future here? How could she raise her daughters here and chase her wild dream at the same time? That would be impossible to do by herself, and she couldn't afford a nanny. Would she leave them in San Francisco, then? With her aunt?

She thought about it when she returned to San Francisco. She finally told her aunt and uncle that she had met an actor, an American one. They asked her what she wanted with him, and Vivian didn't know. Was this someone to alter her life for? She went back to Los Angeles to film the movie. On days when she wasn't needed on set, she was with Richard. He took her to shows and to restaurants with delectable, intricately plated dishes. Wherever they went people stared, and Vivian could feel their gaze on her. It was strange. For so long she had been ignored, if even registered at all, and now there was a kind of indignant, awestruck incredulity to the stares. She felt most comfortable in the moments they were alone but learned to revel in this new public attention.

Directors started giving her a second look. Vivian had known she possessed a certain type of beauty, with her rounded, searching eyes set upon sharpened cheekbones and her full lips. There was a reason she had gotten the role of Lin Daiyu back in the day. One of the casting directors had called her a "precious China jewel" at the auditions for *Song of Lovers*, in a tone that made Vivian glow in the moment, only to make her skin crawl when she thought about it later.

But Richard never said any of that. On long drives with her he only continued his questions, asking her about her day, about what she thought about the movie, about her co-stars, the costuming. At night as the stars swept the sky, he leaned in and kissed her, slowly. She kissed him back, tasting his cigarettes, which she'd eventually come to enjoy, in spite of herself.

She knew this would have to end someday. She was only on set in Los Angeles for a few weeks, and then this would all be over; this rapturous and eternal joy that seemed to beam from the billboards and thread through the streets, the fixed attention of this man that Vivian had only known for months but suddenly didn't want to be away from for even a full day. Still, she didn't tell him. Knowing him was good for her job, Vivian thought, and that excuse held for a while. But now that he had started talking about introducing her to his family and bringing her to Paris with him to an awards show there, she couldn't ignore it. She couldn't make a life here in Los Angeles. The more she thought about it the clearer it became. She'd been abandoned once. She couldn't do the same to her children. She couldn't continue this.

"So," he said now at this dinner over appetizers—*appetizers*, a luxury Vivian only came to know with Richard. "I was wondering what your thoughts were on the Paris trip."

Vivian took a deep breath. "I need to tell you something first."

Richard looked up. Vivian could hardly make herself meet his eyes, his clear gaze.

"I . . . ," Vivian said. "I don't know what I can be to you."

"Vivian," he said plainly. "You know I'm in love with you, right?"

Everything around her seemed to still.

"I love you, too," she whispered, wanting to retract it as soon as she'd said it because she knew it was true. His eyes softened. She steeled herself. "I do. But I need to tell you something. I was married before."

She watched his lips part in shock.

"I had a husband. Back in San Francisco. But he left me." Vivian took a breath. Her eyes smarted. "And my daughters."

"Oh," Richard said.

Vivian waited for him to take in this new information. "My children are in San Francisco with my family. But I miss them, and I want to bring them here. I want to be here with them."

Surely he would withdraw from her. She must look like a ruined woman to him, she thought. Or foolish, scorned. A Chinese divorcée with children. She waited for him to leave. She stared at the tablecloth.

"I love you, Richard," she said softly. "But I don't think you should love me. Because then you will have to love everything. My children, too."

He said nothing.

She stood up. "I will always think about you," she breathed through trembling lips. *And what could have been.* "I'm sorry. I really am." She then ran back toward the entrance of the restaurant. She could barely see through her tears to hail a taxi. She wept into her palms the whole way home, furious with herself for flirting with the impossible. She ran inside her hotel, wanting only to bury her face in the pillow. But she had to tell him the truth. She needed to be with her children. The dream had to end.

Vivian slept fitfully that night. The next morning the hotel concierge called her and told her that someone was downstairs to see her. Vivian dressed shakily and headed down. Richard Lowell was in the lobby, and he didn't look angry. His eyes were gentle as he reached out a hand and asked her if she would like to go for a drive. He took her to the top of a mountain road overlooking trees and meadows. He parked the car and turned to her.

"I thought about what you told me."

She swallowed. "I'm so sorry. I didn't mean to be dishonest."

"You weren't." There was a pause. "I don't think you gave me time to respond, though. That wasn't fair."

Her stomach twisted in on itself.

"I'm almost thirty," he said. "And I've been alone for most of my life. I just bought a house with some land and I've been thinking about the life I want to build for myself. The family I'd have."

She looked up and his fingers brushed her cheek. "I want it all with you, Vivian."

Her heart swelled. A trick, a flash of fate. But Richard was in front of her. His hands were holding hers.

"I knew it was you after our first conversation," he professed breathlessly, his voice tender and deep. "I'll never forget the sight of you in that red dress. I knew you would fascinate me for the rest of my life."

Vivian blinked. Tears rose to her eyes as shock and happiness surged through her.

"And I didn't . . . I don't have a ring, or anything, not yet. I didn't quite plan to have this conversation right now. And I know this is soon, but I know I'll never meet anyone else like you. So. I am yours, if you'll have me. I'll love your daughters like my own, and we can make our own family."

His, theirs, together. Vivian didn't realize she was weeping until things started to look blurry again. "Richard, I—I'm a divorced Chinese woman. Are you sure?"

Richard nodded. "I know that's a part of your history. And I love the whole of you. But you know you're so much more than those things, too, don't you?"

Vivian tipped forward and kissed him, and he kissed her back, his fingers lacing through her hair. She kissed him like they did in the American movies, with her tongue tracing his. Against her lips he inquired, "So, about that Paris trip."

"Yes," she said, giddy. "Yes, yes, of course. And then I'll return to my family."

"And I can meet them," Richard said. "If I may?"

Wordlessly, Vivian nodded, laughing a little and swiping at her eyes with the hem of her sleeve. Was this really happening? She had resigned herself to the things her aunt's neighbors said: that she and her daughters would always be an abandoned family. But now here was a man who was willing to love them and take care of them. Who *wanted* to.

She took a moment to compose herself. "And you said you were building a house?"

Richard grinned. "My family used to have an estate that's fallen into disrepair. I've always wanted to buy it back and fix it up."

A house, Vivian thought. She dug her nails into her palm; this dream had taken a surreal twist, but it was time to wake up before reality became unbearable in comparison. Instead, she focused on the sharp pricks of pain in her hand until she realized Richard was waiting for her to say something. "Really?" was all she could manage.

He nodded. "You're going to love it. We'll renovate it together. It's going to be the perfect house for us," he said, looking in her eyes. "For our family."

Vivian learned that the house and its lot of four acres was nestled near the San Gabriel Mountains, among cresting hills draped with olive and citrus trees. The five-thousand-square-foot estate had been in Richard's family for decades. But he'd told her that he'd dreamed of buying the property back for years. And now, finally, he would have a family to live there with.

It sounded almost mythic to Vivian: he was the prince, and this his fated kingdom. His mother had lived in that house before she moved out East. She had inherited it when her father passed, then sold it to a family who lived there for less than a decade. They'd foreclosed on it eventually, and the house fell into ruin.

Richard resented his mother for selling it. Her family had been Californians ever since the gold rush. He'd attended boarding schools with rolling lawns and stiff shirts in New England, and yet he dreamed about going West. He wanted to be a movie star and had finally made his way to Hollywood the spring after he graduated college. He participated in war protests and narrowly avoided the draft. One meeting with his Yale drama connections buoyed him to the next. The old guard took him under their wing. Richard described learning film in a new age in Hollywood, defined by a renegade recklessness and the dazzling advent of new ideas. Anyone could become a filmmaker, he'd said. Anyone could cut tape, and anyone could act. He charmed his way into parties and smoked on lush lawns with actresses he grew up admiring. He was becoming a self-made man.

It took him a while to find the old family home, he told Vivian. But in the summer of 1974 he drove up the cracked driveway and saw the pillars for the first time. He took in the moss-covered walls, the grounds crawling with undergrowth, and the floorboards that were splintered with rot and mold. This is what his grand abandoned family home had been reduced to. But—and this he described to Vivian in incredible detail—he'd looked upon the house again, and a vision had come to him. He saw, clear as day, how the walls could be restored with new brickwork, how the marble foyer could be polished, and his grandfather's ballroom could be renovated into an elegant library. The fountain behind the house could rush again. He saw the house filled to the brim with people, gathering and laughing under the benediction of a southern California sunset. He saw that vision and was irrevocably altered by it.

Something magical lingered in this place—*his* place. To him it was prophetic. It was as if this land had been waiting for his arrival, to offer itself up for him to build his future. And at last, he was ready. He would claim what was his. He had bought back the house, he told Vivian. And whatever its history, he would remake it new.

eleven

VIVIAN and Richard got married in the backyard of one of Richard's friends, who owned a beautiful Spanish-style house in Simi Valley with red-tiled roofs and a backyard that sloped into a vineyard. Everything around them burst with vivid, sun-drenched green. It was a cloudless day in late July and Vivian stood in front of a white trellis arch, looking up at her husband.

Her hands shook a little as she unfolded the piece of paper with her vows. She'd crafted them painstakingly in the month leading up to the wedding. Daisy had helped her. She'd helped Vivian pick out her dress, too, teaching her to discern between designer names Vivian had never heard of. Together they had settled on ivory chiffon, with cap sleeves and a lace bodice dotted with iridescent pearls leading up to a high neck, like a qipao clasp. The lace trailed like fallen leaves down her skirt, and the chiffon fanned out on the grass around her as her tulle veil fluttered in the breeze.

She was keenly aware of over a hundred guests in attendance: former directors, Richard's friends, mostly, the cast of *Song of Lovers*, her family and new in-laws. Her hair was tucked up with beaded pins her aunt had given her, family heirlooms. A jade pendant settled on her sternum.

She'd spotted her aunt and uncle in the audience, along with her small group of friends, Chinatown actors who'd driven down for the occasion. Bà had flown in from Hong Kong. It had been nearly five years since Vivian had seen him, and he felt frailer in her arms than she remembered. His hair had grayed. The jade pendant was a gift from him. It was carved with 囍, which meant "double happiness," the symbol of a joyful marriage. May you have a good union for a hundred years," he'd said to her in Cantonese, then Mandarin when he fastened it around her neck that morning. "May your hearts be bound forever."

Mā had refused to come. She'd expected Vivian to return to Hong Kong eventually. To not only refuse to do so, but to marry a white American actor was seen as an intentional betrayal. It hurt Vivian to hear that her mother couldn't understand that she had made a life here.

The guests were quiet as she carefully enunciated her vows. Somewhere in the crowd, someone blew their nose and it sounded like a duck. Vivian smiled. She knew it was Daisy, welling up with emotion and as incapable of subtlety as ever. When she was finished, she looked to Richard in front of her, his smile wide enough to reveal crinkles around his brilliant hazel eyes. The words of his vows floated over her; she could only look on in awe at her prince.

This wasn't a small wedding, like her first, which had just been a meal in the back of a restaurant. This was an American wedding, and he was saying these words in front of everyone he knew. He was hers. And with it, his family, his good fortune—she was a part of it now, their legacies intertwined. They kissed, the guests cheered, and the live orchestra swelled with music. He held her hand tightly as they walked down an aisle lined with rose petals.

The sun dipped behind the mountains and painted everything in a golden glow. The drinks flowed and Vivian drifted away to talk to her family on the dance floor. She saw her father with her twins for the first time, and Lucille looked at Vivian with so much adoration that her heart filled almost to bursting.

Richard joined her then. He talked to her aunt and uncle, who each held one of the girls. They toasted to her and marveled at the splendor of the wedding. And as the live music kicked up, Richard led her to his family. "This is Vivian," he exhaled happily to the line of extended family members waiting to meet her. They hugged her and fawned over her, telling her what a beautiful bride she was, what a vision she was in that dress. Some looked at her puzzlingly, as though even at her wedding, they had yet to decide whether she belonged. Richard's mother, whom Vivian had met twice before, stepped forward and kissed her cheek.

"What are the lovely newlywed's plans?" A man that Vivian dimly remembered as Richard's uncle asked.

"We're going to France for the honeymoon," Richard said smoothly, looking over at Vivian. "And then we're renovating the house."

"A house?"

"That's right. The one in Altadena. The one that used to be our family's."

Vivian beamed, and only when she looked away from Richard did she notice that his mother's face had gone ashen, and his family members suddenly went unusually quiet. Vivian watched uneasily as Richard and his mother stared at each other. When the song changed, Vivian took the cue to slip away, toward the music and the food, toward her daughters.

It was only later that Richard's mother found her again. "Champagne for the lovely bride?" she asked.

Vivian gratefully accepted.

"What a lucky man Richard is," his mother said, looking out over the reception. Her dark, graying hair was swept up in a severe twist.

"I'm the lucky one, I'm sure," Vivian said. "He makes me happier than anything."

"Does he?" His mother turned back toward her. "You know, when Richard said he was marrying a Chinese woman, I wasn't sure. But your English is excellent."

Vivian chafed but kept a smile on her face. "Thank you. My father was an English teacher. He's over there with the blue tie."

"Isn't that lovely." Her pale eyes bored into Vivian's. Green, with no flecks of golden brown and devoid of all warmth. Wrinkles webbed around her taut lips. She was beautiful once, Vivian could tell. Unsure where to look, she focused on the pearl necklace that framed her mother-in-law's collarbone. "I wish my son had informed me. Then I wouldn't seem like such a careless mother-in-law."

Vivian sensed a bit of hostility, as if she were being put to some kind of test. "You're not—you've been very kind to me."

Richard's mother ignored this. "This house you're renovating," she said. "It was the house I grew up in. Richard never forgave me for selling it."

Why did you? Vivian wanted to ask. But she held her tongue.

"But he's headstrong. What he wants, he makes for himself. Precocious, too. The world has always been good to him. I tried to tell him, but I don't think he understands."

Night was settling and the overhead lights twinkled to life. A hot breeze brushed the back of Vivian's neck. "Tell him—?"

"Just old history," his mother said airily. "Perhaps he has more luck and fortitude than the rest of us." She placed her cool fingers on Vivian's arm. "Take care of my son. I know you will." She gave a thin smile before walking back into the crowd.

After the music had died down and the champagne had run dry, after toasts were made, and Richard took Vivian's hand and they ran down to the red Polara that waited for them in the driveway, they checked into a Malibu hotel that overlooked the coast. Richard swept her up from the car and carried her into the suite. They tipped into bed, laughing and giddy. Richard kissed her, and Vivian savored it, tasting the sour whiskey on his tongue. He pulled her to him and fumbled for the zipper on her dress. She laughed as she guided his hands away from the expensive fabric. Delicately, she unclasped the dress's closures and stepped out of it, feeling the cooling night air on her shoulders, on her breasts, on her hips that still bore the stretch marks of childbirth. She undid her hair, and it crested around her shoulders in long, dark waves. He looked at her with eyes wide and lips parted for a moment, before he hungrily pulled her to him again.

Vivian fumbled with the buttons on his shirt and tugged it off, feeling the heat of his skin against her hands, the bulge of him straining against her. His fingers trailed down her stomach toward the heat between her legs, slowly, carefully, and she arched toward that desire, crying out when he finally touched her.

"I want to adore you like this," he said, his voice raw. "Forever."

He pressed a kiss above her left breast, his tongue tracing lower, circling her nipple. She gasped, her head humming with nothing but need, her body on fire. She laced her fingers through his hair, pulling him to her and crushing her lips against his, reaching for his hardness to pleasure him the way she knew how.

With a teasing, wicked smile, he gently pushed her back down onto the bed. He put his mouth to her inner thigh, and then his tongue found the center of that heat, so lightly at first, and then with more pressure. Vivian threw her head back and gave herself over to him fully.

This was everything she needed, she thought, as she trembled beneath him, dazed by his power over her, the intensity of his focus on her. Their life stretched out before them that night, their dreams, their house, their new family. What was his would be hers now, forever.

Vivian watched her husband stalk across the empty foyer. "Fuck this," he hissed. "The pipes burst."

"Again?" Vivian turned away from admiring the new bay windows. "I thought we just put them in."

"They were caked with rust," Richard said. "And they burst overnight."

"But they're new."

"Supposed to be. There's no way. New pipes don't do that." He ran his hands through his hair and lowered his voice. "Maybe we got scammed. I'm going to fire that contractor, I swear to God."

Vivian reached for him. Their hands were still tanned from their honeymoon. What a Western concept; a honeymoon, as if one couldn't be sated by that lavish wedding alone. There was a sun-drenched week in Paris and Provence. She came away draped in billowing floral dresses from charming boutiques, carrying wines and perfumes with names she couldn't pronounce. She savored their sweet, honeyed aftertaste on her husband's lips at night. Her *husband*. Her husband, who was building a house for their family. Though Vivian saw now that his jaw had tightened. His loose, collared shirt was opened at the throat and his sleeves were pushed up. His hair had become unruly in the humidity. She loved this new ruggedness. A dim desire rose inside her. "Be patient, qīn ài de."

"We were supposed to move in by November. Now it's looking like next year." He was pacing now.

"We have all the time in the world," she said soothingly.

He looked at her. The sunlight touched his eyelashes into tips of gold. His eyes softened behind his glasses. "You're right." He kissed her gently.

The first time Vivian set eyes on the skeleton of the sprawling house with its filthy walls and uneven patches of grass, panic hit her like cold water. But with her husband's fervent vision, the house came to life. Old pillars were struck down and replaced with new white sandstone ones with bracketed cornices. The original concave mansard roof was maintained, with crested dormers. Paired windows were installed, with window crowns of leaves and flowers, an old French style, and ornamented keystones. The vines were cleared away. The original stone terrace was cleaned. The old, cracked fountain behind the house, which seemed to be mired in a mass of weeds that were cut away, was replaced with a new one carved out of limestone, with ridged bowls that seemed to ripple, petal-like. The tall, uneven grass was sheared and watered to become a sprawling lawn. With every decision, he asked her if she liked what he'd envisioned and what he was choosing; *yes, yes*, she'd responded at each turn.

For now, they were living in a rented house two miles away. Vivian was between films, and so she stayed at home with her daughters. In the evenings she and Richard would bring them to the new house to see the day's work. In the twilight she stood on the stone steps as they ran around the freshly mowed grounds. They chased each other until their legs were tired, and still there was more land to run on. On the drives back to their rental house at night, Richard would let down the roof of the Polara so they could all feel like they were flying through the hazy California dusk. The girls always screamed with delight and threw their small hands in the air.

Her husband obsessed over the exterior of the house and structural parts of the interior. He spent days poring over choices and made sure that the foyer was constructed with ivory granite and the doors made of glazed mahogany and the walls paneled with walnut and redwood.

But the decorative choices were hers. In her mind she conjured up the palaces of Versailles and Yí Hé Yuán, the Summer Palace. She would imitate their opulence. She could imagine it now: the panels of the walls lined with silk screens and scrolls of brush paintings, shelves of delicate porcelain bowls. Chinese books on the library shelves alongside the English.

This would be a home where she could raise her daughters right. She would make sure they learned Mandarin and developed palates that yearned for light winter melon soups and dumplings. They would have rooms to play in and separate rooms to study in. Richard would take them to see great films. They would spend winters skiing in the mountains and summers swimming at the beach. They would get to go to college, each of them. But they wouldn't have it easy all the time, either, Vivian thought. She wouldn't allow her children to grow up soft. They would learn how to 吃苦, to take in hardships. But they would have every privilege that they could be given. Vivian would make sure of it.

One early evening, right after her daughters went to bed, she looked out the window of their rented house, over the rolling hills and winding roads, up in the direction of the new house. Richard offered her a glass of wine. As the stars rose overhead, his hands curled around her waist.

"I've been thinking about that fountain," she said. "I think I want a new garden. Around that fountain." She'd seen the gardens of Versailles on her honeymoon, and she couldn't help wondering what they could do here in California.

"Seems like there used to be one." Richard kissed her shoulder. "Tell me what you want and we'll build it."

"Hmmm," Vivian exhaled, resting her head against his chest. "I want roses."

"What else?"

"And . . ." Vivian sighed as he brushed another kiss against the nape of her neck, and for a moment her thoughts dissolved. "茶花. And honeysuckle. And . . . lilies."

"So we will," Richard agreed. "We'll have them all. I want it to be your paradise." And this time he tipped her jaw up toward his, as his hips pressed her against the edge of the countertop. Yet, as she flung her arms around his neck, a dark fear echoed in the corner of her mind— *what if he leaves too?* But when she looked into the face of this man who wanted to build her a house, a *garden*—she saw a devotion that her ex-husband could never have summoned, that wouldn't have interested him, even if he could have. She and Richard were meant to find each other. She could have happiness again. This was the new spring of her life.

They moved in February when the pipes were finally fixed, the final coats of paint were dry, the paneling installed, and the crown molding connected from room to room. It was impressive and elegant, but sometimes Vivian caught herself wondering if it was almost too spacious. Why had she agreed to so many bathrooms? Her voice and footsteps echoed off the walls eerily when she was alone. But she told herself it would be different once they had picked out all the furniture, and she set her mind to perusing velvet chaise lounges and ornate dressers.

A month in, she woke in the middle of the night in discomfort. She was pregnant again, expecting a child in three months. She walked across the room to open the window, hoping for a breeze. The curtains billowed softly around her and the air chilled her enough that her arms prickled with goose bumps. From the bed, her husband sighed in his sleep, and when she got back in, he curled his arms around her. She kissed his forehead and stretched her limbs out, feeling like she was swathed in an ocean of silk.

The next time Vivian's eyes opened, she was alone.

She sat up. Her heart beat wildly. She looked around for her husband, but he was nowhere to be seen. *He left*, Vivian thought, with a familiar lurch of panic.

"Richard?"

There was no answer, and suddenly the room was unbearably hot. The curtains hung limp; the air reeked of rust. Sweat trickled down her temples, and the sheets around her were soaked.

"天啊," she whispered. "It's *so*—"

She looked down and screamed.

She scrambled back, trying to throw off the sheets, but they were sticky, saturated with blood. It pooled on the floor next to the bed. Gasping, she realized the scent of rust was filling her throat until she was certain she would choke on it. She could only watch, dazed, as blood poured from a gaping wound in her stomach.

The next time Vivian's eyes opened, her skin was slick with sweat. She shot up in bed and pulled cool air into her lungs. The windows were open. The curtains drifted gently. Her husband was by her side, his arms stretched out. She clutched her stomach protectively.

Vivian's shoulders sagged with relief. A low pressure mounted behind her eyes, and she closed them tightly.

It was a nightmare; that was all it was.

Richard mumbled her name in his sleep.

"Sorry," she whispered, settling against him again. She welled with love for him in that moment; she kissed his hand that draped over her collarbone and felt her mind quiet.

twelve

VIVIAN'S husband wanted to give the house a name. All important houses had one, and he wanted to name it after her. Yin Manor. This place was hardly a manor, but still, it sounded like a proper, established estate that had been around for decades and would last for generations more. Vivian loved it. Now all that was left was to show it off.

This part Vivian was a bit more discerning about. She had young daughters, three now including the new baby, Renata. She knew, kids or not, some houses in Hollywood had parties that could last a full weekend, with people showing up at all hours and then sleeping it off in every corner. This house would first and foremost be a home for her family.

So they only hosted dinner parties every weekend. She and Richard approved the guest list together. Sometimes they hosted two guests, sometimes seven. Sometimes Vivian cooked and Richard made their drinks; sometimes they hired a chef who would construct a five-course meal with inventive appetizers and desserts, more things encased in gelatin than she knew was possible. But somehow the exclusivity made the invitations even more sought-after.

These dinners helped them both. They could talk to directors and invite producers and line up roles, all from their dining room. Vivian also wanted to show the house to her family.

Nearly ten months after they moved in, Vivian's aunt and uncle from San Francisco came down by train. They practically fell over when they saw the house rise before them. "天啊," her uncle said, his eyes gleaming. Inside, their eyes roved over the imported Ming-style vases and brush paintings, as Vivian swelled with pride. That night she made them all dumplings herself. They shared platters upon platters, all crowded around the kitchen to eat instead of at the long dining table, which made sharing impossible. Her uncle drank 二锅头 with Richard, and they both made funny faces at Lucille, who shrieked with joy, her lips streaked with vinegar from the dumplings. Her aunt cooed over her new seven-month-old daughter. Vivian translated effortlessly between them, and somehow, Richard's jokes came through.

Her aunt and uncle stayed in one of the guest rooms on the first floor. The next day they were quieter. They ate breakfast quickly. Richard drove them to the train station, and before they boarded, her aunt clasped her hands.

"Come back," Vivian said. "Whatever you need, let me know."

Her aunt nodded and pulled Vivian close. "Be careful out here," she said, words for Vivian only.

Vivian pulled away. "姑姑, of course. What do you mean?"

Her aunt looked at her, mouth open as if to say something. But the train sounded and she simply turned away.

The following month, Richard finally convinced his mother to visit. Dishes were polished twice. A French cook was hired, who made a soup, braised veal with a wine sauce reduction, and perfectly tender potatoes. Cecilia Lowell arrived by taxi. Vivian could tell Richard was nervous by how much he adjusted his shirt collar, and it made her anxious, too. In Mandarin she told her daughters to be quiet.

Richard's mother scrutinized the couple's choices as she walked through the house's halls. She was expressionless taking in the same Ming dishes Vivian's aunt and uncle had gasped at. She evoked some warmth when Vivian and Richard showed her Renata, held the infant, even, and helped put her to bed, but otherwise remained indifferent.

During dinner, the conversation was quiet and controlled. They talked about Richard's and Vivian's recent roles, about a new tennis club that opened up near where Richard's mother lived, the inauguration of the new president. Jazz played on the turntable. Forks and knives screeched against the dishware. Lucille's face puckered as she chewed the veal, and Vivian felt her temperature rise. She drank her wine in small, rationed sips. Richard's mother had never been openly disdainful of Vivian. But still, she had thoughts on politics that Vivian didn't have the context to possess, mentioned names she didn't know, and used words that she had never had any reason to learn, so that when her mother-in-law asked Vivian her opinion, she could add nothing. She felt childish and humiliated when Cecilia did this, like she had failed a test.

"So," Richard asked his mother later on. They were still around the dining room table. Vivian had just put her daughters to bed. "What do you think of the house?"

His mother looked up, her gaze settling on Vivian. "What do you think, dear?"

Vivian swallowed. Her husband turned to look at her. "It's beautiful," she said. "Richard did a beautiful job with the renovation." She winced at saying *beautiful* twice.

Cecilia nodded.

"You should move back out here," Richard said. He fidgeted with his napkin, the only sign of his nervousness. "You could live with us. Have your pick of the rooms."

Vivian shot her husband a look. They'd never discussed this. Did they really want this cold woman to reside in their house? To eat formal dinners like this every night?

"I wouldn't want to intrude on the happy family," Cecilia said, and Vivian felt at first a flash of relief that quickly soured into anxiety. Her mother-in-law hated her, she was now certain of it. And her children, too.

"You wouldn't be," her son reassured her. "Here, stay the night at least? We have guest rooms downstairs."

His mother stood up. "I should call a taxi," she said. "I'll use the phone in the living room." She gathered up her wool coat. Vivian watched her go with her stomach in knots.

Richard shut the door. "She won't even spend a night here."

"It's me," Vivian said, suddenly realizing she was exhausted. "She doesn't like me."

"That's not it." He shook his head, defeated. "It's the house. She's always been this way. I thought I could change her mind if we built it up the way *we* wanted. If we cleared out the old. But—" He grimaced. "She's still superstitious."

"Superstitious," Vivian said slowly. "Of what?"

Richard didn't answer her for a long time. "She's convinced she saw a ghost in her parents' bedroom when she was a child," he said. "But she didn't. That's all."

In May they hosted a late dinner for Eugene Lyman, a producer who was an old friend of Richard's. He'd been three years above Richard at Yale Drama and had become a producer of action movies.

Vivian put the children to bed before she got dressed and greeted Eugene and his wife, Jeanette, a tall, imposing, woman who showed up in a mink-lined tapestry coat and bright jewelry.

They drank wine and looked out over the half-finished grounds behind the house as Vivian told them she'd been looking into hiring a gardener. At dinner Jeanette regaled them, in her low, raspy voice, about the producers who were booking trips to see mistresses, the substance habits of well-known actors, and the romantic trysts of a certain senator with an up-and-coming actress. They were rapt. Eugene dropped in with a joke from time to time. Vivian rubbed her husband's shoulder when she placed a platter of fresh potstickers next to the salad, and he squeezed her hand. One thing she didn't like about show business was how people gossiped. Surely if they were talking about other people this way, someone must be talking about her.

"These dumplings, Vivian," Eugene admired. Vivian remembered coming in to audition for him once. He'd barely focused on her monologue and had dismissed her the moment she was done speaking. But now his eyes sparkled. "I might have to hire a Chinese cook myself."

Vivian's cheeks warmed.

"How you act and raise children and keep up this beautiful house, I have no clue," Jeanette said. She had perfectly applied lipstick that matched her nails. She tapped her cigarette into the ashtray. Vivian winced inside, thinking of how the smoke would rise and stain the walls. "You must tell me your secrets."

Vivian smiled gratefully. "Thank you. I try my best."

Eugene drained his scotch and looked around. "It is a hell of a house, Richie."

Jeanette nodded. "The classical influences are gorgeous. I see the Beaux Arts design on those windows. And the decorations, too. A flair of the Orient."

Vivian was drunk to the point where the lights on the low chandelier were slightly expanding. Eugene rattled the ice around in his glass. "You know, I remember when you first told me about this house. It was a pipe dream, wasn't it? But you really made it your own."

"I remember," Richard said. "You told me not to do it."

"Well," Jeanette said. "What with everything that happened with your family—"

Eugene set down his glass, hard. "Jennie."

Everyone went silent.

What? Vivian wanted to ask. Her dinner guests were looking at one another. Her husband's face was perfectly blank. She met Jeanette's eyes, and the other woman quickly glanced away. Her drawn lips puckered. "Don't mind me. I'm a *nuisance* when I'm drunk," she said. "We just wanted to toast to this beautiful family."

"Yes," Eugene said. He tipped his glass up. "To this house of your dreams."

Finally, Richard smiled. "It's called Yin Manor," he said, looking over to Vivian. "I named it for my wife."

"Isn't that grand. To the Yin Manor." Jeanette raised her drink.

As they clinked glasses, Vivian thought back to Cecilia Lowell's cold eyes, the warning in her aunt's tone. The look exchanged between Eugene and Jeanette.

What had happened in this house? And why hadn't her husband told her?

"Now, Richard." Jeanette leaned forward. Her heavy pendant earrings clinked. "You must tell me. What was Gene like at Yale? I hear you two were quite the pranksters."

"*That* requires more drinks." Eugene laughed, reaching for the decanter. Vivian watched her husband relax.

Vivian smiled. She was starting to feel a little queasy. A sharp, metallic taste filled her mouth. She excused herself and went to the bathroom. She held herself up over the sink. Why was she feeling so *sick?*

She felt almost feverish. The headaches were frequent these days, and another one was beginning to press behind her eyes. It smelled like rust, still, everywhere, tasted like it. Could it have been the wine?

Another wave of nausea brought her to her knees. Her mouth filled with spit, and she vomited into the toilet. The vile taste of her stomach acid almost made her vomit again. Shakily, she pushed herself up and studied her pallid reflection. For a moment, someone appeared behind her. A man with mottled skin, his eye sockets filled with crumbling dirt. The skin rotting away to show the cheekbones underneath. He opened his mouth and bared his blackened teeth.

This time she lurched forward and vomited into the sink. Again, she forced herself to lift her eyes to the mirror.

The figure was gone. *Am I hallucinating?* She took shaky breaths and turned on the faucet, which sputtered. Water ran brown for a moment, then clear.

Vivian was dizzy. She needed to get out of here. She washed her hands and left, only to stop short.

Her daughter stood in the foyer.

"Lucille," she whispered. "What are you doing here?" Her daughter blinked at her, her thumb in her mouth. "Let me get you back into bed." She scooped the girl up, feeling her solid weight. Lucille was four. Almost too old to be carried, but Vivian did it anyway. She heard voices rising and falling from the dining room as she kissed her daughter's head and hummed softly to her. She was glad to not have to return to the dinner just yet. To have an excuse to take this moment to collect her nerves. Drink some water.

She set Lucille in bed and went back downstairs. By the time she reentered the dining room, she was smiling at her husband and her guests.

"Sorry," she said. "I was just checking on my daughter. Where were we?"

They clinked glasses again, and the conversation once more began to flow. Jeanette offered Vivian tips on hiring nannies; Vivian said that there was already a woman named Edith Fan, who took care of her daughters. Edith was married to Josiah Deng, whom she'd thought about hiring as the gardener; he would be coming over to the house that following Monday, and Vivian would meet him. The conversation circled back to Hollywood. "It's a small world, you know," Jeanette said. "Don't piss anyone off, smile more than you think you need to, and you'll do just fine."

What happened in the house? Vivian wanted to stand up and shout. She couldn't stop thinking about the man with mottled skin. Richard reached for her hand. When she looked at him, her stomach lurched again. The figure in the mirror had looked too much like her husband.

"You all right?" he asked, staring up at her with wide eyes.

She couldn't make sense of what she wanted to say, so eventually she just nodded and squeezed Richard's hand. "Of course." She rose to pour more wine, skipping her own glass. Eugene told another story, and they all laughed.

The next morning Vivian woke up and saw Richard leaning over the bathroom sink, a towel around his waist. He glanced up at her in the mirror. His wet, tousled hair fell in front of his eyes. "Did you feel the house shaking last night?"

She looked at him in alarm. "What? Did something happen?"

He straightened up. Something—relief?—seemed to come over him. "Never mind."

"What do you mean, shaking? Is something else wrong with the house?"

"It's nothing," he said lightly. "Just a dream."

She stood at the sink and deliberately washed her hands and then her face. She still felt nauseated, especially so this morning. Was it the wine? Had she eaten something bad? "Qīn ài de," she said.

"Hm?"

"What did Eugene's wife mean? Did something happen with your family here?"

He looked at her straight in the mirror. "Just a . . . it's complicated. There's been a couple of family tragedies. It's all too sad, really."

"Is that why your mother doesn't like to stay out here?" *Family tragedies.* When she blinked, she saw the figure from the mirror the night before burned into the backs of her eyelids. Where could such an awful vision come from? Could Richard's mother have seen something similar when she was a girl?

"For many reasons. But I think she didn't have an easy time growing up. The family stuff really got to her. I don't like to dwell on it." His tone became irritated. "I don't know why Eugene would tell Jennie that in the first place. At least now we know she's a gossip." He finished at the sink and went into the bedroom. "Are the girls awake? We should make them breakfast."

The mood had turned. Vivian's questions had upset him. She got the sense he did not want to be pressed further.

thirteen

NORA heard a knock at the door in the morning. When she went to answer it, Mā stood on the other side, visibly brightened. "早," she said.

"Morning," Nora said cautiously. "Are you feeling better?"

Mā nodded. "I was going to make breakfast. None of those sisters are up yet. Have you eaten?"

Nora glanced down. Suddenly she remembered everything from last night. The garden. Madeline. The pictures in her phone.

"You should eat. I'll make some tea for you, at least."

"I think we should leave."

Her mother frowned. "What?"

What could Nora tell her without sounding like she'd gone insane? Could she tell her about what had happened with Madeline? "This place . . . doesn't feel right."

It sounded ridiculous, but so did saying that vines tried to kill Madeline. She wasn't even going to touch how the flowers seemed alive and bled from their centers. Mā *had* told her never to go into the garden.

"We can't leave," Mā said. "We can't let them have the house. Just this one week, Nora. Okay? And then this is ours. And we can keep it or sell it and have it pay for school. We can even . . . You know, I'd started thinking of housing justice orgs to donate the rest to. Places that help families find affordable places to live or help families with legal assistance. . . . Like I said. Whether it's the house or the money, it's better with us than with them."

Nora imagined not having to think about how many loans to take out or which schools would give scholarships. This could be staggering, life-altering money. Still, she persisted. "But is it really ours?"

"Jiā-Jiā. Vivian gave it to us. She *owes* us."

Her skin prickled. "What for?" Mā didn't answer. Nora stood. "Did Vivian truly give us the house?"

Mā crossed her arms. "What do you mean?"

Nora stared at her mother warily. Could Lucille be right? Nora pulled her phone from her back pocket and showed her mother the picture she'd taken of the security camera screenshot. The one from July 20, 1:28 p.m.

"Mā," she said quietly, her eyes trained on her mother's face. "Was this you?"

Her mother froze. She looked up from the phone and her expression slacked. "What is—?"

"I'm asking you," Nora said, "if you were here. This is your car, isn't it?"

Mā shrank. Finally, in a quiet, hollow voice she said, "Yes. That's me."

Nora's head spun. This whole time she'd assumed that Vivian's daughters had been throwing around false accusations. They seemed so desperate for the house, it made sense they would do something as diabolical, as insane, as to frame her mother. But now—

July 20: two weeks ago, almost three now. What happened that day? Mā had told Nora she needed to go to a doctor's appointment. She didn't come back until well after dinner. *Ran into a friend*, was the excuse when Nora asked her what had taken so long. Mā had lied. Why had this been something worth lying about?

Mā's eyes didn't leave the photo. "How did you get this?"

Nora waited. She didn't trust how her voice would sound and she wanted to be firm. She deserved answers. "Doesn't matter. Why were you here?"

"It's not—" Mā's hands fell limp to her sides. "Okay." She took a deep breath. "Vivian called and asked me to come."

"*What?* Why?"

"Our families have a complicated history. She wanted to settle some things between us. 把事情给摆平了。"

"What did she want to talk about?"

"Many things in the past," her mother finally admitted. "But mostly about Ada. Her daughter."

"Who?"

"Ada." Mā looked at her squarely. "The one who died thirty-four years ago."

The words sank between them. "Died—here?"

Mā nodded.

There had been no mention of this. From Nora's research she knew that Vivian had lost her husband to a drug overdose in 1990. But she hadn't seen any mention of Vivian Yin losing a daughter, too. The two sisters above used to be three. What else did she not know? "How? What happened to her? And what did you have to do with it?"

Mā just kept shaking her head. "Nora. I can't talk about this."

"Then how can I trust you?"

Mā leaned against the doorframe and closed her eyes. "You don't believe me. You still think I did something to Vivian."

Mā had always been opaque. Nora could never figure out what she was thinking, but that didn't mean she was capable of murder. Nora was letting the Yin sisters get to her. "I'm sorry. I believe you." Nora exhaled a long breath. "You knew about the will, then? She told you she was giving you the house?"

"Not then," Mā said. "I really didn't know she was going to do that."

"Okay."

"Do you think that I need to call a lawyer?"

"I don't know. Maybe. Just in case."

Mā went to her room and closed the door behind her. Nora heard the ringing tone of her mother's phone through the wall. *Ada.* The name ricocheted around her head. The hallway lights flickered once, as if in response.

Nora squinted into the kitchen sink later that morning. There was some kind of grit collected at the bottom. Nora rinsed it away. The drain plugged up for a moment, and then the water gurgled down. Hadn't she just done this yesterday? Something skittered around the drain, and she jumped. She peered closer and then heard someone approach behind her. Madeline stood at the kitchen counter. "Oh. Hi."

Madeline looked calmer now. Her long hair fell loose over her shoulders. She was wearing another sweater this time. Not the white cardigan. It all came back to Nora then. The roots writhing and pulling Madeline into the ground. She felt a jolt of panic. She shouldn't have said what she said to Madeline. She should have offered to take care of her wound. To make sure she was okay. Why didn't Nora do that? "Are you . . ." Nora looked toward her arm.

"Oh. Sure. I'm fine."

Madeline was holding it at a strange angle, across her stomach, as if there were some invisible sling. Nora still felt anxious. But Madeline wasn't saying anything more, so Nora turned to go.

"Wait. I need to ask you something."

Nora stopped.

"What you said. Last night. Your mom had told you not to go into the garden. Has something like that . . . happened before?"

Nora tried to avoid eye contact with Madeline. She instead looked toward the glass door that led to the garden. It was firmly shut. She could see spots of pink between the balusters in the stone terrace. The roses were still there. How *had* her mother known? Another question to ask. When she stood at the edge of the garden the other night, what had she seen? Were the roses out there then? "No. I've never seen anything like that."

"Me neither," Madeline said. "I wonder what your mother knows that we don't."

Nora was still.

"Well. I wanted to say thanks." Madeline stepped around the kitchen counter, toward Nora. "Whatever happened last night would have been much worse if you hadn't been there."

Nora finally allowed herself to meet Madeline's eyes. It was like touching static. "You're really okay." She'd meant it as a question.

"Now I am. Are you?"

Before Nora could react, Madeline reached for her hand. Her touch felt cool. She turned Nora's hands slightly, so the cut from the thorns caught the light. She peered at it intently. "Does this hurt?"

Nora shook her head and swallowed. For some reason she couldn't think of what to say. Instead, she lifted Madeline's sleeve, baring the long, jagged cut. It had been hastily wrapped in what looked like shredded paper towels and hair ties. A little darkened blood had seeped through. Around the bandage, her forearm was marred with ugly scratches and spotted with purpling bruises. Nora sucked in a breath between her teeth. "This doesn't look good."

"I'll be fine," Madeline said mildly. "Really."

"You should clean it."

"I did." Madeline pulled down her sleeve as if to end the conversation. Nora stepped back. Why did she feel protective of Madeline, anyway? It was clear she didn't want any help.

"You're giving me this very intense look," Madeline observed. "Like you're trying to figure something out about me."

Too late, Nora glanced away and scrambled for something else to say. "Can I ask *you* something, then?" Madeline nodded. "What did your grandmother want from us?"

"What?"

"Why did Vivian ask my mother to come see her? Do you know what they talked about?"

Madeline looked confused. "Your mom came up here?"

"Do you not know what I'm talking about?" Nora was getting frustrated. "It's all in that folder your mom's been toting around."

Madeline pressed on. "What folder?"

Nora had assumed that Madeline was in on all of it. Wasn't she with her family all the time?

"Wait," Madeline said. "Where is this folder? And what's in it?"

Nora chewed on her lip. *Shoot.* "Never mind. It's not— It's not important."

"No, tell me. You're saying your mom did come to the house? And . . . my grandmother wanted her to?"

"I don't know? I didn't even know about it until yesterday."

"Let's work together." Madeline leaned in. Her herringbone neck-lace glittered. Nora reminded herself not to stare at Madeline's collar-bone. "I feel like our families each have their own agenda. But we both want to know what really happened. And between the two of us, we can figure it out."

The morning light shifted. *The two of us.* There was a slight furrow between Madeline's brows. Her eyes were wide. Trusting. She really *did* look like Vivian Yin, Nora realized. She had the same high cheekbones and full lips. The dreamlike expression. The profile of a starlet.

Nora had to be careful. "I'm not supposed to talk to you," she insisted, stepping back. "Not without a lawyer present."

Madeline's mouth dropped open in disbelief. Nora walked out of the kitchen and retreated down the hallway, back to her room.

fourteen

JUNE 1982

VIVIAN was sitting alone in the kitchen when her husband returned. He nudged the tie from his neck. Vivian smiled up at him. "Have you eaten?"

Richard settled down across from her. "Already did." He reached out to squeeze her shoulder as he rubbed his eyes with the heel of his other hand.

"Qīn ài de, did you not sleep well last night?" He was a light sleeper, and it had gotten worse over the past few years. He'd been having violent and specific dreams that happened over and over again, in which he was thrown from an explosion, or swept away by an avalanche. He would wake up shivering, with frigid, blue fingertips that he'd run under scalding water in the sink, as though he'd been out for hours in the cold. Sometimes he would lurch awake, certain that the house was shuddering. He'd recently been prescribed sleeping pills. Barbiturates.

"It was just a long day." He blinked hard. "I've got to get in all my meetings before I go film in Scotland."

"And how were they?"

Richard shrugged. "As good as could be. They say I need more films under my belt before I can be a director. But I think at this point they're looking for an Oscar or something. What else can I do to prove myself to them?"

"You're young," Vivian said, "to them. They think of you as their . . . their—"

"Protégé," Richard said, filling in smoothly the word that she'd been searching for in English.

"Yes."

"They're just testing me." Richard reached for his cigarettes. "They ask me to jump, just to see how high I can."

"Aiyah, my love, don't smoke," Vivian chided him. "Not in the house with children."

Richard gave her a long look. "Fine," he relented, and slotted the cigarette back into the pack.

Vivian stretched across the table, gazing sweetly up at her husband. "How about we open a bottle of wine instead?"

"Ah, the kinder poison," Richard teased. He extracted a bottle of red wine from the pantry and uncorked it. Vivian took in the ripple in the lean muscle on his forearms. Once again, she felt desire tighten inside her. He poured them both full glasses and handed her one.

"You know, my grandfather used to own a winery." Her husband fiddled with the cork with his long fingers.

"Oh? Here?"

"One of my mother's . . ." His expression dimmed. "Doesn't matter. It folded in the Depression."

"Why?" This was something else she hadn't heard. After that dinner with Eugene and Jeanette years ago, she'd gotten little from her husband on the history of this place. Nor had she bothered him about it. In general, when Richard's family came up, he tended to fall silent or change the subject, and in the end, what Vivian knew sounded like the story of any other family; cycles of fortune and misfortune. That was the way of the world, and even the Lowells weren't immune. Her mother's family had been wealthy once in Zhejiang, until they had to flee their homes because of the Japanese invasion. And Vivian wasn't exactly forthcoming about her family history, either. But now she felt the need to press him. "How did the winery fold?"

Her husband rubbed his forehead. "My grandfather's brother was a broker when the stock market crashed. Shot himself when the family lost half its money, and Pops was never the same. Or so I heard."

"天啊," Vivian whispered. "My God. I'm sorry."

So this—*this*—was the family history that Eugene's wife, Jeanette, was talking about.

They sat in silence. Her husband gave a slight, smooth shake of his head and a reassuring smile. "All in the past, sweetheart." He refilled their glasses. "God, I hope this movie is it. You know, I've done my time with movies that go nowhere. I need some serious roles. And then I can direct something. I mean, they *know* I can. It's crazy to make me keep proving myself."

At this, Vivian stiffened. She'd been naïve and assumed that once she was in Los Angeles, the film world would embrace her. But the same scene that had welcomed her husband was indifferent to her. At a single party, Richard could collect invites to several premieres and dinners; Vivian was practically invisible if he wasn't physically introducing her. Her film agent barely returned her calls. Richard went out to dinner with his all the time and could get up to three auditions booked over the course of a day. When she expressed her resentment to her husband, he tried to comfort her. He'd told her, over and over again, in the morning while she was putting on her makeup, during late nights while they were curled up together on the couch, during weekend afternoons when they helped each other rehearse lines, just how much of a star she would be. The industry didn't see how talented she was, he'd said, but they would one day. It was just a matter of time. Her big break was right around the corner. He'd made it sound so certain, so inevitable, as if it was simply a matter of waiting around. But she'd gotten impatient. Why couldn't anyone else see it in her the way her husband did? Here she was, driving all over Hollywood in the baking summer heat, waiting for her turn in her car, remembering the advice he gave her on how to speak, how to express and emote, how to make a good impression on casting directors, just to audition for supporting roles with so few lines. They dismissed her and told her she didn't look Chinese enough. Who were these men to determine what looked Chinese or not? What kind of specific, twisted visions did they have in their heads?

The roles she did get were miniscule. She hovered at the edges of sets as a maid, or spoke one line as a waitress, or dropped into one scene to give a clue to a policeman. All she'd wanted were longer speaking parts. She'd finally, after years, landed a role in an upcoming movie called *Fortune's Eye*, with actual lines and stunts. Maybe it would be different this time.

Like now, when her husband complained to her about starring in roles she couldn't even dream of having, she was careful not to betray her irritation or jealousy. He was never happy with what he had. But part of her did admire that keening, endless hunger in him. That was a part of the ambition they shared. It was good for them and for the life they were trying to make together. They still needed to pay off the construction bills on this house they'd built.

"You don't have to worry this time. The Academy will love this one." It was true. His next film was *Hamlet*. He would be performing some of the most famous monologues in the English language. The entire project was geared toward setting him up for awards season in a few years. "This will be it."

"I feel like I have that creative *instinct*, you know? And vision." He drummed his fingers around the stem of his wineglass. "And maybe I can produce one day, too."

"And you will. Who knows? Maybe I could even write a screenplay for you to star in," Vivian said. She got up to go to the kitchen counter to pour more wine.

Vivian had been nursing a small dream of writing for years. It would be set in San Francisco. A family comedy, maybe. Or a drama. Either way it would have a happy ending. Filming would be a chance for her to go up there for a while and be with her own family.

Her husband raised an eyebrow. "Screenplay? This is the first I'm hearing about this."

"I've been thinking about it for a while now," Vivian said. "If no one is going to let me audition for the roles I want, maybe I should write my own movie."

"Instead of acting?"

Vivian gave a nonchalant shrug. "Who knows? Maybe I can do both." She peeked at her husband to see his reaction. Was it too much of a leap?

But her husband's expression opened up into a brilliant smile. He joined her, his back against the counter so they faced each other. "Of course you can do it. The typewriter's all yours. Whoever you want to send it to, I'll make sure it gets to them."

Vivian's heart rose. Her husband reached to pour the wine and kissed the top of her head. "I can't wait to read what you come up with." And then he stopped short and frowned at the countertop. "It's cracked."

Vivian straightened up. "What is?" She peered at the ivory granite. It was smooth all over.

"No, here. How did it—? Do you see it?"

The crack was nowhere to be found. He was playing a joke on her. Vivian turned around, expecting to see his smile, but she was distracted by the sound of small footsteps padding toward them. Their youngest daughter stood at the edge of the living room, clutching her blanket around herself.

"Renata?" Vivian liked her full name, but Richard nicknamed her Rennie. It was easier for her other daughters to pronounce. At birth she was Richard's exact copy, with his features and a curled brown tuft of hair. Over time, though, she grew into Vivian's heart-shaped face. Her hair had darkened.

She stared up at them now with wide light brown eyes. Her hair was a mess of curls. It didn't matter that she'd been raised the most carefully, pampered with expensive toys and nutritious infant food. Their youngest couldn't sleep. She would cry and kick as an infant, and still woke up from time to time, looking alarmed and frightened as she did now.

"Sweetheart," Richard said gently. "What are you doing up?"

Renata simply stared at them.

"Bǎo bèi." *My treasure.* Vivian sighed and reached for her. "Can't sleep?"

She felt her daughter shake her head. "噩梦," she whispered in a small voice.

Vivian's gaze met Richard's. *Nightmare,* she mouthed. He was sympathetic. Immediately he reached toward his daughter. "You want to watch TV?"

"She can't watch TV this late," Vivian admonished. "It's bad for her."

"Just this time. It helps her fall asleep."

They settled on the couch. Rennie snuggled between them. They slotted in a recording of *Tom and Jerry* into the VHS player. It always worked. As the cartoons went on, her eyes blinked closed, slowly, until she was softly snoring, her lips lightly puckered.

"I'm going to put her to bed," Vivian said in a low voice. She carried her daughter upstairs, taking the steps carefully. A headache was gathering, maybe from the wine. She kissed the top of her daughter's head. Rennie was six years old and had long lost that sweet milk smell. She had grown too fast.

Gently, she lay her daughter in bed. When she stood up, she looked out the window, toward the back of the house. She stared at the reflection of the moon in the still water of the fountain and noticed that vines had begun crawling up the sides. She would bring this up to the groundskeeper, Josiah, in the morning. The fountain was so expensive. She got an aspirin for her headache before she slipped back downstairs, where her husband was watching the news again. "I'm worried about her," Vivian said as she sat back down.

"She'll be okay," Richard said, without looking away from the television. "Everyone has nightmares."

She settled into the crook of Richard's arm, watching the coverage of space explorations and gas prices, feeling warm and sleepy from the wine. "What happened with the counter?"

"It's nothing," her husband said. "I think it was a trick of the light."

"You need sleep. We should go to bed."

"You're right." He shut the television off and reached for the turntable. He put on an Anita Baker record. He leaned in conspiratorially, as if he was telling her a secret among a crowd of people. "There's a beautiful woman here in this room," he said in a low voice. "If I ask very nicely, do you think she might dance with me?"

Vivian laughed. "It's late," she said, but she was smiling all the same. How could she not? Here he was, his hand outstretched, his head tilted to the side, with his bright eyes and his patient smile. She rose from the couch, more than a little drunk now, and she felt the smooth fabric of her dress grazing her legs as she stood. They swayed from side to side to the very muted music. Vivian relaxed into her husband's arms, breathing in the faded scent of his cologne, wishing for the pressure in her head to ease. "Be safe in Scotland," she murmured. "I'll miss you."

Her husband left for filming early the next morning with a sweet note on her vanity table. Vivian had two weeks before she was headed to the set too. *Fortune's Eye* was her first western, about the life of men who traveled to mining towns to seek out riches during the gold rush. She was playing the part of Jia-Yee, a daring, devious Chinese woman who escaped a controlling and violent marriage to a merchant and traveled through the towns in search of her brother, learning to survive on her own. It was her most ambitious role yet and she wanted to get it right. Late in the day, after she'd wrapped up her table reads on one of the last afternoons before filming started, she drove to the local university library.

The set location was a hundred miles north of San Francisco, in the real ruins of a ghost town. She'd be away from her family for a month, making this the first time both she and her husband would be gone for an extended period of time. Richard was coming back in a month and a half. Edith would be taking care of the girls in the meantime.

Vivian had grown up hearing about the gold rush: that her father's great-uncle from Fujian had sailed east to find his fortune, only to never return. When she came over to America, she heard the latter half of the story from her uncle: that one of his sons journeyed over to find him and never did.

"He was looking for mountains of gold," her aunt said. "That was what they promised him. In his letters he wrote that the gold was all gone, but that there could be work found on the railroads. Then he disappeared into the Sierra Nevada Mountains and no one ever heard from him again." She clicked her teeth. Vivian had been scrubbing her daughter's underclothes in the washboard over the sink. She had peered out the window, over Chinatown. The wound of her first husband's disappearance was still fresh at the time.

But now she was far from that cramped apartment. She'd worked her way to *this*. Vivian sent her aunt and uncle a check and helped them buy a house in the Richmond district. At the beginning of her marriage, people passed on all sorts of requests through her aunt and uncle: an auntie next door who was short on cash for her emergency surgery, a neighbor who couldn't make rent, someone's daughter who needed money for her wedding. Vivian had tried to fulfill them all until her husband stepped in.

"They're not your family," he said. "When people think that you have wealth, that's all you become to them. Someone who has money. If you give it to them now, they'll never stop asking."

"But this ā-yí's like family," Vivian had said. "She always brought Lucille and Ada their favorite treats. She just needs a hundred dollars for rent. I'll do it just this once."

"Just this once," Richard admonished her. "After all the money we put into this house, we need to start saving for our family, darling. We still have three girls to raise. We can be more charitable once we're more secure."

The house *had* been expensive to build—and to take care of, even if most of it came from Richard's trust fund. Now, Vivian parked the convertible her husband had gifted her in the UCLA lot and traipsed across campus through small gatherings of students, who stared at her curiously. She loved the way this college looked, like a little village. All of her daughters would go to college. She would make sure of it.

The library intimidated her. Staring at English books for too long made her head hurt. But when she'd started auditioning for historical roles, she'd taught herself how to do research in the library so she could be prepared. Now, she sifted through catalog cards as she strung the key words together in her head: *mining towns, railroads, Chinese workers.* She followed the reference numbers deep into the stacks, dimly lit with only bare bulbs. She was poring over pictures of gold mine towns up in Northern California when she saw a familiar name: *Dalby.*

Vivian paused. Carefully she set her other books aside. She read the passage about Dalby. And then another. Soon after, she abandoned her research for the movie altogether. Dalby was Richard's mother's maiden name. Cecilia Dalby Lowell; Vivian had seen it on the wedding invitations.

It wasn't a particularly unique name. It could be a coincidence.

Vivian scoured the surrounding books and peered carefully at the back indexes. Finally, tucked between dusty biographies with worn covers and pages brittle as dead leaves, she found a thin book about the men behind the Transcontinental Railroad. She flipped to the index, and then to the pages directed.

Dalby, Amos iii, 46–50, 55

Slowly Vivian read all about Amos Dalby. He was one of the first sponsors of the western construction of the railroad, along with his college friend and business partner, William Kerr. In his first unsuccessful bid for state assembly he'd made remarks on "containing the urgent threat of the Chinaman," a phrase that made Vivian uncomfortable. He paid Chinese rail workers inferior rates and suppressed strikes by withholding their food and wages. He oversaw construction through the High Sierra Mountains amid the most brutal winters and searing summers, pushing all the way to Utah, where the Transcontinental Railroad connected.

She'd heard other stories about the railroad before. An elderly man who owned the medicine shop she'd briefly worked at in San Francisco had talked about it. His father had survived work in the Sierras. "They had to blast dynamite through the mountains," the apothecary owner said. "And accidents happened all the time. One time there was a misfire and twelve workers were blown out of a cave. It rained blood and flesh. Bà was splattered in their intestines."

Vivian had felt sick at the gruesome image. "What happened to him?"

The bronze scales clattered as he turned back to Vivian. "He kept working," he said simply. "Twelve workers replaced the dead ones the next day. But you couldn't forget about them. Oh, they wouldn't let you. If you died in that place with no one to take care of you, there was no way to send your remains back home for a proper burial and offerings. Those men became hungry, abandoned ghosts in those cold, cold mountains. 可怜. Pitiful. Bà said he could hear their cries at night in the wind."

And now she was looking down at the picture of the man who was responsible. She stared into his pale eyes and knew with increasing certainty that this man was related to her husband.

She knew her husband's family was wealthy, but she never knew it came from the railroads. Was it possible that their families' paths had crossed before? Could her father's great-uncle have been one of Dalby's underpaid workers? What if his disappearance into the mountains meant *he*—his spirit, his ghost—was stuck there too?

She could feel the pressure of a headache building behind her eyes, but she kept reading. Amos Dalby crushed unions and assigned the organizers to the most dangerous work in the dead of winter. Despite his public sentiments about the Chinese, he hired many into his house as servants. He threw extravagant parties with his wife, Laura, and his young son, Archibald, in the mansion he built on the outskirts of Los Angeles.

Vivian rocked back on her heels. It was her house. She was sure of it. Not *their* house, but a house that had once stood in the same spot, maybe the foundations of the very house she and Richard had built upon and giddily decorated, that they filled with their lives, their family's life.

She wanted to stop. But now she had to know.

Dalby's gilded life was also rife with controversy—and later, tragedy. Dalby and his business partner, William Kerr, once close confidants and loyal friends, became bitter rivals when they ran against each other for a state assembly seat, which Dalby lost. There were even rumors that Laura Dalby had an affair with Kerr, which was later confirmed in archived letters.

In the winter of 1889, Kerr died of poisoning at a party hosted at his own residence. One of his servants was charged and convicted of the murder. After a period of mourning, Dalby stepped up to be executive director of the railroad company that following spring and, eventually, ran for the House of Representatives, winning his district.

After Kerr's death, Dalby's personal life became more turbulent. His marriage to Laura deteriorated. He was said to have erratic behavior and outbursts, and he ultimately lost his congressional seat in the next election cycle. In 1894, Dalby was away in Sacramento on a trip with his son, Archie, when their Los Angeles home was broken into. Laura Dalby was found fatally stabbed the next morning. Though there was an extensive search and investigation, the murderer was never found. Bereft over Laura's death, the Dalby family receded from the public eye.

Ten years later, Dalby's twenty-four-year-old son, Archie, set out on a grand arts tour of the Mediterranean when a storm sank his ship, leaving no surviving crew. Dalby spent his remaining life alone, dying eighteen months later. The once-great railroad titan and politician is said to have perished of a broken heart in his own garden, leaving behind an estate that would become embroiled in a bitter legal battle before it eventually passed on to his nephew, Thomas Dalby.

She braced a palm against a dusty shelf to steady herself. How much did Richard know about this? She'd only heard his personal history. A private school childhood, a mother who'd moved out East from California, from the same house that Vivian and Richard would eventually tear down to build their own. His mother, who'd once proclaimed to see a ghost. Was it the ghost of Amos?

Vivian had thought that Richard's family's misfortunes only extended back forty, fifty years. But now she knew it stretched further into tragedy. A poisoning; a murder; a shipwreck; how much bad luck did this family have? For Amos to see his friends and family die, one by one . . .

Suddenly what Cecilia told Vivian at the wedding came back to her. *I tried to tell him, but I don't think he understands.*

Richard must have known, or at least been warned. He himself had told her that his family had been out here since the gold rush. That's why he'd insisted on scrapping the old walls and pillars, maintaining only the foundation, the frames, and structural systems. He wanted to build most everything anew. *We don't want the old walls,* he'd reassured her. *They're rotten. And this way we can design it exactly the way you want it.* But maybe it went deeper than that. Maybe he'd wanted to wipe the past clean.

A quiet terror punctured her. She could hear the jagged rush of her breathing. Without thinking, she yanked the pages from the book. They tore into her hand, the words split apart. What was she *doing*? Quickly, she looked around but saw no one. She stuffed the pages into her purse and slammed the book shut.

Vivian stumbled out of the library and into the sunset. The simmering heat had cooled. Shakily, she lit a cigarette in the parking lot and after she smoked, she drove home. On the way she was soothed only by the roar of the engine and the breeze flapping her silk scarf. She clutched the wheel tightly. She thought she had been the only one hiding parts of her past, but her husband had been too.

When Vivian finally got home, she stopped in the kitchen to get a cup of hot water. Edith, the housekeeper, was washing the last of the dishes.

"I'm back," she said in Mandarin, pouring from the canteen. "Where are the girls? And Josiah?"

Edith turned, her hands in rubber gloves holding a dripping sponge. She stood straight, making her seem tall despite her small stature. Her hair was pulled back and fastened with a silver clip. "Rennie's asleep. The twins are upstairs. My daughters are in their room. Josiah's watering the fuchsias in the backyard." The housekeeper paused her washing. "It's late. Would you like me to make you some dinner?"

"I ate on the way home." It was a lie. Vivian was far too on edge to be hungry. She stared down at her purse. The pages she'd torn out of the library book were still there. She peered around the house, taking it in anew. Amos Dalby had lived *here*.

Laura Dalby had been murdered here.

"Lian-er?"

Vivian jumped. "Aiyah! Don't frighten me like this."

"I'm sorry." Edith peered at Vivian more closely. Her eyebrows knotted together. "What were you looking at? You look pale."

Vivian yanked her scarf off. "Oh. Sorry. I've had a long day."

"What happened? Can I cut you some fruit?"

Vivian gripped her keys so tightly they pressed into her palm. Should she tell Edith what she'd learned in the library? They told each other everything, and when Richard wasn't around, they were free to speak in Mandarin as much as they pleased. But right before she opened her mouth, she decided against it. The kitchen counters were spotless. The girls were in bed. This house seemed so peaceful right now, she didn't want to disturb it.

Instead, she unbuttoned her blouse cuffs, grabbed a bottle of red wine off the rack, and smiled. "*Please* come drink this with me."

"There's still dishes to do."

"You can do that later. Richard is filming and I can't finish a bottle by myself. You know I'll get sick."

Edith wiped her hands on a towel, shaking her head as though this was a terrible imposition. "All right." She smiled as she pulled the rubber gloves off. She rolled down the sleeves of her plain cotton blouse and rebuttoned them.

When Vivian had asked Richard if she could hire a Chinese housekeeper, he agreed immediately. They had hired Edith first, and then her husband, Josiah, when Edith said he took good care of plants. Edith took care of her daughters and cooked them Chinese dishes when Vivian was away on set or at auditions. Josiah coaxed the garden to bloom like it never had before. He was the one who suggested dividing it into four sections in a cross shape around the fountain, divided by walking paths, sculpted in perfect symmetry. During the summer months the garden burst with roses and hydrangeas and honeysuckle and chrysanthemum; in the winters he took careful care of the camellias and sweet pea shrubs. It was only a matter of time before Vivian invited them to move their two daughters into the lower wing of the house, into the guest rooms that were never used. The Dengs were churchgoing and fiercely loyal, with no shortage of gratitude, and Vivian liked feeling generous. The first time Edith stepped foot in the house, she looked around her in wonder, at the sloping spiral staircase and the chandelier that twinkled with hundreds of crystals, and then at Vivian. In that moment, Vivian knew what Edith was thinking: that never could she have imagined a Chinese family occupying a house like this.

Things were different when it was just the two of them. When Richard was around, they all spoke English to one another and maintained a certain sense of formality, even if he was nothing but warm to the Dengs. But Vivian and Edith shared recipes and celebrated holidays together and sang karaoke in the car. Double happiness, 囍. That was the phrase that decorated the rim of their porcelain bowls. To Vivian it no longer just represented her happy marriage; it represented their two happy families, too. Now Edith knew her way around the house as well as Vivian did. And when Richard was gone on trips, or away filming like he was now, the formality melted away.

Vivian poured Edith a full glass of merlot.

"Lian-er," Edith chided, watching the glass fill. Edith called her by her nickname. It warmed Vivian's chest. When she called her Lian-er, Vivian knew she was safe to tell her everything. "We can't get drunk in the middle of the week."

"Why not?" Vivian tried to sound playful. "Who's to stop us?" She took a sip of wine and massaged her neck. Edith tapped her fingers around the base of the glass and smiled. "Well. Meng-Meng might come down for a cup of milk later." Edith used Rennie's childhood nickname, too.

"She was the most peaceful one to carry, you know. The twins were the worst. 天啊, the two of them would kick me so much I couldn't sleep. But Meng-Meng, she slept when I did. Through the night." She leaned forward. "I have these bad dreams sometimes . . . nightmares. My mother had nightmares too. But the whole time I was pregnant with her, I rarely had one."

She said this absentmindedly, but immediately she could feel the weight of Edith's gaze settle upon her, and a new fear swept over Vivian. Could Renata have inherited her dreams, and that's why she could never sleep? Was it possible she had absorbed Vivian's nightmares in the womb?

"What kind of nightmares?" Edith asked, interrupting Vivian's spiral.

"Just . . ." Vivid images rose behind her eyes. A nondescript face, the eye sockets filled with dirt, turned directly toward her. Floors slick with blood. Then something clicked. She thought of what she'd read that afternoon, how Laura Dalby had been murdered here and she hadn't been found until the next morning. There must have been so much blood . . . .

She jumped and knocked into her wineglass. It tipped over and shattered on the countertop.

"Lian-er!"

Vivian looked down. The wine had splashed onto her dress and pooled in her lap. She gasped and pushed herself off the chair.

"Don't touch the glass. I'm going to clean this up." Edith was tugging back on the rubber gloves. "Lian-er, what's going on?"

"I don't know what's gotten into me today," she said in shock. This was her good skirt and her crepe blouse. She'd probably stained it forever.

"I have bad dreams sometimes, too," Edith said. She carefully swept the glass into a paper bag and got a towel for the wine, pausing before she bent down to look into Vivian's eyes. "But they're just dreams, at the end of the day. They can't hurt us."

Vivian looked up. She wanted to ask Edith about her dreams, but just then she heard Renata's voice.

"Māmā."

"Oh— Bǎo bèi, what is it?"

Her daughter stood in the living room, dressed in her satin pajamas. "I wanted to drink some milk. Ā Yí said it would help me sleep."

"Ah," Vivian said. She glanced over at Edith, who was smiling now that her prediction had come true. "Here, let me microwave some milk for you. Ā Yí is busy right now."

Rennie stared at them. "What happened?"

"妈妈 was having some wine." Vivian put a cup of milk into the microwave. Her ruined skirt clung to her. "I spilled a bit."

"Can I have some?"

Vivian laughed and retrieved the now-warm cup. She set it down on the kitchen counter and kissed her daughter's forehead. "Milk is better for you."

She watched Rennie hold the cup with both hands and sip from it. Behind her, Edith swept up the remnants of the glass.

"I'm full," her daughter announced. "But I don't want to go to sleep. I want to stay here with you and Ā Yí. Can I watch TV?"

"No," Vivian said firmly. This was Richard's fault: now her daughter couldn't fall asleep without the television on. "You have to go to bed."

Renata didn't budge.

Vivian tried something else. "How about I tell you a story? Sūn Wù Kōng?"

Her daughter reluctantly nodded.

Vivian glanced back at Edith apologetically. Her housekeeper nodded toward Vivian with a small smile, as if to say, *Go on, it's fine.* The tips of her gloves were red.

Vivian led her daughter up the stairs. She paused at the top for a moment, listening to the voices coming from the room to her left. The twins had gathered in Ada's room, whispering and giggling. From downstairs, Vivian could hear Edith and Josiah murmuring quietly.

This house was full. She was surrounded by family, preparing to tell her youngest a story. Edith was right. Dreams couldn't hurt them.

Rennie crawled into bed and pulled the blankets all the way up to her chin. She blinked expectantly and Vivian spoke.

"Once upon a time, there was a mischievous monkey god named Sūn Wù Kōng. After he wreaked havoc on heaven, he was imprisoned under a very heavy mountain for thousands of years. But then a monk came and freed him, so Sūn Wù Kōng could help him look for sacred texts out west . . ."

Vivian sat at the desk in the small glow of the lamp, staring out over the polished floors and crowded shelves of the library. This used to be a ballroom, Vivian recalled. A decaying ballroom with no chandelier and a warped ceiling that was caving in on itself. They'd torn it all down and put in wall-to-wall built-in bookshelves. The ceiling was repainted a solid olive.

This was her home now. Yin Manor. There was nothing here she hadn't deliberated on herself, and yet she still felt like an intruder. Unwelcome, but trapped.

Here she was, a Chinese woman, distantly related to a railroad worker, living on the estate of a former railroad magnate. She hadn't known that's where the family money came from, but did it matter? Amos Dalby had bent the land to his will by crushing the labor out of immigrants until death.

She pulled out her address book. The number for the apothecary she used to work at wasn't in there, though it should have been. How often she'd wanted to call and ask for recipes that would calm her nausea during her pregnancy with Rennie. But now she didn't need to ask about specific herbs. She wanted to ask about the railroad.

She tried hard to summon his phone number. The screech of the dial tone startled her. She tried another, similar number. Nothing.

Then she dialed her aunt's house and leaned back, stretching the phone cord as far as it could go.

"Hello?"

Her relief was immediate. "姑姑!"

"Ah, Lian-er!" Her aunt's voice was bright. "How are you?"

"Good, good. I'm filming for another movie soon. Listen, I was wondering. Do you remember 苏伯伯? Do you remember him? I wanted to make a medicine brew. Do you know his number?"

Her aunt paused. Then her tongue clicked. "It's no longer there, Lian-er."

"The—apothecary?"

"There's another one on Grant now. Mr. Siu passed away a few years ago. Stroke, I think. I remember him. We used to get cold medicine for the twins there, remember? Aiyah, he knew everything."

"Yes, I remember," Vivian said faintly. He had been old, even back then. It had been seven years since she saw him last. Nine years since he'd mentioned the story about his father working on the railroad. The stories, the history, her history—that was all gone now. "I'm sorry to hear that."

"Do you need something from the new apothecary? I can ship it to you. Is something wrong?"

"No, nothing," Vivian said hurriedly. She scrambled for an excuse. "My . . . husband is just having trouble sleeping. But that's okay. He's going to the doctor for it."

"I can try to ask for him. And what about you? What about the girls?"

"We're all right," Vivian said. "No need to worry."

"That's good. They should visit San Francisco sometime."

"Of course. We'll try to find a time when we're both off work. Maybe in the summer."

"Great. Listen." Her aunt's voice caught slightly. "Remember Wu Ā-Yí? The woman who works at the market downstairs from our apartment?"

"Yes, I do." She'd always given Vivian extra coconut bread for her daughters.

"Well, she's going through a hard time right now. Her rent just went up. They're evicting people all over San Francisco, Lian-er. She's also paying for her daughter's college and . . . is there any way you could help her out, do you think?"

There it was. A small bit of discomfort curdled in her stomach. "I . . . I'll see what I can do. I have to ask my husband."

There was a pause. "Okay. Okay."

They hung up soon after and Vivian sat in silence. Every time she called her aunt there was always another of these requests. It was starting to grate on her. Maybe Richard was right.

She stared at her international phone cards. It occurred to her then that the person she really wanted to talk to about all of this was her husband. He was fast asleep now, and it would be the middle of the night over there. But she longed for his steadiness. She imagined them sitting on the living room couch. She could see his patient smile, the way he tilted his head to think of something to reassure her. He'd clasp her hand and rub the inside of her wrist with his thumb until she felt calmer.

But what could he say to—this? If he had reacted badly to Jeanette Lyman making a passing reference, how would he react if she brought up the ghosts of his past by name? Told him she'd found them in a book? What if she was the first to tell him about what Amos had done on the railroads? Did it even matter, now that nothing could be done to change it?

Her panic became a strange, sympathetic pain. Vivian couldn't tell if she felt sorry for her husband, or angry that he had kept her in the dark. But what did she want him to do? Why did she feel like he needed to speak for his ancestors? Hadn't he given her so much? He'd loved her and supported her in everything she did. His wealth had let her order decor and hire help without a second thought. They were rich enough that each of her daughters got a room to themselves. And here she was, anxious about ghosts and history.

Besides, her husband had loved her in spite of her past. How could she not do the same for him? How could she resent him for a past that he had no say in? He had protected her from this; he'd wanted to imagine a way forward, with her and with their daughters. Wasn't that exactly what she had hoped for?

Vivian heard her cry out.

She was standing at the doorway and looking at the woman in her bed, who was hunched over, clutching her neck. The woman looked up through matted cords of hair and her dark eyes found Vivian's.

It was *her.* Laura Dalby.

Bright, viscous blood spurted between the woman's fingers. Her mouth twisted in pain. Blood bubbled through her teeth. Her lips moved and her chest heaved, but Vivian could only hear a strained, wet rasp.

Vivian finally started toward her. But before she could reach the woman, she felt something grab her by the shoulder and drag her back.

"Stop—" In her startled state only Mandarin came out. "She's *dying!*"

Too late—it was all too late. She heard a hiss behind her and she turned, slowly, to see a stranger. He bared his teeth and looked straight at Vivian. "*You're not supposed to be here.*"

Vivian scrambled awake, shivering in sweat, tangled in her own sheets. She leaped from her bed and stared at it. She circled it. The bed was different from the one in her dream. But the room—it was this room. The same bedroom she had dreamed of years ago when they'd moved in. The time she dreamed that *she* was the one bleeding out.

fifteen

MADELINE woke up early in the morning so that she could go downstairs before Mā. She pulled a sweater over her head and gritted her teeth when it brushed the long gash on her left arm. The dull pain was persistent. There were smaller cuts. Her bruises around the cuts were purpling. It still looked ugly.

She made her way downstairs and pulled open the library doors. Miraculously, her mother wasn't there. She crept toward the desk, which was piled high with stacks of papers. She picked through them gingerly. An old, stiff magazine was tossed to the side. Then she spotted the manila folder.

Everyone in this house knew something about her grandmother that she didn't. Even Nora, who had apparently been trying to siphon information from her family all this time. *And yet she saved you.* Of all the things she could not figure out about Nora, this was what puzzled her the most: that after days of total silence, Nora pulled her free from the garden. Then scolded her and disappeared again, then told her they couldn't speak to each other. The confusion had compounded over days into a kind of maddening frustration; she wanted to know everything that was going on in Nora's head, but she knew Nora would never divulge anything to her. Her stoic expression revealed nothing.

Madeline plucked the manila folder up and set it on top of the other papers. There was the preliminary autopsy report; Madeline flipped through it. And then something stopped her. Finally, she saw the full-page printout of what looked like security camera footage. In the center of the page was a car that looked familiar to Madeline. A car that was parked outside right now.

She was looking at Elaine Deng's car. And sure enough, the date and time marked at the bottom matched up with what Nora had told her: July 20.

Elaine *had* come to the house after all.

And from what Nora had said, Wài Pó had wanted her there.

But why? Maybe Nora was lying. Or maybe—

"What are you doing?"

Madeline spun around and faced her mother.

Mā's eyes widened. She shut the door behind her and marched across the room to grab the manila folder.

"Why did Elaine come here in July?"

Mā set the folder on the desk. "Why do you think?"

Madeline was afraid to even say this part out loud. "You think that she came up here to . . . ?"

Her mother nodded. "And now we know for sure."

"Well, we know she came up here. We don't know what for."

"The autopsy places Wài Pó's death around the weekend of July 20. The timing, Madeline. This, the tox report—it all adds up."

"But *Wài Pó* called the lawyer to change the will. Not Elaine."

"This shows Elaine here at one-thirty p.m. The will was changed at six. You don't think Elaine could have broken in and forced her to change the will? Held her at gunpoint? Poisoned her to a state of delirium? You don't understand that family. I do. They're leeches. They'll do anything to get this house."

"What do you mean? What were they like?"

Mā drew herself up. "Elaine was always jealous of what we had. Everyone could see it. Even though Mā gave her family everything. She even paid for part of Elaine's college degree." She scoffed. "But it was never enough for her. Some people just can't be grateful for what they're given until they take everything you have."

Madeline frowned. "But what if Wài Pó gave it to her? Didn't she ask Elaine to come?"

"What do you mean? She asked Elaine to come?"

"I—" Now Madeline realized that she knew something Mā didn't. An instinct she'd likely inherited from her mother told her to hold on to that for a bit. To feel things out first. At least until she knew what she believed. "I don't know. I just assume it's hard to break into a house."

Mā looked around as though surveilling for an enemy. "Never assume. The nurse could have left the door unlocked, for all we know." Suddenly she focused her sharp gaze on Madeline. "What's wrong with your arm?"

"Oh." Madeline looked at her arm, which she realized she had been holding horizontally against her stomach. She peeled her sleeve up a little, to where the scrapes showed. "That's the other thing I wanted to talk to you about. I was just walking behind the house, and—"

"Were you in the garden?" Mā's voice rose. "Madeline, I *told* you to stay inside."

Madeline felt, again, like a scolded child. "I know. But I was curious, and there were roses growing out there, so I went to see." She stopped. What could she say next? That she was attacked by the garden? It felt ridiculous in this moment under Mā's probing eyes, even if her arm did ache. She peeled back down her sleeve. She didn't even want to show her mother the large cut.

"This is *why I told you.* No one's been back there for decades. God knows what's out there, animals or ticks. Stay inside. Okay? I can't be worrying about both the house and about you getting scratched up in whatever grows out of that mess these days." Mā's eyelids fluttered. "And just . . . keep an eye on . . . that. If it gets worse, we'll have to do something about it. But go get yourself some breakfast for now. I got some food from the store. I'm going to work."

"Fine," Madeline said curtly. "Let me help you."

"I've got this under control. Don't worry."

Madeline insisted, "This matters to me. I've got nothing else to do. I'm losing my mind here."

"Find something to occupy yourself. This case is delicate. I don't need you in it."

Case? A flush of rage came over Madeline. This was all it was to her mother, then? "Well, God forbid I get in the way of your big fucking *case.*"

The room was silent for a moment until Mā turned toward her. "*What?*"

"That's how it's always been, hasn't it? There's always some big case or campaign event. Nothing will ever matter to you more." Madeline stepped back. Her eyes started to smart. "This isn't a case. It's our family. And you're cutting me out!" Dimly she thought to calm down. But she felt wounded. She said quietly: "It's exhausting being your daughter. I just ruin everything for you, don't I?"

Mā recoiled. Madeline didn't know what she would do.

"This is all *for you,*" Mā finally spat. "I'm doing everything I can to set things right for our family." Her eyes flashed. "You want something to do? Go apply to jobs and stop feeling sorry for yourself. I can't believe I raised you to be like this."

Madeline stood there for a moment, seething, before she stalked out of the library. She gnashed her teeth on the inside of her cheek until she could taste blood.

Madeline stomped through the silent house and up the stairs. The door to her aunt's room was closed. Locked, probably. Madeline stood at the threshold, fuming. Trying, like she always had, to rationalize on behalf of Mā. *She's anxious. Grieving. Processing this in her own time.* This is what she got for starting an argument. Hadn't she learned? To challenge her mother was like starting a fire and putting her hand in the flame. She knocked on her aunt's door with more force than she'd intended.

She heard shuffling inside, then the door opened. Aunt Rennie peered out. "Madeline?" She took stock of her niece. "Are you okay?"

"Can I come in?"

"Yes—of course." Aunt Rennie wavered, and then the door opened wider. Madeline entered a room strewn with clothes. They hung over the bed frame and piled up on the white chair in the corner. The wallpaper was printed with a pattern of ferns. Her aunt had changed into baggy jeans and her hair was clipped up. A stained T-shirt lay on the floor. Aunt Rennie kicked it away. "What's going on?"

"Did something happen in the house between Elaine and Wài Pó? Or something between your families?"

Aunt Rennie's face fell. "What do you mean?"

"Please tell me the truth, Yí Mā. I want to know." Madeline's voice lowered. "There is security footage of Elaine coming to the house before Wài Pó died. But apparently she asked her to come. Would you know why?"

Aunt Rennie looked slightly bewildered. Then she sank into her bed. "I don't know, Madeline." Her voice was barely audible. "I really don't."

"Can *you* ask? Maybe Mā will tell you."

Her aunt shrugged, although it looked more like a shudder. "What good would it do?"

"Don't you want to know the truth? Doesn't it bother you that my mother has shut both of us out of this?"

"That's just her way of doing things. But she's either going to win this fight or she'll scare them into settling. I know she'll get us the house back."

"It's not about the house."

Aunt Rennie stood up then, alarmed. "What happened? What did your mother say to you?"

"She just—" Madeline's breaths came out in short bursts. "She doesn't trust me. I wanted to help her, and she said that I would ruin it. I'm just—always—another problem to her."

Aunt Rennie folded Madeline into a hug. Under her aunt's usual floral perfume, a stale sourness lingered. "I know what your mother is like," she said quietly. "I know she's difficult. But it's just the family history. Some things are too painful to know about. It's better you didn't."

What did that mean? "But it's *my* family too. I hate feeling like the only person on the outside. I feel like I'm going insane here. I see things that disappear. I can't make sense of anything."

Her aunt peeled Madeline away from her. "What do you mean?"

"The vines in the library. I saw them, and then they were gone the next morning." Madeline paused. She unfurled her palm, revealing the scrapes. "I was out in the garden, too. And it . . . it hurt me."

Aunt Rennie stood perfectly still. There was a brief pause. Then she said, with sudden force: "Stay away from that garden. Didn't we tell you?"

"Okay. But—?"

"Stay in this house. Or even just—in your room. You're safer there. And we'll leave soon."

"Safe from what?"

"Just do as I say."

"What's out there? Does Mā know?"

Aunt Rennie's dark brown eyes trained on her, but they took on a strange, fevered look. Her high cheekbones were flushed with color.

"She never sees anything," she said hollowly. "Or believes anyone. She called you crazy. Didn't she?"

sixteen

LUCILLE stared straight ahead at the bookshelves.

It is exhausting being your daughter.

Her eyes smarted. She tried not to think of how wounded Madeline had looked. But was she wrong? What good could her daughter do? Hadn't this all been to protect her?

Lucille sat down at the desk. She laid the magazines to one side and sifted through years of pamphlets, take-out menus, stamps, and newspaper clippings. A righteous fury consumed the sick feeling. Hadn't her entire life been about trying to provide her daughter with the opportunities she herself had? What more could Madeline demand? The words swam in front of her. She felt a heavy pressure behind her eyes. When she couldn't take it anymore, she picked up her phone and called Daniel.

Mā had liked her ex-husband. She barely acknowledged whatever Rennie's marriage with that art collector was. Neither did Lucille, to be honest. But *she* had taken pains to do everything right. She met Daniel Wang at law review in their Stanford days, and from the moment she spoke to him it had been a meticulous battle of wills. He had a quiet, ruthless confidence, and Lucille fell faster than she could ever allow herself to admit. She went to his house for the holidays and his parents made her beef noodles. Lucille ached with happiness to see a Chinese family that still gathered around the kitchen table. She and Daniel both made partner at their respective law firms within two years of each other. They competed with each other, fought with each other, fucked each other with that same reciprocal ferocity. She liked that she was always trying to impress him, and vice versa. They'd raced each other to become their most successful and virtuous selves.

But recent years had strained them, her congressional campaign most of all. Missed school pickups and events wore on him. When she found out she had lost her county by a few points, Daniel turned away from her, tense with shame, before he reached out to halfheartedly comfort her. She'd shut herself away from him; she preferred to process her pain in private. They both did. She'd failed him and herself. It was unforgivable. Two months later, she discovered photos of his firm's female partner on his phone.

Now he picked up on the second ring. "Lucy?"

She swallowed. "Am I a bad mother?"

"What?"

"I just want to know. Tell me. You were there. Did I never care about my daughter?"

He sighed. "What exactly are you trying to say? What did Madeline do?"

"Was I a monster who focused on her future career and nothing else? After all the years I put her through private school and all her extracurriculars? Is that it? Is that true?" She waited a beat. Already she was lining up arguments in her head to eviscerate his points.

But when he spoke his voice was gentle. "You're just ambitious, Lucy. You know I loved that about you. I always have."

She was taken aback by the tenderness of it. To her shock, tears spilled out.

"But you did . . ." He paused. "You had your own agenda. You always prioritized your achievements. I don't know. Sometimes you did leave us behind. And that hurt me. And our kid."

Neither of them spoke. She heard the background noise of his office through the silence. "It was the campaign, wasn't it?" *That ended us.*

She heard him exhale hard through his nose. "In a way, yes."

"So I'm responsible for everything that happened," Lucille said icily. He loved her ambition and yet couldn't stand her *actually* doing what it took to accomplish her dreams. "I ruined everything."

"I'm not—"

"My ambition fucked your coworker and ruined everything we built between us. Right?"

"What—" There was a pause. His voice lowered. "Jesus, Lucy! What the hell? Are you okay? What's going on? Are you still at your mother's house?"

"Yep. I'm saving it for us."

"Still? Are you serious? You haven't called my contact? Or an actual estate lawyer? I can reach out—"

"*Don't*," she snarled. "I've got it under control. *I* can bring the case."

"Right, but—it's not that. Believe me, I know you're good at what you do. But this is *not that*."

Lucille contemplated hurling her phone across the room and imagined it splintering against the doors. Instead, she hung up and tossed it on top of the papers. She missed when she could snap a phone shut decisively or slam it onto the receiver. She sat for a moment, full of rage.

Focus.

She looked back at the desk. Her mother's leather-bound address book lay in the far-right corner. There was a stack of papers wrapped carefully in a brown pocket sleeve. Lucille unwrapped it. The words on the title page were still legible, despite the paper being brittle:

ALL HAPPY FAMILIES

VIVIAN YIN

Lucille flipped through the papers. It was a screenplay. Mā had never shared it or talked about it, as far as she knew. It must have been locked away for decades. It was about a hundred pages. Lucille was just about to settle in and start reading when she noticed that the last pages in the stack were on different paper, smoother and thicker, and typed with a different font. They were letters. One read:

DEAR MRS. LOWELL, THANK YOU FOR SUBMITTING ALL HAPPY
FAMILIES FOR OUR CONSIDERATION. I REMEMBER BEING

INTRIGUED BY THE CONCEPT OF A FAMILY COMEDY WHEN
EUGENE PITCHED IT TO ME.

HOWEVER, I AM NOT SURE THIS FITS THE TONE OF MY
CURRENT SLATE OF PROJECTS. I FOUND MYSELF AT TIMES NOT
BEING ABLE CONNECT WITH THE STORYLINE. FOR NOW I MUST
PASS—

Eugene Lyman. Reid's father, the producer. Lucille flipped to the next one.

I AM SO SORRY THAT—
WITH REGRET, I MUST PASS—

Rejection letters.

Lucille sat up. Mā had been a screenwriter. Why did she never know? Were there other scripts, too? Lucille could imagine Mā now, hunched over this desk, typing furiously on their old Smith Corona, and then on the word processor that replaced it.

The first letter was dated November 18, 1987. So she'd written the screenplay after she won the Oscar. Maybe becoming an actress had only been the beginning for her. She must have had her own dreams and private ambitions. Dad had always wanted to produce. He'd launched his production company in 1988. Two years before his overdose.

One last page was stuck to the back of the stack, and Lucille pried it away gently, trying her best not to crack the stiff paper. But as she slipped it out, she realized it wasn't a rejection; it was a form. She scanned the letterhead.

PALISADES PSYCHIATRIC CENTER

She sat back. In clear handwriting below, Lucille read:

This recommendation for consultation is for: Vivian Yin.

· · ·

Lucille didn't move from her chair for hours as she read Mā's screenplay. The light waned outside and she didn't get up to turn on the stained-glass lamps, until finally, she put down the screenplay because it had gotten too dark to read. A few pages were missing here and there, but she could piece the story together. The script followed the dismal love lives of three cousins against the backdrop of a big San Francisco Chinatown family. It was full of dry wit and sharp characters. Studios would love it today, probably. But it didn't matter. They hadn't wanted stories like this back then.

Had Mā wanted to be a screenwriter? Was that why she gave up acting? Lucille remembered the buoyant joy she had felt when she watched her mother win the Oscar. Mā could have done anything after that night, it seemed. There were dinners with producers, and paparazzi that lingered wherever they went as a family. But she hadn't booked many roles the next year, or the year after that. Instead, their mother drove out to auditions and came home and fought with Dad. They stopped watching TV or making weekend breakfasts together. Dad started coming home late and going on longer filming trips. When he was home, plates were broken and doors slammed.

Dimly, she heard voices and a knock at the library door, with Rennie asking if she wanted dinner. Lucille ignored it. When she finally shook herself out of her stupor, she returned to the last piece of paper. The printed letters were faded, the pen marks even more so, but she recognized her father's large, looping scrawl.

He had been the one to recommend her. That summer. 1990.

Reasons for consultation: *signs of erratic behavior, signs of paranoia, disturbed dreams. Exhibits signs of mental distress.*

Lucille did have one stark memory of her mother throwing herself against the balustrade of the terrace during that summer. And then she'd left the house and driven away. Her parents had been arguing about the smallest things: which plane tickets to buy to France, the roles Mā should audition for, whether to send Rennie to a performing arts camp. It all seemed so minute now compared to what had happened. But had her mother been unwell? Was she agitated over her marriage? Over her screenplay? Or something else?

Signs of paranoia. Disturbed dreams.

She went back to the psychiatric facility recommendation and pulled the hospital website up on the computer. The homepage featured serene, smiling faces. She imagined her mother's face among them.

She picked up her phone and called the number on the website.

"Palisades Hospital."

"Hi. I'd like to inquire if you have history of patient records—"

"That information is confidential, ma'am."

"I'm her daughter. My mother had a consultation scheduled?"

"Do you have the consent of the patient in question?"

"Well, my mother's dead."

There was only a short pause. "I'm so sorry to hear. You can request information only if you had the permission of your mother prior to her death."

Lucille bit her tongue. "Thank you. Take care." She hung up.

There was no point to this. The recommendation was given in 1990, thirty-four years ago. The likelihood that they could even access her mother's records, if she had any, were slim.

She searched "Vivian Yin" on Google images. There were grainy photos of her in her signature silk red dress in 1986, the Oscar clutched in her hands. There were pictures of her dust-streaked face in *Fortune's Eye.* Lucille scrolled further. There was a picture of her mother with other actresses; she recognized Daisy. Daisy had been Mā's friend; she had talked on the phone with her all the time from the living room. Lucille searched for Daisy's number in the address book and called.

A deep voice answered. "Hello?"

"Is this Daisy Rubin? This is Lucille Wang. I'm Vivian's—"

"I don't know who that is."

She faltered. "Sorry," she said shortly. "Wrong number." She hung up.

She typed Daisy Rubin into the search bar and sat back. Daisy had passed away from breast cancer in 2015.

She pushed the keyboard away from her and started to panic. She rooted through the address book. There were screenwriters and producers and cleaning agencies and schools. She turned to the front. On the first page, in the rudimentary Mandarin that Lucille recognized, were the words for aunt: 姑姑.

Lucille snapped up her phone again.

"Hello?" The voice was stiff and raspy with age.

She tipped forward. "Is this—"

"Mary Fang. Who is this?"

"I'm Vivian Yin's daughter. Lucille. I was wondering if you knew my mother."

The line went silent.

"Hello?"

"No," Mary said bitterly. "No, we didn't. Your mother made sure of it."

Lucille frowned. "I'm sorry?"

"You know, I always wondered what it would be like to meet you." Mary sounded spiteful. "Mā always talked about it. Our cousin she took care of. Who married and moved to Los Angeles in her fancy house with the wealthy actor and became too good for the rest of us."

Lucille curled her fist around the pen in her hand.

"I heard you grew up with live-in nannies. Did you eat dinner on plates of gold? Have expensive paintings on your walls?"

"You seem angry. Did my mother do something to you?"

There was a long silence.

"You know, our mother used to call yours every year. Chinese New Year and the holidays. She'd send letters. She was worried. Your mother seemed alone, all isolated out there with him. But she stopped answering." Mary paused. "Families look out for each other, you know. Mā cared for Vivian and took her in like she was her own daughter. But once she got where she needed to be, she cut the rest of us out. She chased her dreams and left us behind."

"She—" Lucille's words wedged in her throat. There was nothing more she could say, nothing that could move the conversation where she wanted to. "I'm sorry for bothering you. Take care."

She hung up. Mary's words grated on her. What, was it a crime to pursue your own career? No wonder Mā didn't want to be involved with them. They seemed insufferable.

But at the same time, Lucille was coming to the realization that there was no one alive now who knew her mother, not any more than she and her sister did. There were no more connections. Her mother had died alone, truly alone, and all Lucille had was a screenplay, photos, magazine clippings, and a form from the psychiatric facility.

Lucille stood. Was she just hotheaded with anger or was this room warm? She wiped sweat from her forehead. She faced the bookshelves again and noticed that a new book seemed to be jutting out today. Someone had been touching them, and she hated the thought that it could be Elaine or Nora. Lucille reached out for Mā's copy of 红楼梦. *Dream of the Red Chamber.*

A pressed flower fell out, along with a few crumbles of dirt.

Lucille jumped back and slammed the book shut, scattering dust. She went to a different shelf and pulled out another. There, between the cover and title page, was a bright orange poppy that looked so fresh and vibrant, its colors seemed to bleed onto the page. She threw the book on the table. Now she was shaking. Even though she didn't want to know, she couldn't stop herself after that from taking out book after book after book.

Flowers were pressed in every copy.

There was no way.

Had *she* been here all this time? Was she living in this house right now, watching them? Slipping flowers between the pages just to mess with Lucille's head?

Lucille picked up the next book and found a rose petal inside. She hurled the book across the room and it struck a wooden panel with a splitting crack.

She stood in shock. *What was she doing?* She rushed over and picked the book up, brushing the dirt off, she checked the inside cover again.

Nothing. No mark or residue. No flower.

She sat back on her heels, on the floor of the library. The wall panel that she hit had splintered and a corner had come loose from the wall. Had she really thrown the book with such force? She tested the wood like she would a loose tooth. It came away under the slightest pressure, and a rotten, fleshy odor oozed from the gap.

Lucille lurched back for a moment. Then, holding her breath, she probed farther into the crack, behind the back of the paneling. Her fingers met something spongy and warm.

Something crawled onto her arm. She yelped and scurried away backward on her hands and heels, stomping at the thing as it fell. She stared at her stained fingertips and then looked down at the crushed shell of a small bug.

These walls were packed solid—filled—with dirt.

Dirt trickled from the gap in the loose paneling. Something, a tendril, a vine—slithered out.

Lucille shoved the panel back in place, trapping the vine, and tried to force it to stick. The wood felt skin-warm, and she swore it pulsed for a second, bulged slightly, before it went still.

Panic seized her now. She stood and kicked it, once, twice, and finally it stuck.

Lucille stared at the wall, breathing heavily. Dirt in the walls. Dirt in the sink.

She wiped her hands on her pants. She felt hot and sick. She focused on holding back the revulsion that shuddered through her body. The smell lingered; that earthy, ripe, rotten smell.

She went back to her desk and paged through the books. Still no flowers.

Was she seeing things? She couldn't stay in this room for another minute. It could be grief. Or lack of sleep. But above all, she needed to be able to trust herself. The address book was open in front of her, and she finally remembered what she was doing an hour ago.

Lucille stared at the name: Eugene Lyman. She called the number. A terrible screeching sound emitted from the phone; the line was long out of use. Finally, she called another number— the one she had saved only days ago.

"Hello?"

"Reid," Lucille said, her voice cracking in relief. "Can we meet up?" She shut her eyes. "I want to talk to you."

RENNIE returned to her room after scrounging up a dinner of leftovers from the fridge, accompanied by a few glasses of wine and some disapproving looks from Lucille. She felt sufficiently buzzed and sleepy now.

She opened the door and the first thing she saw across the room was the Oscar trophy.

Rennie scrambled for the light switch. Hadn't she buried it back in the bottom of her mother's vanity drawer? But even with the lights on, the trophy was still there.

Could she have some strange gap in her memory? Had she blacked out? Forgot that she carried it back? God, was she drinking *that* much?

Rennie shuffled forward uncertainly. She reached out her fingertips and brushed the surface. Then she grasped the trophy in her hand.

This had happened once before. Nearly forty years ago, the night she saw the broadcast of her mother at the Academy Awards. Rennie had sat so close to the television, nose almost pressed to the glass, that Edith later joked that it was like Rennie was about to jump into the TV itself. She didn't tell anyone what had happened earlier that day. That she had sat in front of the mirror at Mā's vanity, and for a moment, seen an older version of herself, all done up with makeup, clutching an award in her hands. That night she'd gone to bed vibrating with excitement after seeing her mother win the Oscar on live television. The next morning she had woken up to the same award perched on her nightstand. Her fate was there, laid out in front of her, sure as the turn of time.

It had been the beginning of her dream of becoming an actress. A dream that buoyed her through boarding school and all the way to New York City. She persisted through early morning wake-up calls and long audition lines, rehearsing until her voice went hoarse, hoping for it all to happen in due time. Rennie imagined her mother talking to her, hearing her voice as if she were right in front of her in the dressing room, fixing her costume before the community play. *Chin up. Keep that smile. Look at a place beyond the crowd. I made you beautiful,* 宝贝. *Go make me proud.* She wanted to make it just like Mā had.

But somewhere along the way her dream sharpened into desperation. She remembered New Year's Eve in 1998, on the cusp of the new millennium. Twenty-two-year-old Rennie had wandered home in the snow to her windowless apartment in the East Village with hallways that smelled like oil and old paint. She was alone and yet she felt held by this wondrous city and carried by its incandescent vitality. She remembered how anxiously she had waited for that call from her agent; oh, how *badly* she wanted to hear that she'd beat out the other two girls in the final auditions. She would have done anything to be able to call her mother and tell her she'd gotten the Scorsese role.

She had sat on the floor of that apartment, eating deli chicken in measured mouthfuls to stay slim in the heavy sequined dress she was planning on wearing to her friend's party later that night. She thought about her family. Lucille was probably being boring and pre-studying for her next semester law classes out in California, in an apartment strung up with Christmas lights that she shared with her boyfriend, Daniel. Rennie wondered if she would ever find someone.

She spent that evening watching the landline for a call that never came. In another world, that moment could have been the start of it all.

Now Rennie sat on her childhood bed in her childhood bedroom, cradling her mother's trophy in her hands.

The lights flickered.

"You always wanted this, didn't you? Now it's yours."

Rennie's head snapped up. In the reflection in the window, her mother stood behind her, her eyes drilling into Rennie's.

The trophy fell to the floor. Rennie hunched over, squeezing her eyes shut.

She's not there. It's in your head. It's all in your head, don't you see?

Rennie stayed trembling on the floor, trying to focus on her breath, her pulse thumping in her ears. The room stayed quiet. She looked up. She was alone. But the room was dark.

Rennie ran to the light switch and flipped it. Nothing. The lights must have short-circuited again. She brushed dust and dirt off the light switch and walked back to her bed in a daze and sank into it. The Oscar was still on the floor.

Rennie felt a crushing ache in her chest and furiously swiped the tears from her eyes. She wanted to stomp the trophy and smash it against the walls. Instead, she picked it up and righted it on her night-stand. She was drunk and useless.

Even now, Rennie could recall walking into the cold that New Year's Eve night, her cheeks hot, her agent's words and the buzz of static ringing in her ears: *Martin said you were luminous. He really did. You were second in line for the part.* She could remember ducking inside that crowded dive bar on Second Ave and feeling the rush of being surrounded by strangers. She'd meant to go to her friend's party, but ended up staying at that bar all night. She'd tipped back drinks and kissed someone forgettable, and the sting of the rejection had dulled. But this would all be redeemed in time, wouldn't it? The city hurtled into a new year and Rennie made a promise to herself. The next time she had good news, she would call her mother.

She would call everyone.

seventeen

VIVIAN wore a Valentino dress of sweeping red silk and organza for the Academy Awards. Richard loved it. He always said that red was her color, and Vivian always teased him that it was just because she was wearing red the first time they met. He leaned in and told her that the moment he had seen her in that red dress, he had known he wanted her to be his. Vivian loved it when he said that. She let herself imagine him slipping the dress off her later.

Red was the color of luck. She was sure luck would grace them tonight. Richard was nominated for Best Actor, she for Best Supporting Actress. With his handsome aquiline features and classical drama training, Richard had been a perfect English prince, summoning every bit of his Shakespearean upbringing for his thunderous monologues. Vivian had poured herself into the role of Jia-Yee in *Fortune's Eye*. She didn't just memorize her lines; she plunged into the mind of a desperate woman fending for herself in the Wild West with a keen, vicious will to survive. She'd spent grueling hours training in the searing, late-summer heat, her hands caked with dust, her mouth dry, her feet blistering and sweating in her boots. She still had a faint scar of a large scrape on her side from one of her stunts where she'd landed wrong. But she'd loved it. For the first time she had a significant speaking role. She did choreographed fight scenes. She even cried on-screen. Sometimes, late at night on set, she'd lean against the open door of her trailer and smoke a cigarette. Looking up at the sweep of stars above, she would feel, in her weariness, that she had *become* Jia-Yee that day. This was the acting she was meant to do.

That her husband would win was all but assured. But Vivian alone believed they would both be walking out with trophies in their hands.

She had seen a vision in her vanity mirror a year after they'd moved into the house. It didn't matter if it was a hallucination or a trick of the eyes. After a long day of auditions, she had sat down one night to take off her makeup and her reflection had changed. The woman in the mirror wasn't tired and haggard. Her skin was smooth. Her shoulders were bare and pale in the beam of spotlights. She was wearing a red dress and pearl drop earrings.

And her hands clutched a gold trophy.

Vivian had stood suddenly, knocking into her vanity and rattling the perfume bottles, and then she sat down again, hard. When she lifted her eyes to the mirror, it was her again, in the bathrobe. Makeup smeared around her eyes.

She had hung on to that brief vision ever since, and now it had turned into a premonition, like lucky tiles racked up. She had poured every bit of herself into every role. The day she was nominated for an Academy Award, she had leapt into her husband's arms. She knew what she was going to say if—

If she won.

After all, she had had years to prepare.

Now the limo pulled up to the curb. Camera flashes blinded her as she linked arms with her husband and let him lead her in. They stopped for cameras and journalists, but it all barely registered. The crowds swelled and dissolved around them as they made their way to their designated chairs. Vivian fixated only on the stage.

The lights dimmed. She felt anxious, such that her limbs began to numb as the music played and the awards ceremony began. Could this be her moment? What if the mirror had been nothing but a delusion? Somehow the sickness of anticipation was worse than thinking she didn't stand a chance. But she scarcely had the time to collect her thoughts when she heard the presenter's voice.

"And the award for Best Supporting Actress goes to—"

She sucked in a breath, her head dizzy.

"Vivian Yin for *Fortune's Eye*."

Her husband looked at her, and she remembered, years later, that his first expression had been shock. Then it melted into adoration. He cupped her face and kissed her and pulled her into his arms, and Vivian let herself be held for a moment. She locked eyes with her co-star, Ernie MacDowell, who'd received a Best Actor nomination, and he gave her a beaming grin. She gathered her sweeping red skirts and walked carefully into the dazzling beam of spotlights. She looked directly at the presenter when he handed her the award and said, "Congratulations, Vivian." She mouthed a breathless thanks, and then there she was. On the stage, holding the delicate statue in her hands. It was lighter than she had imagined.

"Thank you to . . ." These were the words she'd spent years practicing. "The Academy, and my director, Sheldon, my co-stars, Will and Ernie and Anita and Yuen . . . those who have helped me in my career, to . . ." She looked over at the crowd and her gaze landed on the man she loved.

Except his eyes were gone. The sockets were dark pits, filled with crumbling dirt. His lips were gone too. Mottled shreds of flesh hung off his cheekbones over a grotesque smile. He *was* smiling at her. No, he wasn't moving.

Those were the worms, writhing, crawling where his teeth should have been.

Vivian's words dropped away.

There was only silence now. The presenter, who had been serenely looking out over the crowd, now turned to her. But she couldn't stop staring at the corpse sitting in the place of her husband.

She felt sick. She tore her eyes away and her gaze trailed over the crowd again. Her fingers trembled so much she was scared the award would drop. "To . . ." She took a deep breath. "To my f-family and community, for supporting me, and to Chinese actors, this . . ." She steadied her shaking voice. "This is for all of you. Thank you." And with those last words she was free. She stumbled for the stairs at the edge of the stage. She was dimly aware of the applause that greeted her and the smiles that beamed at her. She didn't want to be in the auditorium anymore. She wanted to bolt for the doors. But she forced herself to walk toward her seat as she took very shallow breaths.

She dared to glance up. The gruesome vision was gone. Her husband's face was once more his.

Her staggering relief gave way to the slow realization that she had forgotten his name in her speech.

As she moved closer, she saw the effort in his placid smile. His eyes were leeched of all warmth. He kissed her lightly on the cheek and Vivian thought of the corpse again and felt faint. The lights panned away from them and she dropped the award in her lap. But Richard didn't reach for her. He faced forward. Vivian kept her eyes wide-open as they ran through the rest of awards. She knew that the moment she closed them she would see the image of her husband's skull filled with earth and maggots. She winced at how each winner joyfully thanked their spouses and loved ones by name. She *had* wanted to thank Richard, truly.

The night dragged on. She was relieved when they got to the Best Actor category, because she knew that only this could salvage what had happened. The names of the Best Actor nominees were called, and Vivian reached over and squeezed her husband's hand tightly.

"And the award for Best Actor goes to . . ."

She waited. For his name, for the roar of applause that would follow.

It never came. She didn't realize that Ernie's name had been called until heads started turning.

Stunned, she gaped toward the stairs, where her co-star loped gracefully toward the award that belonged to her husband. She half rose from her seat in indignation, and then sank back down.

She looked back toward Richard, but he wouldn't look at her. His gaze was fixed on some point on the stage.

Soon they were swept into a limo to an after-party, where Vivian was swarmed with her co-stars' excitement. Ernie swept her up in a hug, and their director congratulated them both. All eyes were on her. It was just like she had pictured all those years ago. And yet everything about it felt wrong. Her husband stood stiffly to the side. She'd upstaged him. She'd gotten what he had coveted all his life. Vivian drank champagne and laughed, but the guilt settled sourly in her stomach.

The ride home was quiet.

"I'm sorry," Vivian said, trying to be diplomatic. "It's late. We should have gone home earlier."

Her husband didn't respond at first.

She said, haltingly, drunkenly: "I'm—sorry. I'm so ashamed."

When he finally spoke, his voice was perfectly even. "Of what, sweetheart?"

"I—" Vivian faltered. The award felt like ice in her hands. What could she say? That she had seen his decomposing face in the crowd and forgotten his name? She shook her head. "I meant to say your name, I promise, it's just that my mind—I blanked out on the stage."

Her husband said coldly, "Was this everything you dreamed of?"

Her neck felt like it was on fire. "I—of course. But you deserved an award too, I swear, it was all yours—"

"Will you shut the *fuck* up and just enjoy your night?"

Vivian shrank back from the tone of his voice. He didn't look at her. It wasn't that he had never raised his voice at her before. But she had never seen this kind of wrath.

"I'm sorry," she whispered a third time, with tears in her eyes.

Vivian watched Richard stalk off to bed the moment they entered the house. She stood alone in the foyer, clutching her heels in one hand, the award in the other. A headache was setting in. She padded toward the kitchen and wiped her tears away with her fingertips.

The kitchen light was on. Vivian peeked around the corner.

"Congratulations!"

Edith and Josiah stood behind a cake on the kitchen island. Edith rushed forward and embraced Vivian. "You were brilliant," she gushed in Mandarin. "The dress, the speech—*wah*, you looked beautiful."

Vivian hugged her tightly in relief. She set the statue on the table, and Josiah's normally stoic expression had become one of admiration. "May I . . . ?"

She nodded and smiled toward it. "Please."

Edith and Josiah held it in their hands and marveled at it from all angles. Vivian let herself sink into a chair. "Are the girls—?"

"I finally got them all to bed." Edith's eyes shone. "I couldn't pull them away from the television. The little one couldn't stop jumping when they called your name." She clutched Vivian's hand. "You should have seen them. We're so proud of you, Lian-er." She looked closer at Vivian's expression. "What's wrong? Where's Richard?"

Vivian let her voice drop to a whisper. "I forgot his name in my speech."

Josiah frowned. "But you thanked your family."

"But I was supposed to thank *him*. And I—I didn't."

"It's all right," Edith said. "He knows. It's your night!"

How could she tell them about his anger, the way she tumbled from joy into shame? How to describe the strange, horrific face that had flashed in front of her? How eerily that face had looked like the one she had seen in the mirror, so many years ago. She looked at the trophy. "He didn't get an award. This was supposed to be *his*."

Her friends looked at her with a mix of pity and disbelief.

"No, Lian-er," Josiah insisted, the first time he had used her nickname. His eyes were earnest. "It is yours. You earned it. We're proud of you. You hear me?"

She met his gaze and nodded.

"Come, have some cake," Edith said.

Vivian finally let herself smile. "谢谢. You're so kind."

"Of course we had to get you something. We had it delivered from your favorite place."

They ate the cake, huddled in the kitchen. Edith mimicked Renata leaping in front of the TV with her nose pressed up against the screen. "She kept asking when she would be 'inside the screen' like 妈妈," Josiah said, shaking his head and smiling. Finally, Vivian allowed herself to laugh. She had come to this country alone, and now here she was, a household name, wearing a designer silk dress and eating a heaping slice of cake with the people she considered family. Happiness seeped back into her and didn't dissipate until the early hours of the morning when they all cleaned up and went to bed.

Vivian ascended the stairs alone, the award clutched in her hand. She couldn't bring it into their bedroom. It would be almost disrespectful. So she crept into her youngest daughter's room. She looked at her

Meng-Meng curled in her blankets, cheeks flushed, sleeping peacefully at last. Yin Zi-Meng, she'd named Renata at birth. *Dreamer.* Richard chose her English name, Vivian her Chinese name. She wanted to sweep her up and hug her to her chest. But instead, she carefully placed the Oscar on the nightstand.

She looked back at her daughter before she closed the door, her entire being flooded with joy at this sweet image. She knew her youngest would love it.

She walked to her bedroom with a cool resolve.

Her husband was asleep, but making jolting, sudden movements beneath the sheets. A whimper escaped his lips. He was having one of his nightmares again. How could it be? His bottle of sleeping pills was open on the nightstand. Maybe he didn't take enough. She took an aspirin in the bathroom for the headache, stepped out of her heavy dress, put on her night slip, and went to bed.

She wanted to reach for her husband and pull him out of whatever nightmare he was in, but instead she stared dazedly at him. She couldn't stop thinking about him in the audience, decaying before her eyes. It reminded her of her disturbing dreams of Amos Dalby. These dreams made sense; since she'd learned about Amos, she'd sometimes think about the horrors that had helped build her husband's family fortune. But what could explain these waking, grotesque visions? Was it something about this place? Could the ghost of the old house and what had happened here find its way into her mind? The foundation of the old house, with its rot and rust, making itself felt in the new?

She told herself to stop. This was her problem. She had brought this evil here by thinking about it all the time. Her husband had planned to erase it. She'd only mentioned Amos Dalby once to him, when she called from the set of *Fortune's Eye.* She hadn't mentioned his name, but she'd asked if Richard could tell her more about his family member who'd worked in railroads. It was clear from her husband's response that he didn't know a thing about trains or railroad tycoons. He'd only said that the person lost his entire family, and it was all too tragic and morbid.

Maybe he was right. But every time he woke from a nightmare

shivering and complaining that he couldn't feel his fingers, or gulping for air and saying he had dreamed of being buried alive, Vivian couldn't help but think of the stories 苏伯伯 had told her, of the Chinese workers who had experienced just that.

She tried to banish the thoughts from her mind, like Edith and Josiah had advised. Tonight was about success, fortune, and happiness. She reached over and took a sleeping pill from Richard's bottle. She swallowed it without water and felt it force its way down her throat.

The next morning she sat in front of her vanity as she unhooked her earrings and rubbed the red from her lips. She felt better. Clearer.

Everything she had seen in the mirror years ago had come true. She was Vivian Yin, an actress who had just won an Academy Award. Years ago, she imagined that this moment would be the beginning, something that would define a long and illustrious career. But now she sat in front of the mirror and could think only about the screenplay she'd just started writing on the side.

This was just the beginning. She would write a screenplay and Richard could help her. They would make their movie and be back on that stage, together, next time. She would do anything in the world to make it happen.

eighteen

NORA knew better than to go out into the garden now, but still, she leaned against the window in her bedroom. The pale pink roses were still the only blooming plant in the dismal, barren garden. Nothing stirred under the glow of a bright moon. The calm felt sinister, knowing as she did what could happen out there.

Something clattered in the kitchen. Maybe her evasive mother was finally up again. She'd been eating at odd hours and otherwise staying in her room. Maybe Nora could catch her and try to get more information out of her. She slipped from the bed and crept to the kitchen.

The clattering stopped just as she rounded the corner. Madeline whirled around, wielding a spatula. She visibly relaxed when she saw Nora. Her hand fell to her side. "Oh. It's you."

"What are you doing?" Nora said.

Madeline gestured to the kettle. She was wearing an oversized T-shirt and had her large cardigan wrapped around her. "I was making tea. I couldn't sleep."

"With a large wooden spatula?"

"Oh, this." Madeline waved it around. "I heard a noise and didn't know who . . . or what it was." At Nora's look she continued, "This place is strange, okay? I'm not ruling anything out."

Nora crossed her arms. "Fair."

They glanced toward each other, though not quite at each other. Finally, Madeline spoke. "Uh, would you like some? Tea?"

Nora didn't know what to say, which was ridiculous. "If you have some left over?" she managed.

"Can I make you some without a lawyer present?"

Nora blinked.

Madeline's smile dropped. "Sorry."

Nora sighed. "No, it's deserved. I know I sounded like an asshole."

"Well. My family *is* kind of one big asshole conglomerate, so I get it."

Nora almost snorted in disbelief. Had she just heard *asshole conglomerate* come out of Madeline's mouth? But the person who'd sat across from her days ago with rigid posture in a pristine blouse seemed relaxed now, despite everything. Her cardigan was loose around her shoulders. Pieces of her long hair had fallen out of her ponytail.

"What? I feel like I can say that." Madeline put in the tea bag and carefully poured Nora a cup. "It's herbal fruit tea, by the way. I found it in the cupboard. I hope it's still good."

"We'll probably live." Nora accepted the cup, surprised to find that the tea was still fragrant. It smelled like peaches. "Thank you." She took very small sips. When she glanced out toward the garden, Madeline followed her gaze.

Nora said in a very faint voice, "You see them too, right?"

"The roses?" Madeline moved toward the door.

Instinctively, Nora reached out to stop her. "Don't." Her hand knocked against Madeline's arm, and Madeline winced. Immediately Nora drew back. "Sorry." She looked down. "Are you— Is this—?"

"I'm fine," Madeline said. She had focused on the garden again. "Is it me or do there seem to be *more* out there than before? What's going on?"

Where had the roses come from? Nora was certain there had been no flowers when they first arrived. Did they grow on their own? Why would someone plant roses, only to abandon the rest of the shriveled mess? Did they trap everyone who stepped foot out there? Would that happen again? Nora didn't want to test it out.

"What are you thinking?" Nora looked her way. "Sorry," Madeline rushed. "I know you don't want to talk to me."

We're not supposed to talk. It sounded so childish. "No. It's . . . It's not me. My mom just told me not to."

"Not to talk to me?"

"Your family."

"Why?"

Nora simply shrugged. "She just said. I am sorry, though. I know I come off as rude."

"You know," Madeline said, studying her. "It's funny. You may be the person who talks to me the most in this house."

Nora cradled the bottom of the cup with the pads of her fingertips. "Really?"

Madeline leaned over the counter. "I tried to find out why your mom came to see my 外婆 or what happened between our families." She paused. "Don't worry," she said, seeing Nora stiffen. "I didn't tell them I found out from you. But it doesn't matter, because I got nothing." She sighed. "I thought we'd come here to, I don't know. Grieve together? Understand the person my grandmother was. Do what families do. Share stories. But my family didn't talk at the funeral. And even now we can't bear to. We just hide in our rooms." Madeline seemed nervous. She twisted a slim gold ring on her middle finger. "We can't stand each other."

Nora didn't know what to say to this.

"You probably resent me." Madeline bore a grim smile. "Which is valid. These are all such trivial problems."

Nora barely shook her head. It only hit her now that Madeline was, after all, someone who had just lost her grandmother. Stuck in this dysfunctional family. Sickly wealthy or not, entitled or not, Madeline seemed lonely. Nora said softly, "I don't resent you."

"So you pity me, then," Madeline said. "Which is arguably worse."

Nora couldn't answer that. Not truthfully, at least. The dim light caught Madeline's eyes and made them soft.

"I take it you got your questions answered," Madeline said. "Or I hope. At least one of us deserves to know the truth."

"I know as much as you do. Vivian asked my mom to visit her. She came to the house, and they talked about your aunt. I don't know what happened after that."

Madeline tilted her head. "About Renata?"

"The other one. Ada."

Madeline looked perplexed. "Ada?" Shock rippled through her expression. "Ada." The second time, it was as if she was testing the name out.

Too late, it dawned on Nora that she might have said something she should not have. Again. Nora remembered how her own mother had paled when she'd said the name. "I'm sorry," she said. "I didn't mean to bring her up like this."

There was a long silence.

"No, I'm glad you told me," Madeline said. "Really, I am."

Told? Nora's breath caught in her chest. God, did Madeline not even know about her? "I thought you knew."

"I should have, shouldn't I?" Madeline said weakly. "What happened to her?"

It was like all the warmth had been sucked out of the room. Nora swallowed. "My mom said she died thirty-four years ago."

"Of what?"

"I . . . don't know." It sounded so inadequate, so trite. "I'm sorry."

Madeline exhaled. Her eyelids fluttered shut. "Don't be sorry. Not you."

"But this shouldn't be happening. Our families shouldn't keep secrets from us." Nora paused. "I can tell my mother's hiding something too."

"I always thought they were protecting me," Madeline said faintly. "But I didn't know what from. We inherit their history. Whether they know it or not."

"Whether they want us to or not," Nora added.

"You know," Madeline said, pressing closer. "If it weren't for you, I would think that I made everything up in my head. About what happened the other night."

"You didn't. It really did happen."

Madeline nodded. "I guess so." She fidgeted with her necklace. Her sleeve fell back, and Nora could see the deep gash on her forearm. She reached out and picked up Madeline's wrist gently, and Madeline let her. It didn't look infected, but it concerned her that it wasn't bandaged when it was still an open wound. "We should do something about this."

"Well," Madeline said, "too bad this Chinese family has absolutely no doctors."

"I'm not quite," Nora said. "But I am pre-med and I have a first aid kit. Does that count?"

Madeline smiled. "I'll take it."

"Okay. Come with me."

They set their mugs down in the sink. Nora led the way. Behind her, Madeline shut the lights off. Nora shivered. What was it—fear of the dark? A premonition? Some kind of anticipation? Either way, she was wide awake now.

Madeline followed Nora into her room and closed the door behind her. The bedroom was dimly lit by a nightstand lamp between the two twin beds. Nora rummaged around in her first aid kit and found Neosporin, medical tape, and gauze. "I should have done this days ago," she said. "I don't know how effective it'll be now."

"Worth a try," Madeline said. She knelt on the floor next to Nora.

"Here," Nora said. She pushed up Madeline's sleeve. The other shallow cuts and scrapes were scabbed over and healing, so she didn't bother with them. She held Madeline's arm delicately. The skin was hot to the touch. Nora dabbed at the cut with some water and squeezed a bit of gel out of the tube, lightly smoothing it over the wound. They were so close it was unnerving.

Madeline asked, "So why pre-med?"

In spite of everything, Nora laughed. "What is this, an interview?"

Madeline shrugged. "Just curious."

Was Nora imagining the blush on Madeline's cheeks? "Well, I like taking care of people and I'm good at my classes, I guess. My mom has always had these paralyzing migraines. I wanted to help her somehow."

Nora applied more Neosporin. Madeline's expression didn't change, except her jaw tightened. Nora taped the wound and wrapped Madeline's arm in fresh gauze from her kit. "Do I get a question?"

"Seems fair."

"Why'd you keep walking around that garden?"

Madeline's shoulders dropped. "I don't know. I guess I wanted to figure out if there was a way to fix it. My family said I could help. In case—"

"You got the house back."

"You make it sound like I'm scheming."

"That's not what I meant," Nora said.

Their eyes met. "It's not going to happen now, anyway. But—" Madeline hesitated. "Sometimes I think about how beautiful the garden must have been. I can just imagine it. And the thing is, I studied ecosystems in college. How to restore them. And I couldn't *not* think about it here, you know? How to bring it back to life." She held up her arm. "Turns out, it is very much alive."

Madeline said it so calmly it was almost funny. Until Nora looked at the dressed wound and thought, in panic, of Madeline being pulled into the earth once more. "What do you think is out there?" Nora asked.

"It was like something was possessing the vines," Madeline recounted. "It was . . . too strong. I could not have escaped on my own. It was going to bury me."

She said this last part so quietly, it terrified Nora. "Do you think it's—?"

Haunted?

The word hung in the silence between them.

"And if it . . . was," Madeline pressed on, "do you think we should leave?"

Nora studied the wood grain of the floor.

"I'm not saying this to—convince you to. Obviously I know our families are still working that part out. I just wonder if this place is . . . unsafe," Madeline said. "I mean. What happened to me was . . ."

"Absolutely terrifying? Yeah."

"Yeah." Madeline sighed. "But I don't know. I don't think I can get my mom to leave this place."

"Did you tell her what happened to you?"

Madeline laughed bitterly. "I tried to. She didn't believe me. How could she?"

Nora's head started to hurt. Things didn't add up in this place. Her mother told her not to go into the garden but wouldn't tell her why. Strange things happened, but then people pretended not to notice them. "I don't think my mom would leave either."

"So we're just stuck here."

"Seems like it."

"Part of me still does want to stay," Madeline said. "Is that twisted? Aside from whatever's in the garden, I feel like . . . so much of my family history is here. My mother got to grow up in this place when it was beautiful. I wish I had that. But even if I can only live with the remains of it, I want to." She sighed. "So, I guess I'm not leaving."

Nora nodded. "We avoid the garden, then. And keep an eye out for each other."

Madeline looked at her. She seemed to be taking her in fully for the first time, and Nora realized suddenly that she was still holding on to Madeline's arm. She let go as if it were scalding.

Madeline glanced down quizzically. "Well. Thanks, Dr. Nora. For this. And for saving my life."

Now what? Were they going to go back to their silences? Nora said, "Thanks for making me tea."

"Equally heroic."

They laughed. Madeline's laugh was a beautiful sound. The room felt warm, and they were standing close now. It took everything in Nora not to pull away. Madeline was entirely still, too. Nora's breath was loud in her ears as time seemed to dilate. She started to say something, but whatever words had been on her mind dissipated the moment Madeline leaned in.

Nora felt Madeline's lips meet hers, soft at first, and then with more pressure. Madeline put her hand on Nora's waist. Nora deepened the kiss, her tongue trailing gently, lingering for long seconds or minutes; she lost count. She had already felt like the night had transcended into an alternate reality. Now they were in a parallel dimension.

When they finally drew apart, Nora looked at the floor and realized she was squeezing the Neosporin with sweaty fingers. "I . . ."

"'Night," Madeline said softly. Nora kept her eyes on the floor. Her cheeks were burning. She was still thinking through a response when she heard Madeline get up and close the door behind her.

MADELINE didn't sleep for a long time. She lay in her bed staring up at the round light, her body buzzing and filled with euphoria. She thought about Nora, about the kiss, about her soft, low voice and her careful touch, over and over again. So Nora *had* wanted her too—maybe even as much as Madeline did. That thought elated her. What would happen next? Would they talk about it? Acknowledge it? She lay back down and tried to slow her breathing.

There was something else. The longer the night stretched on, the more her thoughts shifted to what Nora had said. The name.

Madeline had only heard Ada's name once before. When she was eleven, she had gone through her mother's desk when she was away on a work trip and discovered a thick paper envelope filled with pictures of her mother as a kid. She had never seen photos of her mother when she was young. And yet here she was, in what looked like vacation photos. Her mother, leaning against the side of a car. Her mother in ski goggles. Her mother, framed by the portraits and paintings behind her in an art museum. Her mother had the same the telltale straight posture, the thick eyebrows, the angular features, the prim set of her lips, the pressed collared shirts and the baggy jeans. Then there had been a photo of her mother and Aunt Rennie. And a third person. A cousin, maybe, one who looked exactly like Mā.

She asked, days later, when her mother came back and they were eating dinner, who the cousin was. Mā set her bowl down. "What cousin? I don't have any that I know of."

"The one who went to Europe with you and Yí Mā."

Her mother's expression had paled, and she slammed down her bowl so hard, Madeline jumped. "That's my sister Ada," she said. "She's gone."

And that was that. After Mā left the dinner table, Bà leaned over and told Madeline, very quietly, to never mention Ada's name again.

In the morning she got up and paced her room. She wanted to go downstairs and see Nora again. But already she heard voices from the kitchen. The quiet pocket of night they had between them was long gone, and now she had to think about what Nora had said. She had to find her mother.

Madeline marched out of her room just as Mā was opening her bedroom door.

Madeline intercepted her. "I need to talk to you."

Mā's carefully pinned hair was stringy and pulled back with a clip. Her lips were chapped and pale. "I'm busy."

"I don't care. We need to talk."

Mā gestured to her. "Then talk."

"It's about Ada."

Mā jolted as if she'd been electrocuted. Her fingers clamped around Madeline's wrist, and she pulled her into her room.

The room was dark. The curtains were drawn. Why did her mother keep this room so dimly lit? "Don't ever mention her."

Madeline didn't let up. "Why? Tell me about her. What happened?"

Mā retreated.

"She's your *sister*. Why did you never talk about her?"

"Because it's too hard to!" Mā was yelling now. Her eyes flashed and her breathing was quick. "She died in a car crash when we were seventeen, and it was the most painful thing that has ever happened to me. It killed all of us. Mā most of all." She stared at the wall behind Madeline's head. "And now you know."

"Know *what*?"

Mā flung an arm out. "Why we're like this. Why we're so—*damaged*." She was panting, her teeth bared, tears in her eyes. "This is the last time I want to talk about her."

"Why, though?" Madeline, too, found her eyes smarting. "Why *don't* you talk about her? Why won't you talk about Wài Pó? Why do you shut yourself away like this? Does it ever help? Does it make it more bearable? *Does it?*" Mā's hands hung limply at her sides now, like that outburst was all she had energy for and now she was completely drained. "Talk to *me*. I'm here, Mā."

Mā lifted her eyes to Madeline's, her face blank. "Talking with you does nothing. This is my family. You don't understand." She drew in a ragged breath. "Just go." Her voice broke. "*Go*, Madeline. I shouldn't have brought you."

Madeline felt like she had been struck. *I'm your daughter*, she thought. *This is my family too.*

nineteen

ADA Yin-Lowell never tried to be the best at anything in her family. Everything she thought about trying, her older twin sister had already gotten to first. Top scores, captain of the debate team—that was Lucille. She spun like a cyclone, picking up activities and academic awards around her. Rennie, on the other hand, was the natural favorite. She had a sweetness and wit that endeared everyone to her. When Mā and Dad were in town, they never missed one of Rennie's community theater performances.

Mā's Oscar stood on a shelf in the library. It was a reminder to everyone that it wasn't enough to be perfect; they had to be the best. But Ada had never wanted to push her way into the spotlight. Instead, she sat back and watched, picking up on the things that others missed. It was a big household with two families. Her parents and her sisters. Edith and Josiah and their daughters, Elaine and Sophie. There was no shortage of people—or things—to observe. She predicted when things would turn still and stagnant during the summer, when people's tempers would change. She knew when the dust would kick up in the fall, when the winds would rattle the windows at night, and she secured things on the shelf so they would be safe from falling when small tremors and earthquakes would pass through. The night her mother won the Oscar, everyone pushed for the spot on the couch in front of the TV and watched her speech. Rennie shrieked and clapped, but the first thing Ada thought was: *she left out Dad's name.*

In school she always took careful, detailed notes, so much so that Lucille would copy them to help her study, especially for physics, which was Lucille's hardest class and Ada's easiest. Around the house, she watched the way everyone moved around one another. She made peace in the heated debates that sprung up between Lucille and Elaine. She noticed how Rennie spent close to an hour getting ready for school and always made them late, so Ada set her clock to be a little faster than everyone else's. And she knew that something was wrong between her parents. Mā and Dad were arguing more. They were flying to France in late May to attend a film festival, and every other day they fought over it. What flights to take. What their travel plans were and who they would see while they were there.

The longer it went on, the more anxious it made her. She went to Lucille's room one night and asked, "Do you think they're going to get a divorce?"

Lucille looked up from vigorously highlighting *King Lear*. "What?"

"I don't know. They argue all the time. They didn't used to be like this."

"It's just their midlife crisis," Lucille intoned. "Everyone's parents are fighting these days."

There was a knock on the door. Sophie, Edith and Josiah's younger daughter, peeked her head in. "I'm bored. You guys wanna get iced lemonades?"

Lucille threw her book down. "Please."

Ada looked up. "Who's driving?"

Lucille opened her mouth, but Sophie spoke up first. "Obviously me. Because your dad's car is gone and your mom would kill you if you took her convertible."

Lucille huffed. "One of these days."

"Dream on." Sophie smiled, jingling her keys. The house was mostly empty. Rennie was at her after-school rehearsal, and Mā was upstairs taking a nap. They crowded into Josiah Deng's Camry. Lucille took shotgun. Ada sat in the back seat. Sophie rolled her window down.

"You have to actually come to a complete stop at the sign, you know." Lucille rolled her window back up as Sophie drove. "It's a miracle you passed your driver's test."

"I stopped *enough*." Sophie looked up at the rearview mirror, where she met Ada's eyes. Ada offered her a reassuring smile.

They got fries and iced lemonades from the local burger place and ate leaning against the hood of the Camry. The heat rippled off the pavement in dry waves. Palm fronds fluttered limply in the hot gusts of wind.

"I'm thinking of throwing a party." Lucille shaded her eyes against the bare sun. "When our parents are in France."

"What, with your debate club?" Sophie said. She wiped her mouth with the heel of her palm. Her freckles were more prominent now, Ada noticed. She fixed her gaze on Sophie's shoulders. They were getting pink.

"An *actual* party," Lucille said sharply. "I want to invite a ton of people. That reminds me. Do you think you could ask Elaine to get us stuff?"

Sophie took a long sip of lemonade. "First of all, she's in San Francisco this summer, so she's not even around. Second of all, she's nineteen. She doesn't have a fake."

"Right. I forget she's more with the stoners."

Sophie shot Lucille a look.

"What? It's true. That was her whole high school friend group. I swore she came home baked one day. I didn't tell your parents. She owes me for that one."

Sophie didn't say anything. Ada brushed fry crumbs off her lap and cleared her throat. "What's Elaine up to in San Francisco?"

Sophie looked at her gratefully. "A lot. Volunteering for Democrat campaigns, organizing for housing justice on the side. She was going to try to get involved with earthquake relief and gentrification, too. That kinda stuff."

"She should be on the Hill." Lucille scooped the last two fries. "Working as a Senate intern or something. Dad probably knows someone from Yale. He could put in a good word on her behalf."

"It's okay. She doesn't need it."

"What? Why not?"

"Well," Sophie said, and now Ada could hear the irritation in her voice. "She probably wants to figure it out on her own."

Surely Lucille would stop pressing now. But she said bluntly, "Our parents are already paying for her degree. What's the matter with a few more connections?"

There was a silence. Then Sophie crumpled up the bag. "Are we good?" She got her keys. Lucille opened the door. Sophie said, "Isn't it Ada's turn in shotgun?"

"It's fine," Ada said in a neutral voice. "I like sitting here anyway."

"See?" Lucille sat down in the passenger seat. On the way back, Sophie cranked the radio up when the Cure came on. No one spoke. Ada tipped her head back, in the saturated beams of light, and gazed at the blue mountains in the distance. She glanced at Sophie through the rearview mirror again and their eyes met. This time it was Sophie who smiled at her. When the sun flashed through the window just right, it pooled her brown eyes to honey.

Ada noticed that Dad hadn't been coming to dinner for a week straight. Mā was agitated. The food Edith made for him grew cold and sat out on the table. Later that night, Ada couldn't focus. Lucille had already finished writing her essay and gone to bed, but the words in the heavy thesaurus swam in front of Ada. She heard the front door open downstairs. She tensed, waiting for her parents' voices to rise. A plate clattered and Ada flinched.

Her stomach was still in knots long after the voices faded. Downstairs, the kitchen was spotless, no broken dishes. It looked peaceful in the garden, so she went onto the terrace and descended the cool stairs, down to the gravel walking path.

Ada jumped when she saw something move behind the fountain ahead. Sophie emerged. Her eyes widened. "Oh. It's you." She pulled off her gardening gloves and tilted her head in question. "What are you doing out here?"

"I couldn't sleep," Ada said. She hovered next to the fountain and peered into the bowl, at the puckered reflection of the moon. "What were you up to this late?"

Sophie folded the gloves. "Just doing some watering. The flowers soak up water better at night because the sun's not out." Her fingertips broke the still surface of the fountain's pool. "There are some things that bloom at night, too, so I wanted to check on them."

"Oh? Which ones?"

"Want to see?"

Ada followed Sophie into the garden. The main walkways branched off into smaller, meandering paths. There, next to the delicate lavender and bursting pink hydrangea bushes in the left section closest to the house, was a cluster of small, peaked white flowers, with a clear, fragrant scent. "Jasmine," Ada said in wonder.

"They're doing really well this spring. They like being in partial shadow, I think. Bà didn't think they'd survive with how dry it's been."

Ada reached out and brushed the leaves. "Well, they're beautiful."

"I had something to prove." Sophie gently disentangled the leaves and guided one of the flowers into Ada's palm. Their fingers brushed and Ada was stilled by the tenderness of the gesture, but Sophie had already moved on. Now she bounded closer to the fountain, to the roses. The pale pink buds hung suspended in the breeze, arching from their elongated stems and ethereal in the moonlight. "And these *are* liking the sun." She glanced at Ada. "What?"

"They look like they're telling you a secret."

"What would they be saying?" She tilted a bud toward her, holding it like a receiver. Her eyes widened as she feigned hearing a secret. "There is some *very* juicy gossip going on."

Ada laughed. "I'm serious." She cupped a rose toward her, one that had already burst into bloom, so full that the fragrant petals seemed to unfurl and settle in her palm. "You know people used to send messages with flowers?"

"Really?"

"They told us that in English class. During the Jane Eyre unit. Remember?"

"Didn't pay attention like you did, I guess." Ada blushed, but Sophie smiled at her. "What? I've seen the notes you take in class." Lucille always teased Ada for taking perfect notes but never raising her hand in class. Sophie loved looking at Ada's notes, though. When they sat together in English, Sophie was always admiring how pretty her handwriting was and how everything was cataloged carefully by date and time. Those comments still made Ada glow inside.

Sophie asked, "Do you know what this one means?"

Ada shook her head. "I don't know the secret language of flowers," she confessed. "I just know it exists."

"Oh. Then we could make our own. What do you think?"

She tilted her head and gave Ada an inquisitive look. And from that spring day on, Ada couldn't stop noticing: the lightest of freckles across the bridge of Sophie's nose, her curious, impudent smile, her animated expression, the soft skin of her cheek, the way the flowers seemed to reach for her in the moonlight. The way everything around her seemed to come alive.

Ada watched her sister begin to plot her summer party with her typical obsessive fervor. She'd always been so straitlaced, turning down the few invitations that came her way in favor of studying. But now it was the summer before senior year, and suddenly Lucille had a list of things she was determined to do in the year before college, one of which was throwing a party. Far be it for Lucille to half-ass a party. Their parents' upcoming Cannes trip, combined with Edith and Josiah's trip to Northern California to help Elaine move, would create the perfect opportunity. On the days when Sophie worked her job at the library, Ada would go with Lucille into Glendale to pick out new records. Rennie celebrated her fourteenth birthday in the second to last weekend of May, and they all stayed up eating strawberries and cream cake, her favorite. That night, high on sugar and sparkling juice, Lucille finally clued Rennie into the party, and she nearly leapt from the bed in excitement.

"You can invite your friends," Lucille said. "But none of them can drink."

"Okay!"

"I'm serious about this."

Rennie nodded solemnly. "Swear."

The next day Edith and Josiah drove up to Northern California to help Sophie's sister, Elaine, move off the Berkeley campus and into an apartment in San Francisco. Then Mā and Dad headed to Cannes for ten days. The Yin-Lowell sisters and Sophie were all alone in the house together. Lucille spent the afternoon in the living room, calling everyone she knew. Later that night, she came by Ada's room while Ada was in her pajamas reading a superhero comic. "I called seventy people and told them to bring their friends. Do you think that's enough?"

Ada sat straight up. "Can our house *fit* seventy people?"

Lucille paced. "I'm sure. I feel like they're not all going to show up."

Ada said dryly, "Then you just have a tiny, cozy gathering with fifty people, I guess."

"Invite your friends from Chem."

Ada turned a page. "They don't party."

Lucille plopped onto the edge of the bed. "I feel like you really don't care about this."

Ada set her comic down. "It's *your* party. I don't even know why you're doing this in our house. We'll be in college in a year."

"I want to be in college having already hosted a party. And what's the point of having a big house if you don't use it? Our parents are gone."

"Mā will still find out."

"Not if Rennie doesn't snitch. Which she swore not to."

Ada shrugged and returned to her comic. Lucille lingered at the foot of her bed, and then said sharply, "What's with you lately?"

Ada glanced up. "What do you mean?"

They stared at each other for a moment. Then Lucille declared, "You're unhelpful. I'm going to bed." The door shut behind her. Ada lay on her bed and waited until the house got quiet.

Sophie was waiting for her in the garden, perched on the steps. This time, though, she held up car keys. Her eyes glittered with mischief. "Want to go for a drive?"

"Now?"

Sophie smiled and hopped up. "Who's stopping us?"

They got in the car. The key rattled in the ignition. Ada looked up at the house, but the windows stayed dark. They drove to the end of a long road. Sophie said, "Lucille would have given me shit for this stop sign again."

"Well, she's not here."

Sophie looked over with a raised eyebrow, one hand on the steering wheel, the other fiddling with the radio knob. She grinned. "True. Where do we want to go?"

"Anywhere. I don't know many places."

"Let's go to that lookout in Pasadena, then."

Ada had never even been out this late before without her parents. Cars moved fluidly around them, their taillights winking. Sophie rolled the window down and the cool breeze skimmed over them. She took a winding road, driving them around giant, imposing houses, until she pulled over. The city beneath them was blanketed in soft lights. The inky ocean spilled out beyond the veil of mist.

Ada stared in wonder. "How do you know about this place?"

"My sister. She'd go here with her friends."

"How is Elaine?" Ada asked. "I feel like she doesn't come back very often."

Sophie leaned back against the car. The wind picked up strands of her hair. "She really likes it there."

Ada swallowed. Finally, she asked something she had always wondered. "Does Elaine not like us?"

Sophie hesitated. "She's just a very proud person. I think staying here bothered her."

"Because . . ."

"Because of your parents. And my parents."

Was it really like that? "But—my parents don't—"

"I know. But what our parents do is different than what yours do, isn't it?"

Ada had nothing to say to that.

"My sister begged my parents to move, you know. But then we'd be living in some small apartment. 妈 would be working at a laundromat and 爸 would be doing landscaping work. Elaine wouldn't be at Berkeley, that's for sure."

Ada blurted, "I'm sorry about what Lucille said the other day."

"What for?"

Ada shifted. "I don't know. What she said. About Elaine and her summer job."

Sophie shrugged. "Just Lucille being Lucille, I guess." Her voice lightened. "At least they're not arguing over Marx at the dinner table anymore."

People at school called Lucille a know-it-all. A stuck-up bitch, sometimes. Ada never thought that about her sister and resented the people who did, but sometimes she did witness small moments of cruelty from Lucille that grated on her. Like how she made fun of the way Elaine dressed when she came home, in her baggy jeans and loose shirts. Or how she openly talked about how dumb she thought some of her classmates were, and how none of them had a chance at becoming valedictorian next to her.

"Okay." Sophie picked up her keys. "Want to go get food?"

They drove to a late-night diner and sat in the parking lot, sipping their milkshakes. Ada asked, "Do *you* like us?"

Sophie laughed. "How could anyone not like you?"

Too soon they were hurtling on the highway back toward home. They could do this tomorrow, and the night after, all week. Ada felt a weightless thrill. Their parents were gone and they had the house to themselves. Could they keep doing this when all the adults returned? She certainly wanted to. This was fleeting, and already she ached with impending nostalgia. Sophie parked the car on the curb. They crept through the house and toward the garden and sat on the steps of the terrace. Sophie fidgeted with the car keys. "I'm still thinking about what you said the other day."

Ada wondered what she'd said that could be so remarkable.

"How people used flowers to send messages."

Oh. "A secret language."

"It's like when we speak in Chinese so your dad can't understand. Or when my parents talk in their dialect from Jiaxing just so it's between the two of them." She leaned in. The corner of her lips curved up in a playful smile when she said, "Except this one would just be between you and me."

Between you and me.

"Hmmm," Ada exhaled. Except she wasn't really thinking; she couldn't quite think when Sophie was looking at her so intently like this. Ada wasn't used to being the one observed. She waited. Sophie didn't pull away.

Ada also was never one to make a first move in anything. But suddenly she wanted to. It was like a predetermined course had set in, like they had been inching toward this moment for weeks. Suddenly she found herself closing the space between them. Closer, as if she was telling a secret. Even closer; a finger's width apart. She pressed her lips to Sophie's cheek and a quiet triumph blazed through her.

When she drew away, Sophie was looking at her in surprise, her eyes wide and lips parted. Ada's own cheeks flared with heat. Triumph molted into shame. She rose quickly. "I'm going to go to bed."

Still Sophie said nothing.

Ada turned back toward the house. When she looked up, she swore she saw Rennie peering out her window straight at them. Her heart jumped, but the light flicked off, and the next time she glanced up, the windows were dark. She tiptoed up the stairs and laid in her bed for a long time, thinking that she'd ruined something, until she finally descended into a fitful sleep in the early light.

The next morning something was different when Ada came down for breakfast. Lucille was making peanut butter toast for herself in the kitchen and talking with Sophie. Ada wanted to look at Sophie, but she also wanted to melt into the ground. Lucille asked Ada a question and she answered, not making eye contact. She retreated into the library, and after a while the door opened. Ada recognized the footsteps.

"Hey," Sophie said. "You disappeared so suddenly last night."

For a long moment they stood looking at each other.

Ada swallowed. "I'm sorry if I messed something up. It didn't have to mean anything."

There was silence. Then Sophie said softly, "You didn't mess anything up. I promise." Sophie glanced behind Ada, at the shelves. "I left you something in that book, by the way," Sophie said before she slipped away.

Ada peered at the shelf. One book jutted out from the others, and she opened it.

On the title page was a single pressed daisy, and Sophie's scrawl. *Tell me what this means. I want to know.*

twenty

RENNIE woke in the middle of the night and couldn't get back to sleep. She knew if she made a little bit of noise, Ada would wake up and offer to make them hot chocolate or have some snacks. Ada was a bad sleeper too, but mostly because she was sensitive to noise. Rennie felt kind of awful waking her up on purpose.

Sometimes when she was little, she'd hear the wind pick up around the house and shriek as she was falling asleep. It sounded like people screaming. No one else ever heard it, though. One time, she dreamed that she looked out the window and saw a man with a beard standing in the garden. He was dressed in a suit and looking up at her, though she wasn't sure exactly how she knew that, considering his face was gone. Out of the socket where one of his eyes should have been, a perfect, horrifying rose bloomed, the petals unfurling and then withering as she watched. It had terrified her for months.

Sometimes she couldn't remember what she dreamed about at all. She just woke up feeling like she was breathing funny. She could never describe it to other people because it didn't make sense to her, either. Instead, every night she aimed to push sleep off for as long as possible. She put on one-person skits in her room, cast herself in all kinds of scenarios, and created costumes out of what she found in her closet. Sometimes she'd slip jewelry from Mā's vanity to try on at night.

Tonight, she settled on her bed in front of the small round mirror on her nightstand and clasped together a long pearl necklace she had borrowed from her mother's drawer. She held her hair up and smiled softly at her own reflection, then glanced absentmindedly out the window. Two figures sat in the garden.

What were the twins doing out there this late? As Rennie peered closer, she realized that it wasn't Lucille out in the garden with Ada. It was Sophie. Rennie craned her neck toward the window, her fingers fiddling with the necklace as she peered down at them.

They were talking. She saw Ada lean close to Sophie and—

Rennie went perfectly still. Had Ada just kissed Sophie's cheek? She teetered over the edge of her bed, trying to get a better look.

Another moment passed, and Ada was walking back toward the house. She looked up for a moment, and her eyes met Rennie's. Rennie gasped and ducked, hurrying to switch off the light. She lost her balance and pitched forward off the bed, putting her hands out to break her fall. Her fingers snagged on the long necklace, and only when she toppled forward, landing hard on her knees, feeling the sharp pain throbbing down her legs, did she realize she was surrounded by scattered pearls.

"Oh, shit."

She sat there for a few moments in silence. She heard Ada's footsteps on the stairs and in the hall, pausing outside Rennie's room. Rennie stayed hunched on the ground until Ada walked away.

Rennie let out the breath she was holding. She rose to the balls of her feet and scooped up the pearls in the darkness, trying to slip them back onto the string. But it was no use: the holes were too small and the chain was torn from the clasp. She stuffed what was left of the necklace into a drawer.

Maybe Mā wouldn't notice it was gone, she thought ruefully as she climbed back onto her bed. She wrapped her blankets tight around her and tried again to sleep.

LUCILLE knew she was sometimes difficult. Stubborn and judgmental, too. Even her own mother said so. Lucille was just honest. Sometimes she knew what Ada was thinking and she would say it for her, because she knew Ada didn't want to say it herself. Lucille would do anything for the people she cared about. Especially for her twin sister.

But something was going on with Ada and Sophie. A strange tension had settled between the two of them, like they were fighting. Over what, Lucille had no clue. They no longer looked each other in the eye. Her sister had always been the lighter sleeper between the two of them, but now she was going to bed later and later. Lucille had had to nudge her awake in the mornings for the last days of school.

Ada also seemed nervous around their parents. Lucille was, too, to an extent. Before her parents left for Cannes, she'd tried asking her mother what was going on with Dad, and Mā had been short with her. "We're just figuring out what to do in France," she said curtly, and turned in a way that signaled to Lucille she was done with the conversation. Was that marriage? At a certain point their parents seemed to get so sick of each other that there wasn't anything they couldn't fight about. She wanted to talk to Dad about it. She missed him. They no longer spent afternoons together in the library. He always came home late and seemed on edge and distracted. He'd become too busy for his family, and that annoyed her.

She also needed to figure out what Ada and Sophie were fighting about. Late at night, after Rennie's birthday, she'd come downstairs to sneak some birthday cake and heard something coming from the library. Ada hadn't been in her room. Lucille had checked. She slotted her body next to the hinge of the door and heard Ada and Sophie talking and laughing.

She stepped closer. A split second later, she backed away, a layer of ice forming inside her. They weren't fighting. They weren't speaking to each other in front of Lucille because they wanted to talk, just the two of them. To tell each other things they didn't want her to know. All at once it made sense. Their strange glances. Their silences. In the hallway, Lucille's limbs became leaden. She almost wanted to barge in so Ada could see the hurt in her eyes and crumble and apologize, like she always did, sweet as Ada was. But Lucille stayed there. After a moment more she turned around and headed back up the stairs.

Lucille was no longer her sister's confidante. Sophie was.

Lucille spent the night strategizing. She was going to be precise about this. She wasn't going to lash out. She would let silences linger and refuse to talk over them. She would wait for Ada to confess.

Instead, infuriatingly, over the past month, Lucille watched her sister slip away from her. When Ada and Sophie exchanged glances over something Dad said at the dinner table, a bitter fury curled at the pit of her stomach and the rice felt like glue in her mouth.

During the second to last week of junior year, when they got let out of school that Friday, they all got ice cream to celebrate. But that night, Lucille heard hushed voices in the hallway. She peeked outside her room and saw headlights diminish from the driveway.

Ada's door was open, and she wasn't in her room.

Lucille had been the one who first invited Sophie to play with them as kids. Who was the gardener's daughter, now, to try to break them apart? To exclude Lucille?

Lucille paced around the house. She went downstairs to Sophie and Elaine's room. It was empty. She marched back to her room and sat on her bed. An hour later, she heard the car pull into the driveway.

She asked her sister about it the next morning, when they were making breakfast. Sophie had already gone to the library. Ada just shrugged. "Sophie and I couldn't sleep. So she went for a drive and I went with."

"You didn't ask me?" Lucille had said. "What's going on between you two?"

And then her sister stopped buttering her toast. She was going to apologize now, Lucille thought. She would tell her everything. "You were asleep," Ada said. And then a pause. "You and I don't have to do *everything* together, you know."

Lucille's face grew hot. She retreated into her room and felt like a scolded child.

ADA didn't see Sophie much during the day because of Sophie's job, so at first it was nothing more than pressed flowers tucked between pages. It was almost as if they saved their thoughts for each other, carefully compressing them in the pages of their favorite books. Ada would wait until after dinner to go into the library, and as she slipped through the door, she'd thrill at the feel of Sophie's gaze on her back.

Today, she reached for the copy of *The Great Gatsby*, its blue spine sticking out slightly on the shelf. A sprig of lavender fell out when she opened it. Ada searched for a note, but there was none. Back in the kitchen, where Sophie, Rennie, and Lucille were talking over bowls of ice cream, Sophie slid her a secretive smile that slipped away as soon as Lucille looked over. Ada turned and went upstairs, holding the book. She looked at it for a long time in her room, trying to figure out what it meant. In the morning, she put it back.

"You're being kind of weird these days," Lucille said. She sat on the floor of Ada's room while she was taking in a shimmery satin slip dress that she'd bought for her party. "Why aren't you and Sophie talking?"

Ada shrugged.

"Are you guys fighting? I could talk to her." Lucille's finger slipped and she let out a hiss of pain. "Ow." She sucked on her thumb and shook it out.

"It's nothing." Ada usually told her sister everything, but she wanted this for herself.

"Fine," Lucille said tersely. She gathered up her dress and thread and went back into her own room.

The weekdays passed; the flowers were secret messages, and it was Ada's job to decode them. She'd deduced that the pale pink daisies symbolized joy, lavender a sense of calm, bright red poppies a sort of anxiety. They were always tucked between the first page and the inside cover, so she couldn't miss them.

She kept thinking about the time she kissed Sophie's cheek. She kept waiting for Sophie to make a move, but she didn't. At school it was so simple. Boys asked girls out to prom with elaborate posters and passed notes scrawled on binder paper. They made out against lockers and in front of classrooms before the bell rang for everyone to see.

In the mornings before school, Sophie helped her dad out in the garden. She'd been doing it for years; working alongside him as he transplanted a new species of roses, or constructed a trellis for the bougainvillea, or clipped hedges around the stone terrace. Sophie was particularly deft in taking care of the jasmine, which was best tended to late at night. Josiah always talked about it at dinner, praising his daughter easily. Sophie tried to suppress her smile. After the hottest mornings she spent in the garden, she'd come in for a glass of iced water with her cheeks flushed and damp, her tank top stretched tight against her collarbones and chest. Ada would watch her tip the glass back, a strange sort of anxiety twisting up in her.

That night, a book of poems by Emily Dickinson had been pulled forward. Between the pages lay a violet. The violet was new. And this time, something was penciled on the page.

To A— p. 41
—S

Ada flipped to the page, her fingers trembling.

XI.

THE OUTLET

My river tuns to thee;
Blue sea, wilt welcome me?
My river waits reply.
Oh sea, look graciously!
I'll fetch thee brook
From spotted nooks, —
Say, sea, take me!

Ada stared at the poem for a long time, trying to decipher the meaning between the lines. Finally she gave up and read the poem out loud, quietly, to herself. The second time, something stirred in her chest. She set the book down and went into the garden. She cupped a soft pink rosebud and the petals fell into her palm. She carried the petals into the library. She picked a book and pressed the rose petals into the inside cover. She returned the book to its place, but left the spine jutting out, just like Sophie did.

Sophie went to work her shift the next morning at the local public library. When she came home, she went straight to her room. Ada lingered around the kitchen, and then in the garden. She couldn't take it anymore and walked back into the library. The book was gone.

The doors opened behind her, and without even turning around, she knew it was Sophie. She stayed facing the wall.

"Hey." She heard Sophie's soft voice behind her. She held the copy of the collection of Yeats poems.

"You did . . ." Ada paused. "The violet. And the poem. What does that mean?"

Sophie tilted her head and took a step closer. "What do you think it means?"

"I . . ." Ada's voice faltered. "I feel like it's about how you feel. About how we feel. About each other. But I could be wrong and maybe that's not what the poem means, and maybe I've been reading things wrong the whole time."

Sophie seemed to swallow. Gently, she took Ada's hand and leaned in. Ada closed her eyes. She felt Sophie's lips press against hers tenderly. Suddenly, Ada's insides were hot oil.

Sophie smelled like oranges and honey and sun. Ada took a breath. Then the pressure eased. They pulled away and Sophie said, softly, looking up from beneath her lashes, "Does that answer your question?"

Ada nodded wordlessly.

"I didn't want to do something you didn't want," Sophie said. "And sometimes I think you're too good for me."

"I'm not," Ada whispered. "And I do want this. That's what I've been trying to tell you."

The dim light of the desk lamp cast muted shadows over everything. It was Ada's first kiss. Heat bloomed in her chest. Ada closed her eyes and reached for Sophie again.

twenty-one

MAY 1990

ADA had been wanting to kiss Sophie again ever since their first kiss in the library. This time, she knew what to do. She pressed Sophie among the fur coats. Their fingers trailed instinctively across each other's hips, waists, collarbones.

The door creaked and they pulled apart.

Sophie's eyes widened. "Did anyone—"

"Don't think so," Ada said against her lips. "No one can hear. Everyone's getting drunk downstairs with Lucille." It was true. Beyond the doors of her mother's walk-in closet, Ada heard music swell from the living room. There was a clink of glasses, and then Lucille's loud laugh.

"You don't want to join?"

Ada looked at Sophie's flushed cheeks and parted lips. The room was saturated with the cloying, floral scent of Mā's perfume. They were hidden by satin and bright nylon shirts and velvet and wool. *This* was what Ada wanted to cling onto. She pulled Sophie in and kissed her again, hard, one kiss imploring another. She tasted like honey. "I thought about you last night."

"You did?" Sophie gave a coy smile. Ada could only register the way the dim light played with Sophie's jawline and brought out the lashes that adorned her sharp, angular eyes. "What about?"

"The library."

Sophie teased, "The books?"

Ada blushed. "About *what happened* in the library."

Sophie hesitated, finally earnest. "I've been thinking about that, too. A lot, actually."

Ada whispered, "What are you thinking now?"

Sophie met her eyes. Ada felt her fingers tremble with the strap of her dress. Ada smiled and slipped the strap off her own shoulder. She used to sneak in here with her sisters when her mother was away and try on her fancy clothes. They'd zip up the dresses and feel the cool satin against their skin. Now Sophie's fingers reached for the zipper of Ada's dress as she fumbled with the button on Sophie's pants, feeling the heat of her waist against her palm. "Careful," Ada said. "We have to be quiet."

"Of course," Sophie breathed. She reached up and kissed Ada, her hand cradling her neck, as her other hand pushed down Ada's dress until it puddled around her feet. Sophie's palm slid down Ada's stomach and pushed her back until Ada's shoulder blades touched the cool wall behind her. She gasped.

"Shhhh," Sophie murmured against Ada's cheek, her thigh nudging its way between Ada's legs. "Quiet, remember?"

Neither of them noticed the dresses around them sliding off the hangers as they started to move together. Or that the door beyond had opened just a crack.

LUCILLE had kissed Reid Lyman and the first person she wanted to tell about it was Ada. She searched for her sister in every room downstairs. She jumped up the stairs and took two at a time. There was no one. Mā's door was open, even though she had explicitly told people to stay out of her parents' room. She crept in and heard voices coming from the closet.

They weren't just talking. Lucille could see Sophie close to Ada, surrounded by Mā's dresses. Sophie kissed Ada's collarbone and Lucille reeled back. All of a sudden she felt leaden again, except this time she understood the truth of it all. They wanted to be alone together because they were *together.* And now the secret weight of this fell upon all three of them. Lucille was hit by a wave of nausea, from disgust and sharp anger and the guilt of seeing something that she shouldn't have.

More hushed sounds came from the closet. She swallowed the acidic taste in her mouth and ran out of the room. Downstairs, she reentered a party that didn't feel like hers anymore.

SOPHIE Deng stood in front of the mirror in Vivian's closet as she got dressed. Ada had already headed back to the party. She fumbled with the buttons on her shirt. Smoothed down her straight, short hair. She stared in the mirror at her bright eyes and her swollen lips. "Oh, Sophie," she said to herself, and then laughed shakily. "You are *so* done for."

She made her way down the stairs and through the crowds that had gathered in the hallways. She saw people who'd never even looked twice at her in school. None of her friends were here. Lucille was reaching over the dining room table, pouring herself another drink. She didn't acknowledge Sophie at all. Unsurprising, really. Rennie was giggling on the couch, surrounded by all her eighth-grade friends. Ada sat next to them, sipping wine and fiddling with the speaker knobs. Lucille breezed right past Sophie to go say something to Ada.

No one noticed as Sophie slipped through the crowd. She couldn't look any of them in the eye. Wind coasted through the windows and the curtains billowed. Bracelets clinked and nylon tops shimmered. Sophie emerged into the cool night and ran barefoot down the stone steps. She headed to the one place she knew she could be alone.

The grass was still warm under her feet from the day's heat. She wove through the flowers, through the hydrangeas and lavender bushes and lilacs, and sank down on her knees next to the rose. She squeezed her eyes shut. The memory of the kiss radiated through her, and it was as if she could feel the roots deep in the ground pulsate to her wild heartbeat, to the dim rush of the fountain. The roses had burst into vivid bloom this spring, and now she carefully cupped a bud toward her and breathed in its perfume.

Sophie didn't know exactly when her feelings started. This spring? Or maybe it was years ago and she didn't realize until recently. When did she start looking at Ada and thinking of her, the way her shoulders trembled with her quiet laughs, the pointed look she gave when it was like she was holding a secret just between the two of them, the way her long black hair rippled over her shoulders? Sophie alone caught the quiet moments of kindness, when Ada claimed she was full and slipped Rennie extras of her dessert, or when she talked Lucille down when Lucille was scared she'd failed a test, or when she alone admired the acrylic paintings Sophie proudly took home from art class and looked at them thoughtfully, then at Sophie—and there it would be, the sweet dimpled smile that would make her lose her momentary thought.

These days, her heartbeat quickened every time Ada was near her, every time they shared that furtive smile. Every time a flower appeared between the pages of a book in the library it was a miracle.

But it was wrong. All throughout her life she had been told to keep her wicked desires to herself. To resist sin and strangeness. She was the daughter of a housekeeper and a gardener. *Ada's* housekeeper and gardener.

Her parents had already gotten them this far. Bà found fortune in this place. 福气. They were so lucky that Vivian treated them like family and allowed them to live in this house and paid for their school. Sophie had to do everything right. She and Elaine were raised in gratitude and virtue. They would go to college and set out beyond the house, on their own. They would be able to be the things their parents could only dream of.

But now Sophie wanted to stay.

She *could not* want Vivian Yin and Richard Lowell's daughter. One kiss, she'd told herself, then she would be able to end it. But she knew now that it was only the beginning. Sophie opened her eyes to the darkening sky and unraveling clouds. A breeze tipped through the gardens and she felt the roses sway toward her.

She wanted one more kiss. And then another. She wanted this secret to hold. She dreamed of being with Ada tomorrow, next week, all summer—and she didn't know what happened after that. As long as Ada was near her, was with her, Sophie wasn't sure she cared.

twenty-two

VIVIAN had longed to return to France ever since her honeymoon, and now she was here for Cannes. It was nothing like Paris. Between the sleepy green forested hills and the endless horizon of tranquil sea, cobbled streets knit together shops and homes and hotels. Words rolled off people's tongues as if they had all the time in the world. Maybe one day she'd learn French too.

Vivian now wore a dark blue satin dress with a beaded bodice and a skirt that rippled out loosely around her legs. It looked like deep water, the way it shifted in the light. Her husband's hand rested around her waist. She wished she could grab a drink without his watchful eyes on her. She tried to predict what he would say to her later: that she slouched when she walked, that she drank too much, that she talked too loudly. They needed to be perfect together. Someone came around with a platter of champagne flutes. Richard took two and gave one to Vivian. She gratefully accepted.

Recently, she had been thinking about expanding to international films. She could go back to Hong Kong. Or maybe she could go to Europe. That's what Anna May Wong had done, gone international when roles had gone stale in the U.S. The only question was what to do with her daughters. California had been a good home for her family, but her daughters would be grown and out of the house soon. This was a chance to seek out and talk to some directors.

Richard was trying to get his newest movie funded, a spy thriller, under the umbrella of his new production company. Vivian took a small sip of the champagne. She and Richard approached the table of a French film director. They talked while Vivian stood there awkwardly. The bubbles stuck in her throat. She laughed when the others laughed and drank more champagne to calm herself down.

And then Vivian and Richard were alone again, until Richard broke free, saying he'd spotted a friend of his. Vivian was left in the middle of the room, conspicuous and relieved all at once. She took another sip.

"Vivian, what a vision."

She turned to see Eugene Lyman, his tall, imposing figure in a clean-cut gray suit. He looked tired. His beard was furrowed with gray. Vivian had seen him just weeks before, when they were meeting for his sci-fi drama that Vivian had auditioned for. He'd passed on her and it hurt.

"Eugene." She swallowed her bitterness. "It's lovely to run into you."

"Gene, please. And likewise." His voice dropped. "How are you feeling?"

Vivian paused. He was looking at her intently, cautiously. What did he mean? She was in Cannes. It was the weekend of celebrations. "I'm doing well." She looked around. "Where's Jeanette?"

"She's home," Eugene said. "Went up to see her mother in Seattle. Where's Richie?"

"Oh, over there," Vivian said lightly. "Talking to studio leads, I think."

"Shaking them clean?" Eugene laughed. "I'm sure he's charming them all."

Vivian found herself smiling. "I suppose he does often do that."

"Always has. Runs around showing off all his ideas like a little kid."

"Young at heart," Vivian mused carefully. She wondered if she should've changed the inflection of her voice to show that she adored her husband. She wondered if Eugene could tell.

"Listen. I wanted to apologize for *Dawn Light*," Eugene said. "I really did want you."

"It's all right," Vivian said cordially. "Thank you for considering me."

"Maybe next time," Eugene said. "When you're . . ."

"When I'm what?"

His eyes narrowed. "Never mind."

They sipped on their champagne. Everything was starting to soften a bit around the edges. The pressure in her chest eased. Eugene Lyman drained his glass. "Speaking of young at heart," Eugene said, and his gaze settled on her neckline. His fingers brushed Vivian's bare arm. "You haven't aged a day since I've met you."

Vivian suddenly felt very exposed. Her eyes met with Eugene's. He had always had warm eyes, but now his expression sharpened into something akin to hunger. Vivian let his hand rest on her wrist for a moment longer before withdrawing her arm to reach for her champagne glass. She tried to sound polite. "Thank you, Gene. I'm going to get myself another."

She walked away, feeling his gaze on her. Heat swept the base of her neck, and she couldn't tell if it was tension or disgust or fear. She crossed the room and accepted another champagne flute and looked instinctively to her husband to see if he was watching her, but he was deep in the middle of conversation. She eased out a breath and walked over to him, where he offered a small smile and slipped his hand around hers. He didn't see, she thought. 天啊. Thank the heavens.

"My greater half," her husband said as he introduced her to the director. "Have you met my lovely wife, Vivian?"

After the festival awards had been announced and Vivian clapped politely for them, after the night settled and the stars had come out over the French Riviera, Vivian found herself a bit cold. Her husband gave his jacket to her and she took it gratefully.

She would be lying to herself if she said she hadn't been jealous when others had won awards. She'd once auditioned with one actress who was always a wreck with remembering her lines, but now she was on the stage. Polished. It was her time, Vivian tried telling herself. Everyone had a golden era, if they were lucky. Maybe Vivian's started and ended with *Fortune's Eye*.

Was she terrible for wanting more? After the Oscar she thought she would get big drama and monologues, but it was like she was back to the beginning. They still weren't writing roles for Chinese women. Not to mention her anxieties about her fading youth. What roles she could audition for could be closed to her now. After the awards she went out to dinner with a few of Richard's friends. She knew them, too, through movies she'd heard of, awards show appearances and industry parties. She let the conversation float over her and drank the wine that her husband poured for her, and by the time their taxi pulled up to their hotel, Vivian was relaxed and warm and tired.

She unlocked the door to their hotel room and threw Richard's jacket over a chair. "I think I'm going to draw a bath."

She'd hardly finished her sentence when the door slammed behind them. She jumped.

Her husband said, "You have one chance to explain yourself tonight."

Vivian put her palms on the dresser behind her, steadying herself. "What part would you like me to explain, Richard? The part where I was at your side all night, like an obedient dog?"

"Don't lie to me. You thought I wouldn't see you practically entangled with Gene Lyman?"

Her heart dropped. So he had seen her. She'd been foolish to assume otherwise. "It was nothing," she said calmly. "I swear."

"You were *alone* with him."

"Because you left me there!" Vivian cried. "You *left* me to go talk to someone else."

Before she knew it, he had grabbed her by the hair and there was a sharp pain in her skull. Her right cheek slammed into the wall and his fingers clamped down on her arm, hard enough that she cried out.

"Don't raise your voice at me," her husband said quietly, in her ear. "Not when you've been whoring around some other man who's about to divorce his wife. Who *rejected you* for a movie."

Vivian tried to stay still. The hand twisting her hair tightened and tears came to her eyes. Her mind scrambled, protectively, for rational thought. She could kick him and run. But then where would she go? She was all alone in the middle of France. "I'm sorry. He was the one who approached me. I didn't want to offend him. He could give me a role in the future."

"Oh yes, your *next* movie," her husband said softly, letting her go. Vivian stumbled away. "Because it always has to be about the next movie, doesn't it? Nothing is ever enough for my dear wife, not your Oscar, not even your husband. What will you do? Fuck your way through the Academy until you have another?"

"Fuck you," Vivian spat, matching his vitriol. "The worst thing I ever did was marry you."

Her husband's eyes sparked with anger. For a moment she wondered how he would hurt her next. But then his hands fell limply to his sides. "So you want to leave me."

Vivian said nothing.

"I've only ever loved you." He sank into an armchair, tugging his tie loose. "I'm the most faithful husband you'll ever meet. I love your children like my own, and you want to leave me."

Suddenly Vivian blinked and there were tears. Before she knew it, she was closing the space between them. "No, no," she said. "That's not true. I didn't mean it."

"This isn't the wife I know."

"I'm sorry," Vivian whispered. Her cheek throbbed and her eyes still smarted. She was going to bruise, but this was not the first time. Nor the second or third. Since that first night, though, her husband had been careful. And she covered for him even more carefully. A polite phone call to the front desk when they were staying in a New York hotel, to tell them that the plate accidentally dropped to the ground and cracked. Long sleeve options for every trip, and full-coverage foundation she had overheard a makeup artist recommend to another actress hoping to conceal a birthmark, for her face and neck. Yet now she reached for her husband, and he collapsed onto her shoulder.

"You know I love you more than anything," her husband murmured into her ear. "It just hurts me so badly to think of you with someone else."

"There's no one else," she sighed. "Let's go to bed."

"I'm going to kill Gene Lyman."

"Please don't. Let's go to bed."

She opened the windows to let in the light sea breeze. She glanced backward and when her husband didn't object, she let the windows open a bit wider.

She lay in bed that night, feeling Richard's breathing settle beside her, when a sudden pressure seized her chest. She started to lose feeling in her limbs. She clenched her fists. Maybe she was dying; maybe this is what dying felt like. Maybe she would let it happen and Richard would wake up next to a cooling body. A muffled whimper emerged through her gritted teeth, and her husband stirred. He sighed her name, and she clenched her fists again, tears streaming down her cheeks. He rolled over and held her as she squeezed her eyes shut.

"Were you all right?" her husband asked that next morning.

"Yes," Vivian said. "Sorry. Just a bad dream."

"Don't apologize," her husband said. He stood and walked to the windows. "Come, look."

She joined him. There was no screen. Soft, warm air floated in. It was the cusp of summer. From this point of view, the French Riviera spread out before them, the buildings with their terra-cotta tile roofs cascading upon the beaming sand and the turquoise sea. It was hard not to be besotted with the romance of this place. Vivian felt his arms around her and she let him hold her.

twenty-three

VIVIAN thought she deserved it, that first time he'd hurt her. That was what he made her believe. They'd gone out to dinner with a producer who was Richard's new friend, Elliot Sargent. Vivian had just been interviewed over drinks that afternoon for a profile in a local paper. The journalist wanted to talk to her about her Academy Award, but then they had gotten to chatting, and she'd shown up to dinner a little tipsy. She had laughed loudly at Elliot's jokes, and accidentally spilled a bit of red wine on the table. The producer waved her off good-naturedly. "So," he'd said at one point with a small smile. "Congratulations. What's next for our star actress?" She'd smiled at the tablecloth and told him that she just wanted to keep getting roles. "And try screenwriting, maybe."

"Well, the first, I'd imagine you'd have no problem with. And as for the second, if you ever have something, I'd happily take a look."

She'd nodded at the tablecloth again, unable to hide her smile. When she glanced over at her husband, he was nodding too. But she also noticed his hand was wrapped so tightly around his glass that she could see the white of his knuckles.

He had said nothing then. He drove them home, racing over ninety miles an hour on the highway. When Vivian told him to slow down, he shot across two lanes of traffic and screeched to a halt so abruptly her head smashed into the window. She screamed, and before she knew it, he'd grabbed her by the front of the dress, her pearl buttons tearing.

He'd pulled her toward him and seethed, "Don't ever embarrass me like that again." She'd stared into his livid eyes and gone still.

The next morning he'd cried. It was the first time she'd seen him really weep. He didn't know what came over him, he said. He was more sorry than anything. She apologized for being drunk at the dinner. She hadn't just embarrassed him. She'd embarrassed herself.

For a while things went back to normal. But at the same time, everything became her fault. If she was twenty minutes late to pick up the kids, she was a bad mother. If she spoke up during dinners with other film stars, she was seeking attention. Vivian had auditioned for a role in an action movie and had forgotten to tell him until she'd made it to the final round. It would be her first big role since *Fortune's Eye*. When she mentioned it to him, his expression darkened. "You're keeping secrets from me," he said. "Why didn't you tell me?"

"Why would I? You aren't my agent, are you?" Vivian laughed, half-mocking. She'd tried to shove past him on her way to the door, but he pulled her back by the shoulder and threw her against the wall of their bedroom. Her head knocked into the wall. "Do not speak to me like that," he said, his voice low. The next morning, she woke up to a headache and a bouquet of flowers on her nightstand.

It didn't matter. In the end, she didn't get the role. She auditioned for others and got a smaller part, a hostess in a restaurant in a gritty crime movie. When she told her husband he was happy for her. When they wrapped filming, he'd taken her out to dinner and bought her favorite red wine for the table, a cabernet. They'd stumbled back to his car and he helped her in gently, kissing her forehead before he closed her door.

He was a good husband, Vivian thought. And a good father. He never so much as raised his voice at her in front of the kids. He still made them breakfast on the weekends. He loved her so much, he couldn't always control how he expressed it. That was all.

She went to audition after audition. She got dinner with producers. She saw eyes light up when they recognized her name, but then she wouldn't get hired. Meanwhile, Richard kept getting parts. The lead detective in a thriller, a side part in a war drama, dashing in one role, meek and conniving in the next. He got to direct one movie, and then another. Nothing brought either of them award consideration again, but still, he was steadily employed. Her roles were spotty. Her screenplay had brought nothing but rejections. She kept waiting for something like *Fortune's Eye* to come again, a project written for a Chinese actress, but when it didn't happen, she started to audition for more general roles. Maybe the right director would see something in her and make some revisions just to cast her. But they always said she wasn't a good fit.

Richard started getting restless. He spent more and more nights out with his friends. He had sunk nearly half their savings into the production company he'd started with his mentor, Elliot Sargent. Except the films they were producing weren't doing well. They'd been bleeding money for months, and Vivian hadn't known about any of it until he'd asked her if they could cut back on paying for Elaine Deng's tuition. Then she came across a statement from the bank. She waited all night for him to come home. When he stumbled through the door at three in the morning, reeking of alcohol, she followed him to their bedroom.

"We need to talk. We *can't* be spending our money like this. We are sending the twins to college soon."

"*Our* money? *I'm* the one who's booking everything, sweetheart."

"Look at you right now," she said, gritting her teeth. "You're a *mess.* What are you on?"

"We'll talk about this in the morning."

"Tell me." She went after him. "You're not going to bed until you do."

He whirled around, clamping his fingers around her throat. "Stop— *talking*," he spat. There was a horrifying, blank look in his bloodshot eyes. He shoved her, and she staggered against their dresser. The sharp corner struck her side. Her knees buckled and she cried out. She steadied herself on the dresser and raised her shaking fingers to her throat. He'd never done this before.

"He's been different lately," she said on the phone later that week with Daisy, trying to keep her tone neutral. Her rib still throbbed dully when she took a deep breath. "I don't know what to make of it."

"Oh? How so?"

"He's more . . ." Vivian searched for a word. "Agitated."

"Aw, Vivi, you know he's just jealous, right?"

"Of me?" Vivian asked in disbelief, even though she knew that Daisy was right. Vivian understood. After all, she felt envious of him, too. But after telling herself for so long that she had mishandled her career in every possible way, she struggled to fathom what there was for her husband to be jealous of. "I don't know," she said faintly. "I mean, I'm the one who can't book roles."

There was a pause on the other end of the line. "You're just being selective," Daisy said. "Which, good for you! Means you get to spend more time with family." Daisy laughed. "Now, before I go to my pool's happy hour. How are the kids?"

And Vivian felt herself relax then. "Oh, just great. The twins are juniors and Rennie is just about to enter high school. She's going to theater camp this summer. . . ."

She had sustained herself on the glow of that conversation for a while. *Everyone wants to be you.* They saw the woman profiled in the magazines, this house, her family. She was successful to them. Her children were happy. She remembered the raucous nights with Daisy—fifteen years ago now, wasn't it? She remembered the drive that Richard took her on when he proposed marriage; how Los Angeles seemed like a secret she'd stumbled upon, a treasure she'd discovered. The place that held her future and everything she could ever want.

She'd done what no one else had. Couldn't that be enough?

The next time they fought, it was in an underground parking lot. She'd accused him of being on cocaine and threatened to call a taxi and report him to the police. He dragged her into the car by her hair. That night, she leaned over the bathroom counter and carefully washed the blood from her roots.

She got up the next morning and went to her audition. Afterward she called her aunt in San Francisco from a pay phone. She realized she had missed some hair matted with blood at the back of her head. She cradled the phone to the side of her jaw that wasn't bruised. She hadn't called her aunt in ages, ever since her husband told her not to, that her family no longer cared about her, only her money. She'd listened to him then, but she regretted it now. What if her aunt didn't want to see her?

Her aunt picked up the phone. When Vivian heard the Mandarin, she was so relieved she almost wanted to cry. "姑姑," she'd said. "I'm not happy at home."

"Is it him?" her aunt asked bluntly. There was a pause. "I knew he wasn't good for you. What happened?"

Even after all this time the words caught in her throat. "We had a—a fight."

"What *happened*?" her aunt asked again. "Did he do something to you?"

"I—" Her voice dried up.

"Come here. Bring the children."

Oh *God*, the children. "I can't bring them. They have school. It's March." She paused. "But maybe . . . I can come up for a—week or something."

"Yes. I will come get you at the airport. Just call and tell me what flight you'll be on."

She packed a small bag. That evening, she told her husband.

"I'm going to visit my family in San Francisco."

"You're leaving."

"Just for a week."

"Why?" His brow furrowed. He stood from the bed.

"I need to get away from this house. For a bit." She straightened up. "Maybe that's the best for both of us right now."

His face fell. "What does that mean?"

"You know what I mean, Richard." Her fingers were trembling as she tried to fold a blouse. She just threw it in. The twins and Rennie were home. He wouldn't do anything to her now. "We're so angry with each other. It's not good."

"You want to leave me." It wasn't a question.

Finally one of them had said it. Vivian said in defeat, "So what if I do?"

"Say what you mean."

"What if we made it easy? We could sit down with an attorney and figure it out. Custody. Everything." She stared at him for a moment. His eyes glimmered green in the low light. Then his shoulders folded. He crumpled on the bed and buried his head in his hands.

"I gave you everything I had," he whispered. "I loved you, Vivian. And now you're going to run away from it all."

Blood rose to Vivian's cheeks. "I'm *not*—"

"You're going to abandon this life we built together. Our *family*."

Vivian stopped packing. *Abandon?*

"The girls are so happy. The Dengs are happy. Why would you take that away from them?" He sat up, held out a hand toward her, and she automatically reached out. He twined his fingers with hers and pulled her to him, then he slipped off the bed and onto his knees. From the floor, he held on to her legs like a child. Vivian stood over him. He said, "Double happiness, remember?" 囍; that was the phrase she'd always used, the phrase that came painted on their ceramic bowls. How lucky that two happy families could live under one roof. It was such a radical notion to so many, that she could be loved by Richard as a Chinese divorcée; that her children could be loved by him. But when her husband invoked the phrase, it sounded like a threat. Their two families lived in fortune because of him. She'd signed a prenuptial agreement; his mother had made them. Richard had brought Vivian into this world, and he could take her out of it, too. Everything hinged on him: the money, the happiness of her girls, their access to a better future. The livelihood of the Dengs. Without him she was the sum of a few meager roles. She was nothing.

"You're right, qīn ài de."

His voice was plaintive. "Don't leave me."

"I won't."

"Please don't go."

"I won't. We can go to San Francisco together sometime."

She'd knelt on the ground with him. They wept in each others' arms. He in relief, she in despair. He kissed her gently. In the morning she called to cancel her flight. And then she called her aunt and told her she wouldn't be coming, that everything was fine, that it was just a fight.

• • •

In Cannes the day after the festival ended, Vivian lay back with Richard on a pile of cushions in a private cabana overlooking the beach. Over the course of the afternoon, they emptied a bottle of wine and dozed in the shade. Vivian tucked her head into the crook of Richard's shoulder and pulled her loose linen dress around her. Her permed hair fanned out on the pillow.

A younger version of herself could never have imagined being here, lounging on a beach chair with her striking, tanned husband, ordering lavish food and drinks without thinking of the cost, and having it appear in front of her. She was surrounded by so much blue on all sides. The sand was softer than silk. The sun touched everything: the wine, their shoulders, the water. Still, she felt so empty inside. She thought of what it would be like to float into the ocean; to sink into it and dissolve like seafoam. She closed her eyes. Light filtered through her eyelids and she saw only a muted shade of red.

twenty-four

LUCILLE pulled into the parking lot of Reid's office. It was late enough that the sky was darkening. When she went inside, the lights clicked on. No one was at the reception desk, so she headed straight to Reid's office.

He stood to greet her. "Am I your last appointment?" Lucille looked around. "What's keeping you here?"

Reid ran his fingers through his rumpled hair. "This really complicated will for a producer. I'm currently following up on eight NDAs. It's like pulling teeth."

"I assume you won't tell me who it is."

Reid gave her a cryptic smile. "You can probably google it."

"It's warm in here."

"Yeah. They turn the AC off after seven." He rolled up his sleeves.

"Can't you pass this one off to an associate?"

"I told her to go home. I wanted to handle this. I know the producer's family."

Of course he would. Reid was Eugene Lyman's son, after all. He had Eugene's height and his smooth voice that could captivate the attention of a room. He could have been an actor, but instead he chose to parse out their legacies in fine print. *I want to be a writer*, he'd told her at that party. And yet he was here. What had happened? "Can I sit?"

He started. "Right. Come in." As he guided Lucille toward the chair, his hand slipped to the small of her back and she glanced at him again. He sat back down on the other side of the desk. "So, what came up?"

Lucille sank into the chair. "This isn't really related to the will . . . I just wanted to talk." She exhaled. "To someone."

"Lucy, are you okay? You seem shaken."

That question. To be asked if she was okay was a sign of weakness. It meant that she must be visibly unraveling. To be fair, maybe she was. She was seeing flowers in books, seeing her sister in the mirrors, seeing walls filled with dirt, rippling as if it were alive. "I'm okay. I'm trying to make sense of what happened between my parents." She reached into her tote and laid it all out in front of her: The screenplay. The divorce documents. The slip of paper. "I went through my mother's things." She lowered her voice. "They'd been fighting that summer. About money. And their careers. But I didn't know how bad it was. And I didn't know—" She swallowed. "Mā had tried to file for divorce that summer. And Dad recommended her to a psychiatric facility."

She saw Reid's eyes widen. She said slowly, "I know . . . they were happy sometimes. They took trips together. They went to film festivals together. They went to Cannes that summer. Dad brought home flowers for her all the time . . ." She flung her hand at the papers. "And yet all this still happened. I don't know what to make of it."

There was an unnerving silence. Reid reached across the desk and laid his hand on her arm. "I don't mean to pry. So please stop me if I am. But was something going on with your mother that spring?"

Lucille looked up. "What do you mean?"

That spring. Lucille said, "I think she was . . . frustrated? She didn't like Dad's production company. And she wasn't . . . getting many roles. I thought that was all it was."

"I remember that, actually," Reid said. "My dad talked about it. He'd been all set to cast your mother in a movie."

"Right, I remember that. But at the last minute he picked someone else."

"Because your dad talked him out of it."

Lucille stiffened. "He did?"

Reid nodded. "He told my dad to reconsider. That she wouldn't be a good fit for the role. Because her condition was . . . fragile."

"What do you mean, *fragile*?" Lucille asked sharply.

"I don't know. Mentally unwell, it sounded like. I just remember overhearing at dinner." Reid sounded almost apologetic. He didn't quite meet her eyes.

"What else were your parents saying?"

"Well." A shadow crossed his expression. "You know. My parents loved to speculate. My mom especially. They couldn't face the fact that their own family was a mess. So they projected outward at other families."

"And?"

"They said that something wasn't quite right between your parents. My mom guessed some kind of jealousy, infidelity, maybe—" He met her eyes. "I don't know. It was just my mom."

"And then what? What else did they say?"

"That's all I heard." Reid's shoulders sank. "I don't know any more. I'm sorry."

Lucille ground her jaw. There were two possibilities here why Dad had talked Eugene Lyman out of casting Mā. Either her mother's mental condition really was unstable enough that she couldn't act in movies. Or—

Dad had purposefully tried to sabotage Mā's career.

Which one was it? Mā was angry that summer. Lucille had heard her scream over the terrace and then drive off one day. But that was the only incident she could think of. It didn't seem like behavior that warranted a recommendation to a psychiatric facility.

Lucille considered the second possibility. Even she had sensed a subtle and mounting envy from Dad. He hadn't seemed stable that summer either. He'd come home late sometimes, jittery, stomping too loudly around the kitchen. She had realized later in life that he was probably on coke. Other substances, maybe, too. After his overdose, she'd had to accept that there were things about him she didn't know. He wasn't the person she thought he was.

But would he have gone this far?

She tried to gather the papers together quickly, but there were too many. Her breaths came short and fast; she could feel the panic starting to take over.

"Lucille?" He jumped up and came around the desk, reaching out to steady her. "Hey, hey. You need water? I'm sorry; I didn't mean to trigger all this—"

Her voice shook. She fought to control it. "All these things I wish I knew about my parents, and now there's no way to find out."

Reid knelt near her; his hand on hers. She could smell his cologne: wood and spices. Again, she felt this unbearable tenderness. She wondered if Reid would turn away like her ex-husband would and let her tend to her wounds in private. Lucille had always considered that detachment a mercy. Trained herself to think it. But still Reid looked upon her intently, and she felt the same familiar warmth rekindled in her from his gaze. It wasn't questioning or critical. He looked upon her simply as if he wanted to carefully consider everything she said.

She asked faintly, "Did she hate me, do you think?"

Reid startled at this question. Lucille blinked hard. "I don't know why I'm asking you this. It's just that you're the last person she talked to."

"She didn't," Reid said gently. "I promise."

"How would you know?"

"I asked."

"About me?"

"When she told me to give the house away to the Dengs, I asked her. '*What about your daughters?*'"

"And that was when she said this house would ruin us." Lucille's voice hardened. She kept coming back to that critical detail again. It was one of the last things her mother had definitely said, confirmed by a witness.

"But it didn't—" He faltered. "She did say that. But she also said she wished it hadn't come to that. She said that she had wanted to give you everything."

"And what did that mean?"

"I don't know. The conversation happened so quickly. I wish I'd followed up. I wish I'd reached out to you then. I was thinking about it, actually."

"You should have."

"Well, I didn't exactly have a way of reaching you."

She smiled through her tears. "You could have found me on the internet."

"I could have," he conceded. "But I didn't know how you would feel about it. Me just calling you out of nowhere."

She considered him plainly now. She remembered his shyness all those years ago. So flighty then, fiddling with his sleeve, glancing at her and then away. He had become much more still. His thick, wavy brown hair, streaked through with gray, now fell to his shoulders. The sharp curvature of his jaw was dusted with stubble. There were smile lines around his gentle eyes. She felt it then, intrigue that hummed into desire. "Better decades late than never."

"What do you mean?"

Was he not going to acknowledge what happened after her party? There was his call the next day and the party later that night in Laurel Canyon, the night before her parents came back. There was the day she snuck out of the house the week after, when he picked her up and they spent the day at the beach outlook. She'd remembered him turning the music up in his car on their way back from the beach, pulling over to kiss in the back seat of his car, their lips rough with salt. It was the first time she'd been touched by someone, and it felt right with Reid. He'd called her and they'd talked in secret the next day, and the next. *What could we be?* she'd wondered in one of those late-night calls. *I don't know*, he'd said. He'd sounded uncertain. They ended the call. She never heard anything from him again.

"I waited," she said finally, "for you to call me. You'd just—stopped one day." It surprised her now, how frank she could be about her own teenage yearning. She hated herself then, for sitting by the phone, waiting for it to ring, the hours seeming like eternities. She'd felt pathetic. But it didn't matter now. None of it did.

"But I did call."

"What?"

Reid leaned against the desk. "Two hours later. I wanted to talk things through with you. Your mother answered. She told me you didn't want to talk to me anymore. So I stopped."

Lucille sat up. "That wasn't me," she said slowly. "That was—*my mother* wanted you to stop calling me."

There was a long silence.

"I wish I'd tried to reach you, then," Reid said. "I wanted to be there for you, but I didn't know if you wanted me to. And then your family stopped speaking to mine. And—"

And then there was the rest of that summer.

"I thought I scared you off," Lucille whispered. "I thought you didn't care."

Reid met her eyes, finally. "You don't know how much I did. I thought it was me. I—I'd wanted to say, then, that I wasn't sure what was happening with—you know, with me leaving for college after summer and all. But I did want to be with you. Really, Lucy, I did. I thought I ruined everything."

Lucille was incredulous. "You *didn't*. You said all the right things. You even humored my ridiculous aspirations."

"What, about being president?" Reid gave her a small, fond smile. "It wasn't ridiculous. You had this . . . certainty, Lucille. You still do. I'm sure you know that about yourself. I remember you looked—I don't know if you remember that night we met, but at some point we were outside overlooking your garden and you were in this kind of magnificent golden light. I would have believed anything you said."

Lucille was stilled by this immediate sincerity. He wanted her too. She was sure of it now. The desire now expanded and saturated the rest of her. She remembered what he'd said to her over the phone once. *I want to know everything about you.* "Spoken like a true writer."

"Don't worry. I didn't get my Pulitzer, either."

"No?"

He crossed his arms. "I'm here, aren't I?"

Had he tried? Given up? Now Lucille was desperate to know what had happened to him since that summer. They could have spoken on the phone. Stayed in contact all these years. There could have been a version of her that loved him all this time. But Lucille had changed beyond her own recognition. And it was impossible to work backward; to reach that night and the selves they were when their eyes first met over the dining room table.

Instead, she stood. "I should go."

Reid stepped back. He nodded. "Here, I'll walk out with you."

He stood, gathered his briefcase. She straightened her jacket and slung her tote over her shoulder. In front of her, Reid flipped the light switch off, settling the room into darkness. She said, "Wait."

He turned abruptly. "What?"

Lucille stepped toward him, tilted her head up and teased his lips with hers.

He stumbled back against the door, shutting it. Her tote dropped to the floor. He pulled her to him, and Lucille felt her thoughts dissolve. His once youthful, slim frame had broadened, and now she heard his low voice whisper, "You sure?"

She nodded. He deepened the kiss, and she felt his hands grip her hips, lifting her onto the desk. She sighed, with need and in relief. She was exhausted from having to hold herself and her family up through this brutal, unyielding week. She deserved this. She leaned back, pulling him with her, feeling him get hard. He reached his hand beneath her skirt and his thumb trailed down until it hovered over the peak of her desire. When he pressed down, she gasped at his touch. Her fingers deftly maneuvered the buttons on his shirt.

They were no longer seventeen and hesitant. She felt his teeth trace down her neck and his tongue on her collarbone. They remembered each other, and she reveled in the familiarity, in the heat of him. A moment ago she had felt lost and unmoored, gaping with pain, but here she was. Here was reprieve.

twenty-five

LUCILLE heard tires skid over the driveway. Rennie flew down the stair-case and waited by in the foyer as Lucille scanned the house around her. Everything was in place. She'd swept up the bottle shards on the terrace and collected beer cans the day before. Today she double-checked that were no wine stains, or none that she could see. She had painstakingly unfurled and replaced the rugs and moved back all of her mother's brush paintings.

The front door unlocked and her parents swept in. Mā had a scarf over her dark, pinned-up hair, every tuck and pleat in place even after an international flight. Large sunglasses obscured half her face.

"Mā!" Rennie was the first to bound up to hug her. Mā set her suit-case down. "Bǎo bèi," she said. She pulled away and adjusted her scarf, which wrapped around her high-collared blouse.

Ada and Sophie came down the stairs together. Lucille felt poison-ous inside.

"How was the trip?" Ada asked.

Before Mā could answer, Rennie piped up. "Did you go see the Eiffel Tower? Can you speak French now? What kind of food did you have? How was cans?"

"It's *Cannes*," Lucille said pointedly.

Dad laughed. "Save the questions for dinner." He looked around. "Mā is going upstairs to get some rest for now. How did you girls do by yourselves? Seems like the house is still in one piece."

"We were okay," Lucille said quickly. "I cleaned the kitchen."

She spent the rest of the afternoon in the library, reading. She could barely register the words on the page. Occasionally she looked over at the phone and willed it to ring. Two nights ago at her party, Reid found her before he left and made her give him her number. He called her that next morning and invited her to another party that night, this time at a house in Laurel Canyon. It was a friend of a friend's, he said. They'd gone together and pulled away from the din of the crowd and sat at the edge of backyard pool, talking as the night cooled. He'd driven her back at two in the morning. They kissed in his car for what seemed like hours before she snuck back into the house. On the way to her own bedroom she passed Ada's empty room. Was she out even later with Sophie? In that moment it didn't matter to her much anymore.

Reid had said he would call. He wanted to take her to the beach this weekend, maybe. Lucille tried to read her book and not think about it all, which meant that this was actually all she thought about.

At some point they reconvened for dinner. Edith and Josiah were still up in San Francisco with Elaine, so Mā reheated dumplings from the freezer and made potstickers. Rennie kept asking questions about their trip. Mā seemed tired. Dad couldn't stop talking about France; how beautiful the weather was, how everyone seemed more relaxed there. "I think we should live there," he said. "I mean, it really is fantastic. How would you girls feel about living abroad for a few years?" He glanced around. "A nice international school? We spend our winter break skiing in the Alps, spend the summers traveling? You get to come with me on set? Rennie seems in, yeah?"

Lucille hesitated. This was coming out of left field. What, were they just going to uproot their entire lives? Dad had certainly been acting a little more spontaneous—or maybe Lucille would say harebrained— these days. He often skipped dinner because he was working. He wanted Rennie to star in his movies. He wanted to produce one movie after another, each one sounding more bizarre than the next. Sometimes he left on trips with little to no notice and it took Mā some time to figure out where he'd gone. And now this.

"So tell me," Mā said when the dishes had been cleared away. Sophie leaned over and said something to Ada. Mā looked around the table. "Did you girls do anything this weekend?"

Ada and Sophie stopped whispering to each other. Lucille set down her chopsticks. "No," Rennie said quickly. "Not much. We just hung out."

There was a long silence. "Hm," their mother said, turning back to her plate. There was a pause. She didn't eat. She looked back up. "Then would anyone like to explain the three vases in the corner of my closet?"

Lucille's heart dropped.

"And why there's a whole shelf of wine missing from the cabinet?"

Everyone stared at Lucille. Dad shot her an incredulous look.

"I—" The words faltered on Lucille's tongue. She was not the one who usually got scolded. "We—invited some friends over this weekend."

"Whose idea was it?" Mā asked immediately.

Lucille looked around the table. Ada didn't meet her eyes or jump to her defense. Sophie raised an eyebrow. She looked almost smug.

"Did—" Dad looked at Lucille, his expression unreadable. "Did our daughter . . . throw a party?"

Lucille swallowed.

And then he burst out laughing.

Mā's gaze darted to him.

"Oh, come on, Vivian," he said. He glanced over at Lucille, his eyes twinkling, his crow's feet deepening. "She threw a *real* party."

"This is unacceptable," Mā hissed.

Dad was still laughing. "Now I really am surprised you didn't burn the house down. Was it good?"

"Everyone is underage," her mother practically spat. "Rennie is fourteen."

"Rennie didn't drink," Lucille said quickly. "I made her promise."

"Swear," Rennie said, her eyes wide.

"Oh, what about the others, then?" Mā turned to Sophie. "Did you?"

Sophie raised her hands in innocence. "*I* didn't do a thing at this party."

Bitch.

"What did I raise my daughters for?" Her mother snapped. Lucille clutched the chair under the table. "To be troublemakers? To invite *strangers* into my house without my permission?"

"Vivian."

"You're supposed to be doing something good this summer. Working like all of your classmates, not doing nothing and *wasting* your—"

"Stop overreacting," Dad said sharply. Immediately Mā shrank. "When I was Lucy's age, I threw all kinds of parties when my parents were away. Younger, even. I threw so many parties when I turned sixteen that I've forgotten half of them."

"But she's not—" Again, Mā stopped mid-sentence. Her chest rose and fell rapidly as she fumed. Lucille wanted to know what the ending of that sentence was. Not—? "She's my daughter."

"She's *our* daughter," Dad said, and there was a finality to his tone. She could have sworn that he winked when he looked at her. "But don't make a habit of it. Or at least let us know. All right?"

Lucille nodded gratefully. She tried not to look at her mother.

They ate the rest of dinner in silence. Afterward, she retreated to the library and stewed. She read in the armchair and watched the phone out of the corner of her eye. She stood and plucked the worn copy of *Pride and Prejudice* from the shelf. The cover fell open and a flattened violet fluttered into her palm.

To A— Page 571. - S

Lucille stared at the words. She recognized Sophie's handwriting. She flipped to the page. There, underlined, were sentences that made her take in a sharp breath.

I cannot fix on the hour, or the spot, or the look, or the words, which laid the foundation. It is too long ago. I was in the middle before I knew that I had begun.

Lucille stared at those lines. She tried not to think about what she'd seen in the closet and what it meant. She didn't know if she felt uneasy because she now knew her sister liked girls or because it was Sophie, of all people. Maybe Sophie was the one who came up with this whole idea and looped Ada into it. Lucille couldn't tell if she should be angry or worried about her twin, if what Ada was doing was secretly devious or perverse. They'd grown up together. They knew everything about each other. But already she felt her own sister slipping away from her, hiding, keeping secrets. And it was all because of the gardener's daughter.

At that moment the doors opened behind her.

"This can't happen again."

Lucille turned toward her mother, still holding the book.

"Listen to me," her mother said quietly in Mandarin. "What you did was forbidden."

Lucille gritted her teeth. "All my friends are throwing parties. Dad threw parties. You throw parties—"

"It's different."

Lucille tilted her chin. "Different how?"

"You are Chinese," her mother said, jabbing a finger at her. "And you always will be Chinese. I will never let you turn into a soft American—"

"I don't even know what that *means*. You're American! I am! Dad is! We all are!"

"Yin Chen!" her mother shouted. Lucille jumped. "I don't care what your dad says. Don't *ever* do this in my house, and don't bring your sisters into it. *You* should be setting the example, not drinking and getting into trouble. This isn't the daughter I know. Even Ada knew better."

Lucille was indignant. "You think Ada did nothing," she said icily.

Mā looked exhausted. "It was *your* party. What did Ada do?"

A long silence passed. Lucille clenched her jaw. "Why don't you ask Sophie?" She set the copy of *Pride and Prejudice* down on the desk with the cover open to the pressed flower so that her mother would see everything. Lucille marched out.

VIVIAN sat at her vanity and thought about what Lucille had shown her. Clearly she was hinting at something between Ada and Sophie. Why were they putting flowers in the bookshelves? And why were they writing messages to each other when they could just talk to each other?

She mulled over this when she applied her lipstick for the day.

Makeup had become her armor. Foundation, eyeliner, brow powder. Her lipstick color depended on the day. Only bright red if the occasion allowed it. Today was audition day. She should appear modest. She chose a muted shade of pink.

There was a knock on the door. Before, Edith could come in at any time. But now, Vivian needed to make sure that everything was properly concealed by the time anyone else could see her.

"早," Edith said. Vivian nodded in greeting. In the periphery of the mirror, she saw Edith dust the nightstand and the dressers. The housekeeper knelt next to the bed and straightened the sheets. Vivian put on her earrings and looked for her layered pearl necklace to match.

She stared at her open jewelry drawer. "My pearl necklace is missing."

Edith met her eyes and her brows knit together. With the back of her hand, she brushed her hair from her forehead and stood. "You lost it?"

Vivian insisted, "No, it was here. And now it's gone."

There was a long and almost intolerable silence in which they could have had a whole conversation, and in a sense they did. Edith shifted uncomfortably. "I don't know where it could have gone. I'll look around for it."

Vivian nodded. She waited for Edith to retreat, but her figure grew larger in the mirror. Edith sat on the edge of the bed. "I wanted to talk to you about something, if you have a moment."

Vivian turned.

Edith wrung her hands. "I want to ask you if everything is all right with your husband."

Vivian steeled herself.

"I don't know if it is my place. I know that sometimes there are . . . disagreements in a marriage. And I don't mean to pry or intrude. But I saw what looked like a bruise the other day. Did he hurt you?"

Vivian went perfectly still.

Edith came forward and kneeled next to the vanity, clasping Vivian's hands with her weathered ones. "You deserve a husband who is good to you, Lian-er. Come, tell me. What is going on? I know something is wrong. Both Josiah and I do."

Vivian finally whispered, "What does Josiah say?"

Edith gave her a small smile and a squeeze. "We pray for you at church. For you both. 囍. Double happiness, for both our families. Remember?"

It was pity, then. Or was it care? Either way, Vivian felt like she had been split open, stunned and defenseless. Edith cradled her hand gently. "Tell me," she said in Mandarin.

囍. Tears came to Vivian's eyes. She imagined what it would be like to scrub away her makeup and tell Edith everything. She would have, at one point. She blinked furiously and saw the two of them sitting at the kitchen counter, laughing over a glass of wine. Walking in the garden together. Singing Shanghainese songs in the car when they went shopping, just the two of them. Watching the girls play in the garden from the terrace. She blinked again and remembered Edith and Josiah coming around the corner with a cake the night she won the Oscar.

It would be so easy to tell Edith everything. But Vivian looked upon the face of the closest person to family she had had in these last few lonely years, and thought of what her husband had said to her.

You're going to abandon this life we built together. This family.

If she told Edith, then the truth would be out and they'd have to do something about it. This would become something she couldn't control. Maybe they'd divorce. But they would all have nothing without him. Her family, the Dengs. He was their root, and without him they would shrivel.

"Your family is happy, aren't they?" Vivian asked. "Elaine is enjoying college, isn't she?"

Edith tilted her head in confusion. "Yes. But we're not talking about—"

Vivian extracted her hand. "I'm going to be late for my audition."

Edith stood up sharply. "Lian-er." When Vivian didn't respond, Edith tried again. "Lian-er, *please,* listen to me. I am worried for you. This isn't normal."

Vivian couldn't stand Edith's pitying expression. She snatched up her jacket and threw it over her shoulders. She stood up straight and looked Edith in the eye.

"I'm going to ask one thing of you. Don't *ever* intrude into my marriage with Richard again. For your own good."

Edith blanched.

"We're fine." Vivian's lip trembled as she lied. "What goes on is between us."

twenty-six

VIVIAN was tense that summer. It was hot and dry and even the air seemed to stand still, waiting. Edith wouldn't look her in the eye. Josiah was on the phone all the time. His father had fallen ill back in Jiaxing. Vivian kept telling him to go back and visit. She offered to buy him a plane ticket. She had been thinking of visiting her bà, too. Sometime next year, she promised herself. Maybe Richard would let her take the girls.

Lucille always locked herself in her room these days. Vivian finally understood what she had pointed to in the copy of *Pride and Prejudice.* Ada and Sophie had feelings for each other. But Vivian didn't know how to confront her daughter about it, not yet.

Nothing in the house was working. There were yellowing patches of grass in the garden no matter how much they watered it. The fountain water had plugged up and gone stagnant. Her car wouldn't start the day she needed it for an audition. And now the word processor was finnicky again.

Vivian fiddled with the knobs and buttons. It had shut down after she'd printed the latest page and wouldn't turn on. Of course Richard was the one who always wanted the newest model of these things. Their old typewriter was just fine. She surprised herself by wishing that her husband was home to fix this. But he was away at another one of his meetings and she wanted to revise a page of her screenplay. She had the page next to her, with her notes in pen. She worked on the script in her spare time, even though it hardly amounted to anything but rejection letters. Her grand hope had dimmed over the years. After this filming in September for yet another background role in an action film, she had nothing booked for the rest of the year. At least if her roles ran out, she still had this.

The door creaked open. Vivian looked up to see Ada slip into the library, but she stopped short when she saw her mother. "Bǎo bèi?" Vivian called out, but the door had already closed behind her.

Vivian turned back to the machine and was observing it curiously as the phone rang.

She heard footsteps shuffle toward the library, and then stop. Ada again? She picked up the phone.

"Richard?"

Vivian cleared her throat. "Richard isn't available right now. May I take a message?"

"It's the accountant. Tell him to call me back."

Vivian paused and cradled the phone receiver. "This is his wife, Vivian. Is there a problem?"

The accountant paused. "Well, there's a discrepancy on the tax forms for this year on his income and he needs to file an amended return. Anyway. No need to stress, Mrs. Lowell. Tell him to call me back. ASAP. We'll sort it out."

"Okay." She hung up and stared at the family portrait across from her. His income. Vivian had never questioned it. It had been enough. There had always been enough. But now with the production company, he was spending money on his trips to see studios and executives instead of earning money through roles. The production company wasn't doing well. Maybe things had changed.

It was *exactly* the sort of thing he wouldn't tell her about.

Vivian unlocked the file cabinet drawer built into the bottom of the desk. Everything important was in here: her daughters' birth certificates, their marriage license, the deed from when they first bought this property. The files were neatly organized with labels in her husband's script. She found the folder with the tax returns and pulled it out.

Don't worry about it, her husband always told her. *I'll take care of it.* This house, their lives, the money.

And she trusted him.

She paged through the returns. She took in the numbers, slowly, and summed them up in her head. They'd taken in far less income last year than she'd thought. At this rate, if they paid for the twin's college tuitions, in addition to Elaine's, they'd struggle to pay Edith and Josiah's salaries. She shoved the folder back in the cabinet. Pushing the files back, she caught a glimpse of a manila folder at the bottom of the drawer. When she pulled it out, a piece of paper fluttered out with her name on it.

Dear Mrs. Yin-Lowell,

Thank you for submitting All Happy Families for consideration. You clearly possess a gift for storytelling, but I'm afraid I can't quite place this script. With deep regret I must pass—

Vivian sat back. Had her husband been collecting her rejections? She knew where she put them; in an envelope, buried underneath the scarves in her vanity drawer. She'd folded up every stinging rejection letter and tucked it in there.

But this letter had no creases. No signature.

Vivian sat back. Slowly, she flipped through the papers. None of them were creased. They were perfectly crisp sheets of paper, all in the same font. The words were different, but they all held the same sentiment.

With deep regret I must pass.

I apologize.

I regret to say—

None of them had signatures.

These letters had never been sent. They could have only come from one place.

Cold sweat prickled on her palms, her forehead. With shaking fingers, she picked up the page she'd printed from the word processor and stared at the matching font.

Vivian stumbled out of the library. In the foyer, Edith stopped sweeping to watch her go up the stairs. In a stupor, Vivian retrieved the envelope with all of her rejections.

They were all on the *same paper.* Same font.

Her heartbeat roared in her ears like the thunder of an approaching train. The clock on the wall continued to tick.

I'll take care of it, her husband had said. *I'll take care of everything.*

She thought back to the beginning of her marriage, where they didn't want to make a decision without asking the other. They were the architects and conspirators of their shared lives. Had it all—everything—been a lie? Had she misremembered all of it?

Them rehearsing lines with each other, him making her laugh with silly voices.

His hand on her knee, at the screening of his movie.

Of course you can do it, he'd said, when she told him about her screenplay. *You write it, I'll read it.*

Him reading the script over her shoulder and helping her revise her lines, his pen patiently hovering next to hers as he thought of the words she'd struggled with.

The way he'd looked upon her on their honeymoon in Provence and said, *I don't think even a lifetime with you could be enough.*

The way he'd gotten her flowers when she got the phone call for the role of Jia-Yee in *Fortune's Eye.*

Their fast drives through the enchanting slip of the twilight hours, the long afternoons reading with their children in the living room, the late-night calls that poured forth when one of them was away.

All these years she had waited by the mailbox for any response. All these years her husband had sat across from her at the dinner table as she dared to hope that one day there could be a movie on the screen that she'd written. A movie about a big, happy Chinese family. He'd offered to mail them for her. She'd opened these letters—*his letters*—right in front of him. Each time he'd told her that there would be more chances.

She had never had a chance. He'd made sure of it.

If he'd done this, what else was he capable of?

This time she didn't stop her thoughts. She let each horrifying possibility tear through her. Eugene Lyman's words from Cannes came back to her: *How are you feeling?* Tears sprang to her eyes. She ran out of the room and lurched down the stairs. Edith rushed to her side. "Lian-er, are you—"

Vivian pushed past her. She ran barefoot onto the terrace and knelt by the railing, sobbing. She looked over the gardens she once dreamed up with *him*. He had promised her everything and he had taken it away from her too. She could barely register the sounds that came out of her, the hoarse, muffled, wordless wails. She bent toward the railing and rested her forehead against the stone balusters.

Eventually, the door opened behind her.

"Mā," Lucille called out. "What's wrong?" The twins stared at her, bewildered.

Vivian drew herself up. The sight of her daughters blurred through her tears. She couldn't bear for them to look at her. "I'm going for a drive."

She pushed through the girls, refusing to meet their eyes. Edith stood in the kitchen with Sophie, both staring at her. She headed straight for her convertible. The car her husband had taught her how to drive.

I'll take care of everything.

Vivian stomped on the accelerator and threw the clutch into gear. The car jolted backward. The tires screeched and she could smell the rubber burning away on the hot pavement. On the road, the kicked-up dust stung her eyes and the wind knocked the breath from her chest.

She pulled over when she saw a phone booth. Shakily, she climbed out of her car. She lit a cigarette, took the address book out of her purse and dialed Eugene Lyman.

"Hello?"

"Eugene," she said. She couldn't stop shivering in this dry heat. *Stop. Stop!* "This is Vivian. I need to ask you a question."

At the end of the day, Vivian waited for him in the library.

Edith called her to dinner, but she didn't answer. She watched the grandfather clock. She knew he would come to her. She couldn't stop shivering. She'd draped her suit jacket over her shoulders. At 6:47, there was a knock at the door. After a moment, Edith's steps receded. At a quarter past eight, there was another insistent knock.

"Mā," Rennie said. How her daughter had grown. It was as if Vivian had walked to the door expecting her toddling figure. But now Rennie was taller than her and long-limbed. "Are you—are you thinking of eating?"

Vivian shook her head. "I need to speak with your dad first." She softened. "Don't worry about me, bǎo bèi. Okay?"

Rennie nodded and retreated warily.

She finally saw his headlights at a quarter to midnight. She heard the front door open, and his steps approach the library. "Hey," he said, unbuttoning the collar of his shirt and running his hand through his hair. "Edith said you were in here. Are you—"

His eyes landed on the sheets of paper in front of her.

"I'm going to ask you a question." She pushed toward him all the rejections she'd kept. All these years he'd let her believe she wasn't good enough. He had made sure her dream died bloodlessly. In silence. "Did you write these?"

He stopped short. "No. What are you . . ." He paused, and then he gave her a strange look. She'd seen that expression so many times. That furrowed brow. The measured, concerned expression. It used to comfort her. Now it enraged her. "Sweetheart, are you okay?" He gestured around him. "What is all this?"

Vivian drew herself up. "You're lying."

His gaze snapped back to her. Her body registered that this was dangerous, but she didn't know if she cared.

"I'm going to ask you one more time." She pushed the stack of drafted rejection letters toward him. The ones that were unsent, uncreased, and unsigned. How many were there? How many more times was he ready for her to send her work out and hope? "Did you write these?"

He said nothing. That was enough for her.

"I tried," he said softly. "At the beginning. I tried talking to everyone about it. I really did. No one wanted it. It wasn't . . . there's not an audience, Vivian." He stepped forward. His eyes softened. "I didn't want to hurt you. I didn't want *them* to hurt you."

Vivian's chest heaved. *I'll take care of it.* "I don't believe you anymore." She lifted her chin. "I called Gene Lyman."

His expression hardened.

"*You,*" she cried. "You took that role away from me. In *Dawn Light.*" Her voice rose and cracked. "I was going to get it!" The walls seemed to close in. "You fed him lies. You told him I was—unstable." 神经病. Nerves shot and frayed.

"Do you not remember that you were having panic attacks? I told him it was best for you to step back. I mean, clearly your career was taking a toll on you. It was better for you to be home, to be with the kids—"

"*What career?*" Vivian slammed the table with both hands. "I'm getting *nothing* now. I audition for—for a waitress, or a shopkeeper, or any other role where I don't speak. I try so hard, and then I finally get an opportunity and *you* take it away from me! You *monster.*"

Pain shocked through the back of her skull before she registered what happened. His fingers wrenched her hair. His eyes were bloodshot, wild. He was on something. She felt his hot breath on her face and smelled stale, sour whiskey. "Are you not happy with what you have? Other people work their entire *lives* for this, and it's still not enough for you."

Vivian went limp. Tears seared her cheeks.

"What a greedy woman you are," he snarled. "You got what no one else could, and you're still not satisfied."

It was about the Oscar. It always was. She knew exactly how to placate him right now. She could apologize. But she had a fierce urge to hurt him back. She laughed, high and shrill. "You *wish* you got it. You never will." She whispered through gritted teeth. "*You're not good enough.*"

That was when his fingers closed around her throat.

He shoved her against the bookshelves and pinned her with his whole weight, raising her up to her toes. Vivian kicked at him, but his grip only tightened. Her head pounded and she fought for air. "Say that again."

She struggled against him. He wasn't letting go.

His eyes were lethal. "Go on." He threw her against the shelf, once, twice. "Say it."

Nothing could make its way out of her throat. Her eyes felt like they would burst. Seconds dragged; the room swayed before her. She clawed at his hands, but he didn't let go.

Spots filled her vision. The room dimmed. She heard a buzzing sound—was that real? Her husband was looking at her with that terrifying look she knew too well, except the flesh around his jaw was sagging, purpling and then becoming green. His eyes clouded over, bloating and bulging in his sockets, until they burst and splattered against her.

She pitched forward and fell on her knees, blinking frantically, sucking air in with rattling gasps. Light poured into her vision. She was on the floor of the library. She pushed herself to her feet and staggered into a chair. Her husband was facing away from her and she was relieved not to have to look at him.

Seconds, or hours, passed. She kept swallowing, as if it could open up her throat. The room still spun. There was still this buzzing in her ears. "I'm filing for divorce." Her voice came out so hoarse, she was surprised he was able to hear her.

"We're not divorcing." He still wouldn't look at her.

Look at what you did to me, she wanted to scream.

"Let's make this clear," he said quietly. There were scratches down his wrist. He rolled down his sleeves to cover them. "If you leave me, that is your choice. But let me tell you exactly what will happen next. You will ruin this family. You will never get another cent from me. I will get full custody of Rennie—"

"You won't," Vivian rasped.

"I will. I'll get the best lawyers. You won't see her again. And I will make sure you never, ever, come near Hollywood again, Vivian. I will make sure you are never on another screen in my lifetime. You will be a ghost here. No one will remember your name."

"I'm your wife."

"I brought you here," her husband said. "I gave you everything you have."

There was a creak from behind them. Vivian turned. The door hung ajar.

Her husband jerked away from her.

Ada stood there, her eyes wide.

"Hua-er," Vivian whispered, Ada's nickname. She swallowed, again. "Go back to bed, Ada."

This time Ada didn't move. "What's going on?" Her eyes narrowed and she stepped forward. "What are you fighting about?"

He walked toward Ada. "We were talking. Just go back to bed."

"*No*," Ada said, and her voice trembled. "I'm tired of not knowing. Tell me!"

Her husband lunged forward and slammed his fist against the door. He roared, "*Get out!!*"

Her daughter froze. She stumbled back and opened her mouth, but then she ran.

Vivian staggered after her. "Bǎo bèi," she croaked. Ada ran up the stairs. Vivian tried to follow her, but she got dizzy and fell on the first step. Ada's door closed and the lock clicked.

It was the first time she had seen her husband's violence turn toward her children. She felt both trapped in her body and as though she was floating outside of it at the same time. Her breaths were ragged and painful. *Wake up*, she told herself. *Wake up.*

But this was not a dream.

Her husband came into the foyer and when he looked down at her his expression was empty. "Look at what we've done to ourselves." He shook his head. "Look at what we've done to our family. Let's just go to bed."

twenty-seven

JUNE 1990

VIVIAN searched the house the next morning, but the letters were gone. In the kitchen she saw Edith talking to Richard. Their heads lifted when they saw her. Her husband had his hands on his hips. His sleeves were rolled down. He held his bag at his side.

"Morning." His gaze lingered to the scarf she'd tied around her neck. He kissed Vivian's forehead and then left. Vivian tried not to recoil from his touch. Edith didn't meet her eyes. She busied herself with breakfast. In the kitchen, Lucille, Ada, and Sophie sat at the table. Edith had driven Rennie to her theater camp. Ada stared into her bowl of cereal. Vivian looked at her. Was her daughter going to say something? Had she told everyone? How could Vivian possibly explain it away? She tried to think of what she could say to comfort her daughter. "Does anyone need breakfast?"

Lucille spoke up. "Ā Yí already made us hard-boiled eggs. What's wrong with your voice?"

"Just a cold," she said. "I'm not feeling very well." It hurt so much to speak that tears came to her eyes. So she poured a cup of white tea and retreated to the library. She sat at the desk and stared ahead listlessly.

She'd start calling up directors herself. She would be spare with the details: marriage troubles, a husband who would fly into a rage. *That's not the Richard I know*, they would say, and she would brace herself for the answer. *I know. That's not the man I married.*

She had to try.

She rifled through the drawers and pulled out the magazine feature she'd done with him.

The Power of a Dramatic Duo.

"What a beautiful couple," the photographer had said. He'd told Richard that he could run for president, and Vivian had known exactly what the photographer meant; Richard captivated. You wanted to confide in him. Do anything for him. Before, she'd been proud. Possessive. Now she felt sick. She felt like she was going to vomit. She closed her eyes and waited for the room to stop spinning.

Richard came back in the late afternoon. She greeted him with a cool kiss. He made dinner for the girls, which she skipped, saying she had a headache. She lay in bed for hours as dusk sank into night, her head pounding, feeling like the room was still spinning. There was still that buzzing sound in her ears, that low roar. She heard her husband come in. He kissed her shoulders, the top of her head, the back of her neck, and she felt revolted.

In the middle of night she lay awake, still thinking about the rejection letters. She went downstairs and searched her husband's briefcase for any remaining copies. She had to know that she didn't make this all up, but she came across something else instead.

PALISADES PSYCHIATRIC CENTER

RECOMMENDATION FOR VIVIAN YIN LOWELL

She stared at her name on the paper. She remembered how her daughters couldn't look her in the eye. How Edith was whispering to Richard. Her own family thought she was crazy.

When she finally fell asleep that night, she dreamed that she stood in the doorway of her bedroom. This time, Laura Dalby just sat on the bed. Her bloodied nightgown hung from her in shreds. She looked directly at Vivian with an empty gaze. Her eyes were sunken, her lips pale. She bared her neck and Vivian could see the flesh slashed at her throat, exposing the severed tendons.

"He killed me," she said, as blood spurted between her teeth and splattered onto her nightgown. "He'll kill you too."

• • •

Vivian was not safe. The next day she woke up and was possessed by a numb sense of dread. When she drove, her hands shook at the steering wheel until she had to pull over. She felt like she was wading through fog. That night, and then the next, and the next, she let herself be held by her husband. He didn't raise his voice at her again. His kindness felt like a threat. A truce forced by sheer will.

He'll kill you too.

She sat at her vanity that morning and stared at her reflection.

Her skin was uneven and dry. Divots probed between her brows and wrinkles lined her eyes. Her eyes were puffier than they used to be. The skin on her neck, once taut, now sagged slightly. She pressed her fingers lightly to the splotches of bruises that trailed down the left side of her neck and on her collarbone. They were just beginning to yellow around the edges.

It was still painful to swallow. She started to feel light-headed again. What day was today? In the mirror, a hand slipped around her throat. Panic clamped down on her. She couldn't breathe. Vivian clawed at her throat, yelping in pain when she scratched into flesh.

The dizziness passed and suddenly she was able to draw a breath again. Vivian looked back up at the mirror and the hand was gone. She had dug her nails into herself and scratched her own throat. She was safe. There was no one else here.

"神经病," she muttered to herself. She *was* ill in the nerves. She was seeing things that were not there. No wonder her husband wanted to put her into a mental institution. But she couldn't leave him alone with her daughters. Not ever. She saw how he'd acted toward Ada. If she wasn't around, Vivian couldn't begin to think about who he might take his anger out on instead.

That night, after she finally sank into sleep, she opened her eyes to find that she was being buried in an open grave. Dirt piled up on her body as she screamed her daughters' names. They stared at her with blank eyes. When Rennie turned, she saw that the side of her jaw was covered with bruises. Her mouth filled with earth.

Vivian lurched up from her nightmare. She went to Rennie's room and eased open the door. Her daughter slept peacefully, her hand curled up next to her on the pillow. Vivian closed the door in relief.

She went downstairs, then down the terrace steps and felt the dirt crumble under her feet. Sophie was trying her best, but in Josiah's absence, a few weeds had sprouted. Vivian knelt. She couldn't shake herself from her nightmares. The one she just had, with her daughter being hurt. The one she had nights ago, where Laura Dalby was murdered.

She stared around her. Everything—this serene garden, the house they'd built, was not a peaceful place. Amos Dalby had died in this garden. Laura Dalby had died in the house.

She shuddered with another horrifying speculation. What if the robbery had not been random after all? Even if Amos had been out of the house at the time, that didn't mean he couldn't have arranged his wife's death. That notion was no longer an impossibility. Vivian now knew her own husband could kill her. He might. His jealousy had festered for years and now it was lethal. If he couldn't kill her for it, he would take everything from her and leave her to rot in a facility, and then he was going to hurt her children.

She ground her fist into the soil. She remembered how long ago she had heard stories from an old woman in the city where she grew up about how Ming dynasty concubines were buried with their emperor when he died. Vivian, Yin Zi-Lian then, had asked her how they all happened to die at the same time.

The woman had looked at her with a chilling expression. "They were buried alive, child. They had no choice."

But Vivian did. She was not going to let her husband ruin her or her children. Vivian Yin had fought tooth and nail to survive in this country. To make sure her children survived. She would not die a good wife.

twenty-eight

SOPHIE nearly had a heart attack when she found Vivian, surrounded by a cluster of potted flowers, in the middle of the night. The actress had a wild look in her eyes; her hands were covered in soil.

"Ā Yí?" On instinct, Sophie moved to hide the flowers she'd plucked, and fixed her hands behind her back.

Her mother had told Sophie that Vivian had been acting erratic recently. And now, finding Vivian out here pawing through the soil in her satin pajamas and some leather gloves, surrounded by pots of flowers Sophie had never seen before, it seemed like Mā was right.

Vivian's eyes narrowed. "What are you doing out here this late?"

Sophie cleared her throat. "Um. I was just taking a walk. Couldn't sleep."

"I couldn't sleep either," Vivian said softly. She stared around her as if she were trying to get a sense of her bearings. "I thought I'd . . . plant some new flowers."

"What flowers?"

Vivian's gaze shifted down. "What are you holding in your hands?"

Shit. Sophie hesitated. "I . . ."

"Go on, show me."

She could do nothing but hold out the flowers she had cut at the height of their bloom. Their petals were still fresh. She tried to rush an excuse. "I didn't mean to take your flowers, Ā Yí. I just saw that some of them needed pruning. Since Bà is away." She didn't dare look up.

"Are these the flowers I see pressed in my books?"

Vivian saw them? Sophie's mind raced. "No, they—"

"I see your notes in those books," Vivian said. "Are those for my daughter?"

The petals dropped to the ground. Sophie was trapped. They weren't careful enough, and now Vivian knew. And she'd tell Bà and Mā and then they'd drag her to church and force her to pray for forgiveness.

Vivian could have her thrown out.

But when she looked up, the actress's eyes were kind. "You can tell me."

She couldn't.

"There's something between you and Ada, isn't there?"

Sophie needed to calm down. She had to talk herself out of this.

"You can trust me," Vivian said. "I think it's sweet."

Sophie stopped still. "You do?"

Vivian nodded. "My daughter is lovely. I'm not surprised you think so too."

"Please don't tell my parents," Sophie whispered. "They can't know."

Vivian lowered her voice. "Then your secret is safe with me. And don't leave these on my account." She gestured at the petals on the ground between them.

Warmth flooded Sophie's chest. Suddenly she was glad that of all the people, she'd told Vivian. All this time, whenever Sophie wasn't with Ada, she felt wrong and monstrous for the way Ada made her feel. She knew her parents would never understand, but she could see now that Vivian, too, had made a path of her own. She knew what it was like to be different. It made sense that she would be accepting. Now the actress smiled at her and there were no more secrets between them.

For a fleeting second, Sophie allowed herself to imagine being with Ada for real. Telling the truth to her parents. Maybe—*maybe*, Vivian could even help.

Sophie tucked her cut flowers into her pockets and surveyed Vivian's work. She cupped the flowers, which had clustered around the stalk, each bud delicately shaped like a butterfly wing. They were a brilliant, deep shade of purple. "I haven't seen these in the garden before. What are they?"

"I don't know. I just found them at the store. I liked the color and I thought gardening might be good for me." Vivian shrugged. "But to be honest, I could use your help. I have no idea what I'm doing."

Vivian offered Sophie her leather driving gloves, which made Sophie laugh. "We'll have to get you some real gardening gloves," she said as she retrieved Bà's pair from the terrace steps and came back to kneel down next to Vivian. No one had requested new flowers to be put in the garden for years. Bà had always been in charge of it. "Let's move these over there. The soil is better." She and Bà had taken care of the claylike soil so it could drain well, padding it with layers of compost in the spring.

Sophie and Vivian hauled the plants over, past the roses that ringed the fountain, past the section of poppies, to the hydrangeas, and gently loosened the soil around their roots. Sophie showed Vivian how to slowly tip the plants into the ground and take care to set them upright and then pack in the dirt around the roots again. When they were done, she leaned back and examined their handiwork. The flowers blended in well against the pale hydrangeas. "There. We'll water these every few days and check on them. Make sure it's properly draining."

Vivian appraised the flowers, too. "You're right. They're beautiful here." Her knees were stained from the dirt, but she looked calmer than Sophie had seen her in weeks. She turned to Sophie. "You're good at this. You have your bà's gift."

Vivian stared at her for a second more, as if she wanted to say something, but then she simply headed for the house. Vivian's robe billowed out behind her as she climbed the stairs to the terrace. Sophie followed. Her pockets bulged with flowers. Her head buzzed with Vivian's praise.

Before they entered the house Vivian stopped. "One last thing. We'll keep this a secret between us. Just between you and me."

Sophie nodded. "Of course, Ā Yí."

"All of this. Not even with Ada. I want her to tell me about you two herself. Promise me you'll let her do that?"

"I promise," Sophie said. Vivian seemed serious, and she was too. Ada deserved to tell her own mother in her own time. A secret for a secret. "I won't say a thing."

. . .

Sophie helped tend to the new flowers throughout the week. She watered them close to their roots at night, after she came home from the library, and then checked on them in the early morning. They seemed happiest in the partial shade, so Sophie made sure to arrange the hydrangeas so that they shielded the new flowers from most of the sun. In the early mornings the flowers were still sparkling with dew, as if candied. Toward midday, the cone-like stems stretched proudly toward the sky, complementing perfectly the hydrangeas that opened in the honey-like sunlight, almost drooping under the weight of their buds, the geraniums, the Spanish lavender. The beginning of the summer had been dry, but with constant watering and mulching, the plants were finally wilting a bit less. The particular jasmine was even back into steady bloom.

Vivian trusted Sophie with this task, and she wanted to prove herself. Bà would be proud of her when he came back. He just had a few more things to work out with Sophie's grandfather's will. Soon, everyone would be back. It would once again be a full house.

Everything was the same and different. Her sister called home. Already Elaine was making a life for herself in Berkeley. She chose to stay in the Bay for the summer. She would phone home every once in a while, talking excitedly about handing out flyers, organizing a protest on Telegraph Avenue, attending events for tenant rights, helping phone bank for a local progressive city council candidate. She talked about being a city council member one day, maybe state representative. Her sister was bursting full of newfound aspirations. She'd always hung out with an odd, nerdy crowd at school, but now she'd finally found her place. "Oh, by the way, I got my first tattoo last weekend. Don't tell Mā yet." She paused, then said, in hushed, exhilarated tones, "Just wait until you go to college." Car horns sounded in the distance.

During the day Sophie drove around with Lucille and Ada. They got ice cream. Her and Ada's hands brushed in the parking lot. She went to her shifts at the library and stood under the blast of the air conditioner, punching numbers into the catalog cards. At night, after she'd carefully washed the dirt from her fingers, she'd hear a knock and

Ada would slip in. She loved that Ada reached for her before the door had even finished closing.

Days dripped by. One night in late June, when Sophie was working alone in the garden, she found herself entranced by Vivian's small flowers. Thinking of which books she could press them into for Ada, she caught a bud that was detaching from the stalk. She cupped the flower in her hands and observed it closely, rubbing the petals between her fingers. The flower had no distinct perfume; it only emitted the bitter, damp scent of the earth.

Suddenly she imagined something so clear that it startled her. She was looking out over a haphazard and rugged garden, filled with lettuce and tomatoes and rhubarb and wild dandelions, lined with moss and rich compost. She knew somehow that it was *her* garden. There was a house, too. The windows were open and she was painting the shutters. Ada was stepping out of the back door in a tank top and shorts. The light was warm on her skin, and she shaded her eyes against the sun.

Sophie tumbled forward and suddenly she was back in the dirt of Vivian Yin's garden. But the vision had been so vivid and the joy so visceral that she ached with the hope of it.

She looked up at the house. Yin Manor, Mr. Lowell called it. This house was dedicated to Ā Yí. This was the garden that Bà had helped build for her. Sophie tore off her gloves and dug her fingers into the dirt, until they touched root. At this she radiated again with the memory of her own garden. Was it in her mind or could she now feel the flower vines threading under the dirt with their own pulse, the roots all reaching to intertwine? She drew her fingers back and giddily plucked some of the purple buds and tucked them into her pocket.

In what seemed for a moment like a mirror of her vision, she saw Vivian come out onto the terrace. Sophie expected Vivian to appraise the flowers, but she barely looked at them. Instead, she came straight for Sophie.

"He's coming home tomorrow," Vivian Ā Yí said. "My husband." She paused. "You should probably take the flowers out of the books."

"Oh." Right. Vivian wanted to protect them. "Okay. I will."

Sophie brushed the dirt off her pants and walked back to the house.

In the library she pulled out all the books she or Ada had pressed flowers into and removed them. Then she erased the penciled notes she'd written. Back in her room, she put the now-dried flowers in her drawer. The violet butterfly-shaped flowers she tucked under her pillow.

She looked over at the empty twin bed where her sister used to sleep. It was strange, having had this room to herself for the past year. She missed her sister. Elaine had rarely visited the last year. She seemed happy there and reluctant to come back. She'd only come back when dormitories were closed down for winter break. She dressed differently now, with plaid shirts and baggy jackets and jeans. Her hair had been chopped short, too, unevenly, as if she cut it herself. She brought tattered books to the dinner table and stirred things up until Bà took her aside and quieted her, and she seemed sullen for the rest of break until she got to go back to Berkeley again. Sophie wondered if Elaine would ever return to this house, or if she'd put it all behind her and Sophie was now on her own.

The next day when she went into the garden, Vivian's flowers were gone. What remained were only gaping, clotted holes in the dirt, as if they'd been ripped out.

"They didn't look right," Vivian said when Sophie asked about them. "I changed my mind."

Sophie felt slightly hurt. She'd tended to them so carefully and had been looking forward to showing their progress to her bà. Now the only evidence left was in her room.

That night, after she came back from Ada's room, her head rushing and her cheeks flushed, she reached under her pillow. She cupped the petals, hoping to bring back that vision, that faintness, the elation, that happiness. Her heartbeat stuttered as if in response. She fell asleep with the flowers curled in her hand.

twenty-nine

MADELINE carefully poured the kettle of boiling water over the loose-leaf tea. "Sometimes it feels like we're the only two people staying in this house." The steam warmed her cheeks. She held it out to Nora. "Careful, it's hot."

Nora lifted it to her lips anyway and flinched. "Fuck."

"What did I just tell you?"

"I'm bad at taking other people's advice," Nora said. "Personal flaw."

"At least there's self-awareness."

Nora set her mug on the counter. "Everyone keeps locking themselves in their rooms. I haven't seen my mom in twenty-four hours."

"Is she okay?"

Nora sighed and pushed up the sleeves of her flannel shirt. Her short hair was up in a blunt ponytail. Nora was taciturn with her thoughts, so Madeline focused on her expressions. The way her jaw would set, the way her voice lowered. What made her eyes narrow. Her perfectly controlled eyebrow raise. But despite so much observation, Madeline still was unsure what Nora was thinking most of the time. "I think so. I'll check on her again tomorrow morning."

"My mother hasn't spoken to me," Madeline said. "Ever since I asked about Ada. I tried looking her up, but cell service sucks. And I couldn't find anything."

Nora glanced her way. "I'm sorry."

"Don't. I wanted to know." Madeline fixed her eyes on the

refrigerator across the kitchen. "It explains a lot, actually." Mā had a twin sister who died. She had always thought that it was Mā's stepfather's death that splintered the family, but it had been two deaths, that same summer, in catastrophic succession. A double tragedy.

Richard Lowell existed on the internet. Madeline had found him. She could read about him. *Actor, director, producer. Died of an overdose.* But Ada was a ghost everywhere. Nothing about her, on her, from her. Madeline only heard herself say, faintly, "There's so much I didn't know about my family. Ada lived *here.* I keep believing that maybe if I stay here, I can understand what happened."

Nora faced the door that led into the gardens.

Madeline cleared her throat and reached out. "I'm sorry. That wasn't pointed, I promise."

"But you're right. The house shouldn't be ours."

"My grandmother gave it to your mom for a reason, though. Didn't she?"

Nora exhaled and turned. "And what would that reason be?"

Madeline shrugged. "A footnote in the will would have been nice."

"A clarification."

"A sign from beyond, maybe. It would make our lives a lot easier. I'll even take messages in tea leaves." Madeline glanced up. "Maybe 外婆 will give us a sign right now."

Nothing shifted, though they both looked around the kitchen warily.

Nora finally laughed. "What are we doing, a séance?"

"Worth a shot."

"Not that I'm an expert on communing with the deceased, but I'm pretty sure you need more people for this. You can't do it with someone you barely know."

"Oh, so we're strangers?" Madeline smirked.

"Well, what would you call us?" Nora peered at her curiously. "Friends?"

Madeline chewed on the inside of her cheek. "I don't know," she said. Something like that. "You're right. Maybe we have to get to know each other better."

"Hm." Nora tilted her head.

"Any questions to send through your legal rep?"

"Come on." Nora laughed. They were standing close now.

Madeline took in Nora's arched brow, the faint freckles across the bridge of her button nose. "You're turning red."

"It's just the tea," Nora said faintly. "It's hot."

"Too hot?" Madeline said. She was teasing, but it was making Nora blush, and that gave her a thrill. "I thought making a good cup of tea was my only redeeming quality."

Nora laughed again. Without another thought, Madeline leaned in and kissed her, long and slow. She felt Nora's fingers brush her waist and heat pool in her chest, then lower, in her stomach. "Let's go upstairs," she whispered against Nora's lips.

Wordlessly they set their mugs in the sink and ascended the stairs and into the hallway. The second Madeline's door closed behind them, they reached for each other and then Nora was kissing her, urgently. Nora's fingers found their way under the hem of Madeline's shirt, ice cold against her flushed skin. Gingerly, she lifted Madeline's shirt over her head, peeling it away from her wounded arm with care.

Nora reached up and delicately unhooked Madeline's bra. They stumbled against the dresser, then the bed frame. Nora laughed and Madeline blushed, but it sounded like a conspiratorial laugh. Nora shrugged her shirt off. Madeline leaned forward, her long hair falling around them like a curtain, and kissed Nora again. She finally pushed Nora's underwear aside, feeling her wetness, teasing her with light touches. Nora let out a soft moan, almost a whimper that lit Madeline's entire being on fire. Confession and concession, she thought, feeling euphoric. *I've finally gotten something out of her.*

Nora reached up, crushing Madeline's lips to hers. Madeline let herself be pulled in. They'd spent days in this house slowly circling each other. Madeline wanted to know everything in the world about Nora, and this desire was an extension of that curiosity. There was no other way to express that somehow, in this vast ocean of silence, Nora had become her life raft.

· · ·

Afterward, Madeline lay her head on Nora's chest. She could smell the sweet vanilla of Nora's lotion. She whispered against Nora's sternum, "Was that okay?"

Nora laughed, and Madeline felt it tremor in her, too. "More than okay, I think."

There was a long pause. Madeline closed her eyes. Her limbs felt like they were made of softened butter.

"Is this weird?" Nora finally asked.

Madeline looked up. "Why? Do you regret it?"

Nora met her gaze. God, she looked so hot with that slow smile, with those sleepy, half-lidded eyes. "No," she said. "I don't."

"Good. I don't either."

Nora's fingers traced her jawline, and Madeline felt herself dissolving under her touch. She felt the rhythm of Nora's breath, the steady rise and the fall. "I don't care if this is weird. I like it," Madeline said, smiling to herself. "Besides, nothing about this place is normal."

"Agreed," Nora said. Madeline saw her reach down to cradle Madeline's forearm and raise it to the light, so gently that Madeline barely felt it. "Let me change this out. Does this hurt?"

Madeline shook her head. It only ached, and it wasn't unbearable.

"Okay. Good."

"Do you remember . . ." Madeline sighed. "I wish I'd brought this up sooner. But when I was out there, I saw the flowers. And they were strange. Something was coming out of them. It was like they were—"

"Bleeding," Nora said.

So you saw it too. "I tried looking again the other day. But it wasn't happening anymore. They were just there."

She felt Nora tense. "We talked about this. We can't—"

"I know," Madeline insisted. "I know we talked about it. Something is fucked-up out there. But things are weird in here, too." Madeline paused. "Do you see the vines?"

"The what?"

Madeline pushed herself up. "It's like . . . vines are coming through the walls. I saw it in the library the other day. Did you?"

Nora frowned. "No. I don't know? Maybe this house messes with us in different ways."

Madeline played with a loose thread. "A personalized experience."

"Did you feel the earthquakes?"

Madeline looked up. "Earthquakes?"

Nora stared back. "The first two nights we were here. But maybe that's because I'm staying closer to the ground? You haven't felt them?"

Madeline shook her head. "I don't feel anything at all up here."

NORA came down from Madeline's room eventually. She couldn't stop thinking about Madeline, the way she laid her head on Nora's chest and brushed her collarbone with a kiss, the way Madeline looked up at her, full lips pursed into a small, trusting smile.

And Nora didn't deserve it.

She had become certain of one thing that night: the house shouldn't be theirs.

Of course she'd wanted it at the beginning. The plan was to sell it and pay for school. It was retribution, wasn't it, taking this house from them? But now she felt uncomfortable even thinking about it. It was the last piece Madeline had of her family history.

The next morning when Nora woke, she steeled herself and headed across the hallway. She listened to the pacing footsteps from within to confirm that her mother was awake, and then knocked on the door. "Mā."

The footsteps stopped.

"Can I come in?"

"I'm busy."

Nora said, "I need to talk to you."

A pause. The hallway light flickered. Something crumbled down from a jagged crack in the wall. Nora looked up and collected it in her palm. Was that *dirt*?

The door opened.

"We can't have the house," Nora started. "We can't be doing this."

Then Nora saw her mother for the first time in two days.

Mā's hair hung limp around her face. Her eyes were frenetic. She clutched a leather notebook in one hand and held on to the doorknob in the other.

"What?" her mother asked blankly.

"Let me in. Jesus." Nora pushed past her. "Listen. We can't—"

She stopped short. Inside, the room was hot and smelled stale. Plates were stacked high on the dresser and the nightstand. Clothes were strewn across the floor. Nora pried away the notebook her mother was now holding to her chest and opened it. "What's this?"

Diagrams were scrawled all over the page in bleeding blue ink. Nora made out the outlines of a room. An arc that represented a door.

Before, Mā had had the dulled expression of someone in chronic pain. But she no longer seemed dazed. Her eyes had a feverish light in them. She was flushed. "Do you like them? I haven't finalized anything yet. But it's getting somewhere." She spoke quickly.

"Mā," Nora whispered. "What are you doing?"

Her mother smiled strangely. Her lips were pulled taut over her teeth. "I'm planning for our house."

Nora stood still. "This house? What—to flip it? You didn't even want to keep this place. You wanted to sell it! And donate the money to all your nonprofits, remember?"

"But this is *ours*," Mā said, throwing her arms wide. "Why not keep it? We can make it into whatever we want!"

"What if I don't want to—live here? What, we're just going to uproot our lives?"

"What life?" Her mother clutched the notebook back to her chest. "Me driving an hour every day through traffic just to sit in a city government cubicle? Sitting in council meetings and trying to persuade people on policies they don't care about? Taking money from my retirement account to save for your school?"

"But I thought you wanted to give back? All those—housing organizations? You hated living here."

Mā shook her head. "Our family comes first. This is our way forward.

We deserve this house, Jiā-Jiā." Mā stepped toward her. "We'll sell our house back in San Bernardino. It'll get you through school. We'll keep this place and make it ours. And when I go, I'll hand it over to you. You can raise your family here."

"I don't want to raise anything *here*," Nora cried out. "This place feels cursed." She was dizzy. Had she imagined it all? The ground trembling, her mother's tear-stained face contorted in a silent cry? The roots, pulling Madeline into the ground . . .

There was something sinister here.

A drop of red fell onto the notebook between them. Nora looked up. "Mā. You have a nosebleed again."

That meant that her migraines were getting worse. But her mother stared ahead unblinking.

"Are you okay? Do you need water?"

"We'll remake this place." Mā wiped the blood from her upper lip and it streaked across her cheeks. "We'll make it ours. We'll scrub their poison from it. It could be beautiful."

"This house isn't ours, okay?" Nora's voice rose. "It never was. It belongs to the Yins. They've lost so much. We can't take this away from them too."

Her mother jolted back. "You're *sympathetic* to them?"

Nora stood still.

"You don't think—" she hissed. "That their family ruined our lives?"

"How?"

"You don't even know what I lost. You don't know what they took from me."

"And what did they take from you?" Nora paused and took a deep breath. This wasn't going anywhere right now. "Okay. You need to lie down. Let me get you some water. You don't look good."

"I'm fine." Her mother turned away, and blood dripped onto the floor. "My head has never been clearer."

"You don't look fine."

"Go," her mother demanded. She frowned as if it pained her to look at her own daughter. "Get out." She advanced and Nora stumbled back, past the threshold. The door swung shut in her face. Nora stood, stunned, as she listened to the lock click into place.

"Mā!" She knocked. "Mā. Let me in." She wrenched the doorknob and rattled it. "Come *on*!"

The pacing footsteps started up again.

thirty

AUGUST 1990

VIVIAN lay in bed alone and did not sleep. Her entire body felt numb with fear. She clutched the bedsheets already damp with her sweat, while the pressure mounted between her temples.

Her plan had been set in motion. It was only a matter of time.

Vivian had harvested what Sophie had grown, root and flower, so that no traces remained. Her husband had come back from filming and was only home for the weekend before he went back to New York, which was all the time she needed. He had three sleeping pills left in the bottle she'd found in his suitcase. She'd tapped the contents of each capsule out, washed it down the sink and refilled the casing with her own mixture.

Then she waited. First for him to pack, then to leave for the airport. He had phoned when he arrived at the hotel a few hours ago. It was three hours ahead in New York, and nighttime there. He could have already taken the pills. He would have.

But she could have measured wrong. Or chosen the wrong combination. A part of her wanted to halt the clock hands that ticked toward her husband's fate. Let her exist right now, in the peaceful night, with her husband out of the house and her daughters sleeping soundly around her. A part of her knew that she would never get peace after this.

This was the only way to keep her life.

She heard muffled footsteps on the stairs. She bolted straight up. Was there someone walking around the house? Richard? Could he have come home? Had she been found out? She wanted to move but she was also seized with dread. Her sheets had cooled under her. Vivian forced herself to step out of bed.

She heard the soft sound of laughter. In the dim light of the moon, she looked at the digital clock on her nightstand: 5:04. She edged toward her door and peered out. No one was on the landing.

The night dragged into morning. Just when she thought it was too late, that nothing had happened, just when she was about to prepare breakfast for her daughters, the telephone rang, sharp and shrill.

Vivian froze. She walked down the stairs toward the living room in a surreal state.

She fell into the seat and picked up the phone. "Hello?"

"Is this Vivian Lowell?" The voice was shaking.

"Yes," she answered slowly. "It is."

"This is Mount Sinai Hospital calling. Your husband Richard Lowell was found unresponsive at the Warwick Hotel this morning."

She couldn't speak.

"They . . . think it's a possible drug overdose. Paramedics were on the scene to try to revive him, but they were too late."

The phone dropped from her hand and clattered to the table.

Just barely, she registered "I'm so sorry, Mrs. Lowell."

Vivian slid to her knees on the living room carpet and started to scream.

Ada was the one who found her first. "Mā! What's wrong? What happened?"

Then Vivian felt hands on her back. She knew that if she turned around, she would see the faces of her daughters.

Her *daughters.*

She was struck with a slow horror. Richard hadn't just been her husband. He had also been the father of her children. And she had taken him away from them.

She heard the voices of Edith and Josiah, stirred from sleep, who came into the living room.

She rose to her knees and saw them all gathered through the blurry film of her tears. She told them what had been said to her in the call.

And she watched the light fade from her daughters' eyes when she told them that their father was dead.

THE LOS ANGELES TIMES

OBITUARIES

Los Angeles, CA—Richard Frances Lowell, aged 44, producer, director, and renowned Academy Award–nominated actor known for his roles in Hamlet, The Great Gatsby, and Fifty Days of Sun, among others, was found dead on Friday, August 17, in New York City at the Warwick Hotel. The cause was determined to be a possible accidental overdose. He is survived by his wife, actress Vivian Yin, and their children.

Vivian sat in the library armchair near the heat of the lamp. She looked over the uneven words on the pad of paper in her lap. She had written and then struck them through with enough force that the tip of the pen had torn into the paper. Ink bled into splotches. English words faded from her mind. She tried writing in Chinese instead, but she only managed ten characters before she slashed them all, too.

What could she possibly write about her late husband? How were widows supposed to grieve? This would be her most demanding role yet, she realized. She thought of the Greek myth he had told her about, the wife who had faithfully waited for her husband to return from war for twenty years. The woman who married Richard Lowell that day fifteen years ago would have waited lifetimes. She would have given herself to him, body and marrow, had he loved her like she had adored him. But he would have killed her. She would be the one at the morgue right now having her jaw sewn shut for the funeral, and her children would have been hurt just like she had been.

天啊. Vivian closed her eyes. *Wake up*, she used to beg herself. Wake up, and maybe this will all be a nightmare. She would be sitting in his convertible, and he would be enchanting her with stories all over again. She would be on the front lawn, her girls small again, watching him race them across the garden, or patiently dividing their treats at dinner, so no one would feel left out. Wake up, and she would be tucked into his chest on a blanket on a day trip to Dana Point, listening to his steady heartbeat. Wake up, and they'd be across the room at movie premieres and events, their eyes meeting amid the camera flashes, with a thrill that at once felt exciting and ancient, like they had been searching all their lives for each other, and they couldn't believe they had found each other, again, and again.

What a great lie. What a ruined promise.

At some point exhaustion overtook her. Her pen fell to the pad and blotted the paper.

She woke up to her husband standing in front of her.

He wasn't more than a few paces away, pale, his skin almost translucent in a shirt that was open at the collar.

He came back.

"Richard?" she whispered.

But her husband did not speak. He did not move. He stared straight at Vivian.

Until he buckled to the floor. His eyes bugged out as he writhed, clutching his midsection, clawing at his throat. On his side, he convulsed and vomited onto his shirt. Vivian rose to her feet and swayed, clenching back a scream.

She started backing up, only to trip over the leg of the armchair and fall. She landed hard on her tailbone with a yelp of pain that was the only thing Richard seemed to register. He went rigid, staring at her. His eyes paled and then went milky before collapsing inside his skull. His flesh bruised and dripped away into the pool of vomit, until only the stark-white bone of his skull remained.

And when she thought it was over, his jaw unhinged and his teeth crumbled into dirt.

Vivian scrambled backward, shutting her eyes as she huddled against the shelves, clamping a hand against her whimpering mouth.

When, shaking, she finally opened her eyes, she was alone. The floor was bare where her husband had just been.

Paralyzing panic gouged through her. After what felt like hours of ragged, wheezing breaths, the most she had managed was to curl into the fetal position and weep.

She couldn't wake her daughters up, but she shuddered with the force of her terror.

She had seen this before. It was always going to end this way. Ever since the night she won the Oscar. The night he almost killed her. It hadn't just been a nightmare—it was a warning. And it was her doing all along.

thirty-one

AUGUST 1990

SOPHIE wore the only black dress she owned to the funeral. It wasn't really even black; in the sunlight it was dark blue. She wore Mā's cardigan over it and pulled it tight around herself.

She pressed a palm to her chest to calm her erratic heartbeat. She had the sensation of constantly falling. She tried to suck in small gasps of air in the heat, but ended up hunched over, trying to suppress the sharp, monstrous pangs that cut through her stomach. Elaine, who'd taken the train down for this, looked at her like she was crazy. Bà, who'd come home days earlier, now sat at the end of the row in his worn suit. He held Mā's hand.

Sophie held a fistful of her dress in her hands and her fingers gripped it so tightly that her nail snagged and tore a hole in the pantyhose. She was sure she was going to pass out. The pastor was speaking, but the words drifted right through her. She could only focus, deliriously, on the figures in front of her. Vivian in the front row. Rennie leaned against her, sobbing to the point that she was hiccupping. Lucille sat stiff and unmoving. And Ada—Sophie could see her trembling.

Their dad was dead. Only hours had passed between waking up to Vivian's screams echoing from the foyer and when the first cameras arrived. Sophie grasped what had happened through hushed whispers. Mr. Lowell had been found in his hotel room in New York the morning after a party. There was an open bottle of liquor and empty bottles of sleeping pills and painkillers. His heart had stopped. That was it.

She'd barely seen him that last weekend he was home. And now they were in the cemetery under a cloudless sky in the late summer heat. So-phie's dress clung to her back with sweat. Groups of people dressed in immaculate black suits poured in. A slow panic dripped through her.

"He was a loving husband and a devoted father of three daughters. He was the gifted son of the late Mark and Cecilia Lowell. He was a prolific actor, Oscar nominee, emerging producer, and one of the most beloved and influential members of the film community. He will be dearly missed." The pastor spread his arms out. "Now, we will hear a eulogy from his wife, Vivian."

Vivian rose. Gently she untangled Rennie from her. A sharp pain stabbed through Sophie's stomach, and she lurched forward again. Her fingernails dug into her thigh. Vivian spoke, but Sophie couldn't grasp her words. At one point, Vivian's eyes settled on her, but she couldn't meet them. She doubled over and squeezed her eyes shut.

She couldn't say it. She couldn't even think it.

Vivian had finished speaking and everyone was standing up now. The coffin was being lowered into the ground. Sophie stood unsteadily with her family. She followed as they walked up to be near Vivian, who was talking with a dignified woman whose face was partially obscured by a wide hat brim. They stood there for a moment in silence, on the grassy slope. Bà reached out and held Vivian by the arm. The woman came over and folded Rennie into a hug, kissing the top of her head. Lucille faced away, her face contorted as if she were trying not to cry. Elaine stood staring at the ground. And Ada looked at Sophie, glassy-eyed. Ada reached out and clutched Sophie's hand. Sophie squeezed back another wave of nausea.

The families took separate cars home. On the way back, Sophie met her mother's eyes in the rearview mirror. Her mouth was dry and she knew there was sweat on her forehead. They had barely walked into the foyer when she raced for the bathroom on the first floor and vomited. She sat back, trembling with effort.

On the cold tile, it was finally quiet enough to consider the ques-tion that had prodded at her ever since she learned what happened. The question that was consuming her from the inside out. There were hints: Ā Yí's sudden interest in gardening. The upended dirt next to the roses the day before Mr. Lowell came home. Hearing Ā Yí on the phone, requesting no further autopsy in a low, firm voice.

And then the final piece that made everything clear: The next morning, when bouquets poured into the house from every corner of Hollywood, Sophie saw Vivian alone, looking at the cards calmly. But the moment Vivian saw Rennie, Sophie watched as her expression crumbled and her shoulders began to shake. An actress, through and through.

Sophie snuck out of the house later that day with one of the flowers from her nightstand tucked in an envelope her pocket. At the library, she scoured the catalog cards for a book in the gardening section and tore through the pages, comparing photos to the plant in her hand until she saw something that made her blood run cold.

Bouquets piled up on every surface in the house. The sweet smell made Sophie feel even worse. She stole a bottle of aspirin from her mother, took two, and then another two. The pain in her stomach dulled momentarily as she climbed the stairs to Vivian's room.

She knocked on the door. "It's Sophie."

Vivian's hair was loose, and she wore her silk robe. "What is it?"

Sophie leveled her gaze. "Ā Yí. I need to talk to you."

Vivian looked at her, then at the book in her hand, and wordlessly she gestured her in. Vivian went to her vanity and picked up her wooden comb, brushing it through her long hair. Sophie sat on the armchair in the corner. "What is it?" Vivian asked, looking at herself in the mirror.

Sophie held out the book. *Mansfield Park*. She flipped to page 241. The violet petals were perfectly preserved, so thin and bright. "I looked up what this flower was. Every part of it is poison. The roots most of all."

Vivian's eyes snapped up and saw Sophie looking at her reflection.

"Sophie." Vivian turned to her slowly. "I told you not to keep these in books."

Sophie tried to keep her voice level. "What did you do?"

"What did I do? My husband overdosed." Vivian's eyes bored into Sophie's with a bloodless stare. She knew, beyond certainty, that her worst fears were true. "I don't know what you're trying to say."

The book clattered to the floor.

"Ā Yí," Sophie pleaded. "Why would you do this?"

Vivian looked at the floor. Finally, she spoke quietly in Mandarin. "If I told you he hurt me, would you believe me? If I told you he tore my hair out until I bled and choked me until I thought I would die, would you believe me?"

She had heard her parents talking about it, once. Her mother had seen a bruise on Ā Yí. Sophie heard the fights. Heard the plates shatter. So her mother's suspicions were right. He had been abusing her. She whispered, "I'm so sorry, Ā Yí."

"He was going to kill me," Vivian said. There was a tremor in her voice. "That much I was certain of. And then he was going to hurt my daughters. But if I left him, he would have ruined us all. Your family and mine." She set her jaw. "Now he can never hurt us again." She lowered her voice. "And now we will never speak of this."

How could they not? "But—"

"Besides, you were the one that grew this," Vivian said, glancing down at the book. "You're as responsible as I am. But we shouldn't think about it, should we? What's done is done."

Sophie jerked back. She remembered kneeling in the garden, her palms buried in the soil. Tending the plant gently. Wanting to please Vivian, who had been so much more accepting of her feelings for Ada than she had ever thought possible. She squeezed her eyes shut. "I didn't know." She was crying now. "I had no idea."

Vivian stood up and moved toward her. "You and I have been protecting each other. And we're going to keep doing it. It's better for us—for everyone—if we keep each other's secrets. Didn't we already agree to that?"

Sophie stared, horrified, into the eyes of a woman she no longer recognized.

"You understand why I had to do this, right?" Vivian tilted her head. "I've kept up my end of the bargain, haven't I? I could have told your parents about you and Ada. And I didn't."

Sophie was falling again, her heart stuttering in her chest.

"Sophie?"

"Yes," she whispered. "You have."

"Good. So we understand each other. That won't change." Vivian reached out and cupped Sophie's face. "We will survive this. It will be hard. But our families will be whole again. Together. I'll take care of all of us." She turned back to the vanity and set down her comb.

Sophie sat in her room and looked out the window that night. The house had quieted, but she had barely moved since returning from Vivian's room. Pain pulsed through her. She needed water. She reached for the painkillers on the side of her bed and swallowed two more dry.

This couldn't be from the flower, could it? Wouldn't it have killed her already? How much did it take to kill Mr. Lowell? She'd touched the flowers with her bare hands. She'd fallen asleep holding it, tucked under her chin. Could she have absorbed the poison through her skin?

Why would it only be affecting her now? The flowers were taken out a week ago. But she couldn't eat. She felt feverish. She was never religious like her parents were, but she knew without a doubt that she was being punished right now. She deserved this, whatever it was. She had to endure it.

A small knock sounded at the door and Sophie jumped. Ada slipped in. "Hi." Sophie rose to her feet. Ada came forward and reached for her.

Wordlessly Sophie held her and stroked her hair. She ached everywhere, but she forced herself to stay standing. It was the least she could do. *I did this to her.*

"I'm sorry," she whispered against Ada's hair. Ada's shoulders trembled. "I'm so sorry."

Ada looked up and their eyes met. Then Ada kissed her. On instinct, Sophie kissed her back. Ada's tongue was warm, but Sophie's lips were numb. *No.* Ada slipped her fingers under the hem of Sophie's shirt, and Sophie gently pushed her away. She swallowed. "I can't."

Ada's expression shifted in the lamplight. "Okay. Not tonight."

"No," Sophie said. She looked at the girl in front of her and her heartbeat surged. She was so beautiful and in so much pain. It hurt Sophie to look at her. She desperately wanted to fully love her and comfort her. She wanted to kiss her again.

All this time Sophie thought she had been safe confiding in Ada's mother. But Vivian had been using her. She asked about Ada every night because she wanted something to hold over Sophie. Now Richard had died because of what Sophie had done; because of her wild and reckless emotions. "I can't do this."

Ada stepped back, looking as shocked and hurt as if Sophie had kicked her. "You don't want this anymore?"

Sophie squeezed her eyes shut. "It's not good. I'm not good, Ada."

"No. That's not true. You know how I feel about you."

"We can't be doing this. It isn't right."

"Why are you saying this?" Ada pleaded. "Did someone find out about us?"

Sophie felt faint. "I—"

"Who found out? Was it one of my sisters? Is it Rennie? My mother?" Ada probed. "Mā found out about us, didn't she? Was that why I saw you talking to her the other day? What did she say to you?"

"I can't— It's not—"

"What did she say?"

"I can't tell you!" Sophie's burst out. She felt like she was going to throw up. "Stop asking. Just—stop. This needs to end. Trust me. Please."

"Needs to? Or do you want it to?"

Sophie said nothing.

Ada whispered, "Tell me that you don't care about me. I won't believe you until you say it. As long as you care about me, I still want this."

Sophie's throat constricted. She couldn't look at Ada at all. She took a shuddering breath and stared at the floor. A moment passed, and then two. The door closed and Sophie crumpled to the bed in relief.

thirty-two

ADA lay in bed for most of the next day in shock. The phone kept ring-ing with condolences and requests from journalists. Edith made food only for it to sit out on the table.

She felt trapped. She wanted to leave the house, but she couldn't drive and didn't want to ask Lucille. Most of all she couldn't bear her mother's absence through all of this. She finally got up and went down-stairs to the library.

Surprisingly, Mā was there. She looked up from her desk. "Bǎo bèi? What is it?"

Ada closed the door behind her. "I thought you were gone. Where were you?"

"Meeting with the lawyer." Mā sighed. "Going over the proceedings. Dad didn't have a will."

Ada took stock of her mother's appearance. She had lost weight over the last few months and her face had a gaunt weariness to it. "What does that mean?"

Mā shrugged. "Everything goes to us. It's what he would have wanted."

Ada nodded. She focused on the bookshelves with the titles she'd practically memorized. The collection of Yeats poems was missing. Her mother followed her gaze until they locked eyes.

"I reorganized the shelves a bit," Mā said in Mandarin. "Actually, now that you're here. Is there something you want to tell me?"

Ada stared at her.

"About what's going on between you and Sophie, maybe?"

So *that* was why Sophie had ended things with her. Ada tried to formulate a response. She could say the notes were from her English class. She could deny it. Or she could plainly say the truth. What then? "How did you find out? Who told you?"

"Does it matter? I'm your mother. Of course I know. You should have told me a long time ago."

Her mother looked strangely calm. Was she furious underneath? Upset that Ada had kept this from her? Ada couldn't tell, and it terrified her.

Ada picked her words carefully. "What did you say to Sophie last night?"

Mā flinched. "*What?*"

"I saw her go up to your room. And afterward she told me she couldn't see me anymore." She took a deep breath. "Did you tell her to say that?"

"I didn't." Her mother's eyes narrowed. "Sophie ended things with you?"

Mā was pretending not to know. Ada was sure of that. "What did you tell her, then? We—" Her voice caught. "We care about each other." And then, even quieter, she confessed, "I care about her. A lot."

Mā watched her, and Ada fought the urge to hide.

"You should probably respect her decision, shouldn't you?" Mā said. "I know what it's like at your age. It's easy to get swept up in your feelings. But you should be cautious about this. If Sophie came to her senses, then so should you."

Came to her senses? "Mā," Ada said slowly. "What do you mean?"

"You know what I mean."

Ada stiffened. She'd kept her feelings a secret all this time because she'd wanted to protect what she and Sophie had. She didn't want to have to explain it to anyone. She'd thrilled at realizing that the things she'd only observed in the past between other couples at school—the electricity, the tension that passed between them with a look in the middle of class, or the murmured words between lockers—she felt all those things and more for Sophie. Being with her was the easiest, most natural thing Ada had ever done. Of course she knew the words other people around her would use to describe it, words they spat and hurled at each other, and it made her skin crawl. But did her mother think those things, too?

She'd heard her parents whisper about it in disparaging tones, how Dad's co-star had been fired from a movie because he was seen with a man at an awards show after-party. And now Mā was finally looking at her just like she'd feared. Like something was wrong with her.

"Bǎo bèi, I am trying to be prudent. I want what's best for you. You know that, right? She's the housekeeper's daughter. I know you'll get some sense. We can forget this before anyone has to know." Mā said this as though she thought Ada would be relieved.

Housekeeper's daughter? Ada thought of what Sophie had told her. That they'd all grown up the same, gone to the same schools and lived in the same house. But she realized now that in Mā's eyes, they would never be equals. That even if Mā was okay with her and Sophie being together, she'd always think of the Dengs as less than.

"You don't know me, then," Ada said. "At all."

Mā's expression turned cold. "I am a tolerant mother," she said. "I could have thrown her out for this. Or sent her away. But I didn't." Mā stood up from the desk to face the bookshelves again. The conversation was over.

Ada paused at the foot of the stairs and looked up at the closed doors. Who could have told Mā? Lucille? But Lucille always came to Ada first. She and Mā always fought. And she'd been preoccupied at the party.

Which left Rennie.

It dawned on Ada. Of course it was her little sister. Ada remembered the night when she kissed Sophie's cheek in the garden and had glanced up to see Rennie's light wink on for just a moment. Rennie *had* been watching them.

Ada knocked on her door.

"Come in." Rennie was sitting on the floor, looking up at the wall. She jumped up when Ada came in. "Do you think Mā would let me repaint my walls?"

Ada shut the door behind her. "Did you tell her?"

Rennie's eyes widened. "What?"

"About me. And Sophie. Did you tell Mā about us?"

Rennie frowned. "No." Ada knew she was lying. "Why? What's going on with you and Sophie?"

"Come on, Rennie," Ada snapped. "*Stop* putting on this act. You saw us. You were spying on us."

"What?"

"You saw us that night in the garden," Ada insisted. "And you went straight to Mā."

"I didn't." Rennie shook her head vehemently. "I don't know what you're talking about."

"Rennie!" Ada's voice came out sharper than she'd meant.

Her sister's bottom lip began to tremble. "Fine! I just couldn't sleep," Rennie said. "I wasn't trying to watch you, swear. I just saw, and then *you* saw me watching you—"

"You always do this," Ada accused. "You always go to Mā about everything. Even when we were kids." Rennie would trail behind her and Lucille and Sophie, crying to Mā when they didn't include her. "But this is different, Rennie. This isn't your secret to tell. Do you know what would happen if everyone knew?" Her voice rose. "If people found out? You ruined everything between me and Sophie. I hope you're happy."

Ada didn't want to stick around and hear Rennie try to talk her way out of this. She turned to find Lucille in the hallway.

She had heard everything.

Ada pushed past her twin sister and went to her room, but Lucille followed her. "What's going on between you and Sophie?"

Ada used to tell Lucille everything. But she looked at her sister's mocking, expectant expression and realized she was tired of it. "I don't want to talk about it."

"What the hell? What is going on with you? Come on. Tell me. I should know."

"Why?" Ada retorted. "Because you always think you deserve to be in my business? Because you want to control every part of my life?" She knew her words were sharp and she reveled in it. She'd never so much as raised her voice at Lucille. She heaved a breath. "Stop—*pretending* like you understand me."

Lucille stood still. She opened her mouth, and then shut it. She heard Lucille slam the door behind her as she left.

SOPHIE had never again touched the dried purple flower from her nightstand. And yet she was still in pain. She'd been trying to sleep, but night after night she couldn't stop thinking about Mr. Lowell. Did his heart seize? Did it happen suddenly or over the course of hours? He was alone in his hotel room. He didn't call for help. Did that mean he was unconscious at that point?

His last moments consumed her. She kept dreaming about him dying over and over, in front of her. Falling to his knees. Thrashing on the floor. Froth bursting from his lips. Sophie would wake up tangled in her sheets and shivering as daylight came.

She knew that Vivian had gotten a lawyer because she saw his business card on her desk. The others thought he was Mr. Lowell's, just informing her of the terms of his assets and inheritances. Which Ā Yí got all of.

But Mr. Lowell's family was closing in. The phone kept ringing. Her own mother answered it at one point and went to find Vivian.

"Tell her I can't come to the phone right now," Ā Yí said.

"It's his mother. She's been asking for you this whole weekend."

"I can't. I need my own time to process. Tell her I'll call her later."

"Okay." Her mother set down her dishrag. "I'm going to pick up Rennie." She turned. "Girls, get ready for dinner."

Sophie watched all this from the kitchen counter, where she was trying to force down leftover rice. She couldn't eat. The grandfather clock ticked, and her heartbeat knocked erratically with it. She watched Vivian, but Ā Yí didn't even look at her. She couldn't fathom the thought of this continuing. Tomorrow she would have to go back to work at the library. And then—?

Ada came into the kitchen, followed by Lucille. Sophie looked away and clutched her chopsticks tightly. She could feel Ada's eyes on her.

Sophie ducked her head and brushed past them. When she looked back, it wasn't Ada staring at her, but Lucille.

Sophie shut herself in her room. Elaine had already gone back to San Francisco. She watched Bà out in the garden as the light fell. Her parents were so focused on taking care of Vivian's daughters and making sure that the house was in order that Sophie slipped by, invisible to them. She had to stay that way, too; if they asked too many questions, she knew she would fold. About everything. She knew that. The pain pummeled her in waves, seizing her stomach. Her lips were numb and cold, but she was sweating. She went to the aspirin bottle and swallowed three more.

The phone rang again after dinner. This time Vivian went to get it. Sophie watched her stand over the phone while it rang. She picked up the receiver and let it fall. And then she went into the library.

Sophie followed her. Ā Yí looked up when she entered. Sophie closed the door behind her. "What do they want?"

Ā Yí's voice was calm. "His mother wants an autopsy."

"They'll find out," Sophie choked out in terror.

"Lower your voice," Vivian said sharply. She sat and shifted her papers. "He's not getting one."

"Why not?"

"Because only the next of kin can authorize it. And I'm the next of kin."

"You can't—" Sophie balled her hands into fists. "She must already suspect something."

"She shouldn't. My husband died of an overdose. Everyone knows that. He was no stranger to that possibility. You mix sleeping pills and alcohol and you take that risk."

"But they don't believe you."

Finally Ā Yí looked up but said nothing.

"What if the police get involved? What if we get put on trial?"

Vivian slammed her palm against the table. "We won't." Sophie jumped. There was a dangerous look in the older woman's eyes. Her hair was disheveled; her clothes hung off her too-thin frame. "You need to calm down. 醒一醒."

"Ā Yí," Sophie said. Her whole body was shivering now as tears fell down her cheeks. "Please."

"*Stop crying.* You can't lose your mind." Her voice dropped. "You put us all at risk." Vivian straightened up. "Everything will be fine. Just do as I say." She reached out and held Sophie by the shoulders. "We keep this to ourselves. All right?"

Sophie nodded. She swallowed. At the door, she swore she heard footsteps. "Did you hear that?"

"What?"

But when Sophie opened the door, the foyer was empty.

That night she went for a walk in the garden. She stopped in front of the roses and looked down at their perfect blooms. Bà had clipped the tops where they'd grown too tall.

If only she hadn't kissed Ada in the library, if only they'd stopped there, if only they'd never tried to—

She had seen that vision so clearly. She and Ada in a house of their own. In a garden of their own. A part of her still clung to the possibility and she hated herself for it. Her insides contracted in searing pain and her head spun. Sophie fell forward, her palms braced against the ground, and vomited into the dirt. She knelt there, her stomach heaving, as a final, horrible thought entered her mind.

Vomiting. Lips numb. She'd been feeling ill for days.

You can't lose your mind. You put us all at risk.

What if—

Her pulse thudded wildly. She remembered Vivian's cold eyes on her, judging her, but now Sophie realized Vivian had not been judging. She had been calculating.

Could Vivian be poisoning her, too? What if it was slow this time? Little by little, until Sophie dropped dead?

She would never, Sophie thought in a panic. She was paranoid. But she didn't know what Vivian was capable of anymore. What if this was her way of making sure that Sophie could never testify? Could she make this look like another accident?

Sophie was the daughter of a gardener and a housekeeper. Her name would disappear and no one would care. Vivian would explain it away to her parents. After all, hadn't they been in debt to her their whole lives? Hadn't Vivian shown them nothing but kindness?

The clouds above her started to swirl. Sophie clutched her stomach and staggered forward. There was only one way out. She had to escape. Now.

thirty-three

ADA backed away from the library door. She bolted up the stairs and nearly ran into Rennie, who was just leaving her room.

Rennie started after her. "Jiě Jie—"

Ada ignored her and continued to her room. She'd thought that Mā had been scolding Sophie again about their relationship. Ada had been poised at the door, ready to stand up to her mother for once and defend Sophie. But they hadn't been talking about Ada at all. Their voices were muffled, but she could make out Sophie's pleading tone and her mother's own stony responses.

Everything will be fine. Do as I say. We keep this to ourselves.

Ada paced her bedroom for what seemed like hours. It was dark out when she finally walked back down the stairs and snuck across the large foyer.

The light was on in Sophie's room, and there was a rustling and muted clatter from within.

Ada knocked. "Sophie?"

It went quiet. Ada tried to open the door, but it was locked.

"Sophie, what's going on?"

"Go away."

"Sophie—"

The door suddenly flung open. Sophie looked around wildly and put her finger to her lips.

Ada glanced past her into the room. Drawers were overturned. A bag was open on the floor. She pushed inside. "Are you okay? What's going on?"

"Don't tell anyone."

"You're—leaving?"

Sophie stood with her arms crossed, wearing a tank top and jean shorts, her chest heaving. Sweat dripped down her forehead.

"What did Mā tell you? What were you two talking about? Is she making you leave?"

"No. She doesn't know I'm going."

"What about your parents? You're just going to leave them?"

Sophie went back to shoving clothes into her duffle. "I don't want them to come with me."

"And what about *me?*"

Finally, Sophie stopped. Her eyes were red from crying, and Ada wanted to hold her. But she knew Sophie wouldn't let her.

Ada whispered, "Do you hate me?"

Sophie's eyes welled. "How could I hate you? I love you."

The air between them stilled.

Ada took in a small breath. *Oh.* She reached out and laced her fingers through Sophie's, elated by her confession. "Then we'll figure something out. We'll reason with Mā."

Sophie's fingers clamped around Ada's wrist. "You don't understand. Your mother wants me dead."

Ada frowned. "What?"

"Listen. You're not going to believe me. But someone has to know the truth. I'll tell you, and you'll let me go. I'll disappear out of your life forever. Okay?"

"Hold on. Wait, wait, wait. You can't just—"

"*Listen,*" Sophie yelled, then brought her voice under control again. "Your mother had me grow something for her. I didn't know what it was at the time."

"What was it?"

"This flower." Sophie's voice started to quiver. "They use it in—in traditional medicine." Sophie lowered herself to the bed, grimacing.

"It's all poisonous. The roots, the flower . . ." She looked up. "I swear I didn't know, Ada. Until after . . ."

Ada became very still. "After?"

"Until after your dad's funeral."

The room expanded and contracted in front of her. Sophie seemed to get farther away. "*What?*"

"It wasn't an overdose."

Ada dropped Sophie's hand and stepped away. "You're not making sense."

Sophie's words were rushed. "Your dad was abusing her, Ada. She said he was going to kill her. So she needed to . . ." Her words were coming out faster than Ada could process them. "I didn't know any of this. I'm sorry. I'm so sorry." She was trembling uncontrollably now. "And she found out about us. She was so kind to me, and I thought . . . maybe . . . we could be together for real." Her voice dissolved into a sob as she clapped the heels of her palms over her eyes. "But I didn't know what the flowers were! She was just using me. I didn't know what she was planning, I swear—"

She stopped mid-sentence, her hands clenched around her own waist.

Ada remembered the night when she stood in the doorway of the library. Something *had* been going on between Mā and Dad. She remembered the glazed look in Dad's eyes, as if something had possessed him; how he had lunged for her. It all made sense now: the rising voices, the distance between them, the terror on Mā's face.

Had he hurt her? How had they not seen the signs? The bruises? Maybe Mā had covered them up. She knew how to do stage makeup. Mā had endured this all alone, and Ada had never asked. Ada was always the one who noticed things. But this time had been different; Mā had needed her, and she had been preoccupied with her own fantasy. It broke her to think about her mother living in fear like that. She remembered how quickly her mother wanted to leave the funeral and sink into her own grief.

If Sophie was telling the truth—

If.

Then everything in her family was a lie.

Her father was an abuser who had threatened her mother until she had killed him. Her mother had used Sophie to do it.

Ada wished, desperately, to go back to earlier in the summer. She could have talked to her mother. She could have stopped those fights. She didn't know how bad it was. She should have known.

Finally, what she'd overheard made sense: *Everything will be fine. Do as I say. We keep this to ourselves.*

Sophie watched Ada as the pieces came together in her mind. "Now you understand. And now I'm going to disappear. I promise. I'm so sorry."

She zipped her bag and looked at Ada, her eyes imploring. "Please don't tell your mother that I told you the truth. Please. For me. I don't know what she'll do to my parents. Just pretend I never existed."

"What will your parents say?"

"I told them I'm going to stay with my sister for a bit. She has an apartment."

Sophie was going to be gone. Ada couldn't stay behind. No, she couldn't possibly wake up in the morning and continue her life as it was. The walls were closing in on her. She couldn't stay here knowing this.

"I'm going with you," she told Sophie.

"You can't," Sophie said. "They'll come looking for us—"

"Your parents were going to come looking for you anyway," Ada said. "We'll go to San Francisco. Both of us."

"You can't leave them. Your family."

To stay here and say nothing was unbearable. But so was confronting Mā with the truth. Who knew what she would do? There was no other way forward.

"I can't stay either," Ada said. "We'll be eighteen soon. They can't force us to come back here then." She clutched Sophie's hands. "I'm going to get some money and pack a bag of my own. Meet me downstairs in an hour."

Ada had never thought about what it would be like to leave. To be unmoored from Lucille, from Rennie, from her parents. She had once been scared at even the thought of going to college. But now a terrifying new clarity flooded through her. Looking around her childhood bedroom in the darkness, she didn't know if she would ever come back.

Ada heaved her bag up and stepped into the hallway. She tiptoed down the stairs. On the first floor she headed for the library, where she knew her mother kept extra cash for emergencies. To think she had imagined she'd known all the secrets in this house. She unlocked the top drawer of the desk and wrote a note. Her hands wouldn't stop shaking. Her handbag sat on the desk. Ada reached in and plucked out her wallet. She swiped a credit card. They would get found out for sure, but this would buy them time.

She entered the hallway of the left wing right as Sophie closed the door to her room. Sophie held up her right hand, and Ada could see the glint of car keys. Of course Sophie was driving. All this time and Ada still didn't have her license because she was too scared. She'd always been so scared of everything. It was time for that to end.

"Ready?" Ada whispered. Sophie nodded.

They slipped out the door and crept to the car, each of them wincing as they opened and closed the doors as softly as they could. They threw their bags in the back seat and sat in the car for a moment, breathing. Then Sophie reached over and gave Ada's hand a squeeze.

Behind them, the foyer light switched on.

"Shit," Sophie said. She jammed the keys in the ignition. The engine revved and the car jerked into motion.

"Go!" Ada shouted, looking back. The front door opened. Mā ran out. "Go!"

They hurtled out of the driveway and onto the road. Ada trained her gaze on the yellow lane markers in front of them. The mist pressed against the windows, as if to offer them some kind of protection. Terror burned away into pure, insane adrenaline. They were speeding, away from the estate, away from her mother, away from the horrible things that her family had done.

They were free. They were seventeen and they could go anywhere.

"You think she's gonna call the cops on us?"

Ada shook her head. "I don't know. I don't know my mā anymore."

As soon as she said it, she knew it was true. "She might come chase us herself."

Sophie's light smile was long gone. Instead, she gritted her teeth with grim determination. Her hand tightened on the steering wheel. The other clenched around Ada's fingers.

"I'm sorry for what my mā did to you," Ada said.

"I'm going to hell," Sophie said. They lurched through one light, and then another. "I know it."

"It's not your fault."

There was a long silence.

"I need to tell you something." Sophie's fingers tightened. The car jerked and sped onto the ramp to the highway. Sophie was driving erratically, and Ada started to get scared. "I—" Sophie's words were cut off as she doubled over the wheel and groaned in pain.

"The poison . . . I think I'm—I think she—"

Sophie jerked back into her seat with a sharp cough and blood spurted out of her mouth, splattering onto her lap and the steering wheel.

"Sophie!" Ada heard herself shouting. They swerved into the opposite lane. "Pull over!" She grabbed for the wheel. She didn't know how to drive. She didn't know how anything worked.

Too late.

Sophie let go and Ada jerked the wheel to right, but the car swung out too far. They spun toward traffic, the oncoming lights flooding the inside of the car as Ada screamed.

thirty-four

RENNIE watched the house shutter itself. No one visited. No one was permitted in.

Wreckage had been recovered from the highway. Both Ada and Sophie dead upon impact. For two weeks the two families mourned. No news reporters were allowed in. Security surrounded the premises. The lawyers Richard Lowell's mother hired stopped coming to the door, and his family stopped the investigation. No one spoke of why they ran away.

Two separate, quiet funerals were held. Sophie's older sister, Elaine, came back for her funeral. Whereas Edith and Josiah were bereft and lost in their grief, Elaine seemed angry. She comforted her parents as they became two hunched figures and asked them over and over again why Sophie and Ada had been in that car together, with their bags, so late at night. No one could answer her.

Rennie herself didn't know why. She could only think of her last conversation with Ada. In the hallway she would pass Lucille standing wordlessly in the doorway of her twin's room. Rennie wanted to talk to her, but her older sister refused to speak. So did their mother.

Rennie just sat on her bed for days. At night, she could hear Edith's hoarse cries downstairs. She watched Josiah scatter his daughter's ashes in the garden as gently as he had tended the flowers. She sat across from him at the dinner table while he cried into his hands and said, blankly, to no one, that he'd named Sophie for the roses.

Flowers crowded the countertops along with short notes for a while, and then stopped.

Rennie had always thought that their two families would take care of each other. Two families; double happiness, Mā always said. But a month after Sophie's funeral, the Deng family left. Without any water, the flowers started to wither in the heat. Weeds sprouted. Mā stayed locked in her room.

For a brief time, it became known around Hollywood that Vivian's daughter had died in a car wreck: never mind that there had been two girls in the accident. No one knew about Sophie. The news labeled it the tragic combination of an inexperienced driver and the dense fog that had overtaken the road that night. Her mother became the cursed Chinese movie star who had lost her husband and daughter in the same summer. There were hushed whispers about her, sensationalized news stories, speculations and theories galore; and then, the news became sedimented by other events and sank out of public attention.

Weeks later, the roses started to grow again. They sprouted atop the remnants of the past rosebushes. The vines stretching, as if reaching for something beyond the garden's borders. And then, late one night, when Rennie was alone and unable to sleep, she went outside into the garden. The buds had opened up, just slightly, and a deep crimson trickled from their centers. Spooked, she ran back into the house. By morning, when she checked again, the blood had long since seeped into the dirt, and the roses were stained only around the edges.

During the day, Rennie watched the house mourn. And night after sleepless night, she watched the flowers bleed.

thirty-five

LUCILLE had gotten used to the twin bed she had back at Lawrence Academy. That mattress sagged. The slats dug into her back. She'd even gotten used to her roommate's obnoxious snoring. In the mornings she'd wake up and the pale light would stream in and reveal her roommate's wall of magazine cutouts.

The first day Lucille moved in, her roommate introduced herself as someone who sang choir and did model UN. Her dream college was Wellesley because her mother had gone there. She invited Lucille to a party. Lucille went out of politeness. She stood in the corner and didn't speak to anyone. After that, she didn't get any more invitations. The walls on her side of the room stayed blank.

Lucille hated boarding school. She hated that Mā had shipped them off, so suddenly that she had been enrolled in the middle of the second week of the term. She hated its cold, damp halls and its mildewed smell. Mā had to ship them winter coats. She sat in classrooms and read while people leaned over their chairs to talk to one another. She sat in the library writing essays while they got ready for parties. They'd known each other for years, and she was the new kid who arrived senior year. Some people tried talking to her, but she didn't respond. She didn't want anyone to know anything about her. Especially not about her father. Or her mother. Or her sister. So everyone talked about her instead, and she let them. Lucille tucked Ada safely away, deep in her chest. In her mind, her twin was still here with her.

But now she was home for the holidays, and she wished she were back at Lawrence. It was a strange feeling to sleep in her own bed again. In the house, they couldn't hide from one another. They sat at the long dinner table, too vast for the three of them, and ate the bland noodles that Mā made. None of them could look one another in the eye.

Mā had faded into herself. Her garish gray roots grew out into her unkempt perm, which flared out around her bare face like she'd received an electric shock. She hadn't booked a role since the summer. For all they knew, she was done with acting.

Rennie, on the other hand, got cast in the Lawrence production of *Romeo and Juliet* and wouldn't shut up about it. Lucille said nothing. Everything she wanted to say, she only wanted to say to her dead twin sister. Every day she passed Ada's closed bedroom door.

Maybe it was good that their mother had sent her and Rennie to a school on the East Coast, one that cost half a year's college tuition. In school she could lose herself in her classwork and come home to a nondescript room. Teachers wrote blocks of praise on her essays. That was the one thing she could control. She was going to get into Dad's alma mater. She was determined to go to Yale. She faded into the crowded hallways during passing periods. Sometimes she would see Rennie, talking and laughing, surrounded by a crowd of her new friends. A vicious pang would tear through Lucille to see her younger sister happy like that. Their eyes would meet, and Lucille would look away.

At school, she dreamed of coming home. She would get on a plane and Mā would drive her home from the airport, and she would open the door and Ada would be there, asking *where have you been?* Lucille dreamed it was still summer and the garden was blooming. She thought about the two of them, sitting on the terrace, driving around. If only she were home—she'd wake up and realize it had all been some terrible nightmare.

But now that she was home, she saw that this house could never be what she dreamed of. Josiah and Edith had moved away. Weeds had overtaken the garden. Rotted twigs and mold collected in the stagnant fountain, which was drying out. She kept thinking about Ada's last moments. She thought about how shards of the windshield punctured through her eye and cut into her brain as the car burst into flames around her. That's what the coroner said.

She was here for three more days, and the feeling was starting again. A strict tightness wrapped itself around her chest and closed her throat. Lucille's muscles locked up, her body freezing against her bed. She pulled in one breath, then another. She just needed to wait for the feeling to pass. This had been happening for months. The minutes stretched out before her, gaping and eternal.

When it was over, she forced herself to sit up and move. In the bathroom, she ran the sink and splashed cold water on her cheeks. She stared at herself in the mirror, against the backdrop of dark green wallpaper.

For a moment the face in the mirror shifted, and there was a dimple that hadn't been there before. A gash on her head weeping blood.

Ada looked out at her from the mirror and opened her mouth as if to say something.

Lucille stumbled back, crashing into the door behind her. A sharp pain jolted through her back.

She heaved breaths through gritted teeth and tilted up her gaze. The sink came into view first. It was still running. Then she faced her reflection in the mirror. Ada was gone. She was alone.

RENNIE knew that the holidays were for family, but her family was broken. There was a reason Mā had sent her and Lucille off to boarding school. She couldn't bear to be around them anymore. It seemed like she couldn't bear to be around anyone.

And Rennie couldn't *sleep*.

One of her friends, Nancy, had given her some of her sleeping pills. They calmed her nerves down, she said. Helped her relax. The first time Rennie took one of those pills last month, she sank so deeply into sleep that she didn't have a single dream. Oh, it was *heaven*. Nancy had given her a couple more, and Rennie had hidden them in an emptied box of mints. She'd run out right before she came home, and now she had spent five nights turning off the lights and lying awake, trying to will herself into slumber.

I'm going back tomorrow, she repeated to herself, as if doing so would push the clock faster. She felt awful for it.

Lucille was the one who had demanded they go home for winter break. They had crouched around the school's communal payphone after another short call with Mā. They spoke in Mandarin, in hushed tones. People passed by and stared at them. "Mā needs us. We need each other."

But then they came home and no one spoke. Mā shut herself in her room all day, or sat in the library staring into space. Rennie tried so desperately to fill the dead air with stories from school, but Mā only offered her half smiles. Lucille stayed silent and sullen and angry. As if this hadn't been *her* idea.

This was how it was at school, too. Rennie waved to her in the halls, and Lucille's unforgiving gaze barely brushed hers before she'd march on, alone, the other way.

"Your half sister's kind of a bitch," her friends would say. "No offense. You're the normal one."

Rennie would lightly shrug and swallow the burning feeling in the back of her throat. She knew Lucille was angry with her. For making friends in this school, for filling her days with choir and theater, for going to parties on the weekends. She felt guilty for running from one thing to the next. But she was scared that if she stayed still and had even a moment to herself, her guilt would consume her.

So she went to class, and then rehearsal. She gave herself highlights in the communal bathroom. She loved not being able to see past the stage. She reveled in the heat of the spotlights. She got the part of Juliet in the Shakespeare production. And it felt good, acting out a part that was on paper, with lines that were already written. She *loved* it.

Rennie was a natural. Everyone told her so. She glowed with the praise. She had arched brows and expressive, doe-like eyes perfect for an actress. She got invited to parties with the older kids from the theater crowd, and they all said she was like their little sister. She played their drinking games, and they called her affectionate names. If they got sufficiently drunk, they would try to guess Rennie's ethnicity. "You don't look Chinese," they would say. They would tilt their heads. "But you do." They'd turn. "Does she?"

Rennie's insides would burn. She didn't know how to explain that she'd grown up eating Chinese food, that she still perfectly understood the Mandarin that Mā and Edith spoke to each other. She realized with a sinking feeling that this was always how she would be seen by others. In-between, always speculated upon. But when they ruffled her hair and kissed her on the cheek, that burning feeling in her stomach eased, just a little bit. She soaked in their affection, smoking joints with them on the balconies while they harmonized and talked about their dreams: New York, Los Angeles, a casting call that was posted in the Boston area for this one coveted movie role. They didn't see her as the kid who lost two members of her family in one catastrophic summer, and she didn't tell them. She was only what lay ahead of her: a promising actress. A bright future. They took her in. "You're so pretty," someone said, holding her chin and jaw once. "You remind me of someone famous, but I don't remember who."

But no matter what she did, at some point in the night Rennie would be awake.

And then she would think about Dad. And Ada.

Now, in the bedroom she'd grown up in, all those thoughts gripped her. She thought about Ada's soft laugh. The times that she would come downstairs and make a warm cup of milk for Rennie in the middle of the night. When they had been younger and Rennie wanted to tag along with her and Lucille and Sophie, Ada was always the one to relent. Lucille would get annoyed, but Ada was only sweet to her. Except for that last night.

You ruined everything, Ada had said that night. *I hope you're happy.*

Rennie glanced outside the window that overlooked the garden, just like she'd done over the summer. Someone was standing in the garden.

"She's out there."

Rennie froze. She felt a presence behind her and, slowly, she turned around.

Ada was looking straight at her. "Go."

A scream curdled in Rennie's throat. She scrambled backward and squeezed her eyes shut. The back of her head knocked into the windowsill, and pain shot through her skull. She counted to ten and opened her eyes.

No one was there.

You're fucked-up, Rennie. You're seeing things.

She lowered herself to the ground, her knees pressing against the unforgiving floorboards. Ada was gone. Whatever that was—a ghost, a vision, an apparition—had disappeared. And yet a part of Rennie wished she'd kept her eyes open. *Jiě Jie*, a braver version of herself would have pleaded. *Don't be mad at me. What did I do to you? Please, tell me. I'm sorry. I'm so sorry.*

LUCILLE woke up weeks later to an uneven knock at her door. They were back at school and it was the middle of the night. A moment later there was another knock. Her roommate snored. Lucille sat up in bed. The unblinking red numbers on the digital clock told her it was past four.

And then she heard, in a soft, muffled voice, "Lucille?"

Lucille jumped down and slipped outside. "Rennie? What's going on?"

Her sister stood in the hall, arms crossed, wearing a too-tight cardigan sweater. Her eyes were wide and framed with clumped mascara. Her lipstick was half-smeared and blotchy. She said in a blurry voice, "I just want to talk to someone."

Lucille closed the door behind her. "What happened? Are you okay?"

"I just—" Rennie sighed, and Lucille could smell something sharp and sour on her breath. "Can't sleep."

"You can't sleep?" Lucille blinked awake. They stood in the stark dormitory hallway under the harsh fluorescent lights. It was damp and cold, and she shivered in her T-shirt. "That's all? Where were you? Were you drinking?"

Rennie shrank. "Not really—"

"You could smell the vodka from Connecticut."

"*Fine.* I was in one of my friends' rooms. Just hanging out. But now they've all gone to bed, and I don't want to sleep. I don't wanna."

Jesus, Lucille thought. *It's almost five.* "Why not?"

"Because I wake up and I feel awful."

That stopped Lucille. All this time she'd thought Rennie had moved on and happily shed her old life. She reached out and held Rennie's arm. Her sister was slightly taller than her, long-limbed and uncertain. They were no longer eye level. Rennie flattened herself against the wall and closed her eyes. Lucille leaned against the wall next to her sister.

"And I get nightmares about her."

Lucille bit the inside of her cheek to stop herself from crying. She said in a thick voice, "Me too."

"Do you think—"

"What?"

"Never mind."

"No, say it."

"Do you think we'll ever be okay?"

Lucille paused for a long time. Did Rennie expect everything to go back to normal? Was she looking for reassurance? Didn't they both know the answer to that question? Lucille didn't know how things could ever change. The school counselor had told her it would get better as time went on. But she was also becoming aware that the more time passed, the further she got from Ada, and that thought terrified her too. She settled on something that she knew would comfort her sister, but it came out sounding hollow. "I'm sure we will be."

Rennie whispered, "Do you ever see Ada?"

Lucille's eyes flew open. "What do you mean?"

"I keep seeing her. She keeps appearing. I saw her when we were home for break. And I just saw her today."

Lucille started to feel numb. "Okay," she said slowly. Her hands were tingling. "Rennie. What were you doing at this party?"

"I was just—"

"Did you take something?"

"I—"

"You took something."

"This wasn't tonight," Rennie said. "This was the other night. When I was coming back from rehearsal. I wasn't taking anything but sleeping pills, I swear."

"Sleeping pills?" Lucille's voice rose. "Are you *serious*?"

"I can't—*sleep*. It helps."

"You're taking fucking sleeping pills?" Lucille felt hysterical. "After what happened with Dad?" She whirled around and shook her sister by the arms. The color drained from Rennie's face. "Listen to me. This isn't normal. You've been hallucinating. You are going crazy. You need to quit whatever you're taking, *right now*." She felt her chest constrict, but she pushed through. "Or you'll end up like him."

She saw the moment her words sank in, and she felt monstrous. Rennie's face crumpled and she broke from Lucille's grip.

Lucille swallowed and dropped her hands. "I didn't mean it like that. You know that."

Rennie was clearly trying very hard not to cry. She said in a small voice, "Okay."

It was the truth, Lucille told herself, even as she watched Rennie's lonely figure move down the freezing halls. It was cruel, but there was no other way to say it. She couldn't lose her little sister, too.

thirty-six

RENNIE dreamed that she stood above the garden, on the last stair of the terrace. A deep chill cut into the air. The stone was cold beneath her bare feet. A figure clad in white was hunched over among the rosebushes.

Rennie stepped down. Without thinking, she walked over sharp gravel and dirt, over grass still warm from the daytime sun. Gingerly, she asked, "What are you looking for?"

That's when she realized the figure wasn't digging. She was yanking the rosebushes out by the fountain. Tearing them out by the roots with such vicious force that clods of dirt still matted to the stems.

"Mā!" she cried out. "What are you doing?"

A younger version of her mother turned. Her mouth was sealed in an angry line, her shoulders taut. Her raw, mangled palms faced the sky. Fresh blood spurted through her fingers. The remains of the roses lay at her feet. Rennie looked into her mother's dark and fathomless eyes and choked back a scream. When Mā opened her mouth, clods of dirt spilled through her lips. She coughed and convulsed.

When she finally spoke, her voice was low and hoarse. "It's for you, bǎo bèi. Everything I've done, I've done for you."

NORA couldn't take another day of being shut out. She woke up and went straight to her mā's locked door with a cup of water. She heard the rustling of paper. Okay. Mā was up. Nora would talk sense into her.

They would be fine without this house. They always were, weren't they? A week ago, they hadn't even known that owning the house was a possibility. They would leave this place and go back to that reality.

"Mā." She knocked. "I know you're up. Let me come in."

Her mother continued to shuffle. Nora held the cup with one hand and knocked, harder.

No answer. "Let me in!" Her voice rose each time she repeated it. She banged on the door until it shook on its hinges. The handle rattled loose, but the lock held. When the door finally sprang open, Nora pitched forward. The cup fell and shattered. Hot water splashed everywhere.

"What have you done?" Her mother lurched forward to sweep the papers out of the way.

Nora looked up.

What remained of her mother's notebook lay gutted on the bed. Next to it was an open blue ballpoint pen. The pages, marked with dried bloodstains, had been ripped out and flung to every corner of the room. Her mother looked at her, her eyes wild, blood smeared under her nose. Her graying hair had come completely loose out of its bun. "Mā," she whispered. She took in this frightening image. "Are you okay?"

Her mother blinked at her.

"Let's—" Nora tried to keep calm. "You don't look good. Let's go get you cleaned up."

She reached for her mother, but Mā didn't budge. Nora tried tugging on her. With a sudden force Mā pushed her away. "I'm *busy*."

Nora staggered backward.

"It's the seventh day," her mother intoned. She rolled her eyes up, toward the top floor. "They're leaving tomorrow."

Nora steadied herself. "And *we* are leaving with them."

"We're staying. This house is *ours*."

Nora grasped her mother by the shoulders. "Are you listening to me? I don't want this house. I don't want to be here. We can sell this place or—or give it back to them, but we can't stay here. Look at you! *This place is dangerous.*"

Her mother wrested herself from Nora's grip. "These are plans for *our* future."

Nora surveyed the scene. "*I don't care about the plans.*" She lunged forward, grabbed a fistful of the sheets and tore them.

"Stop!" her mother cried. Nora grabbed another fistful and ripped them. The shreds fluttered around them like leaves. "We need to get out of here." She reached for another pile of paper, but before she could pick them up, her mother shoved her. Nora fell, hard.

She froze for a moment, dazed. Her mother stood over her.

"You ungrateful child," she spat. "I'm doing this all for *you.*"

A small prick of pain radiated through Nora's palm. She picked her hand up from the floor to find that a jagged shard from the broken cup had punctured her skin. A drop of blood welled up. Nora pushed herself up, wiping her hands on her pants. "And I'm telling you I don't want any of it. So stop."

They stood across from each other, their chests heaving.

Nora looked at the thin trickle of blood that crept down her palm and then out past her mother, through the window.

Madeline had been right. There *were* vines. A thin blanket of them now wrapped around the stone railings of the terrace. The tendrils reached toward the house. It was as if the garden was closing in on them.

You're going fucking insane, she told herself. *They've always been there.*

But when she thought back, she knew they hadn't.

Nora tried her last resort: "I'm leaving tomorrow. I'm taking the car. Come with me or don't. It's your choice."

thirty-seven

VIVIAN knew it. The garden was finally coming for her.

At night she dreamed that she stood in the empty, dark foyer. Vines burst through the granite floors and redwood walls. They laced around her limbs and brought her to her knees. They wrenched bones from joints in her fingers and limbs, ripped tendons apart. They wrapped around her neck, crushing the breath from her throat, until spots filled her vision; until the roots gouged through flesh and organs, until her blood pooled on the ground. Until the vines covered the floor, until the house splintered and sank into the ground. Until it finally flooded with *her* rage. Night after night for the past few months, Vivian had dreamed of this.

She swore she could feel the roots twist and tremble underneath the foundations of the house. Dreams of her husband's decomposing head had long faded. There were no more visions of Laura and Amos Dalby. Their ghosts, finally, were silenced, overtaken by the presence of the gardener's daughter.

Vivian had been aware of the garden all these years. She'd watched the roses wilt in the fall, and fade into the ground for the winter. In the summer, they would bloom all over again. She'd stare out the window until she could see Sophie's figure, tending to them in the dark. Some nights she'd even seen blood trickle from the roses' centers.

Vivian understood that something of Sophie was trapped in the garden. She sensed her anger and she wanted nothing to do with it. She had stayed in the house, never stepping foot in Sophie's domain, hoping for her presence to fade with time, like everyone had said Vivian's grief would. But years became decades, and Sophie's rage only grew. Repairmen who came to look at leaks in the basement and problems with the pipes said that roots from the garden had pushed their way through the cracks in the rock foundation. The house was buckling. It was only a matter of time.

She had been warned on her wedding day, after all.

Now, Vivian sat at the long dining table with one rice bowl in front of her, and another at the place next to her. She watched the afternoon light shift. She should have left a long time ago. That's what her oldest had told her. *You can't live in that big house alone*, Lucille had tried to reason with her. She needed company. She needed help. But Vivian refused to go. Because there was one final, crucial reason to stay.

She turned and said softly in Mandarin, "It's time for dinner."

Something shimmered at the corner of her vision. Then her daughter appeared by the dining room chair. She still had her bright eyes and rounded cheeks. She wore a T-shirt and jeans, the same as she appeared to Vivian every day.

Ada sat down in front of her meal.

Vivian saw her own spotted hands; her skin had sagged and her limbs ached with sharp pain constantly. But her daughter was seventeen. And she would stay seventeen, doe-like and radiant in her youth. Vivian wanted to throw her arms around her. Ada had once had lifetimes ahead of her, and eras to grow into. Vivian would never forgive herself for the fact that Ada was trapped in this house too.

"Listen," Vivian said. "I'm going to get you out of here."

Her daughter looked at her wistfully.

"You tried, Mā. You keep trying."

"No. This time I'm going to do it. You have to go."

Ada shook her head. "There's just no use anymore."

"Don't you feel *her*?"

Vivian saw her daughter's expression shift to fear. Slowly she nodded. "There's no love now. Only anger," Ada whispered.

"I have these dreams," Vivian said softly, "where the garden is tearing me apart."

Her daughter said nothing.

"She wants me. I know it."

"You need to go," Ada said. "You can still leave this place. I'll stay behind."

"My dear daughter," Vivian said, her voice breaking. "You know I'd never leave you."

This was why she'd stayed. After that horrific summer, Lucille and Renata had floated away, cut themselves from their anchor. Vivian had let them, partly because she knew it was good for them, but partly because her other child was still here, keeping her company. Each night Ada appeared for dinner. Decades of truth lay bare between them. They were mother and daughter; they would always be together.

And Vivian *had* tried, desperately, to free her daughter from this house. She'd tried every ritual she could find. She'd reached for the occult and said prayer after prayer. She'd begged to God and to the heavens and every deity to let Ada go. To let her finally move on, to rest, to be at peace.

"She wants me," Vivian muttered. "She wants to ruin me the way I ruined her."

There was silence.

"I'm going to do it," Vivian said. "I'm too old, Ada. I can't leave you here."

This was her last chance. She had to try. Her daughter looked up at her. The actress steeled herself, bracing her hands on the arms of her chair. "I want to settle this. I'm going to tell the truth about what happened."

There was a knock at the front door. With difficulty, Vivian crossed the library and foyer to answer it. The house was now a minefield of brittle, cracked floorboards. Ada was nowhere to be seen, but she could feel her daughter's presence.

Vivian unlatched the door and opened it. "Hello, Elaine."

Elaine Deng looked every bit as bitter as she did when the actress saw her last, as that radical college student who came home that summer with cropped hair, tattoos, and accusations. The once youthful, angry tilt of her mouth now puckered with lines and wrinkles. Her once-short hair was now pulled back into a graying bun.

She almost looked like her mother. Vivian thought of Edith with a pang.

Elaine's expression didn't soften. She stood at the threshold and looked around. "This place has gotten ugly."

Vivian swallowed. "Please, come in. Let's talk."

For a moment she saw herself as Elaine did. Shriveled and pitiful. The stairs were lopsided and sagging. The chandelier bulbs above them had long burned out. Dust piled up in the corners and stains crawled down the walls. The house stretched in front of them. Vivian didn't know if it was her old age and limited mobility that made it seem more cavernous, but she often felt like giving up before she'd even started to cross a room. She took a deep breath and motioned for Elaine to follow her as she made her way to the table. It was a relief to sit.

"Do you remember this house?" Vivian asked in Mandarin.

Elaine considered her for a moment. She answered back in accented Mandarin. "I try not to."

"Fair enough. You were never very fond of this place, were you? Or of us."

"Vivian," Elaine said. Before that summer she had always used "ā yí," even if it was measured and defiant. But Elaine said her first name coldly. "Why did you ask me here? What do you want?"

"I'm sorry," Vivian said. "I know this place holds grief for us both." She lifted her head to meet Elaine's eyes. "I wanted to talk about your sister. You must promise that this stays between us."

Two days ago, Vivian had picked up the phone and dialed a number she found online.

"Hello?"

"Elaine. Is that you? It's Vivian Yin."

There was silence. Then, "How did you get my number?"

Vivian said, "We should talk."

"I have nothing to say to you."

"I want to tell you the truth," Vivian said. "About your sister."

She waited for a click, or for the drone of the dial tone. When neither came, she continued. "Where are you right now?"

"What?"

"Are you in California?"

Another pause. "San Bernardino."

"That's only a few hours away. Come to the house, then. At your convenience."

"No. I never want to see that house again." Her voice dripped with disgust.

"It's just me, Elaine. I'm alone and I'm not well enough to travel. I want us to talk. In person."

"No."

Vivian sighed. "I know you have questions. If you come to the house, I will answer every question you have."

Elaine finally said, "Why don't I just ask you now?"

"Elaine. I want us to talk in person about Sophie. I believe you deserve that much."

"Fine. I can be there tomorrow."

Now Vivian watched Elaine sit, stiffly, and cross her arms. "Why do you want to talk now?"

"It was about time, don't you think?"

Elaine scoffed. "It's thirty-four years too late. But I guess your conscience finally caught up to you?"

Vivian wished it were her conscience. Living with the consequences of her own decisions was so painful that she had been little more than a shell of herself all these years. A living skeleton of her own making. She felt Ada's presence in the room, in the dust, all around her. She felt Sophie's presence, in the roots that gnarled under the house. She sat forward. "Ask me what you want to know."

Elaine straightened in her chair. "You killed Mr. Lowell, didn't you?"

She had been telling lies for thirty-four years, but now Vivian answered without hesitation. "Yes."

"I knew you did," Elaine's voice was emotionless. "I knew it all along."

"He abused me. He was going to kill me."

"That's what my mother said," Elaine said. "She told me she tried to help you. *You turned her away.*"

Vivian regarded her carefully. How could she tell Elaine about how Richard's wealth had ensnared all of them in the house? Instead, she had said nothing, which she now understood had ruined them just the same. She would not try to absolve herself.

"You poisoned him."

Vivian settled back. "Yes. I did."

"How?"

"With the 附子. The flowers I grew in the garden. They use them in traditional medicine. I knew the roots could kill, so I put it in his sleeping pills."

"So you poisoned him, and my sister found out?"

"She grew it with me."

Elaine's expression went slack with shock. "I don't believe you. Sophie would never hurt anyone."

"She didn't know it was poison. She found me planting it. I couldn't tell her why I was doing it, so I just said I wanted to grow something next to the roses and she offered to help me." Even now she remembered Sophie, luminous with hope in the evening, telling her about Ada and cupping the petals. "She took care of the plants."

"So she helped you," Elaine said with contempt. "Or you forced her to?"

"I didn't force anything," Vivian said. "I'd known about her . . . and Ada. So I let her confide in me. Trust me. She had no one else to go to. And I thought I could trust her with this in return."

"I found those flowers," Elaine said. "In her drawer. After—When I was going through her things. I didn't know what they were. I didn't think to look them up until later." She quieted. "It poisoned her. It must have." She lifted her eyes to Vivian. "Was that what you wanted?"

"It wasn't."

"You're lying."

"No. I swear," Vivian said. "I just didn't tell her it was poisonous. It would be too suspicious. I didn't think she'd take care of it as much as she did . . ." She squeezed her eyes shut. "And it affected her. Which I never wanted." Sophie had knelt on the floor of the study, with pale lips and tears in her eyes. She'd been so young and frightened. How could Vivian let that happen? "I still don't entirely understand what happened myself. I don't know if it was from having too much contact with the plant while she was taking care of it." She lowered her eyes. "That I do regret. I'm sorry for not warning her."

Elaine considered her. "But that doesn't explain why they were in the car, then?"

"They were trying to run away. When Sophie found out the truth about the flower, she got Ada to leave with her." Vivian took a labored breath. "But I think by that time her body may have already been re-acting to the poison." This, too, she could never forgive herself for. She was the one who had ultimately, inadvertently caused the accident that ended her daughter's life.

"*You* promised to take care of my family." Elaine's voice cracked. "My parents saw you as their savior. Instead, you ruined them. My sister never got to grow up with me. Your daughter died because of you. What a monster you are."

Each breath she took felt like the opening of a new wound. Vivian closed her eyes and let herself be eviscerated. Torn clean. "I know I am. I've been paying for it all my life."

"Not enough," Elaine seethed. "You're still here, in this big house of yours. Sitting on all your money. After everything you did, you lived the longest out of any of them." Her voice broke at the last part.

Josiah. Edith. The kindest people she knew, the family she'd made, all gone. "You hate me," Vivian said. "You wish I were dead."

"And yet we're not that lucky, are we?"

"I'm sorry about your parents," Vivian said. "I tried to help your mother, you know. I did everything I could. I'm so sorry she suffered as she did."

Elaine said slowly, "How did you know about her? She never spoke to you."

Vivian lifted her chin. "Who do you think made those anonymous donations to your page?"

Elaine rose from her chair.

"I cared about her," Vivian said. Every few months she had looked them up on the internet, until finally, she saw each of their obituaries. "She was like a sister to me. I know you don't believe me, but it's true."

"I don't. You didn't do that because you cared about us. You did all these things to absolve your guilt. You wanted forgiveness. That's why I'm here, isn't it?" Elaine towered over Vivian now; for a moment she believed Elaine would hit her. "We will *never* forgive you for what you've done. And I want you to live the rest of your pathetic life knowing that."

Vivian nodded once, ruefully. "So this is how it ends, then." She pushed her chair back. "Now you know."

Elaine glared at her one last time. Then she shoved her hands into her pockets. She stalked through the house, pausing at the door. And then she spat onto the floor.

As Vivian stared at the glistening wad of spit, the front door slammed shut, startling her. She was alone in the house again.

She hunched over, her forehead resting against her clasped fists. Finally, she allowed herself to weep. Her shoulders shook; her chest ached. She could feel the vengeful roots under the house trembling. She imagined them tearing her apart and shredding her brittle bones from her flesh.

She felt a hand on her arm and looked up into the face of her daughter.

"She was never going to let this go, you know."

"I'm sorry," Vivian whispered. "I thought confessing might placate her. There's nothing else I can do."

Ada nodded. "I know. So now you have to get out of this place."

"But I can't leave you."

She had thought that Sophie was the one keeping Ada here, but what if Ada was here because she was? Because—beyond Sophie's rage—Vivian herself had never let go? Because a selfish part of her clung to the remnants of her daughter?

She *had* wished for Ada to be set free. She knew deep down that the Ada she ate dinner with every night was not truly her daughter—it was a version of her frozen in time. But after losing Ada, she had treasured the ghost of her all the same. How could any mother not want to be with her child, even if it was just a piece of her? Vivian was terrified of being truly alone in this life. She wanted Ada to be near, to stay here, tethered to her. Sitting down to dinner with Ada's ghost every night had become a ritual. It was both a penance and a comfort.

No, she wouldn't be able to let go of Ada as long as she was alive. But maybe if she died, her daughter would be set free.

She looked up at Ada. "I can't do this anymore. I just want this pain to end. I want to rest with you."

She'd finally said it. Her daughter's eyes widened. "Mā. Are you sure?"

Vivian nodded.

She looked toward the door. There was one last thing she had to do. She shuffled to the living room table, where the landline was. She felt her daughter's eyes on her as she dialed another number.

"Hello?"

The garden—*Sophie*—was going to take her. Probably destroy the house. She needed to save her other daughters from that possible fate.

"Reid." Vivian cleared her throat. "Listen. I need to make some changes to my will."

The day was ending.

Vivian had finished her call with Eugene Lyman's son and handwritten the amendment to the will. She signed the codicil, sealed it in an envelope, and put it in the mailbox. She shuffled through the house, straightening things to the best of her abilities. She couldn't do much. Her joints ached. Her steps were difficult. Maybe her body was finally giving out.

The medicine cabinet in the kitchen was littered with bottles for muscle aches and headaches and blood pressure. Now she reached for a long-expired prescription bottle for heart medication at the back and shook out an unmarked pill.

Vivian had planned out how she would do this long ago. She had thought about it constantly. It surprised her now that she had been able to delay it for so long. But there had been reasons to stay. There was her Ada, but also other joyous and fleeting moments. She'd been in the hospital when her granddaughter was born; she'd held Madeline in her arms, small and wailing with all her might. She'd felt a strange joy that blossomed so fiercely in her that she thought her heart would seize up right then and there. She'd become a grandmother, against all odds. Her granddaughter was so very perfect, free of the terrible history that hung over the rest of their heads. How she wanted to give Madeline all her love. She'd visited briefly. She'd brought her to the park and taught her how to fold dumplings. But mostly, she stayed away. She wanted to keep her granddaughter far from her own rotted fate. She visited each of her children separately, afraid that if they were under the same roof again, something terrible might happen. She watched Madeline grow through photos, and it hurt her more than anything. She saw Lucille march, tight-fisted, through her life as she always did. And she watched Renata fade from her. Her calls coming less frequently, until they didn't come at all.

But this was the end.

Vivian wondered if she should call her daughters. What would she say to them? What if they didn't pick up? If Vivian told them, *I love you*, would they be tipped off?

It was better to slip away. Vivian looked at the capsule in her palm. 附子, aconite. The Chinese name meant *daughter root*. What was once a beautiful violet flower now filled the contents of the pill. Just the same as she'd given her husband. A life for a life. She swallowed the pill.

She had often thought of that fateful, fatal decision. She should have done it differently. Or she should have not done it at all. How many times had she wondered what would have happened if she had just proceeded with a divorce instead? In so many ways, her life now was worse than she could have ever imagined. All that was Vivian Yin now lay around her in shambles.

It was no use dragging all this back up. The sun would dip below the horizon soon, and she wanted to see it. She said her daughter's name and turned.

There Ada was, in the waning light. She smiled, and Vivian's heart broke for the last time.

"I'm sorry, 亲女儿." Tears slipped down her cheeks. "I'm so sorry."

"You tried everything you could."

"No," Vivian whispered, shaking her head. "I'm sorry for what I did to you. Will you forgive me?"

Ada said nothing, but held out her hand. Vivian took it. Ada's grip felt cool. They walked toward the terrace. Vivian felt a tug at her wrist.

Her daughter said, "Don't go into the garden."

"I know," Vivian said. Ada had said this to her so many times before. "I won't." She looked back at her daughter, her flesh and blood. She said in Mandarin, "I love you. More than anything in this world."

Ada nodded. "I know."

Her grip eased. Vivian walked out onto the stone terrace and looked out over the rotting mass. Once this had just been a grassy field that she took her young daughters to. She was going to build a house that was big enough for their dreams. They were going to live a better life than she ever did. They had struck gold.

Now she saw that she had spent decades trying to prove herself to this place. She'd given it everything: her ambitions, her youth, her children, her sense of self, and still it held its mouth open for more. She thought of her ancestors who'd come in search of gold; of the people who made it in, only for their bodies to be blasted through mountains. If you could survive this place, you got to dream. That was the privilege you fought for. It was never a done deal, and it would never be enough. You would bury yourself, hoping that under the weight of it all, your roots would grow strong enough that your children might be able to reach toward the sky.

She had clung to her dreams for herself and her children for so long. She had wanted to give them everything: this house, a good education, this life she thought they had secured the moment she married Richard under that summer sky. In the end, she had killed for it, rather than risk it being taken from them. And even then, when her daughters had been in pain and at a loss, she had kept pushing them—away from her and toward some unknown, better thing. She had cut herself out of their lives so they wouldn't have to bear the burden of doing it themselves. Wasn't that why she had exiled them from this house? So they could excise the poison of this place and continue onward?

Now, far too late, she saw that the rift she had forged had broken her children, too. She couldn't expect them to understand she had done it all out of love, when she had never told them the truth in the first place. But there was no going back now. All she could do was try to save them one last time by offering herself to this place. And maybe this time, it would be enough.

Vivian was ready to die. She opened her eyes to the setting sun and braced herself for the pain.

thirty-eight

LUCILLE ate dinner by herself. Madeline got some food at some point and slipped back upstairs without speaking to her. Rennie didn't come down at all. Bloated wine corks lay in the sink. Mud bubbled up through the drain. A green tendril had emerged.

Now plants were growing *inside* the pipes? Lucille hosed it with brown water that spurted erratically through the tap. She reached to yank it out, but when she blinked it was gone. All that remained was the mud.

Was this what happened to old houses? She had never lived in one. Come to think of it, the house felt strangely hot and damp today. It had begun to truly stink with mold and mildew, though there hadn't been a weather change outside.

Lucille was on her way upstairs to change into something lighter when she saw Elaine at the top of the staircase facing Lucille's bedroom door. Elaine turned. Dark circles ringed her eyes. Limp, stringy hair hung around her face. Her nostrils were crusted with dried blood.

"*Jesus.*" Lucille switched on the hallway light and it flickered above them. The harsh light made Elaine look even more ghastly. Why was she up here? "What do you want?"

"Your week is up." Elaine approached and flapped a sheet of paper. The one they'd both signed a week ago. "You leave tomorrow morning."

Lucille frantically flipped through the days in her head. She had lost track of time. How could she let herself do that? "Only if we found no evidence of wrongdoing."

One of the doors upstairs opened. Madeline drifted into Lucille's periphery.

"And what have you found?" Elaine tilted her head in mock interest. "Anything besides the security footage?"

How did Elaine find out? If it was out in the open, so be it. "That's sufficient." Lucille's voice rose. She wanted to claw that deranged smile off Elaine's face. "You were here in this house on the day she died."

Elaine didn't even flinch. "Your mother invited me. We had a conversation."

"About what?"

"She told me she was giving me the house."

"Why?"

Elaine hesitated. Just then there were footsteps in the foyer below. Nora looked up at them from the foot of the stairs.

Lucille stepped toward Elaine. "Stop lying. Mā was drugged. That's what the toxicology report said. You were the last person to see her alive."

"I had *nothing* to do with that."

"Is that what a jury is going to think?"

Elaine's eyes widened. Finally, she was rattled. "You *promised*—"

"Let's settle, then." Lucille said. "You get half the monetary inheritance. We keep the home. And we never take this to court."

The clock ticked.

"I would think very carefully about this. This is the first and last offer I'll make. The evidence is not on your side."

Elaine's bloodshot eyes darted around the hallway. Nora ascended a few more stairs, inching closer to Lucille. "I'll get my own lawyer. I haven't done anything wrong."

Lucille narrowed her eyes. Elaine should have settled—*she* would have, in this case. It was the smart thing to do. But Elaine didn't look rational right now. "We'll see you prove it in court, then."

"Do it. Spend your mother's precious inheritance on this case. You can drive yourself into the ground over this, just because you can't accept that your mother gave it to me. In the end, it will still be mine."

"You don't deserve it!" Lucille roared.

Nora startled. Elaine's cheeks flushed with color. Even Rennie had emerged from her room.

"You've always leeched off us, haven't you?" A vicious charge ran through her. "That's all you have ever done. Your whole family. A bunch of freeloaders, living in our house. Taking advantage of Mā's generosity."

Elaine trembled with rage. "Fuck you."

"She let you be raised here. Because we're all Chinese, right? And now look at you. You're lying about this house. You're lying about everything. Even in Mā's death you're still sucking her dry."

"Generous," Elaine seethed. "You think your mother was so virtuous, don't you? You don't even know half the truth." She moved toward Lucille. "She was selfish, manipulative, calculating—"

"*Don't* say that about her." Rennie came forward, her eyes sparking with fury.

Elaine looked between them. "You two are so desperate to defend her. You don't even know what she did, do you?"

Neither sister spoke.

"Your father and sister died because of her. Don't you know that?"

Lucille heard her daughter's sharp intake of breath. Nora gaped at her mother in shock.

Madeline whispered, "*What?*"

Elaine drew her phone out from her pocket and tapped a button on the screen.

"*You killed Mr. Lowell.*" Elaine's voice warbled through the speakers. "*Didn't you?*"

"*Yes.*"

Lucille and Rennie locked eyes at the sound of their mother's voice.

"*I knew you did. I knew it all along.*"

"*He abused me. He was going to kill me.*"

Lucille staggered; she reached out for the railing. Everything was going in and out now: the sound. Her vision contracted. Her body went numb.

"*—How?*"

"*With the—*" Here, Lucille couldn't catch the phrase Mā had just said in Chinese. "*The flowers I grew in the garden. They use them in tradi-tional medicine. I knew the roots would kill, so I put it in his sleeping pills.*"

"*So you poisoned him, and my sister found out?*"

"*She grew it with me.*"

"*I don't believe you. Sophie would never hurt anyone.*"

"*She didn't know it was poison. She found me planting it. I couldn't tell her why I was doing it, so I just said I wanted to grow something next to the roses and she offered to help me. She took care of the plants.*"

"*So she helped you. Or you forced her to?*"

"*I didn't force anything. I'd known about her . . . and Ada. So I let her confide in me. Trust me. She had no one else to go to. And I thought I could trust her with this in return.*"

Elaine tapped the phone and the recording stopped. She looked directly at Lucille. "You want to know why I was here July 20? Your mother wanted to confess."

Lucille looked down the dizzying height through the railing balusters to the foyer. All the pieces were coming together in her mind.

How had it come to—murder? Why couldn't they just divorce? Lucille had been reeling all her life from that summer. Trying to reach her mother, trying desperately to put her family back together. And now, here was the answer to the puzzle—and in the end she had offered it to Elaine.

Lucille looked to Rennie, but it was obvious she hadn't known, either.

"You had a *sister*?" Nora interjected.

"Sophie," Elaine said through gritted teeth. "She died in that car with Ada."

"And you never told me?"

Elaine didn't look at Nora. "I think she was being poisoned too. And then she got in that car with Ada . . ." Lucille watched her take a deep breath. "Now you know the truth about your mother. She could have left your father, but she chose to kill him instead." She swept her gaze around. "And look at what she did to all of us."

The grandfather clock clashed into the hour.

"So," Elaine said. "You're going to leave this house tomorrow. And if you bring a case against me, I will make sure the whole world knows what she did."

MADELINE watched her mother let out a bloodcurdling shriek and leap up the stairs, hurling herself at Elaine as if in slow motion.

Together they fell into the railing, cracking the posts under their weight. The phone spun out of Elaine's hands and tipped over the edge, crashing onto the foyer floor below.

Madeline ran to the edge of the stairs. Nora rushed up, pushing Mā off Elaine. Mā reared and struck Nora across the face. Nora yelped. Madeline grabbed Mā's arm, and Mā tried to wrench it away, but then Aunt Rennie was pulling her too. "Lucille!" Madeline heard her aunt scream. "*Stop it.*"

Together Madeline and Aunt Rennie hauled her mother off Elaine and away from the railing, onto the second floor.

Elaine pushed herself up, Nora supporting her. Her chest heaved. She looked over the railing at the smashed phone. "You don't think I'd have this saved everywhere I could? I thought you were the smart one," Elaine scoffed. "You're insane. All of you."

Mā lunged again, and this time Aunt Rennie held her back. "Stop. Stop! We can't fight like this."

Elaine clutched the wall, safely away from the broken railing. And Nora was on the other side of her mother, cradling her cheek. Without a thought, Madeline stepped down to where Nora was.

"Are you okay?"

Madeline pulled Nora's hand away. Nora was scratched, badly. A small bit of blood welled up on her jaw. She'd kissed Nora there gently only two nights ago. An eternity, it felt like. Back before—all *this*—had come to light. "I'm so sorry," she whispered. "Hold on. I can get something."

"No, you won't." Elaine pointed a shaking finger at her. "Get away from my daughter."

Nora turned. "Mā, it's fine."

"Nora—"

"I said I'm fine," Nora said steadily. Her eyes met Madeline's.

"Madeline!"

Madeline whirled around at her mother's voice. Madeline rounded on Mā, brimming with rage. "*You hurt her.*"

Mā faltered. Aunt Rennie blanched. Madeline had never raised her voice to either of them. Now she approached them. "Stay away from them," she said, her voice trembling. "Nora had nothing to do with this."

Aunt Rennie gaped. "Madeline, what?"

Her mother's eyes widened. "What is going on between you two?"

Madeline and Nora looked at each other, but then Elaine grabbed Nora by the arm. "We're going."

"What have you done?"

Madeline was backed up against a wall in the room her mother occupied. They were all gathered there. Mā gripped her shoulder and Madeline could feel her sharp nails. Through the window the sky had darkened. Mā's wrinkles looked harsher in the fading light. "Is something going on between the two of you? Is this what I think it is?"

"It probably is," Madeline said, and then went silent. They'd never talked about it, between the two of them. Madeline had brought girls over to her house when Mā was at work, and the things that had happened at school . . . Mā had never known.

"天啊," her mother said. Her expression slacked. "You're—" She swallowed. "Why *her*?"

Because she healed me. Because she saved me from the garden. Because she was the only person who was honest with me. Madeline tilted her head stubbornly. Her heart thudded in her chest and her cheeks felt hot. "Why not?"

Mā burst out, "It's *Elaine's* daughter."

"It's happening again," Aunt Rennie said faintly, rocking herself on the bed. "A daughter from our family, a daughter from theirs. It's repeating. This place is cursed."

Mā said sharply, "Stop trying to curse your niece." She stepped back and crossed her arms. "Ada and Sophie's relationship ruined them. Don't you see?"

"Are we actually being serious right now?" Madeline spread her palms out. "This didn't all happen because two girls were in love. It was because Wài Pó killed her *abusive* husband."

The room fell silent. Madeline remembered flashes of Wài Pó throughout her childhood. She had helped Madeline eat cake at her fourth birthday. She'd taken her to the park and let her feed the ducks with her gentle hand. And yet Madeline never knew any of this about her. She never was aware of Wài Pó's brutal history and the things she went through. About the choices she'd had to make. And, it seemed, neither did her mother and aunt.

"Will we talk about that? Or do you still want to come after me for what I have with someone who had no part in any of this?"

She stared down her mother.

"You don't know that," her mother said finally. "About Nora."

Madeline looked at her mother in disbelief—for a moment, for a brief eternity—before she marched out the door.

thirty-nine

NORA faced her mother in her room.

"I told you *one thing*," her mother said. "To not speak to their family."

Two, actually. The second rule was to never go into the garden. She'd broken that one, too. But at this point, what did it matter?

Mā pointed to her shattered phone. "Look at what they did. Lucille would have thrown us over the railing if she could. And look at what she did to *you*." She touched the scratch on Nora's cheek. "I'll make sure they leave tomorrow if I have to drag them out of there."

"I'm still going."

"*No.* You're staying with me. I know this has been difficult. But once we're free of that entire rotten family we can finally make this house into our home."

It scared her how much Mā had changed her tune. Now she was going to force Nora to stay?

"I told you," Nora insisted. "I'm *not staying*."

Mā skewered her with a withering look. "It's not because of that girl, is it?"

"What? I—"

"Are you still not listening to me? The rest of my family loved them. *Worshipped them.* My sister fell in love with Ada, and looked what happened to her."

Nora's stomach churned. "Sophie died because of Vivian," she said slowly. "Ada didn't do a thing to her."

"It's all the same. That family protects itself. If you love any of them, they'll destroy you." Her mother's eyes widened. "Don't you see what happened before?"

We inherit their history, Madeline had said, and now Nora's heart stuttered. *Whether they know it or not.* "I didn't know what happened before," she said, "because you didn't tell me."

"I was protecting you! Who was the first to talk? You or her?"

Nora swallowed. "She was."

"You should have told me *that very moment*."

"And you should have told me *everything*!" Nora burst out. "You're my mother. But it's like I don't know you at all. I didn't know you came here to see Vivian. I didn't even know you had a *sister*." She whispered, "Why didn't you tell me about—Sophie?"

Her mother's expression went slack. Her hands fell to her sides. "Because it would have killed me to."

Nora sat on the bed opposite her. Her mother seemed to shrink. Her expression was hollow. The strange, ferocious figure from the past few days regressed back to a childlike self in front of Nora's eyes.

"Stay with me," Mā pleaded. She reached out and clasped Nora's hand with tears in her eyes. "I can't lose you too."

"Then tell me," Nora said. She moved to kneel on the floor in front of her mother. "What happened the day you saw Vivian Yin?"

"Do you actually think I did it?"

Nora steeled herself. "I'm asking you."

Mā put her face in her hands. "After Sophie's funeral, I tried to put all of this behind me. I couldn't live with myself—that I had left home, hadn't stayed in touch enough to know what was going on and protect her. No one in my family could. We left the house so we wouldn't have to be constantly reminded. It was—" Her mother's fists clenched. "An accident. That's all we knew. I couldn't drive for years after that, because every time I would think of my sister and panic. Your grandparents had their own nervous breakdowns." Her eyes found Nora's now. "But I always thought that Vivian had something to do with my sister's death. I just had a feeling."

"So you knew that she was poisoned?" The horror of it cast a chill over Nora.

"I'd suspected," her mother said. "I found dried flowers in her nightstand drawer and didn't think much of it. It wasn't until years later, thinking back, that I realized I didn't recognize them and had never seen them in the garden, so I looked up what they were. When I saw they were poisonous, I couldn't figure out why she would have them. Neither her nor Bà would have planted them, knowing what they were, so I started putting it together. I told Mā that maybe it had something to do with the garden. I brought it up to Bà, and he didn't believe it. Said he never saw the flowers. Even after all that happened, he still refused to think ill of Vivian. So I buried it. For years." Her expression hardened. "Until Vivian found my number and called me."

Nora nodded. "And you got the truth from her. You were right."

"And it was even worse hearing it. But I needed to hear Vivian say it. I needed her to admit that she was responsible for my sister's death."

It all dawned on Nora now, this agonizing, embedded tragedy. The bitterness that had isolated her grandparents and her mother. "She confessed and let you record her."

Her mother shook her head. "She never knew about the recording."

"So you just—"

"I needed proof. For myself."

"Then what?"

"I knew she was trying to ask me for forgiveness. And I told her that I would never give it to her." Mā's mouth set in a grim line. "She outlived everyone. She never had any consequences. There was no justice for my sister." She lifted her eyes to Nora's. "Before I left, she asked me if I wished she were dead."

"And you said . . . ?"

Her mother looked away.

"But you didn't do anything to her. Right?"

Her mother's eyes filled again. "But what if I still caused it?" As angry as she knew her mother had been, Nora could see the true pain in her face. "What if my conversation with Vivian that day made her end her life?"

MADELINE ran down the stairs and into the library. The doors were open, the room empty and dark. She stared up at the dust particles suspended in shafts of light.

Suddenly, vines surged through the cracks in the panels. They snaked upward and squirmed over the windowsills. The walls around her rippled and contracted, as if the room itself was alive. As if it were taking a breath—

She blinked again and there was nothing. Everything was once again still.

She marched out of the room, past the shards of Elaine's phone left behind in the foyer. She went to Nora's room and knocked. When there was no response, she knocked harder.

The door opened a crack, and Nora squeezed out the sliver of open space, shutting the door behind her.

"Are you okay?"

Nora nodded. The scratch on her cheek was raised and red.

Madeline reached for her, and Nora leaned in. But then she felt Nora still. "We can't."

"I don't care what they say." Madeline was filled with a wild, reckless rush. "They have no ground to stand on. They've been lying to us. You're the only one who's cared about me this whole time."

Nora's expression crumbled. When she looked back up there were tears in her eyes. "Don't you see? All our families know how to do is hurt one another."

"But we're different," Madeline said. "We didn't even know some of these people existed! I won't let my family hurt you again."

"It doesn't matter." Nora's voice was flat. "*We inherit their history.* Remember?"

Madeline stilled at hearing her own words repeated back to her.

This time, Nora didn't meet Madeline's eyes as she retreated into her room. "We shouldn't have. I'm sorry."

Madeline stared at the closed door. This was all a mistake, then, to

Nora. How could Madeline have assumed otherwise? She had fallen for her without a second thought. But Nora was never supposed to even acknowledge her in the first place.

Her family had destroyed the Dengs. This she could never answer for.

Madeline was halfway up the stairs when everything started to shake.

It started quietly, but soon became violent. Madeline stumbled, holding on to the wall to steady herself as the shaking worsened. Her knees buckled and she fell hard on the steps. The chandelier above her clanged. She squeezed her eyes shut, trying to remember what she was supposed to do in an earthquake, but her mind was blank.

And then, just as abruptly, the trembling stopped.

forty

RENNIE watched Lucille pace.

"What could have happened between them, even? It's only been a week." Lucille flung her hands in the air. "And for it to be *her*, of all people. She could be in on it with Elaine, for all we know!"

At this, Rennie finally rose from the bed. "She's not. And Elaine's not either."

Her sister faced her. "What do you mean?"

Rennie had held her tongue when Lucille and Elaine were fighting. But she had to come clean. She had to finally talk about that night.

Rennie took a deep breath. "Elaine wasn't the last person to see Mā alive. It was me."

She waited for Lucille to react. She braced herself for the force of it.

Instead, Lucille simply whispered, "What do you mean? You came with her?"

"No." Rennie had to force the word out. "Three days before Mā was found on July 25, I spoke to her here, for half an hour? Maybe less. And then I left." The memory was so vivid, and she had been over it so many times, it was strange to finally say it aloud.

"Why did you—"

"I don't know how you didn't see my car on the camera," Rennie barreled on. "Maybe it was dark, so it didn't show up. Maybe you weren't looking on that day. But I was here."

"That's not even remotely close to my question. Why *on earth* did you not tell me this entire week?"

"I—" Rennie started and then swallowed. "I don't know. I'd been meaning to. But I didn't know where the case was at, and you mentioned settling, so I thought—I thought if anybody could scare Elaine into settling, it would be you. And no one would ever have to know. I'm sorry."

"Oh God," Lucille said. She faced the wall and clutched her head. "Oh my God. I can't even look at you right now." She whirled around. "What did you two talk about? What did she say?"

It all had to come out now. Rennie admitted, finally, "I came to ask her for money. But then I backed out. And I left. She didn't say much to me."

You were the most like me. You became the cruelest.

"But we have nothing now," Rennie said. "We're out of moves, aren't we? So let's just go. Okay? Let's listen to Elaine and take the inheritance and leave this all behind us. Let's go. Please. I don't want to be here anymore."

Lucille stared. "All you know how to do is leave, don't you?"

Rennie flinched.

Lucille started toward her. "*I've* been grinding my fucking teeth out of my head to try to get us this house back. And all the while, you kept vital information about Mā to yourself." Rennie tried to back away but Lucille cut in front of her. "You thought you could use Mā and me to get money, and now you want to back out. Now you're just going to abandon us and disappear like you always do. Right? *Right?*"

Rennie's eyes smarted. "I don't—*abandon* people." Even as she said this her words sounded empty. In that instant she remembered Mā looking at her in the dim light. Her voice, rasping: *You only came here when you wanted something from me.*

"You'd ask for my help and then not return my calls." Lucille's voice trembled. "Sometimes I wouldn't even know what *city* you were in."

"That's just—"

"You cut us out of your life," Lucille spat. "You didn't even invite me to your *wedding*!"

"I eloped!" Rennie was crying now, and it made her feel so stupid and childlike and out of control, but she couldn't stop. "And it was a godawful sham of a marriage anyway, which is how things usually go for me." She swiped at her nose with the back of her hand. "All I ever wanted was to do *one* thing that you and Mā would be proud of me for. And I never could. *That's* all I can think about when I'm with you. That I'm just a fuckup. A mentally unstable addict, and—it's better that I stayed out of your lives, don't you see?"

"That's not true," Lucille muttered through gritted teeth.

"That's what you think of me. And I know it." Rennie dragged in a shaky breath. "I've heard you talking about it with Daniel, and I can *see* it when you look at me. I just—" She tried to offer a teary smile. "Oh, never mind. None of this matters anymore. We need to leave this house, Lucille. It's doing things to me. To your daughter, too."

Lucille frowned. "What do you mean it's doing things to Madeline?"

"I don't know what Madeline is seeing," Rennie said. "But I see *her* again. Ada. "

Lucille backed away. Her stark expression told Rennie everything.

Rennie said, "You've been seeing her too, haven't you?"

Lucille shut her eyes tightly.

Rennie walked toward her. "When was the first time?"

Tears slid from her sister's closed eyes. "Winter break. Senior year."

Rennie had been a freshman at Lawrence then. She remembered sitting together in the waiting room of the counselor's office before they each went in alone; she remembered standing in the hallway outside Lucille's room. How Lucille had told her that she was seeing things, that she was going to become an addict, that she was going to end up just like Dad. *God*, how Rennie held on to that accusation for years, decades, dragging herself in and out of rehab, hurting herself, hating herself for being high, thinking she was damaged and rotten to the core. She remembered the Thanksgiving, years later, when she overheard Lucille telling her then-husband, Daniel, offhandedly, that Rennie seemed a borderline alcoholic and unstable.

She wanted to scream now: *How could you have left me alone all this time?*

But just then the floor tipped underneath them. Lucille staggered.

Rennie threw her arms out against the bed to steady herself. The lights in the room flickered.

The floor jolted again, and Rennie looked at Lucille with terror.

A final tremor shuddered through the room and then everything was still.

Madeline burst in. "Did you feel that?"

Rennie looked at Lucille and pleaded, "*We need to go.*"

"Okay." Her sister was back to pacing, but she wouldn't meet Rennie's eyes. "It's late. I need to gather some last files. We can leave first thing in the morning."

LUCILLE shoved everything in her bag: papers, files, all the things she could look at in more detail later. She tried to fit as much as possible, but she was running out of time. Once they left this house in the morning there was a chance they could never come back.

She blinked hard to stay awake. The sleepless nights were catching up to her. It would be so easy to take a quick nap in the armchair, but she switched on the computer and went to email herself all the security camera footage. She watched it again. There was Elaine's car on the twentieth of July; she arrived in the early afternoon and left an hour later. Then the camera lens got progressively darker, until it was completely obscured by that evening by the leaves.

Could Elaine have done *that*? This was why she hadn't seen Rennie's car in the footage, but what could have made it happen?

The files were massive and took forever to send; the Wi-Fi kept going in and out. Lucille paced. She yanked her thumbnail between teeth until she felt a sharp slice of pain and drew blood. Finally, the files appeared in her phone's email inbox. She scrolled to make sure the videos were all there and then was about to click out when she saw the old email. The preliminary autopsy.

She'd read it already, days ago. Several times. But she clicked on the report again.

This time she fixed on the last line.

Her mother's time of death was estimated to be between July 20 and July 21.

Lucille scrambled to read the line again. Rennie said she visited Mā on July 22. It didn't make sense.

Lucille sank into the armchair. Either the medical examiner was wrong, or— Or Rennie had recounted the wrong dates.

Could Rennie have misremembered? She did seem pretty out of it these days. Could she be on something? Lucille caught herself— she didn't want to accuse Rennie of anything else. She'd already done enough. She couldn't stop thinking about Rennie's broken expression when she admitted that she, too, had seen Ada's ghost. She knew she had exacted cruelty time and time again toward her sister. She wanted it to be different between them.

Lucille wanted so badly to be a soft and understanding person and not human shrapnel. But she had been doing what she thought was necessary. And this was a critical detail. If Rennie *had* misremembered the dates and went to see Mā earlier in the week, then that meant the case was still viable. It was still possible for Elaine to have been involved in Mā's death. It would all fit perfectly, terribly, in this timeline.

Lucille felt that familiar kinetic rush of figuring out the key to a case. She spun the dates and the facts around in her head. She resolved to ask Rennie in the morning, after they left, and sat back in the chair with a sense of relief. Her eyelids started to droop like she was a little kid again, in the spot of afternoon sun, with the library and the whole world in front of her. She was asleep long before the light of the green lamp finally gave out.

Lucille found herself lying in the soft grass. Stars stretched out above her. It was a summer night and the air had long cooled. She breathed in deeply, taking in the scent of jasmine and lavender.

"Jiĕ Jie."

Lucille turned her head. Ada lay on the grass next to her. Her eyes were closed. Her bangs had grown out and swept over the side of her cheeks. She was wearing the Sky High shirt she loved.

Her sister was exactly how Lucille remembered her that summer, 1990.

"You don't have any reason to be jealous, you know," Ada said. "Just because I loved her doesn't mean I stopped loving you."

Lucille couldn't speak. To hear her voice after so long was astonishing. So young, so high-pitched. "It's a different love, that's all," Ada continued.

Lucille opened her mouth, though what came out felt hollow and automatic, like she was acting out a script she hadn't written. "But it's wrong."

Ada's eyes fluttered open and she looked at Lucille with a clear gaze. "Don't tell me you still believe that." She put a hand over her eyes. "She thinks it was wrong now, though. Now she's angry."

"Where is she?" Lucille asked.

"You know."

Lucille sat up and looked around. There was no one else in the garden.

"She was so sweet," Ada sighed. "When I said that the daisies were my favorite, she brought me the most beautiful daisies I had ever seen." She looked at Lucille. "That's why I brought you back here. This is when she was kindest. We're safe here."

"Safe," Lucille asked, "from what?"

"Remember 红楼梦?"

"*Dream of the Red Chamber*?" Mā loved reading the Chinese classic to them. She'd always remind them that she had once played Lin Daiyu in the movie. They would curl up on the living room couches and read the tragic story of Jia Baoyu and Lin Daiyu. How they fell in love as their family dynasties soured into ruin.

"There's a line in there," Ada said. "假作真时真亦假."

When what is false is taken for truth, true becomes indiscernible from false.

"Ada," Lucille whispered. "Why are you telling this to me?"

"Because you've all been living a lie," her sister said. "All this time. About what Mā had done. She did it to protect you."

A slow dread settled upon her. As if she were finally realizing—no, *remembering* what had happened that summer. "Mèi Mei . . ."

"And now that you know the truth, I need to tell you something, too."

Ada sat up.

Her sister was seventeen. They were seventeen. The year was 1990. But was it? She felt a burgeoning sense of fear. Something horrible had happened. "What's going on?"

Ada's eyelids fluttered. "I brought you to this time," she said, "because this was when the garden was safe. But that's not true anymore. And the house isn't safe either. This is what Mā was trying to protect you from."

"Mèi Mei—"

"I've been holding the house," Ada said, her eyes now wide-open and trained on Lucille. "But I can't do it anymore. She's breaking through. She's been angry for a long time, and I thought Mā being gone might appease her. But now that you're here, her anger is growing like a fire, and I can't stop it."

Ada's placid expression twisted into terror. "You need to get out, Jiě Jie." Her voice rose. She clasped Lucille's shoulders and shook her. "Wake up, Lucille. Now. *YOU NEED TO WAKE UP.*"

part three: rot

forty-one

AUGUST 2024

MADELINE woke to her bed shaking. But when she sat up, she realized the entire *floor* was shaking. It must be aftershocks of the tremble she'd felt earlier that night, she thought.

Then she saw the vines.

Tonight they weren't flickering in the corner of her vision. Now they slid up the walls, coiling around the nightstand and the headboard.

Wake up. Surely, this was a nightmare.

She leapt out of bed and immediately pitched forward. The ground buckled under her feet. A vine surged in the window, shattering glass, and curled itself around the sill.

Madeline screamed. She leapt for the door and flung it open, scrambling into the hallway. When she looked down, her stomach dropped. In the slits of moonlight that came through the foyer windows she could make out writhing vines that snaked their way in through the windows, like dozens of arms reaching in. There was a terrible splitting sound as vines emerged through the floor.

The stone foundation was cracking.

Madeline staggered through the hallway. She threw herself against the doors and banged on them with her fist. "Mā!" she shouted. "Yí Mā! Wake up! Wake up!"

No one answered. Madeline peered over the stairs. The door to the library flung open below.

"Mā!"

"Come down!" her mother shouted. "We need to get out! She's tearing down the house."

She?

Madeline turned to watch a vine erupt clean through a wall and splinter a door. Cracks were spreading through every room. Madeline went back up the stairs and pounded on Aunt Rennie's locked door. The floor swayed as she threw her weight against the door. A shock of pain tore through her shoulder. "Yí Mā!" She was sobbing now. "Get out!"

Writhing vines crawled up the banister.

"Madeline! Come down!"

Madeline ducked and scrambled down the stairs, leaping past each tendril that seemed to reach for her. The railings had split and cracked. Her mother was at the front door. Nora ran into the foyer. At the threshold she paused and looked past Madeline. "Mā!"

Nora met Madeline's eyes, then ran. Madeline tried to follow her, but she fell forward. A vine lashed out, faster than she could see, and wrapped around her ankle.

"No." Madeline tried to tug herself free. "No!"

The vine pulled back with a violent jerk. Madeline screamed, pain ricocheting through her knees, her wrists. She scrambled for any kind of purchase, but her fingers clawed smooth granite. The vine wound up her thigh, thorns tearing into her skin. Madeline choked out a cry.

She skidded across the floor. She was being dragged backward, farther into the house.

"Mā!" Madeline shrieked. "Mā—"

The vines were strong and solid as trees. A rose burst from one, trickling blood and oozing a foul, rotten odor. Madeline gritted her teeth. The floor felt slick, and she realized the granite was smeared with her blood. Dimly she heard her name.

Madeline found a smooth spot on the vine around her waist and yanked it with all her might. It loosened for a moment, and she sucked in a breath. But then it shot up with a vengeance, crushing her ribs, and coiling farther up her torso. Above her, the chandelier swayed. Vines reached for it across the ceiling, forming dark, grotesque veins.

I'm not going to get out.

A vine twisted itself around her shoulders and began to constrict.

NORA's eyes flew open.

The walls rattled. The digital clock toppled off the nightstand and cracked. The lamp rattled on the floor and was surrounded by glass from the shattered bulb. Nora sprung out of bed just as a giant vine burst through behind her and drywall scattered to the floor.

She saw her mother in the hallway. Her eyes were wide. "Mā!" The walls around them rippled and splintered. Nora looked back into her room, but her bed was already on its side, tilted by a vine that had sprung up from beneath it. There was no time to gather her things. She ran for the foyer. A crackling sound shot through the house as one of the pillars buckled.

Nora tripped on a vine and watched as it coiled into itself and retreated, almost as if it was clearing a path for her. A chunk of the hallway ceiling fell to the granite tiles with a horrific crash. Nora turned blindly and screamed, "Mā! Get *out!*"

She looked up to see Madeline making her way through the foyer. And then she sprinted for the front door, which was now a gaping hole. The chandelier clattered wildly, shedding bits of glass fixtures to the floor. She threw herself into the light from outside and tumbled down the front steps. A sharp pain split through her knee, but she hauled herself up and ran down the driveway. When she reached the end, she looked back.

The house was being swallowed. Nora could see vines scaling the sides, burrowing into cracks and tearing chunks out of the walls.

Someone shrieked, "Madeline!"

Lucille staggered up behind her in the driveway. One hand covered her eye, and blood dripped through her fingers. "She's in there. She's trapped in there with Rennie!"

Nora whirled. Where was her mother? "Mā?" She scanned the grounds, but there was no sign of her.

A muffled whimper echoed from the front door. Nora's heart dropped. They were both in there: Madeline and her mother.

The pillars sheared through the front windows. Nora screamed. Lucille ran for the house, and Nora followed her inside.

forty-two

LUCILLE threw herself back into the house. She couldn't tell who was screaming anymore. She frantically tried to dodge the vines. If one got her, it was all over.

On the other side of the house, Elaine stood frozen in the living room, staring out at the garden in a daze.

"Mā?" Lucille heard Nora shout. "We need to get out of here!"

Find Madeline, Lucille thought. There was a writhing mass of vines on the floor, in the middle of which was her daughter's head. She wasn't moving. A vine was curling its way around her neck.

Lucille grabbed desperately for her daughter. She tried to pull her by the shoulders, but the vines didn't release. "I can't!" she screamed. Tears streamed down her cheeks. "It's not—" She whimpered. She felt a tug as a vine wrapped around her ankle. *Let them take me.* She wasn't letting go of her daughter.

Nora ran over and stood by her side, wrapping her arms around the vines, her teeth gritted. "There's thorns!" she cried. "Be careful!"

A faint croak came from Madeline. Her eyes bulged.

Drywall tumbled around them along with bits of glass.

"She's losing consciousness." Nora sat back on her heels, her eyes full of panic.

"What are you doing?" Lucille yelled as she tried to grasp at smaller tendrils.

Nora leaned over Madeline. She placed her hand over where a thorny stem had punctured Madeline's arm, and blood was streaming.

She raked her palm over the thorny vines, gritting her teeth, and her hand came away streaked with blood.

Instantly, the thorns recoiled. Nora reached down and, with a grunt, pried the vines from Madeline's neck. "*Help me!*" Nora yelled.

Lucille pulled with her, and the vine slowly gave way, letting Madeline suck in a shuddering gasp.

"Pull," Nora said, her hands now covered in blood. "PULL!"

Lucille heaved backward again, and the vines withdrew from Madeline all at once, so quickly that her head hit the floor. She was going in and out of consciousness, her lips pale, her limbs frantically jerking about, as if she were still trying to free herself.

Painstakingly, they half dragged her out of the living room. "Mā!" Nora shouted over her shoulder. "Wake up!"

Elaine stared at them across the living room. She shuffled forward, stepping on vines that immediately recoiled from her feet.

Lucille looked up. High above them, cracks in the ceiling ruptured toward the chandelier. Rennie's door was still closed.

She turned to Nora. "Get Madeline out."

"You're—"

"I need to get my sister."

Elaine stepped into the foyer, her eyes glazed. "Leave," she said flatly, as if still in a trance. "It's not yours anymore."

Just then, the chandelier detached from the ceiling.

Lucille threw herself at Elaine and they toppled toward the doorway. The chandelier landed with a horrific, screeching crash, glass exploding everywhere. Lucille ducked and pain split through her arm. She uncovered her head to see her arms studded with shards of glass and blood. "Get *out*," Lucille shrieked. She shoved Elaine toward the entrance.

Lucille then ran toward the stairs, dodging the vines that lashed out at her. When she was halfway up, the steps behind her caved in as more vines punctured the wall. There was no way back down but couldn't think about it now.

On the second-floor hallway, the entirety of the railing had been torn away by vines. To her right, there was a sheer drop down to the foyer. To her left was the crumbling wall. Above her, the ceiling split apart.

"Rennie!" Lucille shrieked, her throat hoarse. "Renata!"

The door at the end. She just had to make it to the end of the hallway.

Another block of ceiling crashed down right in front of her.

Her sister was trapped.

She scrabbled her way up the wreckage. She slipped, and something stung her hand. She came away bleeding and saw a shard of the bathroom mirror on the ground, blood staining the edges. There was no way out now.

Lucille grabbed the mirror and held it between her hands.

"Ada," she said.

The mirror was still.

"Ada," she whispered. *Please, please, please.*

Slowly Lucille's reflection flickered and her sister's face appeared.

"Jiě Jie?"

Lucille gasped. "Ada."

She knelt over the shard of the mirror, over her sister's shifting face.

"You need to go," Ada said from the mirror.

"No," Lucille shouted. Beyond her, the window shattered. She didn't move. "I need to talk to you."

"There's no time."

That's why Ada had appeared so often, Lucille thought. She wasn't trying to scare her or frighten her. She was trying to warn her.

That was why Mā gave away the house. This house that Lucille had fought for. Forced them to stay in. Mā was trying to save them all along. If only they'd left earlier—

"I can't hold it anymore," Ada said, her reflection flickering. "I'm—"

She was gone.

Ceiling drywall rained down around her. Lucille clenched the mirror in her hands. She could see the warped, severed pipes through the gaping hole in the wall. "No. No, come back—"

"She's angry," Ada repeated, back in view but nearly transparent now. "I can't reason with her anymore. She's stronger than I am now."

Ada was better than Lucille could ever be. She only wanted to protect them. Had their roles been reversed that summer thirty-four years ago, Ada would have kept her secret about Sophie. She would have done anything for her twin sister.

"I'm not going," Lucille sobbed. Her vision of her sister blurred with tears. "I'm not leaving you again."

There was a pause. "Jiě Jie—"

"I'm sorry," Lucille whispered. Tears streamed down her cheeks. Prideful, stubborn Lucille knelt now on her hands and knees in front of her sister as the house collapsed around them. "I'm so sorry, Mèi Mei. For everything."

The truth tore through her with her own jagged heartbeat. *When what is false is taken for truth, true becomes indiscernible from false.* Lucille left this house in denial, never thinking about what would have happened if she had let her sister confide in her. If she'd let Ada keep her secret, and not handed it right over to their mother with a turn of her wrist. An open book. What if she hadn't scorned her sister's happiness? Would Ada and Sophie still be alive?

This garden—Sophie—wanted her. She knew that she wasn't going to make it out. But she was never meant to live this life without her twin sister. She'd been numb for the past three decades. From the moment she and Ada came into the world, they were together. They were the beginning and the end.

Lucille lost her footing and tumbled, gripping the mirror shard. Her head collided with the wall. Faintly, she heard shouts. She clutched the mirror to her chest, her sister. She could feel the vines wrapping around her, and she closed her eyes and let them take her.

RENNIE woke, her mouth dry. She was being rocked gently, as if lulled into sleep. It was almost like the house was *swaying*. Ink was bleeding across the ceiling.

Rennie blinked and realized that she was seeing vines.

She hauled herself up in bed. Her head pounded. *No. Not again.* Drawing her knees up to her chest, she watched as the vines traced down, drilling into the walls, and making them fracture and split.

This was a nightmare. The house was shaking. The floor itself tilted. Rennie grabbed on to the headboard of her bed to anchor herself. Something shattered. This was how it had been when she was a kid. She'd always dreamed of the walls rumbling, splitting apart. *Wake up, Rennie. Wake up.*

Someone pounded on her door.

"Yí Mā!"

Rennie froze. It was her niece's voice. This couldn't—

This was real. The vines, the house, the cracks in the drywall. Her mind was muddy, but her body knew she had to move.

"I'm coming," she called out. "I'm coming!" She pushed herself from the bed and staggered forward.

When she looked up, her mother was standing in front of the door.

Rennie let out a cry and scrambled backward. A searing pain cut through her foot, and she realized she'd stepped on the glass from a broken bottle. Dark wine puddled around her feet.

Mā tilted her head and looked at her curiously. The wrinkles around her eyes had deepened. She opened her mouth and dirt fell from her lips. "Are you so scared of your own mā?"

Rennie shivered. She had to get out. She forced herself to look the ghost of her mother in the eye. She was wearing the same clothes Rennie had last seen her in.

"Please," she said, her voice plaintive.

"You were the one I wanted to call me the most when I was alive. You were the daughter that flew the farthest away from me. You broke my heart."

Rennie squeezed her eyes shut. She remembered the promise she had made to herself so many years ago, sitting by the phone, that she would only call if she had good news. How new and beautiful and possible everything had seemed then. She could barely register the chaos around her. The wood of her dresser groaned as vines tore it apart. "I meant to call," Rennie whispered. "I really did."

"I can't even remember the last time you came to see me," Mā mused, oblivious to the destruction. Rennie opened her eyes. "Was it New Year's, five years ago?"

"I saw you two weeks ago," Rennie cried. "I came, don't you remember?"

"That wasn't Mā." A voice emerged behind her. Rennie knew, even without turning her head, that it was Ada. "She was dead by then."

Rennie stopped short as a chill poured over her. She remembered how odd Mā had looked that evening; her skin so pale, it was almost translucent. The strange, flat hiss of her voice. Her mottled teeth.

If she had already been dead . . . then Rennie had been speaking to a ghost.

"亲女儿," Mā rasped. Dirt dripped from her lips. Her eyes glittered cruelly. *My darling daughter.* "You had the whole world. I had so many dreams for you. I sacrificed so much for you. And look at you now."

The window overlooking the garden shattered clean through. Rennie staggered back, her breaths jagged in her chest. *Wake up, wake up,* she told herself. She faced the apparition of her mother, the expectations that had tormented her for a lifetime. Now she knew the truth of what had happened thirty-four years ago. What her mother had done— what her father had done—and the aftermath of it.

"You—abandoned us," Rennie whispered. "You failed us too."

"I gave you everything I had," Mā snarled. "Wasn't it enough, Bǎo bèi?"

"This isn't real," the ghost of Ada warned. "This is not Mā. It's this house. Rennie, you need to leave. Before it's too late."

Maybe it wasn't Mā's ghost. It was a hallucination. A specter of her worst fears.

Rennie would have once cowered under Mā's gaze, shriveled in the glare of it. She could have blamed her mother for playing tricks, for allowing them to dream, and then wielding those dreams against them. But now she understood that it didn't just start and end with her mother. It was their family, this house, this place that surrounded them, that had poisoned them with triumphant and ruinous visions. She remembered when she looked in the mirror on the night her mother had won the Oscar. How clearly she had seen that vision, and how hungrily she'd latched on to that fate. How it compelled her for the rest of her life. Maybe each of them had seen such visions, only to be broken by them. They had manifested and magnified their dreams, and in doing so, turned them into curses. This house fed on their hunger, their ambition, until it corrupted love and reason itself. A madness festering inside each of them.

The floor heaved. Rennie crumpled to her knees. Dust hailed down, and with a terrible, thunderous crack, a chunk of the outside wall dropped away.

Her mother started to cry, and Rennie still felt a strange ache to comfort her, even as the floors began to crumble beneath her feet.

"Rennie," Ada cried behind her. "*Get out.*"

Renata Yin Lowell looked at her mother in front of the door, her shoulders shaking with sobs, then back, finally, at her sister. The ceiling pulled apart with a terrible groan.

"Get out!"

She ran.

epilogue

LUCILLE put on the hot water kettle and sank into the couch. She closed her eyes and waited for the painkillers to kick in.

"I've just drawn up the settlement agreement. I'm going to route that over to you and Elaine for your signatures, and then it'll be finalized."

Her phone was perched on her lap and Reid Lyman's voice crackled through the speakerphone. "Okay," she said. "Sounds good."

There was a pause. "I take it you and Elaine sorted things out, then?"

"In a sense."

"What happened between the two of you? If you don't mind me asking?"

Lucille opened her eyes. She squinted at the drawn blinds in her living room. Normally she loved how the light tapered in the afternoons and warmed the white furniture with precision. But she was still concussed.

She stared at her bandaged hands. *What had happened?* For a moment, she contemplated telling Reid everything. What she'd discovered about her family. What her parents had both done, the truth of that summer. About the house that ended up being a trap. How the garden—or the wrath of the dead—had almost taken her daughter. How Lucille had prepared to die, to stay with the ghost of her sister, only to wake up in a hospital room.

Elaine had been the one to save her, Madeline told her in the hospital. After Elaine left the house, she had gone back in to pull Lucille out. Elaine told the doctors that the foyer chandelier had fallen on them, an excuse Lucille first found ridiculous, but eventually realized was the only possible explanation. They had been covered in cuts. Glass had sliced so deep into Lucille's palms that it almost caused permanent nerve damage. Now there were staples in her head.

Why had Elaine chosen to save her? She'd tried to find Elaine when she woke up in the hospital, but the Dengs were long gone. Rennie, on the other hand, was nowhere to be found. It was just her and Madeline.

Madeline was the person who'd seen Rennie last. "She jumped out the window," she'd recounted from her hospital bed, shifting up on her pillows. She'd ended up the worse out of the both of them and was covered in bandages. All in all, her leg had received a combined fifty-four stitches.

"From the second story? That's a twenty-foot drop."

"She was fine. She landed in the bushes. I saw her get up and run toward the back."

"Toward the back? Why? Why would she run *toward* the garden?"

"I don't know . . ." Madeline blinked, clearly exhausted. "I called her name, but she didn't answer."

Where could Rennie have gone? It wasn't unheard of for her to go off the grid and disappear for months while she reinvented herself. She always could extract herself from whatever circumstances she wanted to be free of. Lucille had tracked her elusive sister down so many times she'd lost count. They'd all lost their phones in the house, so Lucille watched her email like a hawk from her laptop, but nothing came. Instead, an email appeared in real time from Reid, saying that Elaine's lawyer had sent him a revised family settlement agreement. Elaine had given them the house. Or whatever remained of it.

"We talked it out," Lucille finally said over the phone to Reid. "We came to a resolution." The hot water kettle hissed. She shuffled over to the kitchen and poured two cups clumsily, with both bandaged hands.

"Right. That's good to hear." Reid sounded relieved. "And did you ever figure out what was going on with your mother that summer?"

Lucille stared at the rising steam. She thought of all the files and papers buried under the rubble of the house. There was one that she'd been thinking of recently, the library pages that Mā had torn out of a book and taken notes on. What was it on, the railroads? There was the picture of that man who looked like her dad. If she thought hard enough, maybe she could conjure his name. But it hurt to think.

And there was Mā's screenplay, too. The one and only copy of it. All irretrievable.

"No," she said faintly. "Still looking into it." She cleared her throat. "I'll get that signature in by end of day, though. Thanks for handling everything."

"Of course, Lucille." His voice softened. "And one more question. Aside from the will."

"Shoot."

"I, ah . . . Do you think you'll be around LA anytime soon? In the near future?"

Lucille shifted her weight from one foot to the other.

"We could—well. Grab a drink sometime. Or a coffee. If you'd like?"

Lucille chewed on her lip. She felt the familiar stirring recall of that early summer night over thirty years ago when their eyes met across the dining room table, but the memory was fuzzier and held less power now. "I probably will. I'll let you know."

After they hung up, she stared at the counter for a long moment and then brought one of the cups to her daughter's room.

The door was ajar. Lucille shuffled in and squinted against the light. Madeline was tucked into the sheets, her arm curled up underneath her cheek. She used to doze like that as a baby, and that memory tugged at Lucille so sharply that her eyes started to well. Lucille used to work on evidence files on the floor next to Madeline's crib while she slept, as if nothing could ever disturb her.

She set the cup of hot water on Madeline's nightstand, next to a roll of gauze, and tucked a loose end of the blanket over Madeline before she made her way back to her laptop in the living room. She then did what she had done every night since she came home from the hospital. First, she sent a text to Rennie's phone, which she knew was probably futile. Next, she sent an email. An email should reach her sister, wherever she was. Maybe Rennie just needed time to process. Whether that took days, or weeks, or months, Lucille would try to be patient. And understanding. And hopefully, one day, when Rennie was ready, she would respond. Then, Lucille vowed to herself, she would apologize and try to undo the hurt she'd caused. She would finally make things right.

MADELINE eventually found her way back to San Francisco in the fall. Things had slotted into place slowly. First, she took two months to heal. In October, she interviewed for a job with a climate nonprofit over the phone and got it. The rest followed: a sublet through a friend of a former classmate, and then a move that Mā insisted on helping with, since Madeline didn't have her full strength yet. They took I-5 all the way up. They stopped for gas when they passed through somewhere around LA, and while Mā paid she kept glancing around. Madeline knew why.

"Where do you think she could be?"

Mā adjusted her sunglasses. She was still a little sensitive to light. "I don't know. She always . . . sometimes it's hard finding her. One time in the nineties, she drove across the country with a band and I didn't know until she showed up on my doorstep in San Francisco. Or there was a time she gave up her landline and moved apartments and no one in New York knew where she was until we found out she was in Paris." She shook her head. "I don't know where she'd go after jumping out a window, though."

"She seemed okay," Madeline said. "I mean, she was running."

"At least there's that." The gas pump released. Mā jammed it back into the nozzle. "Let's keep going."

They passed the exit to 外婆's house, and Mā's hands tightened around the wheel as they sped on. Madeline had no idea what it looked like now. Had the vines swallowed it? Did the garden lay still? It was easy to quell her curiosity. Her nightmares were enough.

Her new place in San Francisco was a yellow Victorian house. She had two roommates and a small room with a bay window. Mā helped her get set up. All those years her mother had left Madeline to move on her own back and forth from college, and now she'd blown all her vacation days helping Madeline put together her bed frame and furniture. Before she left, she'd wordlessly reached for Madeline and held her for a long time with such force it surprised even Madeline.

A week later, Madeline started her job. The stitches came out and the wounds faded into raw, raised scars, which puckered and stretched across her arms and legs. She took the train to the beach with her friends. She found her favorite vantage point from Mission Dolores Park, and sat there with a book to watch the sunset.

One day in mid-November, she looked up from her book and saw someone walking toward her. Nora Deng grinned. Madeline's heart leapt to her throat.

"Hey."

Madeline set her book down. "Thanks for meeting me here."

"Of course. You knew I was around." Nora was dressed in a collared shirt and slacks. Her once-cropped hair was longer and half pulled up.

"How'd your interview go?"

"Okay, I think. I tried to keep it cool."

"It's a really good school, right? UCSF?"

"Only my top choice. I probably jinxed it by saying that." Nora pulled a corduroy jacket around her shoulders. It was getting dark and cold.

"I personally think you're a shoo-in." Madeline leaned back against the grass. "You've already saved lives."

Nora smiled to herself. "I'm not sure where I can list pulling someone out of a haunted house on my applications."

"Well. You kept me from bleeding out."

"You were in a bad state. I was really scared for you. I thought it sliced your femoral artery."

Madeline remembered the excruciating, persistent pain afterward. Her entire body tensed up, but she tried to keep her voice light. "See? You know what you're talking about."

They sat in silence for a while.

"Why did your mother save mine?" Madeline knew her mother wondered about that question, obsessed over it, even.

Nora looked at her. "I don't know," she finally exhaled. "I guess she felt like she needed to."

"Why?"

Nora's lips parted. "I don't know. I asked her the same thing. But she doesn't remember much about what she did. Or being in the house at all, really. It was like—" Her voice dropped. "A dream. Or possession. Or something."

"By what?"

Nora shrugged. "Hard to say. Anything was possible there. It scares me to think about it, so I don't."

"Did your mother see ghosts?"

"Yes. I think so."

"My mother saw her sister. Ada."

Nora nodded. "I think my mother saw hers." She pulled her jacket around herself.

"I didn't see anyone."

"But you saw the vines early on."

"I didn't feel the earthquakes, though."

"Maybe we were all haunted by different things."

The sun had disappeared now, and the sky was streaked with red. Madeline watched the deft way Nora's fingers played with a blade of grass. Silence stretched between them. She caught a flash of a white scar on Nora's hand. On instinct she reached for it and held it up. The long, jagged mark split across her palm.

"I had to get you out," Nora said.

Madeline swallowed. "Does it still hurt?"

"Not anymore."

"I'm sorry."

"For what?"

"I feel like you kept getting hurt because of me. For me."

"I'd do it again." Nora smiled. "For you."

Madeline looked at their hands and focused on breathing steadily, waiting for Nora to unlace her fingers, but she didn't. She looked up and Nora was staring at her with a curious expression, her dark eyes unreadable in the waning light.

And then Nora leaned in and kissed Madeline, a long, slow kiss, her other hand brushing Madeline's cheek. Madeline kissed her back, her heart racing, and let herself fall, unreservedly, one more time. For a moment they were extricated from their families' shared past. They were just two people who wanted each other.

Nora pulled away gently and stood. "I have to go, but I'm glad you're doing okay now. And that you're here."

As Nora crossed the park, she looked back and grinned. Madeline pressed the back of her hand to her lips and knew with a small certainty that they would see each other again. There was still so much she wanted to know. She wondered if they woke from the same nightmares, turned the same events over and over in their heads. These things snag and startle and ebb and consume. The grief, the healing. In between, now, maybe, a beginning.

Madeline was shivering from the cold by the time she unlocked the door to her house. She turned the lights on and slung her cardigan over a chair. Both her roommates were out.

She went to the bathroom and washed the dirt off her hands. She kept thinking about what Nora had said. *Maybe we're all haunted by different things.*

They'd each seen someone—something—in that house. What had Aunt Rennie seen? She was the only one who had been honest about it with Madeline. What was *she* haunted by? What made her do what she did that night? Madeline tried to walk back through each moment with her eyes shut. She remembered her aunt clambering down from the second-story windowsill and falling to the bushes. Madeline had screamed her name in horror, then. But after a minute, Yí Mā had stood. She had started running toward the garden, her skirt billowing, without looking back. Why hadn't she run toward her family, toward escape?

The icy water began to numb her fingers as a new thought unfurled in Madeline's mind. She steadied herself on the sink with her hands. Her breath rose rapidly in her chest. *Unless she didn't escape.*

She looked at her own reflection, at the shock in her eyes, at the dark circles underneath, at the color seeping from her cheeks.

She looked like she had seen a ghost.

acknowledgments

To my wonderful agent, Jess Regel—thank you for your belief in me and in this story and for everything, really, truly.

To my brilliant editor, Margo Shickmanter—thank you for your insight, your enthusiasm, and your magnificent editorial vision. I am beyond fortunate to get to work with you.

To the Avid Reader team, with special gratitude to: Amy Guay, Carolyn Kelly, Alex Primiani, Meredith Vilarello, Rhina Garcia, Caroline McGregor, Katya Buresh, Jessica Chin, Allison Green, Ruth Lee-Mui, Sirui Huang, and to James Tierney and Alison Forner for the beautiful cover design and direction.

Thank you to Professor Marci Kwon for your Asian American Art History class, which has changed my life in innumerable ways.

To my family, immediate and extended.

To my found family, to whom this book is dedicated. DACU, I am so glad I found you all: Chloe, Racquel, Tashie, Zoe. Thank you for being so supportive of this story from its inception.

To Joelle, for your daily wit, support, and pure genius.

To Julia, for your incisive feedback and vast knowledge.

To Andi, for your friendship, your mentorship, and your kindness. And for the generosity of the Princess Writing Residency.

To the wonderful friends who have always been in my corner: Katherine, Lauren, Becca, Rachel, Pranavi. To my beloved Squirrels: Cate, Eghosa, Gaby. To Grace, Camryn, Jake, Michael, Fari, Pietra, Kei, Squish, Abbie, Gracie, Marina, Page, Jen, Kamilah, Audrey, Anna, Lexi, Therese, Aamna, Fiona, Lily, Dan, Katia, Dave, Paula. Thank you from the bottom of my heart.

Thank you to the resources that were especially formative in my research, especially Gordon H. Chang's scholarly work in the field of Chinese workers on the Transcontinental Railroad: *Chinese American Voices: From the Gold Rush to the Present*; *Ghosts of Gold Mountain: The Epic Story of the Chinese Who Built the Transcontinental Railroad*; *The Chinese and the Iron Road*; and the Chinese Railroad Workers in North America Project at Stanford University. To other notable resources: *Surviving on the Gold Mountain: A History of Chinese American Women and Their Lives* by Huping Ling; *Hollywood Chinese* by Arthur Dong; *A Field Guide to American Houses (Revised): The Definitive Guide to Identifying and Understanding America's Domestic Architecture* by Virginia Savage Macalester; and *Deering's California Probate Code*. Thank you to Professor Pearson for the legal insight as well: all errors and liberties are my own.

And lastly, I would be nowhere without the excitement and dedication of readers, librarians, and booksellers. Thank you so very much for what you do.

about the author

CHRISTINA LI is the award-winning author of children's and young adult books *Clues to the Universe, Ruby Lost and Found*, and *True Love and Other Impossible Odds*, which have been selected as a *Washington Post* summer book club pick and one of the NPR and New York Public Library Best Books of the Year. She graduated from Stanford University with degrees in Economics and Public Policy. She grew up in the Midwest and California, but now resides in New York. *The Manor of Dreams* is her adult literary debut. For more information, visit her website at christinaliwrites.com.

Avid Reader Press, an imprint of Simon & Schuster, is built on the idea that the most rewarding publishing has three common denominators: great books, published with intense focus, in true partnership. Thank you to the Avid Reader Press colleagues who collaborated on *The Manor of Dreams*, as well as to the hundreds of professionals in the Simon & Schuster advertising, audio, communications, design, ebook, finance, human resources, legal, marketing, operations, production, sales, supply chain, subsidiary rights, and warehouse departments whose invaluable support and expertise benefit every one of our titles.

Editorial
Margo Shickmanter, *Executive Editor*
Amy Guay, *Assistant Editor*

Jacket Design
Alison Forner, *Senior Art Director*
Clay Smith, *Senior Designer*
Sydney Newman, *Art Associate*

Marketing
Meredith Vilarello, *VP and Associate Publisher*
Caroline McGregor, *Senior Marketing Manager*
Kayla Dee, *Associate Marketing Manager*
Katya Wiegmann, *Marketing and Publishing Assistant*

Production
Allison Green, *Managing Editor*
Jessica Chin, *Senior Manager of Copyediting*
Alicia Brancato, *Production Manager*
Ruth Lee-Mui, *Interior Text Designer*
Cait Lamborne, *Ebook Developer*

Publicity
Rhina Garcia, *Publicist*
Eva Kerins, *Publicity Assistant*

Subsidiary Rights
Paul O'Halloran, *VP and Director of Subsidiary Rights*
Fiona Sharp, *Subsidiary Rights Coordinator*